## Sisters Three

'I didn't think it would work,' Kenny MacGregor said.

'Is that why you followed me here,' said Rosie, 'so I could tell you how my brother-in-law reacted? Sorry to disappoint you. If you must know, I don't see much of Dominic. What he does is not my concern.'

'You do know what he does, though?'

'I was brought up in the Gorbals,' said Rosie. 'I have probably seen more monkey business than you have. I know what my brother-in-law used to do but since he married my sister he has gone on to the straight and narrow. He buys and sells imported goods and has a warehouse in Govan, all perfectly above board.'

Kenny pressed his lips together and frowned. 'That's just not true, Miss Conway, not true at all.'

'Prove it,' she said. 'Go ahead then, prove it.'

*About the author*

Born in Glasgow, Jessica Stirling is the author of twenty-two
heartwarming novels, many with Scottish backgrounds.

# Sisters Three

Jessica Stirling

CORONET BOOKS
Hodder & Stoughton

Copyright © 2001 by Jessica Stirling

The right of Jessica Stirling to be identified as the Author
of the Work has been asserted in accordance with the
Copyright, Designs and Patents Act 1988.

First published in Great Britain in 2001 by Hodder and Stoughton
First published in paperback in 2001 by Hodder and Stoughton
A division of Hodder Headline

A Coronet Paperback

10 9 8 7 6 5 4 3 2 1

All characters in this publication are fictitious
and any resemblance to real persons, living or dead
is purely coincidental.

A CIP catalogue record for this title is available from the British Library

ISBN 0 340 7 3868 5

Typeset by Palimpsest Book Production Limited,
Polmont, Stirlingshire

Printed and bound in Great Britain by
Clays Ltd, St Ives plc

Hodder and Stoughton
A division of Hodder Headline
338 Euston Road
London NW1 3BH

# Chapter One

When word drifted down from Flint that Bobtail Boy would canter home at one hundred to eight in the November Handicap Polly had no option but to place a bet. Heaven knows she didn't need the money. She had everything a woman could possibly want and if anything out of the ordinary did catch her fancy then all she had to do was snap her fingers and Dominic would have it delivered.

Seven years of marriage hadn't diminished Dominic Manone's infatuation with the girl from the Gorbals and so far he'd shown no inclination to acquire a mistress, an omission that suggested weakness to his colleagues on the shady side of the street. Even they had to admit, though, that a guy would be hard pushed to find a mistress who could match Polly Conway for that indefinable quality that envious wives dismissed as spending power but that their husbands perceived as class.

How Flint intended to rig the race was a mystery, for ever since Dominic had pulled out of bookmaking Polly had lost touch with racing gossip. Hot tips from John Flint were few and far between, though, and Flint would be insulted if she ignored the favour. She waited until ten minutes before the race before she sent Tony to the tote to lay a tenner on the Bobtail's nose.

'Splashing out, are we, Mrs Em?' Tony said. 'Know something I don't?'

'I doubt it, Mr El.'

Polly gave him a little pat on the shoulder to send him on his way.

After her husband's Uncle Guido had retired to Italy Tony Lombard had taken over as Dominic's right-hand man. He was tall and broad-shouldered and had dark, lazy-lidded eyes. Most women found Tony irresistible: Polly was no exception. He was smooth and cool and polished, like her husband. In fact the men might have been brothers, except that Tony carried a faint air of menace as if you couldn't be quite sure what he would do if you crossed him, a quality that Dominic had lost over the past few years.

Perhaps she was partly to blame for the change in her husband. It was on her suggestion that he had sold off the book to Flint and had pulled out of the street rackets. Squawks of protest and a flurry of cables came from Dominic's father in Philadelphia, of course, but to his credit Dominic had stuck to his guns.

She watched Tony climb the steps to the top of the stand.

He wore a snap-brim hat and a Raglan overcoat and walked with a straightforward, upright gait, his broad shoulders swaying as if he was just on the verge of throwing a punch.

Polly shivered a little and tucked her chin into her fur collar.

The afternoon was cold and still.

Cloud blotted out the river and the graving docks and the lights of the little townships below. The cold made the horses skittish rather than eager and Bobtail's jockey struggled to bring the animal to the starting-gate.

Polly had no information about the three-year-old's form or what weight he was carrying. She'd hardly had time to glance at the card before Dominic had sent her off to lunch with Tony in the grandstand bar while he went down to meet someone in the enclosure, a short, squat bullish man in his fifties whom Polly had never seen before. She had caught a glimpse of him at the edge of the enclosure just before Tony had steered her into the bar.

Polly wasn't the only good-looking woman in the long room but everyone knew whose wife she was and heads turned when she came through the door. Even the haughty county types who commandeered the big table by the fireplace eyed her up and down.

Tony brought her lunch: a salmon mousse, filet of steak flanked by three boiled potatoes and a spoonful of buttered cabbage. He handed her a gin-and-tonic and settled with his back to the window. He'd bought no drink for himself, not even lager. He was, she realised, working at keeping her out of Dominic's way for a while.

She glanced out of the plate-glass window in the hope that she might catch sight of her husband in the crowd below and the squat little man with the big military moustache. There was no sign of either of them at the railings or among the bookmakers' stalls. She was tempted to ask, 'Who is that man and what business does he have with Dominic?' but she didn't want to put Tony on the spot.

She sipped her gin-and-tonic and dipped her spoon in the salmon mousse while Tony slit open a meat pastry and began to eat.

Dominic didn't join them in the bar. He was waiting on the bench in the fifth row of the stand when Tony and she returned. He seemed relaxed, almost amused, as if the meeting with the little man with the moustache had been unexpectedly profitable.

'Nice lunch, darling?'

'Plain,' Polly replied, 'but wholesome.'

'How much did you drink?'

Tony answered for her. 'One gin.'

'With tonic,' said Polly. 'Okay?'

'Perfectly okay.' Dominic lifted his binoculars. 'Flint has given us a nod that Bobtail Boy is sure-fire. What do you think, darling?'

'If Flint says "sure-fire" then I wouldn't doubt it.'

'I've put something on, something out of the fund.'

'Oh, good,' said Polly.

She was supposed to assume that the moustache had brought a message from Johnny Flint, a hot tip from the horse's mouth. Somehow she doubted it. She had no reason to doubt it: she just did. She was being brushed off again, deceived. For the best part of a year now Dominic had been lying to her, nothing drastic, just a small, steady stream of white lies – or perhaps she was just being over sensitive. Perhaps life in the little mansion in Manor Park Avenue had become too idyllic and she and her children, Stuart and Ishbel, had become too detached from the stresses that added spice and texture to the lives of ordinary folk.

Dominic's business had held up in spite of the slump. Now rearmament programmes had brought full employment back to Clydeside and the ice-cream factory, cafés and restaurants in which he held shares were booming. She had every reason to feel safe and secure – but she didn't. An Italian army had swept into Abyssinia and the left-wing government in Spain had been attacked by General Franco's rebels and Chancellor Hitler had annexed Austria and like Bernard Peabody, her stepfather, she'd been dismayed by a headline photograph of British Prime Minister Neville Chamberlain shaking hands with Benito Mussolini.

Bernard was a veteran of the Great War and the prospect of another conflict in Europe appalled him, though he claimed that he'd have been off like a shot to join the International Brigade if he hadn't been a shade too long in the tooth.

It wasn't just Spain that bothered Polly, however, or the Italian crises or jackboots stamping through the Rhineland. Fanatical fascists rioting in streets much closer to home had her on edge too for Dominic had played both sides of the fence for so long that she had no idea where he really stood on any important issue. He subsidised the Jewish pipe band with one hand, gave money to the Union of Italian Traders and the Socialist Workers' party with the other. He had subscribed to the purchase and renovation of the magnificent *Casa d'Italia* in Glasgow's Park Circus, one of the finest *fascio* flagships in Britain, but had refused to become a member. He continued to back causes redder than ox-blood and causes blacker than midnight without, it seemed, being aware of the distinctions, and when she asked him to clarify his position he just smiled and politely avoided the issue.

Dominic had never set foot in Italy. He had been born and educated in Scotland and had married outside the Italian community. Even so he still paid homage to a father whom he hadn't seen in almost twenty years, a father who, not to put too fine a point on it, was a gangster in America. In addition to all the other woes in the world, therefore, Polly had to live with the fear that one day the forces of law and order would catch up with her husband and that he would be made to pay for his past, let alone his present, mistakes.

She watched the horse-race with hardly a flicker of interest.

The jockey Flint had chosen to ride Bobtail Boy knew his stuff. He didn't draw away from the field until the final furlong and then, with whip cracking and the crowd roaring, brought the Bobtail in by a nose from the odds-on favourite. Polly took no pleasure in the knowledge that she had just won a tidy sum of money. High up in the stands she felt remote from the excitement of the shiftless crowd. The next race would not only be the last on the card but the last of the season. Whitewashed stands would soon empty, snack bars and restaurants would put their shutters up and the judge's box would be locked until April. The punters would mooch away into the burnt-out haze and soon – all too soon for Polly – it would be 1939 and the start of another year of uncertainty.

Dominic's face remained hidden behind the binoculars. He wore a pale grey scarf of fine lambswool. Black kidskin gloves were tucked into the belt of his overcoat. He might have been a general studying a battlefield, all his concentration focused on – on what? Not jockeys and owners and horses, not on the winner's enclosure or numbers posted on the wall of the judge's lodge: he was methodically scanning the crowd, looking for someone.

Tony slid his right hand against the small of her back.

She leaned into him.

'Well, Mrs Em, looks like you're a winner,' Tony said.

Without lowering the binoculars, Dominic said, 'Tony, please take Polly home now.'

'What about you?' said Polly. 'Aren't you coming with us?'

'No, darling,' her husband told her. 'I still have business to do here.'

*What sort of business? Business with that vulgar little bull of a man? What are you keeping from me, Dominic? What are you holding back?* Before the questions could reached her lips, Polly buried her chin in the soft, cold collar again.

Tony's hand in the small of her back spread out like a brace.

'Will you be home for supper, Dominic?' she asked.

Dominic did not answer. He had found someone in the crowd.

Polly followed his line of gaze, saw the little man with the military moustache and beside him, hanging on his arm, a tall young woman with long shapely legs and a helmet of blonde hair who even as Polly spotted her, rose on tiptoe and waved.

Lowering the binoculars a little, Dominic waved back.

'Tony,' Dominic spoke softly. 'Take my wife home.'

And Tony led Polly away.

★   ★   ★

On Saturdays the only way Babs could get to see her husband was to bump the perambulator down the steps of their bungalow in Raines Drive and shepherd her children round the long corner to the garage in Holloway Road.

In spite of the bubble-headed petrol pumps, free air compressor and tyre rack and the great oily cavern round back in which his brothers worked on vehicle repairs, according to Jackie, Hallop's wasn't a garage at all but a 'Motoring Salon' – which showed just how divorced from reality Jackie had become. Manual labour was beneath him now, of course. He had risen above all that. In the office overlooking the forecourt he fiddled with purchase and sales ledgers, licences and registration forms, aided and abetted by old Miss Dawlish who was as steely and efficient as a Rolls-Royce gearbox when it came to refreshing the pedigree of vehicles come by slightly less than honestly.

Babs had no objection to Jackie poncing about the forecourt or posing in the big bow window of the showroom or even lounging in the little kitchenette in the back listening to dance music on his Ultra 500 Magic Eye wireless set. What she did object to was Jackie out on the town, swanning it at dealership conventions or loose with a cheque-book at sales or auctions and, most of all, vanishing for entire afternoons without proper explanation or excuse.

For this reason, Babs would occasionally dress up her offspring, pop baby into the pram, throw on her beaver lamb coat and beret and sail around the corner just to check that Jackie was actually there and doing what passed for his job.

Hand in little hand May and June would walk primly in front of her, baby April would goo and gurgle in the high-sided Roxburgh pram, and Angus, age seven, would pedal furiously ahead on the tricycle that he had definitely outgrown while emitting an uncannily accurate imitation of his Daddy's Excelsior motorbike – *Brrrrrrrooooooommm.*

'*Ang*-gus,' Babs called out sharply. '*Ang*-*gus*. Stop right where you are.'

Angus obstinately pedalled on round the corner, head down, shoulders hunched, *brrroooming* like mad, while May, age six, and June, age five, quickened their pace to keep the daredevil in sight. On Saturday afternoons there wasn't much traffic in Holloway Road, only a few customers puttering into Hallop's, a coal merchant's or greengrocer's cart and now and then a single-decker bus that had gone astray. But the gnashing of trams from the junction with Paisley Road and distant roars from Ibrox football stadium sent little darts of anxiety into Babs's stomach for however selfish she might be in other respects, she was heart and soul a mother and fretted about the safety of her kids.

'There!' June pointed dramatically. 'I see him.'

Babs trotted breathlessly around the curve of the

pavement just in time to see her son pass under the wooden archway that spanned the entrance to the forecourt. Jackie's brother Billy had constructed the arch and fitted the wiring that picked out *Hallop's Motor Salon* in coloured bulbs. Billy had made a good job of it for like all the Hallop boys he was clever with his hands. He had also erected two tall flag-poles, one at each end of the low wall that kept the motorcars from escaping into the road, but on that dreary November afternoon the flags hung limp and rubbery against their whitewashed poles.

Refusing to be beaten by the gradient Angus rose from the saddle, pumped on the pedals as if he were kick-starting a motorbike and shot up the ramp into the almost empty forecourt. The girls, the pram and Babs all followed on.

Babs had learned enough about the motor trade to separate browsers from potential buyers and she reckoned that the couple who were prowling around an almost-new BSA Scout two-seater had the air of seriously interested parties. The man was tall with curly fair hair and a frank and open face. The woman – probably his wife – was small, almost wispy and sported an off-the-peg overcoat a size too large for her. At a hundred and thirty pounds the Scout would be too expensive for the couple even on hire purchase, Babs reckoned, but further along the row was a Hillman, four or five years old but still gleaming and confident, that Jackie would knock down to sixty or sixty-five quid and negotiate on suitable terms.

She quickened her pace and caught up with her daughters. They were very well behaved, her daughters. Indeed, they emanated an air of supercilious patience and precocious dis-approval that they applied not only to their brother but also to Mum and Dad.

There were no salesmen in the forecourt and no sign of Jackie.

Babs followed the tricycle up to the bow-fronted window. There were no lights in the office or showroom and she guessed that Jackie had dropped off in the armchair in the kitchenette while listening to Ambrose or Billy Cotton or a football commentary on his wireless. Billy and older brother Dennis would be back in the repair shop for they only came out front when someone rang for petrol. She braked the pram next to Angus's tricycle and pushed open the showroom door.

Cars loomed menacingly out of the shadows: an Alvis, a Wolseley, a big black Daimler. The girls remained outside to guard the baby and Angus had already gone rocketing through the building, shouting, in his gruff, gravel voice, 'Dad, Daddy, Dad, I've come to see you.' Babs peeped into the office and found no one there, not even Miss Dawlish.

Through the windows she could see her girls, the pram and, beyond them, the customers. The man was looking up at the showroom but the wispy young woman had disappeared. A sudden *frisson* of apprehension ruffled the hair at the back of Babs's neck. 'Jackie,' she shouted. 'Jackie, goddamn it, where are you?' When no answer was forthcoming, she went back through the showroom and left Angus to find his own way out.

The young man was waiting by the door. He smiled optimistically at May and June but they were not to be cajoled into talking to strangers. Baby April chewed the apron of her pram and slavered.

As soon as Babs appeared the young man looked up.

'Are you Mrs Hallop, by any chance?'

Tinged with a Highland accent, his voice was softer than she'd anticipated but as soon as he spoke the prospect of selling the Hillman, let alone the Scout, vanished.

'What if I am?'

'I'm looking for your husband.'

'You're not the only one,' Babs said. 'If you're interested in a car . . .'

'I'm interested in your husband,' the man said.

'I'll fetch my brother-in-law,' Babs said. 'He's round in the repair shop.'

'No, it's Mr Hallop, Mr John Hallop, I want to speak to.'

'Aw, really!' Babs pushed back her shoulders: the girls watched her, eager to learn. 'What, may I ask, d'you want him for?'

Out of the corner of her eye she spotted the wispy young woman in the off-the-peg overcoat coming around the gable with Dennis. Big, solid, reliable Dennis, dressed in baggy brown overalls, was wiping his hands on a cotton rag.

'Who is that woman anyway?' Babs heard herself say.

'My sister.'

'An' who are you?'

'My name's MacGregor, ma'am. I'm a policeman. I've come to serve warrant on your husband, I'm afraid.'

'Uh-huh, uh-huh,' Babs said just as Jackie, whistling unconcernedly, appeared from behind the petrol pumps, holding young Angus by the hand.

It was dark now and the street lamps had come alight, shop fronts blazed and even the dingy pubs looked warm and inviting in the chill wintry haze. Football supporters spilled from side streets jeering and rough-housing or trudged in the direction of tram stops or waded through the traffic heading for the Clutha or the Bon Accord or some other favourite pub. They jostled the women shoppers on the pavements and crabby old widows, flighty young girls and wives burdened by poverty and child-rearing had sense enough to clear out of their way for on Saturday afternoon their men folk were numbed by football and a thirst for hard liquor and cared nothing for common courtesy.

Polly had been raised in streets like these but had remained oblivious to the scars that gender and class can leave on ordinary people. It was only after she'd moved out to Manor Park Avenue that she'd come to realise how much difference money could make and had begun to resent the heartless industrial machine that ground men down until there was nothing left but a few rare sparks of courage and endurance. Her mother had endured, of course: her mother had struggled bravely against the odds all her born days until, thank heaven, she'd shaken off the chains of poverty by marrying Bernard Peabody.

Tony had taken the main road into Ibrox via the proud old weaving town of Paisley which had staunchly preserved its independence through every phase of boom and slump. Heading east now, he turned off into the parkway and the harsh street lights were abruptly screened by trees and the sedate Presbyterian mansions of Belville Road.

Tony hadn't said a word since he'd steered out of the field behind the racecourse. Polly occupied the rear seat as a rule but tonight she sat up front. The family Alfa had been traded in when the first anti-fascist riots had broken out and a few hotheads and Clydeside Bolsheviks had stoned Italians in the streets and smashed up their cafés and fish restaurants. Jackie had found them a nice Triumph Dolomite to replace the Alfa and Tony said he preferred it. Polly didn't care one way or the other for neither she nor her sister Babs had ever learned to drive.

She watched the trees loom behind the pleasing curve of high iron railings. In the park in the half dark she saw a man with a dog, two small boys playing with a rubber football, a couple kissing behind a chestnut tree, and the town was replaced by an air of rustic seclusion. She caught the thumb and forefinger of her glove between her small sharp teeth and tugged off the glove. She dropped it into her lap and let it lie there. She put out her hand and spread her fingers on the leather seat. The car was moving slowly, ornate street lamps and the lamps in the porticoes of the mansions marking Tony's face with light and shadow in a queer, lazy, dreamlike rhythm.

He took a hand from the steering wheel and covered her hand with his.

'Will you come in with me tonight, please?' Polly said.

And Tony, loyal Tony, answered, 'Sure.'


Jackie Hallop had hardly changed since Babs had first clapped eyes on him nine years ago. He had been leaning from a ground-floor window when the Conways had arrived in Lavender Court packed into the back of a Sanitation Department van along with their few sticks of furniture. He had been wearing nothing but an undervest that had shown off his pale, undernourished body to worst advantage and had given Babs – 'Blondie' he'd called her – a real good eyeful of all he'd had to offer which then as now hadn't been much.

Anything less like husband material would have

been hard to imagine even for someone as young and impressionable as Babs had been in those days. During the erratic course of their courtship, however, Jackie had proved to have plenty of steam in his boilers and his willingness to spend money and enjoy a good time had eventually lured Babs into sacrificing a girl's most precious possession. Then, like many a girl before her, she had wound up pregnant and married to a guy she hardly knew, a guy who made his living renovating stolen motorbikes in a junk yard off the Calcutta Road.

Dominic had done all right by Jackie, however, and Jackie had done all right by Dominic. Regular exchanges of money between them kept the relationship cordial. However good Jackie and his brothers were at managing the salon, at home her husband could be a sore trial at times.

According to Rosie, Babs's deaf but outspoken little sister, Jackie fancied himself as Peter Pan, just a boy who refused to grow up. But Peter Pan had never got up to half the things that Jackie got up to, especially in the bedroom where Babs and he joined in raptures so careless that both May and April had been conceived without forethought and if nature had been able to keep up with the hectic pace there would have been three or four more babies to add to the heap.

Though he spent more on clothes in a month than the average man earned in a year, Jackie still retained such a boyish appearance that unwary folk assumed he was either innocent or daft and even his daughters had already begun to suspect that there was something odd about Daddy. And they had their names to prove it.

'April, May and June!' Rosie declared in her clicky, deaf person's voice. 'Dear God, Babs, it is as well for Angus that he was not born in August or September or you would have been saddled with an Auguste or a Septimus. Have you stopped now, by the way? Have you put a sock on it yet?'

Fortunately Rosie didn't know the half of it. It wasn't Jackie's organ of generation that needed muzzling so much as his mouth for when he became excited or upset he would prattle on and on in a quasi-American drawl that made him sound vaguely like the film star James Cagney.

On that particular Saturday Jackie arrived home at a quarter past seven. The crunch of the Ford's tyres on the gravel and her husband's voice seemed to merge even before the car braked to a halt. Ranting, he entered the kitchen by the back door, paused long enough to lift the lid on the pan that Babs had left simmering on the gas stove, then came on through the hall, ranting again. He fired several remarks in the direction of his son who, fed, watered and wrapped in a blue woollen dressing-gown, was lying tummy-down on the rug in the lounge looking at the pictures in *Motorcycle Weekly*. Then, without waiting for Angus to respond, he danced through the hall into the bathroom where, in the absence of a nursemaid, Babs was bathing the baby while May and June, dressed in pink dressing-gowns and floral slippers, observed.

The baby was having a high old time of it playing with a big yellow sponge while Babs, kneeling, supported her and tried to direct suds to unreachable parts of the plump little body.

Red-cheeked, straggle-haired, Babs was smouldering with resentment at having been summarily dismissed as soon as the copper flashed his ID, not politely requested to make herself scarce, mark you, but hastily escorted off the premises by Dennis as if she were an accomplice instead of the innocent wife of an innocent man.

'. . . and told that bugger where to get off. He wouldn't have been throwin' his weight around if Dominic had been there, I can tell ya. Dominic would've told him to stuff his so-called warrant up his . . .'

'Jackie!' Babs rolled her eyes in the direction of the girls.

'Well, yeah, point taken.' Jackie touched each of his daughters on the crown of the head as if conferring a blessing. 'But I mean t' say, it's the truth, Babs, ain't it? Got no respect for an enterprisin' businessman, these guys. Jeez-zus . . .'

'Jackie!'

'Well, they ain't. It's bloody Percy Sillitoe an' his new broom sweepin' clean at police headquarters. Coppers runnin' scared if they don't make enough arrests old Perce'll have them back directin' traffic at Tolcross. Sure, our new Chief Constable might've put the fear o' God into the Irish and the Bolshies and got rid o' half the wild men out o' the gangs but Jee – I mean, cripes – we're not that breed o' person, not me an' not Dominic, so why are we bein' persecuted?'

'Are we being persecuted?' Babs said.

'We're honest citizens. We pay our taxes an' . . .'

'What did he want with us?'

Jackie fell silent for several seconds then said, 'Nothin'.'

'I thought he was wavin' a warrant for your arrest.'

Jackie laughed. 'My arrest? What the heck would they be arrestin' me for?' He looked down at June. 'Why would they be takin' your Daddy in, honey?'

June shook her head and May, not to be left out, shook hers too.

Angus and the girls had known no life but that of the bungalow. They had never suffered hunger or cold or bullying, had never lived in fear of anyone or anything, which was all well and good when things were running smoothly but what would she tell her children, Babs wondered, if Daddy was snapped up by the jaws of the legal system? How secure and self-assured would her children be if they had to trail up to Barlinnie prison on visiting day to peer at Daddy through the bars?

'A search warrant, was it?' said Babs.

'Naw, it wasn't even a search warrant,' Jackie said. 'Even if it had been a search warrant the bastard wouldn't found anythin' incriminatin' at the salon. Is she ready for dryin' yet? Take her out an' I'll powder her while you serve my dinner.' He waited while Babs fished for baby April, then he went on. 'I think they're closin' in on Dominic. The woman wasn't a copper. She was only the copper's sister. He brought his sister along to scare me! Take more than one Highland nance and his sister to drag me into the dock, I can tell ya.'

'Jackie,' Babs said. 'Stop it.'

'Stop what?'

'You're frightenin' the girls.'

'They don't look frightened to me. You're not frightened, are you, sweetheart?' May shook her head. June followed suit. 'Here, gimme the baby an' the big towel an' I'll get her into her gown. By the way, if you think I got the wind up today, think again. They've nothin' on me. Let the buggers lean on Dominic if they like.' He reached past Babs, plucked the baby from the bathwater, lifted her, dripping, into his arms and hugged her to his chest. 'They've leaned on Dom before, remember. If things get too hot Dominic'll fix them. He knows how to handle coppers. Why should I worry?'

'Yeah, why indeed!' said Babs.

He glided away, the baby, towel-wrapped, in his arms.

May and June trailed their father into the nursery, their feet pattering on the parquet. Babs heard the baby's whimper then a petulant wail as her father laid her on the changing table in front of the gas fire.

She leaned on the rim of the bath and listened

to her daughters giggle at Daddy's efforts to talcum April. Jackie might be no prize as a husband but he was more willing than most men to take a hand in raising his children. Sighing, she hoisted herself to her feet and mopped at the puddles on the lino-tiled floor with a damp towel. Luisa, the day-maid, didn't work on Sunday: Sunday was not a day of work but a day of worship, Luisa said. Babs had no alternative but to concede the point, particularly as she had no religious belief to fall back on.

She knew that Jackie was rattled. He couldn't disguise it. Some time next week she would have to have a word with Dennis to find out if the tall, fair-haired policeman was chancing his arm or if the eagle eye of Chief Constable Percy Sillitoe had finally fallen on Dominic Manone and by association on the Hallops.

'Jackie,' she called out. 'Why don't you telephone Dominic?'

Silence in the nursery.

'Call Dominic, let him straighten it out before it gets any worse.'

Jackie appeared in the bathroom doorway, jacket and waistcoat damp, hair ruffled. The baby rode high against his chest, one bare arm about his neck, a nappy pinned snugly about her.

He frowned and said, very quietly, 'Naw.'

'Why not? Dominic will . . .'

'Naw, Babs. No Dominic.' He shook his head emphatically, making April rock in his arms. 'Not a damned word to Dominic about what happened this afternoon, nor to your sister neither. You hear me, Babs?'

'I hear you,' Babs said meekly and drying her hands on the towel hurried through to the kitchen to serve her husband his meal.


The cook was Irish, the day-maid Jewish. Patricia, the little red-haired nanny, was a shy young thing from the Isle of Arran who had taken a course in Domestic and Resident Child Care and thought herself no end of a swell to be working for a well-to-do family like the Manones. There were no Italians on the staff and the bills-of-fare that Mrs O'Shea put up for Polly's approval every Monday contained few traditional dishes though, when the Manones entertained, Mrs O'Shea could produce a magnificent tagliatelle or a cannelloni the very smell of which would make your mouth water.

Most Saturdays the Irish woman and the girl from Arran were given the evening off. They would stroll out arm-in-arm for a fish tea at the Embassy Café before heading off to the pictures. Polly and Dominic would eat supper at the deal table in the kitchen and enjoy having the place to themselves.

If Dominic had been looking forward to a quiet supper alone with his wife when he returned from the racetrack, however, he was doomed to disappointment. Tony was already seated at the kitchen table, making inroads into a fish pie that Cook had left in the oven.

Saying nothing, Dominic slipped off his jacket and loosened his necktie. He pulled out a chair, seated himself, reached for the grappa bottle, poured a shot into a whisky glass and knocked it back.

'Are the children in bed?' he asked.

'Yes,' Polly answered.

'I'll go up to kiss them goodnight.'

'No need,' Polly said. 'They're asleep.'

'Did you remember to collect your winnings?'

'Of course.'

She watched him pour a second shot. She was supposed to be the drinker in the family and it was unusual for Dominic to take anything before dinner. She wondered what had shaken him, if the long-legged blonde had anything to do with it, but she had more sense than to question him in front of Tony, for she was not without secrets of her own.

She laid down her fork and knife and took the pie dish to the oven and put it inside to warm. Tony had taken off his jacket and loosened his neck-tie too. It pleased her to have both her men in the basement kitchen at the same time. Unlike the dining-room the kitchen was an intimate place. A solitary barred window looked out into a garden set higher than the basement and all you could see was a wall, an apron of grass and now and then a cat slinking by.

She waited by the oven while the temperature gauge crept up and observed her husband and his counsellor from the corner of her eye; like brothers, yet not like brothers. She had never met Dominic's brother, or his mother or his father; the American Manones were mere shadows as far as she was concerned. She watched Tony cut through the pie crust with the edge of his fork. He used his knife hardly at all and ate without the finicky mannerisms that Dominic had acquired.

At length she removed the pie dish from the oven and served a helping on to a warm plate. The plates were oval and decorated with vine leaves, the cutlery silver. A fat bottle of frascati and a slender bottle of grappa stood in the centre of the table. Everything in the kitchen was the best that money could buy. Even the fish under the pie-crust was plaice and sole not the scrapings from the bottom of a fishmonger's barrel. The potatoes had been rolled into little crusty balls, spiced with herbs, the salad bowl trimmed with thinly sliced avocado, a vegetable that her mother had probably never heard of let alone tasted.

Polly sipped wine, ate a mouthful of fish.

'How did you get back from the Park then?' Tony asked.

'Flint's boy gave me a ride,' Dominic answered.

'Flint's boy? Which boy would that be?' Polly heard herself say.

Tony looked up at her out of the tops of his eyes but Dominic, working the pepper-mill over his plate, did not seem to notice.

'Skanks, I think his name is,' Dominic said. 'A youngster.'

'Arthur Skanks' boy?' Tony said. 'He's not so young as all that. He has a kid of his own, a girl name of Kate.'

'Really!' Dominic said. 'I don't know how you find out these things.'

'My business to find out these things,' said Tony, not seriously.

'How old is Kate?' said Polly.

'Thirteen, fourteen,' Tony said.

'A little too young even for you,' Polly said. 'Is she pretty?'

'Sure,' said Tony, still not seriously. 'Very pretty.'

'She isn't Italian, by any chance?' Polly said.

'Nope.' Tony loaded his fork again. 'Unfortunately she isn't Italian.'

Dominic gave a little *huh* of amusement and said, 'It seems my wife is determined to marry you off.'

'No I'm not,' said Polly.

She knew that he was trying to draw the conversation away from the events of the afternoon and wondered what soft, waxy secrets he might share with Tony.

'All you wives are the same,' Dominic went on. 'You think that marriage is the answer to all your problems and you believe therefore that it should be the answer to all our problems too.'

'I didn't know you had any problems,' Tony said.

'Not me,' said Dominic. 'You.'

'I got all the trouble I can handle without looking for a wife. What is this? Some feudal rite from the old country, you've got to find me a wife.' He wiped the corners of his lips with his knuckle. Stubble showed dark on his chin, rough to the touch, Polly knew, like a cat's tongue. 'You don't have to get me hitched. I don't need hitched. I don't even want to be hitched.'

Polly laughed. 'If we make another killing like we did today, we can club together and *buy* poor Tony a wife.'

Dominic explored the pastry with his fork in search of tender flakes of sole. Later Tony and he would go upstairs to the living-room to smoke cigars and drink more grappa and chew the fat, while she washed up. She resented her husband's hold over Tony Lombard, though she had no reason to be jealous of anyone, least of all her husband.

'We could all club together,' Tony was saying, 'and buy us a racehorse.'

'Bobtail Boy, maybe?' Dominic suggested.

'Wouldn't be a bad buy, unless Flint's already sold him for horse meat.'

They were keeping her at a distance. Something *had* happened today and Dominic and Tony didn't want her to know about it. If she'd been more like her mother she'd have adopted a good old, straight-from-the-shoulder, hands-on-hips approach, direct as a punch on the nose: *Who was she, Dominic?*

*Who the hell was that woman at the racetrack?* But she hadn't been winnowed by years of hardship. She wasn't big-boned and big-hearted and stuffed with character like Mam. She was a dainty, intelligent, obedient wife who in the opinion of everyone who knew her had everything a woman could want – everything except the one thing she really wanted, the one thing that Dominic could not buy her.

They continued to talk casually about horses, what stabling and training would cost and how, between them, they might turn a profit.

Even Tony had backed away from her.

She got to her feet more abruptly than she had intended, lifted the empty plates from the cloth, reached for the pie-dish and salad bowl and balancing them on her arm looked down at the enquiring faces of her husband and her lover.

'What's it to be, gentlemen?' she said. 'Cake or canary pudding?'

'Why not both?' said Tony.

# Chapter Two

Tony had borrowed the motorcar to collect his parents and drive them to early mass at St Cuthbert's. The Lombardis lived in a tenement flat about half a mile from Manor Park. Tony had left years ago to set himself up in a one-bedroom apartment in a modern block on Riverside. It was a remarkably tidy hide-away but too spartan to have much character, a far cry from a family home cluttered with religious effigies and ornaments and horsehair furniture.

Manor Park Avenue had been dismally traditional when Polly had first moved in and she had insisted on replacing the gilt-framed pictures and dark brown furniture with expensive, lightweight antiques. Dominic had co-operated and various vans would turn up unexpectedly in the driveway and a nice little Regency-style sofa or a pair of eighteenth-century walnut wing chairs would be carried into the house and arranged according to Polly's wishes. Dominic had no study of his own, no office or den to retire to. He claimed the big public room at the front of the house when he wanted to take his ease with a cigar and a coffee pot and the newspapers or when he needed to entertain Mr Shadwell, the firm's accountant, or Carfin Hughes, the lawyer, or other men to whom Polly was never introduced.

On Sunday morning Polly rose early. She had made love again on Saturday night but love-making, however energetic, never wearied her and she carried no guilt about it. She had recently learned to accept responsibility for guilt, to swallow and consume and forget about it, though not about the pleasure that preceded it. Sometimes she wondered if Tony was obliged to atone for what they did together or if his promises to the priest were as hollow as most of his other promises.

Soon after breakfast Babs and the children turned up.

Dominic opened the front door to his sister-in-law and called upstairs to Polly to inform her that 'visitors' had arrived. Polly left Stuart and Ishbel in Nanny Patricia's care and hurried downstairs. Dominic had already lifted his nieces and given each a kiss. He kissed Babs too in a perfunctory sort of way then, leaving the sisters in the hall, padded back into the living-room to his coffee and his newspapers, and closed the door.

'What the hell are you doing dropping in at this hour, Babs?' Polly hissed.

'Need t' talk to you,' said Babs.

'About what?'

'Things,' Babs said. 'Things, that's all.'

Polly had changed a great deal since Babs, Rosie and she had shared a bed in the tenement in Lavender Court but she hadn't shed the conspiratorial rapport with her middle sister for they were linked by experiences that Mammy and Rosie knew nothing about and, God willing, never would.

Polly directed Babs and the baby into the parlour then chased her nephew and nieces upstairs to the first floor playroom. The floor was littered with toys. Flanked by Stuart and Ishbel, Patricia was building a castle out of wooden bricks. Later she would dress the children and escort them to Sunday School at Manor Park Church where they would mingle with other well-to-do children and continue the process of social integration that their father insisted was good for them.

'More for the fray, Patricia. Sorry,' Polly said.

Eager as ever, Angus threw himself full-length on the carpet and gave Stuart a grin to remind his cousin that he was already superior in many important respects. Pert and pretty as daffodils May and June held hands, stared at Ishbel and by force of will tried to reduce her to tears. There was something vulnerable about her children, Polly knew, a gentleness that Babs's brood instinctively exploited. Much as she loved her son and daughter Polly wished that they might be less polite and self-effacing and acquire some of the Hallops' rowdy egotism.

Leaving the children to play, she went back downstairs to the parlour. Babs had unbuttoned her coat and blouse and was breast feeding April in front of the electrical fireplace. French doors opened out on to a flagged path and showed lawn and flowerbeds still rimed with frost, but the room was comfortably warm.

'Do you want something, Babs?'

'Like what?'

'Tea or coffee? Have you had breakfast?'

'Hours ago.'

'Where's Jackie?'

'Sleepin'.' She winced as April tugged her nipple. 'That's why I brought them with me. Give the poor guy some peace.'

'You spoil him, you know.'

'What if I do? He looks after us, I look after him.' Babs brushed her daughter's head in its fluffy angora wool cap. 'I gotta question for you, Poll.'

'Go on.'

'Is Dominic in trouble with the law?'

Polly drew out a chair and seated herself. 'What sort of trouble?'

'I dunno,' Babs said. 'I was hopin' you'd tell me.'

'He's in no trouble that I know of.' The image of the squat little man and the long-legged blonde leapt to mind. 'If he was, I'd probably be the last to hear of it.'

'You could ask Tony.'

'I could,' said Polly. 'But you know Tony; he won't tell me anything. What makes you think there might be trouble?'

'The coppers came round to the salon yesterday, not uniforms, detectives.'

'How many?'

'Just one — and his sister.'

'His sister?'

'They pretended they were lookin' at motor-cars,' Babs explained, 'but they were really lookin' for Jackie.'

'Did they find him?'

''Course they did. Saturday afternoon: where else would he be?'

'Did they have a warrant?'

'Said they had, but they hadn't. Just a card, Jackie said, standard ID.'

'Was she a copper too?'

'What? Who?'

'The sister.'

'Nah,' Babs said. 'She was just camouflage.'

'Were you there?'

'Happens I was, with the kids.'

Polly wore a flowered housecoat and her bare legs were smoothly shaven. No matter how hard she tried Babs couldn't emulate Polly's style. She hadn't the leisure for one thing, or the figure. One more baby, she would blow up like a balloon and any chance of becoming more like Polly would go down the pan forever.

Polly said, 'Did the detective question you?'

'Nah, Jackie wouldn't have stood for that,' Babs said. 'I think he was lookin' for somethin' particular, though I don't know what.'

Polly doubted if Dennis would leave incriminating evidence lying about the garage. Most of the salon's important transactions were conducted between Tony and Dennis who was calm, sensible and pragmatic, at least when he was sober.

'I take it the cop didn't find anything?' Polly said.

'They don't do the work there,' Babs said. 'They do the real work at a yard over in Govan. Everythin' at the salon's legitimate.'

'Including parts?'

'Parts?'

'Spares.'

'Oh yeah, the spares.' Babs shook her head. 'Don't know about the spares.'

Babs was probably lying, Polly thought; there were precious few secrets between her sister and her husband. She wished she could say the same about her marriage. Between Dominic and her lay the whole Italian thing plus a clique of businessmen to whom nothing seemed to matter but pride and profit. She had only a vague notion how Dominic earned the huge sums that flowed into his accounts.

'What do you want me to do, Babs?' Polly said. 'Talk to Dominic?'

'God, no! Jackie would kill me if he thought I'd

blabbed. I just wanted to share it with you, Polly. I admit that the sight of that damned busybody nosin' round our yard fair put the wind up me.'

The baby tugged again on Babs's nipple, her small, newly formed teeth sharp enough to hurt. Babs detached the infant from her breast. Tiny beads of perspiration lined the fringe of April's angora wool cap but the effort of suckling instead of tiring her had made her more eager. She waved a tiny pink fist and staring up at her mother, whimpered for more. At that moment a wail floated down from upstairs. Polly heard a door open and the wail became louder. Feet thudded on the stairs. Patricia called out, 'Stuart, Stuart, Angus didn't mean it,' but both Polly and Babs knew that Angus had meant it, whatever 'it' was.

'I'd better push off,' Babs said.

Ignoring April's demands she hitched up her brassiere, tucked herself into the cups and buttoned her blouse. Polly had never been able to mother in that firm, unhurried manner. She was too yielding and forgiving for her children's good. Any second now, for instance, Stuart would trail tearfully into the parlour and Angus, not contrite but cocky, would protest his innocence against any accusation of bullying that his cousin levelled against him.

Babs cradled the baby against her shoulder. April emitted a loud bark, breaking wind, and dribbled on to her mother's hair.

'Promise you won't say anythin' to Dominic, Poll.'

'All right,' Polly said. 'But tell me if and when the coppers come back.'

'Okay,' Babs said. 'Will you talk to Tony, see what he knows?'

'I'll try. I will. I'll try,' Polly said just as the door swung open and Dominic peeped into the parlour. He had his son, tear-stained, in his arms.

'Ah, there you are,' he said. 'Staying for a spot of lunch, Babs?'

'Is that an invitation?' Babs asked.

'Certainly not.' Dominic laughed in a way that suggested he knew why Babs had called so early and that she wouldn't linger now that the harm had been done. 'But you can stay if Polly asks you.'

'No, thanks,' Babs said, flushing. 'Maybe another time, uh?'

'Any time you like,' said Dominic and while Babs gathered her brood for departure, carried his son safely into the living-room and quietly closed the door.

After the death of her mother-in-law Lizzie Peabody felt more at home in the terraced cottage in Knightswood. Though small, it was a great deal more comfortable than any of the tenement slums in which she'd raised her daughters after their father, Frank Conway, had done a bunk. The only problem in living there was that she'd had to share it with Bernard's mother. Old Mrs Peabody had been understandably resentful that her surviving son had picked a wife who was older than he was and who had arrived in Knightwood dragging a deaf daughter with her. The fact that Lizzie, Rosie and Mrs Peabody had managed to rub along for several years without much friction was mainly due to Bernard's tact.

In the spring of 1933 old Mrs Peabody passed away in her sleep. Bernard was naturally upset. Rosie wept buckets and even Lizzie shed a tear or two and set about arranging a grand funeral tea in the Co-op halls for all Violet Peabody's friends, a gathering of fifty mourners, mostly war widows, who consumed vast quantities of sandwiches and sausage rolls and flirted outrageously with Bernard and Reverend Jacks, the only gentlemen present.

For a month or so afterwards Bernard was very depressed. Then summer arrived, the patch of garden behind the cottage claimed his attention and at Lizzie's suggestion he repapered and painted the back bedroom. Rosie abandoned the bed-settee in the living-room and moved into Mother Peabody's bedroom, and the waters of Lethe closed quietly over Violet Peabody and before the year was out there was nothing much left to remember her by except a few ornaments and a nice little headstone up in the cemetery at Copplestone Road.

In the same year Lizzie's mother also passed away – much less discreetly.

Gran McKerlie had been rehearsing her death for years, of course, walled up in a single-end on the top floor of a crumbling tenement in Laurieston with only Janet, Lizzie's sister, to look after her. The building was one of many ancient tenements that the city council planned to demolish as soon as there was budget enough to replace them. Everyone looked forward to the day when the hammers would move in on Ballingall Street – everyone that is except Gran McKerlie.

In due course council inspectors arrived, then planners, then dapper little men with folders and briefcases accompanied by doctors from the Public Health department and Gran McKerlie was officially informed that her tenement was next for demolition and that she would be transferred to more suitable accommodation. On receiving this information Gran McKerlie went mad, not certifiably, carted-off-in-a-van type mad, alas, which would have solved everyone's problem. Instead the old woman shook off the nine plagues of age, donned the armour of righteousness and, like something nasty out of Norse mythology, elected to go down fighting. Even after the chimneys were removed, walls demolished and the whole rat-infested neighbourhood was disintegrating about her ears Gran McKerlie refused to be intimidated by the ball-hammer that hung ominously close outside her window and remained fixed in the wooden armchair from which she had ruled the roost for so long. Perhaps she saw herself as the last relic of a golden age of hardship and squalor that Glaswegians would look back on with perverse and totally unwarranted affection: whatever the reason, Gran refused to budge.

First the council sent a constable to escort the old lady downstairs, then a second constable, then a sergeant, then two firemen, then a female Public Health official who patiently explained to Gran that a lovely ground-floor apartment awaited her in a refurbished tenement just around the corner in Moorcastle Street, that Janet had inspected the place and approved of it – which Janet had not – and that all Gran had to do to inherit this palace was permit the firemen to ease her out of her chair and carry her down the iron staircase into a waiting taxicab.

Gran's answer was to growl, spit and whack the Public Health official's shins with one of her walking-sticks, a response that finally reduced Janet to helpless tears. After further consultation a council vehicle was sent across the river to Knightswood to fetch Lizzie to come and reason with the thrawn old bat before civic authority was forced to live up to its stereotype and act like a heartless monster.

Lizzie duly arrived: Lizzie clambered up the iron staircase, squeezed past dapper gentlemen, past firemen and coppers, past the red-faced female health official and entered the smelly one-roomed flat where her mother lay in wait. The moment Lizzie stepped over the threshold Gran raised herself out of the invalid chair for the first time in twenty years and, with eyes bulging and a curious white froth on her lips, yelled, *'Now see what you've done t' me, Lizzie, you an' your high jinks,'* and toppled forward on to the dusty floorboards, felled by an almighty stroke.

The reports to the Fiscal's office exonerated police and council officials from blame and Gran's body was released to the family just as soon as the tenement in Ballingall Street had been safely reduced to rubble. Dominic met the costs of the funeral and the head-stone in Laurieston necropolis. He sent Polly round to the refurbished council apartment in Moorcastle Street to offer Aunt Janet financial assistance in the shape of a well-paid job in his warehouse. Janet would have none of his dirty money, his charity. She wouldn't let Polly cross the doorstep, wouldn't speak to Lizzie or any member of the Conway clan, was finished with the Conways for good and all, she said, and thereafter refused to answer letters or accept gifts even at Christmas and New Year. In 1936, Mr Smart's wee grocery store, where Janet had worked for years, was sold to Sloan's dairy chain. Janet was given a new white overall and an increase in wages and, as far as Lizzie or her daughters knew, continued to live out her lonely little life south of the river.

After a year or so Lizzie no longer felt guilty about what had happened to her mother and sister. She snuggled up to Bernard and thanked God for the way things had panned out, for daughters who had gone up in the world, for darling wee grandchildren, for a nice secure house and nice secure husband who, thanks to the influence of Dominic Manone, was now deputy manager of an estate agency in the leafy outer reaches of the city.

In the back of her mind, though, Lizzie suspected

that there were still some dark things out there, nightmarish things, from which neither Bernard nor Dominic could protect her and that Rosie knew what they were and what they signified.

Bernard could have told her if only she'd thought to ask him. He knew only too well what the changes in their circumstances meant and what the cost might be in the long run for he'd wrestled with his conscience for weeks before deciding to accept the opportunity for advancement that Dominic had offered him. In a strange way he had been inspired by his stepdaughter Rosie who had lost her hearing in childhood. He reckoned that if Rosie had learned to cope with that handicap he could learn to cope with something as minor as a bruised conscience.

Rosie had acquired a variety of ways of comprehending. She could lip-read with astonishing accuracy, but how the words conveyed themselves to her brain not even Bernard could begin to understand. He was very close to Rosie, though, for every morning they walked the half-mile to the railway station at Anniesland Cross together and had developed an affectionate rapport.

On wet days they shared the shelter of Bernard's black umbrella. On crisp, invigorating winter mornings with the sun just showing above the trees of Jordanhill, they would step out lively. But whatever the weather Rosie's cheerful presence would send Bernard rattling off on the train to Breslin with a smile while Rosie, travelling in the opposite direction, caught the train into Glasgow for a day's work in Shelby's bookshop.

On that particular November morning, however, the sun failed to penetrate the fog that shrouded the suburbs, street lamps remained lighted and the houses seemed to be cut from thick grey flannel. City workers emerging from garden gates nodded to Bernard and touched their hats to Rosie and girl clerks and shop assistants fluttered gloved hands in greeting. Bowler hats and scarves, newspapers, lighted pipes, after-breakfast cigarettes, the minutiae of the weekday world, Bernard thought, the substance of days that would go ticking on and on, strangely fulfilling in their predictability.

Rosie raised her chin from beneath her scarf and said, 'Do you ever wonder how much money our Dominic rakes in?'

Bernard turned to face her. 'What makes you ask?'

She shrugged. 'The fog reminds me of the old days.'

'You are too young for' – he broke the word into three parts – 'nos-tal-gia. Don't tell me you're hankering after the Gorbals?'

She laughed. 'Nuh, nuh. I was just thinking of Dominic's boys, the street collectors. I wonder what became of Alex O'Hara, for instance, after Dominic changed his spots. Dominic *has* changed his spots, has he not?'

'Why don't you ask Polly?'

'Hah!'

'I don't know if he's changed his spots com–pleet–ly,' Bernard said.

'I can see what you're saying.'

'Sorry.'

'But I do not hear an answer.'

'I don't have an answer, Rosie.'

The hub of the Manone empire was still the Central Warehouse in Govan. Dominic had financed Jackie Hallop's motor showroom, no secret there. He had also bought into Lyons & Lloyd's real estate agency and had installed a new manager, Mr Shakespeare, who was Bernard's boss. Dominic owned stock in several Clydeside cafés and restaurants and supplied equipment for ice-cream factories and a bottling plant. The bulk of his interests were decidedly shady, however, and Bernard preferred not to know about them.

'Does the Rowing Club in Molliston Street still belong to Dominic?'

Rosie definitely wanted an answer. He could always tell when she was trying to wheedle something out of him by the way she slurred her consonants. Why, he wondered, was she suddenly so interested in Dominic? Personally he preferred to forget the dreadful years in Lavender Court when squaring up to Dominic's debt collectors had forced him to acknowledge that honesty and cowardice do not necessarily go hand in hand.

He hesitated, then signed with a firm, flat, emphatic

slash of the right hand to terminate that line of conversation.

Undeterred Rosie continued to watch for an answer.

'I believe he sold the club to John Flint when he gave up bookmaking,' Bernard said at length. 'Polly put pressure on him, I think.'

'Does Polly have influence over him?' Rosie said. 'I know she is supposed to wear the pants in the Manone household but I do not think that is the case.'

Bernard could see the busy junction of Anniesland Cross up ahead. For once he was relieved to be nearing the railway station. He really did not want to be reminded that he, or rather Lizzie, had almost lost out to the gangs and that only the intervention of Dominic Manone, the biggest crook of all, had finally rescued the Conways from the contamination of the slums; Bernard still detected a sinister irony in that fact.

Rosie's job in Shelby's bookshop may have matured her but she would never have her sisters' hard shell. He had constantly to remind himself that married or not the Conway girls were united and that by accepting Dominic's offer of a post with Lyons & Lloyd he too had put himself beyond the pale.

Rosie stopped at the crossing that would carry them over the tramlines between buses and trade vans and the slow-moving drays that came down in convoy from the coal depot and the long horse-drawn carts from the timber yard that adjoined the canal. In the murky morning air the gasometer resembled a zeppelin hovering behind the railway bridge that spanned the Great Western Road. Bernard glanced at his wristlet watch and took Polly's arm to steer her across the thoroughfare. She resisted, not petulantly but firmly.

'Will you not tell me anything about Dominic?' she shouted.

Bernard put his hand to his ear as a tram thundered past.

'Can't hear you,' he mouthed. 'Sorry.'

And that morning at the railway station, for the first time ever, Rosie refused to kiss him goodbye.

Oswald Shelby, Sons & Partners, Books, Rare Books, Bindings & Manuscripts, had been at the centre of the book trade in Glasgow for the best part of sixty years. Their premises in Mandeville Square, just around the corner from the Royal Exchange, occupied all five floors of one of the city's neo-classical buildings. It was not the architecture that caught the attention of passers-by, though, but the two shallow windows in which were displayed a few of the many bibliographical treasures that Shelby's had for sale.

Dressing the windows was a task that Mr Robert Shelby, the junior partner, had allocated to Rosalind Conway. Sometimes she would stack the spaces with leather-bound sets, on other occasions with just a few handsome volumes laid on velvet cloth. Price tickets were never attached, only a simple description of the items written on postcards in the clear copperplate script that Rosie had perfected. She enjoyed dressing windows and didn't object in the least when cocky young stockbrokers or insurance clerks loitered outside to ogle her while she worked. She would give them a smile, sometimes a wink but always modestly ensured that she wasn't giving them an eyeful of her knickers as well. Her main occupation was that of research cataloguer and she spent most of her time hunched behind a long table in an alcove at the rear of the ground-floor book room. She had received her training from Mr Albert Briggs who was almost as old as the building itself, though in recent years Albert's eyesight had deteriorated to the point where he could hardly see print at all and Rosie did all the manuscript work and most of the typing.

Rosie had no brothers and had never known her father. The men who had most influenced her were not blood relatives, not Conways or McKerlies but Bernard, Mr Albert and, of course, Mr Feldman at the Institute where she'd been schooled. As a teenager she'd moped over Mr Robert Shelby and imagined that he would eventually fall in love with her but it didn't take long to discover that love does not conquer all and when Mr Robert married an English debutante Rosie was more relieved than disappointed.

On the table were a pile of books that Rosie had lugged up from the basement last thing on Saturday, choice items from the library of the late Sheriff of Golspie. She laid out her sheaf of lined foolscap, filled the inkwells, renewed the blotting-paper and had just picked out a first edition of Burke's *Reflections on the Revolution in France* when the bell above the main door chimed.

'That,' said Mr Albert, 'sounds like your young man again.'

Rosie frowned. Mr Albert, arms folded, calmly puffed his pipe. She didn't have to ask how he knew who had entered the shop when he couldn't see further than the tip of his nose for she had an odd, almost supernatural sixth sense when it came to picking up sounds that her ears could not hear.

'Is it him?' said Albert.

Rosie peeped over the partition.

'It's him,' she said, trying to whisper.

'Where's Gannon?'

Gannon, now in his twenties, was the shop-boy. He should have been dusting counters and display cases and gener-ally keeping an eye on the book room while Mr McAdam, the department manager, spent his usual twenty minutes in the water closet attending to a call of nature and completing the *Glasgow Herald* crossword. Gannon, though, was nowhere to be seen.

'Your young man's either a shoplifter,' Albert said, 'or he's after somebody. Who could he be after, I wonder?'

'Gannon perhaps?' Rosie struggled to keep her voice down.

'I doubt it,' Albert said. 'If anyone ever comes for Gannon it'll be in a Black Maria. Now, do you want me to hoist my poor old bones . . .'

'I will go and see what he wants,' said Rosie. 'If I cannot make out what he is saying I will come and fetch you.'

'You'll make out what he's saying, I'm sure.'

Albert returned the pipe to his mouth, leaned back and folded his arms as Rosie darted out from behind the desk before Gannon could appear and spoil everything. She put on her best 'Babs' walk, chest out and hips swaying. Unfortunately she didn't have Babs's figure but she was more graceful than her middle sister and hoped that might compensate. She had met the young man several times before, which is to say that he was on his way to becoming a regular. There were a dozen like him, though not so attractive, men who would drop by to chat to Rosie and who made nothing out of her deafness. They were bookworms, however; clearly the young man was not. He seemed uncomfortable in the book room, as if fearful that the shelves might collapse or the stately glass-fronted cases crack if he trod too heavily on the carpeted floor.

'Good morning, Mr MacGregor,' Rosie said.

'Ah!'

'You are the early bird, are you not?'

A pinkish flush spread across his broad cheeks. He considered resting an elbow on the surface of a Globe bookcase but decided against it. He stuck his hands in his overcoat pockets and rocked on the balls of his feet. He wore black polished shoes with thick soles.

Rosie watched his lips move: 'I've an hour to spare so I thought . . .'

'What better way to spend it than browsing among old books?'

'Aye – yes, that's right.'

'Oh, dear!' said Rosie. 'I was hoping you had popped in to see me.'

'Oh, I did. I mean . . . I have.'

Rosie could do little to control the pitch of her voice. To compensate she had perfected the art of body language and could convey much by a wave of the hand or a tilt of the eyebrow. 'Is there something in particular you are after?'

'I've something I'd like you to look at.' He fumbled in the pocket of his overcoat and drew out a brown-paper packet. 'I wonder if it's got any value.'

Rosie hid her disappointment and took the packet. What worthless 'treasure' had he unearthed from a hall cupboard or from his old grandmother's dresser drawer, she wondered. She gave him a professional smile.

'I am not a valuator. Mr Robert is our valuator.'

'Still,' the young man said, 'I'd like you to look at it first.'

'Why?'

'Well, you never know. You might have seen it before.'

She felt a sudden stiffening inside herself. Last time

they had chatted he had mentioned that he knew her brother-in-law, dropping Dominic's name so casually into the conversation that she'd made little of it, just enough to prompt her to ask Bernard about Dominic's present circumstances. She hadn't forgotten the sort of men who'd hung about the Ferryhead Rowing Club, though Mr MacGregor didn't look at all like one of Dominic's runners. Besides if Dominic had an item – a stolen item – that he wanted valued she was the last person he'd send it to. She placed the packet on top of the bookcase and peeled off the brown-paper wrappings.

As soon as the little volume was exposed Rosie's demeanour changed. She lifted the book carefully on the flat of her hand and opened it at the title-page.

'Do you know what it is?' Mr MacGregor said.

Although he was standing close by, she heard his question as a faint bumble-bee drone that had no meaning whatsoever. She did not ask him to repeat himself.

She studied the book's title-page, turned the pages with her forefinger and examined the red and black type, red-ruled margins and stunning woodcuts.

He leaned closer, his lips almost brushing her ear.

'Can you read what it says?'

'Yes,' Rosie answered. *'Heures à la Louange de la Vierge Marie.'*

She pronounced the French words badly but she didn't think Mr MacGregor would notice.

'What does that mean?' he asked.

'Hours in Praise of the Virgin Mary.'

'Oh!'

'It is a prayer book.'

She turned the book over and opened it at the back page.

*'Ex libris Augusti le Chevalier,'* she read aloud.

He pointed. 'Is that a date?'

'Fifteen hundred and twenty-five. Paris – for Geofroy de Bourges.'

'Wow! It's old, isn't it?'

'Not for a prayer book,' Rosie told him. 'An early date does not give it value.'

'What's it worth?' Mr MacGregor said. 'Approximately.'

'I have no idea.'

She continued to turn pages, counting the wood-cuts, checking seaming and pagination: no shaving of the margins, the binding tight: an almost perfect copy of a choice item. Even so, holding the little volume gave her a queer feeling that something wasn't quite right about it.

'It is valuable, though, isn't it?' the young man said.

She could sense his urgency; perhaps he *was* one of Dominic's cronies and the choice little item *had* been stolen.

'Wait,' she said. 'Just wait right here.'

'Where are you going?'

'To find Mr Shelby.'

'For – what for?'

'To make you an offer.'

'An offer, but . . .'

She glanced up the length of the shop in the hope that Gannon or Mr McAdam had returned to the floor. She thought of calling out to Albert but Albert was too old and frail to protect her if the thief decided to cut up rough.

She kept calm and said, 'I thought you wanted to sell it.'

'No, I only want it valued.'

'What for? Insurance?'

'Look, just tell me – have you seen that book before?'

'Never,' said Rosie. 'It is quite a rare item, I think.'

'Are you absolutely sure nobody has ever shown you this book?'

'You mean somebody like my brother-in-law?'

'Your brother-in-law?'

'Dominic Manone. He sent you, did he not?'

'He's the last person who'd send me,' Mr MacGregor said.

For a moment Rosie thought he was about to snatch the prayer book from her hands and make a break for it. She pulled the volume to her breast and followed the movement of his lips anxiously.

'Knew I shouldn't have come,' he murmured. 'Rotten idea in the first place.'

'Idea? Whose idea? Dominic's idea?' Rosie said loudly.

'You're going upstairs to telephone the police, aren't you?'

'I am going to show the book to Mr Shelby.'

He leaned against the bookcase and fumbled with the buttons at the breast of his coat. Rosie was suddenly afraid. She remembered O'Hara, Dominic's persuader, his razors, his knives. The bluff young man with the curly fair hair and frank open face might be an up-to-date version of the same vicious breed.

She opened her mouth to shout for Albert, but no sound emerged, then she was staring at a card that had appeared in the young man's hand. He held it out to her like a badge. It wasn't a badge, however, just a card, open like a little pageless book. She saw the words *City of Glasgow Police*, red-letter stamping, a name printed beneath a signature: *Kenneth Robert MacGregor*.

'Yuh – yuh – you're a policeman,' Rosie stammered.

'Yes, I'm afraid I am,' said Kenneth.

'Thank God for that,' said Rosie, and puffed out her cheeks in relief.

# Chapter Three

The decor of the Athena Hotel did not impress Dominic Manone. There was too much steel and mirrored glass, too many bars and elevators and circular corridors and the pale mock-marble staircases reminded him of nothing so much as great frozen blocks of vanilla ice-cream, all too self-consciously modern and arty for his taste. He ate lunch there with Victor Shadwell from time to time only because Victor liked to appear up to date, though in fact the accountant would probably have been more at home in the Rowing Club than in the cold neon glare of the Athena's bar and grill. He crossed the lobby, presented himself at the reception desk and asked for Mr Harker. He expected to be directed to the coffee lounge or one of the bars. Instead he was given a room number and told to go straight up to the ninth floor.

The elevator was vast, fast, and empty. It discharged him into a featureless corridor of pale blue carpet that curved around the north side of the building. From the little windows he could look out at nothing but sky. He followed the numbers around the bend then ahead of him saw a rectangle of light and standing out in the corridor, arm raised in welcome, Edgar Harker wearing a pair of pale green flannel trousers and a turkey-red sweater.

'Dom,' he called out, 'come away with you, come on in. Found us okay?' He ushered Dominic into the suite with a vigorous handshake and a slap on the back.

Four close-set windows defined the shape of the building and under them, bathed in icy November light, was a black leather sofa, and on the sofa was the girl.

She seemed, Dominic thought, to need that amount of space to accommodate her long slender legs and long-waisted body. She wore a tailored suit in charcoal grey and a white shirt-blouse with a frothy lace collar, jet black patent leather shoes. Her arms were extended along the back of the sofa, long, long arms with the longest most delicate hands Dominic had ever seen. Her head was tilted to one side, a strand of gleaming golden hair dangling over one eye. She gave a little shake of her shoulders and looked up at him, not sweetly but with a kind of taunting mockery.

'Well, here she is,' Ed Harker said. 'All yours.'

'Not so fast,' Dominic said. 'I haven't agreed to take her on yet.'

'Oh, but you will, son,' Ed Harker said. 'You got no choice, really.'

'I'm not ten years old and this isn't Philadelphia,' Dominic said. 'You can't breeze in off the Yankee Clipper and tell me what to do. I'm under no obligation to you, Harker, or to you, Miss – Miss Weston.'

'Call me Penny,' the girl said.

'How about I remind you that she's just escaped from a country where girls like her are being herded into trucks and sent to keep the troops amused,' Harker said. 'You read the newspapers, don't you? Even the Scottish papers must . . .'

'Oh, for God's sake!' Dominic interrupted. 'I don't swallow any of that propaganda claptrap and I'm not going to be taken in by some sob story about how she's my niece or my cousin or my half sister.'

'You told me Saturday you understood the situation,' Harker said.

'Sure, the old man cabled me and told me the score,' Dominic said. 'But that doesn't mean to say I'm falling for your cock-and-bull stories about persecution.'

'Do you not want to help your papa?' the girl asked.

Dominic ignored her. He turned from the windows and looked around. The suite had two doors, apart from the door to the corridor. One led to the bathroom, the other to the bedroom. He noted the double bed's rumpled sheets.

'Ain't nobody hiding in there,' Harker said. 'It's too early for Santa Claus.'

The girl uncrossed her legs and drew them up. She looked as angular as an antelope but not awkward or ungainly. She spoke English with just the trace of an accent. He had met her only briefly at the racetrack on Saturday and hadn't yet figured out where John Flint fitted into the picture, or if Flint was involved at all.

He said, 'Who's paying for all this?'

'You are,' Ed Harker said.

When he grinned the massive brown moustache rose to expose a twisted scar on his upper lip. He was even more ebullient than he had been at the weekend, cockier and more sure of himself too.

'He wants to hear about the money, Ed,' the girl said. 'It's the money not me that is the problem for Dominic.'

'Oh, no,' Dominic said. 'Don't kid yourself: you *are* the problem. I'll get around to talking about the other thing once I've decided what I'm going to do with you.'

'What's wrong? Harker said. 'Don't you trust your own father?'

'I haven't seen my own father since I was ten years old.'

'It is therefore understandable that you are cautious,' the girl said. 'It pays us all to be cautious, does it not?'

'Look,' Ed Harker said, 'take off your coat and

park yourself and we'll thrash out the deal. Penny's right – you're entitled to be cagey.'

'I want you to tell me in words of one syllable why I should take responsibility for this young woman and, while we're at it, just what she has to do with the Manones.'

'I go with the money,' the girl said.

'I can figure the money side of it.' Dominic addressed her directly. 'I can see what's in it for me but . . .'

'More than you can possibly imagine,' the girl put in.

'But I can't figure how you got to be part of the deal. I'm quite capable of setting up the sort of organisation my father needs without some kid peeking over my shoulder all the time.'

'Have you done a similar thing before?' the girl asked.

She was smart, Dominic decided, smarter than Harker. He knew Harker, the type at least. There was something depressingly familiar about Harker in spite of his gaudy clothes and Americanised drawl. Take him out of the turkey-red sweater and tight pants, Dominic decided, and you could put him down in Govan Road and he'd hardly be noticed. The girl on the other hand had no natural protection. Drape her in an old shawl, wrap a cheap cotton skirt about her and she'd still stick out like a sore thumb.

He knew why it had become necessary to get her out of Vienna but he couldn't understand why his father had shipped her to Scotland. She wasn't a blood relative, wasn't even Italian. Unless he missed his guess she was Jewish, a young Austrian Jew who had fled flag-waving, kow-towing Vienna soon after Hitler's storm troopers had marched into the city.

'Have you?' the girl repeated. 'Can you handle something this big?'

Harker laughed. 'Sure, he can. Carlo wouldn't have sent you here if Glasgow hadn't been the right place and Dominic the right guy for the job.'

'I would like to hear him say that I am welcome,' the girl said.

Dominic noticed that she avoided making eye contact with Harker. He wondered if she was ashamed of having to share a bed with a man old enough to be her father, wondered too if his father, Carlo Manone, knew about the sleeping arrangements or if that was something that Harker had negotiated on his own.

'I'm not going to send you back to Austria, if that's what you mean.'

'Say that I am welcome and I will show you what I have brought you.'

'All right,' Dominic said flatly. 'You're welcome.'

She unfolded herself from the sofa. She was taller than he was but somehow he didn't mind. He stepped aside as she strode across the room. Grinning again, Harker pushed the bedroom door wide open and after she'd gone into the bedroom closed it behind her.

'You won't be so shy when you see what she's brought,' he said.

'Shy? I'm not shy.'

'Maybe not, but you certainly ain't what I expected. I thought you'd grow up different. More like your old man.'

'What do you mean by that?' Dominic said.

'I mean, you're a surly wee begger, ain't you?'

'Be careful.'

'Giving that poor lassie such a hard time.'

'What do you do for my father in Philadelphia?'

'Lots of things,' said Harker.

'For instance?'

'I ran numbers for a while.'

'What else?' said Dominic.

'I kept your brother out of trouble.'

'What sort of trouble?'

'Trouble with the law, trouble with the union bosses.'

'The unions?' Dominic said. 'On the docks?'

'Sure, on the docks,' said Harker. 'In the shipyards, the refinery too. We had a lot of trouble at the refinery one time.'

'You were a professional strike breaker, I take it.'

'I did what you do, son: I organised.'

'Why has my father never mentioned you in his letters?'

'No reason to mention me, was there?'

'I suppose not,' Dominic conceded for this was neither the time nor the place to test Edgar Harker's knowledge of the inner workings of the family business on the Delaware.

He watched the bedroom door, awaiting the girl's return.

'Fancy her, do you?' Harker said.

'What?'

'Wouldn't be human, you didn't fancy her.'

'I'm a married man,' Dominic said, stiffly, 'a happily married man.'

'So what?'

'Aren't you married?'

'Not me.'

'Well, I am.'

'I know,' Harker said. 'You married Polly Conway and you've two kids, Stuart and Ishbel. See, I done my homework before I left Philly.'

The bedroom door opened again and the girl emerged carrying an oblong cardboard box. She walked to the coffee table in the centre of the room and placed the box upon it. She lifted off the lid of the box and extracted several layers of white tissue paper and soft cloth padding. She put the packing carefully to one side, sank down on her knees, lifted out the plates and placed them on the flannel then, leaning to one side, beckoned to Dominic.

The plates were of fine steel fixed to thin strips of lead backed by thick wooden blocks. They were obviously heavy, like little ingots. The girl used both hands to lift one. She tilted it against the light so that Dominic could see the tooling.

'Beautiful, is it not?' the girl said.

'How does it print?' said Dominic.

'Perfectly.'

'Do you have samples?'

'Only on rough paper.'

'Where do we get the right paper?' Dominic said.

'We have a contact in Verona?'

'Your uncle,' said Harker. 'Old Guido.'

'Guido isn't in Verona?'

'He is now,' said Harker.

'I thought he'd retired,' said Dominic. 'He's an old man, for God's sake.'

'Old men have their uses too,' the girl said. 'Look at the reverse.'

She held up the second plate and offered it to Dominic. The surface had been treated with a light film of wax. He balanced the block on the tips of his fingers to avoid contaminating the engraving. He would have preferred not to handle the plates at all but it was too late for that sort of caution. He had never seen let alone handled a counterfeit plate before. Three years ago he had shifted a crate of forged banknotes, though, had filtered them down through the *Unione* to finance a shipment of side arms from an agent in Sicily, arms that had probably wound up in the hands of Spanish guerrillas.

He felt oddly stimulated just holding the plate in a hotel room with a beautiful Jewish girl from Vienna looking up at him. So far life had been easy, almost routine, but now his father had thrust him into something much more dangerous than managing a few shady sidelines in the back streets of Glasgow. He glanced down at the girl's long waist and rounded hips, at her helmet of blonde hair. She, not Harker, was the key to the deal, though whether he would like the deal when it came right down to it was another matter.

He gave her back the plate, offered his hand and drew her to her feet. He peeled off his overcoat, tossed it to Harker then seated himself squarely on the sofa and looked up at the girl.

'All right, Miss Weston,' he said. 'Tell me exactly what you need to get started.'

'A house?' Bernard said. 'What sort of a house?'

'Four or five large bedrooms. Detached.'

'Here in Breslin?'

'In the neighbourhood,' said Dominic. 'Outside the city.'

'To buy?'

'To rent.'

'Long term?'

'A year at least, maybe longer.'

'I don't know if we have anything right now. Perhaps Mr Shakespeare . . .'

'Forget Allan Shakespeare,' Dominic said. 'I want you to handle the transaction, Bernard, and keep very, very quiet about it.'

'I see,' Bernard said. 'I take it this house is not for Polly?'

'No, for a friend.'

'I see,' said Bernard again.

The Dolomite was parked outside the office but there was no sign of Tony Lombard. Dominic had driven himself across the river, out through sprawling garden suburbs and over the Switchback, past farms and fruit orchards into the region of mansions and villas that formed the communities of Bearsden, Mugdock and Breslin. The fact that his boss had come calling on a cold, grey November afternoon indicated that something unusual was going on and Bernard began to suspect that the telephone call that had summoned Allan Shakespeare to a 'showing' that afternoon was more than just coincidence.

He knew just the sort of property that Dominic required for his 'friend', not a nice cheap little hideaway but something expensive and discreet. He regretted that Dominic had involved him in the deception. From now on he would be obliged to lie whenever someone in the family praised Dominic for his devotion to Polly and the children. He stepped behind the counter, pulled open a drawer, slid out a ledger and slapped it down on the counter.

'What's wrong with you?' Dominic asked.

'I don't know what you mean?'

'You're mad at me.'

'Of course I'm not,' said Bernard, grimly.

'You think it's for a woman, don't you?'

'None of my business who it's for.'

'Well, it is for a woman.'

'Oh!'

'It isn't what you think, though.'

'You don't have to explain yourself to me, sir.'

'Come off it,' Dominic said. 'You're as transparent as a pane of glass. It's a woman who'll be living in the house but not, let me emphasise, *my* woman. I'm only telling you this because you'll be handling the transaction and I've got to trust you not to tell anyone about it. When you see the girl you're going to assume I've lied to you because she's a peach – but she isn't my peach, Bernard, just remember that.'

'She is your responsibility, however?'

'That's it, that's all.'

'Blackstone Farm.'

'Hah!' Dominic said. 'Of course. We bought the whole site, didn't we?'

'You did,' Bernard said. 'At least Bonskeet's Builders did. You should keep a closer eye on your holdings, Dominic, and you wouldn't have to ask for my help. I take it you've never been out to the Blackstone site?'

'To the farmhouse? No, I've never been there.'

'It's a far cry from a thatched cottage,' Bernard said. 'It's a two-storey dwelling in finished brick. All mod cons. Been empty for half a year simply because nobody's keen to stump up for a farmhouse on the edge of a new estate.'

'It isn't an investment. I don't want to buy it.'

'You don't have to buy it,' Bernard said. 'All I have to do is tell the Bard that you dropped in, checked the ledger and suggested we might do better to lease the damned place than have it standing empty. I'll draft an agreement, have your female friend sign it and attach a separate page with your name as guarantor. Your bank will send us a cheque every month and none of it need show in the ledger.'

'What about Shakespeare?'

'He has his own private files: I have mine.'

'Do you now?' said Dominic.

'Well, I will have when I do this for you.'

'How far off the beaten track is Blackstone Farm?' Dominic asked.

'Half a mile from Roman Road, give or take. It's level track, if a little on the rough side. The building site is a good half-mile to the west so there won't be a problem of disturbance, not for a while. In fact, if there's a war . . .'

'There won't be a war,' said Dominic.

'Won't there?' said Bernard. 'Been in touch with Adolf, have you?'

'Chamberlain will make sure that the agreement with Hitler stands up,' Dominic said. 'Don't you believe in peace in our time, Bernard?'

'Experience has taught me not to put much faith in paper promises,' Bernard said. 'Experience also suggests that it might not be too long before the blackshirts are measuring noses in Argyll Street.'

'At least you'll have nothing to worry about,' Dominic said.

'No, but I'm not a Semite.'

'My friend is,' Dominic said.

'Pardon?'

'My friend – your new client – is a Jew.'

'Really!'

'Does that make a difference?'

'Not in the slightest,' Bernard said. 'Does she have family?'

'She came on her own?'

'Came,' said Bernard, 'from where?'

'You're asking too many questions.'

'Is that why you want some place quiet for her, because she's a Jew?'

'Far too many questions.' Dominic leaned on the counter and inspected the entry in the property ledger. 'As far as anyone's concerned Miss Weston is an American. She has all the necessary papers to prove citizenship in the land of the free and her accent – she does have a slight accent – won't matter because if any of the locals get too curious she'll tell them her father is Dutch.'

'She's a young woman, you say.'

'Yes.'

'She's going to find it pretty damned quiet up at Blackstone.'

'Peace and quiet will suit her,' Dominic said. 'Is this place furnished?'

'Partly,' said Bernard. 'Scrappy stuff. You'll have to dig about in your warehouse to find her something to sleep on.'

'Can we go see it?'

'What? Now?'
'Why not?'
'It'll mean closing the office.'
'Then do so,' Dominic said.

It had been a long day for Lizzie. Splashing about
with suds and boiling water in the wash-house at the
bottom of the garden was quite satisfying but wet
clothes were impossible to dry on the outdoor lines
in winter and she'd had to lug the clothes into the
kitchen, screw the mangle to the side of the sink and
wring out each garment individually. She'd worked
for so many years in a hospital laundry, however, that
domestic wash-days seemed easy by comparison.

She finished about half-past four, hung sheets
and shirts on a pulley in the kitchen, stockings and
underwear on a rack in the living-room. She would
remove the rack before Bernard arrived at a quarter past six for Lizzie belonged to the traditional
school of housewives who believed that the bread-
winner should come home to a neat and tidy house
with a piping hot meal on the table. Lizzie, in a
clean frock and apron, would be waiting to give
her husband a kiss at the door and Rosalind would
arrive ten or fifteen minutes later and then they
would sit down together and, as Bernard put it,
break bread.

That evening, however, Rosie arrived before her
stepfather.

She slipped straight into her bedroom and did not come out again.

Lizzie reckoned that she would by lying on the bed with her 'good ear', the left, laid gently against the loudspeaker of the big old-fashioned wireless set, in which position, it seemed, Rosie could pick up not just music but voices. She wasn't unduly concerned about her daughter's need for solitude. She would keep an eye on the girl, though, for she was plagued by a fear that the germs that had almost cost Rosie her life twenty-one years ago might still be lurking in her bloodstream just waiting to strike again.

Bernard did not rattle the letter-box until a quarter to seven. The moment he entered the hallway Lizzie realised that he too was in an unusually sombre mood. Her kiss was received without much enthusiasm and was not reciprocated.

She hung up his coat, hat and scarf. 'Busy day, dearest?'

Bernard went directly to his chair by the fire and sat down.

'Last minute client,' he said, and opened his newspaper.

Back in the kitchen Lizzie ladled oxtail soup into three bowls, carried them into the living-room and put them on the table in the corner by the window.

Bernard got up from the fireside and came to the table and a moment later Rosie appeared, seated herself too and began to spoon hot soup into her mouth.

Bad news often affected her husband and daughter's mood. Lizzie glanced at the front page of the newspaper that lay on Bernard's chair. It seemed innocuous enough; a blurred photograph of a burnt-out church, not even a church but a synagogue, in a town called Vienna, a long way from St Margaret's at Knightswood Cross or St David's at Polnoon.

'What's wrong with you both tonight?' she asked.

'Nothing,' Bernard answered.

Rosie glanced up, scowling not frowning. 'Wha'?'

'Is there something bad in the news?' Lizzie said.

'Wha'?' said Rosie again, sounding stupid. 'Wha', wha'?'

Bernard faced her. 'Your mother's asking why you're so quiet.'

'Ah-m eating.'

Bernard said. 'Did you catch the evening news on the wireless?'

'Wha'?' Irked at her lack of vocal control, Rosie took a firmer grip on herself. 'Yes, eighteen churches have been razed to the ground in Austria.'

'Synagogues,' said Lizzie. 'In Vienna.'

Husband and daughter glanced at her in surprise.

'How,' said Bernard, 'do you know that, dear?'

'It's there in your newspaper. I *can* read, you know.'

'Of course,' said Bernard. 'I just didn't think you were interested.'

'Is that what's making you both so depressed?' said Lizzie.

'Jewish churches?' said Rosie. 'Nuh!'

'What is it then?' said Lizzie. 'Something happen at the shop?'

'Nuh!' said Rosie again.

They ate, all three, with studied concentration.

Bernard murmured, 'Very nice, Lizzie, very tasty indeed,' but that was all that was said until pudding had been consumed, teapot and cups brought in from the kitchen and tea poured.

Lizzie lifted her cup in both hands and blew across the surface of the tea. It seemed so ordinary, this life, so quiet and harmless that she couldn't believe that anything would ever change, that Bernard and Rosie would grow older, that she would eventually wither into dust like her mother-in-law; Violet lying there in the little back bedroom, face to the wall, eyes open, plump little fists bunched under her chin so that it hardly seemed to matter that she'd stopped breathing; Violet Peabody who'd given two sons to the nation in the Great War, had made her contribution to history, had paid her widow's mite. When she died, Lizzie wondered, what little tract of history would go to the grave with her?

She felt suddenly weepy, no longer protected against the smell of smoke from the synagogues in a place she'd barely heard of in far-off, unimportant Europe where Bernard's brothers had died and Frank, her errant husband, had vanished under the mud of Flanders.

'Lizzie, are you crying?'

There was concern in Bernard's voice now, a note of repentance too.

'No, it's the tea, the hot tea.'

'Stop making a fuss, Mother,' Rosie said. 'They're only Jews.'

'I know,' said Lizzie. 'Silly, isn't it?'

'Tell her, Bernard,' said Rosie. 'Tell her it's got nothing to do with us.'

'Do you believe that, Rosie?' Bernard said.

Rosie paused, shook her head. 'Nuh.'

Bernard got up from the table, pushing his chair back in a manner that suggested a rare outburst of anger, the cause of which Lizzie could not quite grasp. She wished that she wasn't so stupid, so dull. She had understood the world when everything in it was small and hobnail hard and all she'd had to cope with was poverty and petty theft, hunger and loneliness, not the burning of synagogues and the tears of people she had never met.

'It's got everything to do with us.' Bernard said, then to Lizzie's dismay snatched up his newspaper and his cigarettes and headed off towards the water-closet in search of a bit of peace.


'Where are you are taking me?' Penny Weston asked.

'I told you. I'm taking you to supper.'

'Supper?'

'Dinner.'

'Are there no supper rooms in Glasgow?'

'Sure,' said Dominic, 'but I prefer not to be seen with you.'

'That is not very flattering.'

'I just don't think we should be seen,' Dominic told her, 'and I'm pretty well known in Glasgow.'

'You are famous?'

'Not famous, no.'

'Notorious?'

'Known,' Dominic said. 'Familiar.'

'You are familiar for being – what is it?'

'Not for being anything in particular,' said Dominic patiently. 'I'm a businessman. I know a lot of different people.'

'People who might tell your wife.'

'My wife has nothing to do with it.'

'I do not believe you.'

'Believe what you like,' said Dominic. 'Anyhow, it'll be simpler when you're settled at the farm.'

'What is it that will be more simple?'

'Meetings.'

'This farm, I will have to feed pigs every day?'

'No pigs,' said Dominic. 'The pigs are all gone.'

'Horses?'

'No horses either.'

'I like horses,' the girl said. 'Do you go riding?'

'No,' Dominic said. 'I don't go riding.'

'What is it you do?'

'I told you, I'm a businessman.'

'For pleasure?' Penny said.

'My children give me pleasure.'

'Does your wife give you pleasure too?'

He could not decide if she was teasing him or if her questions were signs of insecurity. She didn't seem insecure. She seemed remarkably self-assured for someone who had arrived in a strange country less than a week ago. He'd never travelled, of course, had never been a foreigner in a foreign land. He tried to imagine what it would be like to clamber off a liner in New York, Hamburg or Genoa all alone or, worse, dependent upon the charity of people who were not your people. The very thought of it made him edgy.

He gripped the steering wheel a little more tightly.

'She is like me, your wife?'

'No,' Dominic said. 'She's nothing like you.'

'Her name is Polly?'

'Yes.'

'Polly-wolly-doodle. Polly-put-the-kettle-on. Polly . . .'

'Cut it out,' Dominic said.

'It is not respectful?'

'No, it's not respectful.'

The girl laughed, a soft throaty purr. He had a sudden desire to slap her. He kept his eyes fixed on the empty road ahead. He hadn't driven the moor road for two or three years and had forgotten the landmarks.

'Was it Harker who told you about Polly?'

'Yes,' the girl said. '*Where* is it you are taking me?'

'To dinner. I told you. To a road-house.'

'I think you are carrying me off. It is so dark outside.' She put a hand to her mouth and drew her knees up. He could see the silky shape of her knees in the glow of the dash-lights. She pretended to be frightened, made her voice quaver. 'What are you going to do to me out here in the darkness?'

He fisted the wheel, bumped the Dolomite on to the verge and along it towards a field gate that had come at him out of the darkness. He braked abruptly, throwing the girl forward. He turned on her, glimpsed uncertainty and a trace, just a trace, of fear. He leaned across her lap, forearm pressing on her knees. She felt solid, like vulcanite. He leaned his shoulder into her breast, cupped her chin with his fingers and tipped her head back.

'Listen,' he said, 'you can cut out the nonsense, Penny. You won't twist me round your little finger like you do Harker. So wipe that smirk off your face and don't ever make fun of my wife again. You hear what I'm saying?'

He felt her throat move against his fingertips.

She swallowed, then said, 'I hear you, what you are saying.'

'Good,' Dominic said. 'Remember it and we'll get on just fine.'

He put his hands on the wheel again and edged the car off the verge. He waited for her to say something, waited for her to cry, perhaps even to ask his forgiveness. But she said nothing, not a word.

76

He had no sense of her mood during the last half-mile of the drive down into Rutherford.

Only when he drew the car into the courtyard at the side of the road-house did she speak again. 'What is the name of this place?'

'Rutherford,' he told her.

'I thought it would be the farm you would take me too.'

'No,' Dominic said. 'It's a road-house. Do you know what a road-house is?'

'An inn, a tavern for motorists,' she said. 'I did not know that you had such things in Scotland.'

'You'd be surprised what we have in Scotland,' said Dominic.

He reached across her to open the passenger door but she stopped him, a hand on his arm. 'Why have you brought me here, really?'

'To meet someone.'

'Who is it? Is it a man?'

'Yes, his name's Tony, Tony Lombard.'

'And who is he?'

'Someone I trust,' said Dominic and a minute later escorted Miss Penny Weston across the cobbled courtyard into the Rutherford Arms.

# Chapter Four

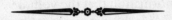

Rosie hadn't expected to meet Mr MacGregor again, especially not so soon. After all he wasn't plain Mister MacGregor but Detective Sergeant MacGregor of the City of Glasgow Police and the offices of the Criminal Investigation Department were in St Andrew's Street off the Saltmarket which wasn't exactly next door to Mandeville Square. She thought of him a great deal, though, for she was still exceeding curious as to what he'd hope to gain by bringing her the *Hours*.

According to Mr Shelby the *Hours* was worth between ninety and one hundred pounds. There were no accounts of it having been stolen from a dealer or library and Sergeant MacGregor had refused to say how the volume had wound up in the hands of the CID.

Rosie was not content to let the matter rest. She traced *Heures à la Louange de la Vierge Marie* through Book Auction Records, noted the names of the three dealers who had purchased a copy in the past decade and persuaded Albert to telephone each of them in turn. The results of her little investigation were very interesting indeed: a copy of the *Hours* that had been knocked down in Christie's auction in 1929 had subsequently been acquired by the University of Glasgow. A telephone call from Albert to Mr Jackson, custodian of the university's rare book collection, elicited the information that the volume was presently 'on loan', but Mr Jackson was not at liberty to say who had obtained permission to remove the valuable item from the collection. Albert thanked the librarian and hung up.

He turned to Rosie. 'Same copy we saw this morning, d'you think?'

'I would be surprised if it isn't.'

'Why would the CID want to show you a borrowed *Hours*?'

'Have a guess, Albert?'

'Your brother-in-law, the Manone chap?'

'Dominic, yes,' said Rosie.

'I can't quite see the point, though, can you?'

'No,' Rosie said. 'But there is one, I'm sure.'

'Most mysterious,' said Albert, and Rosie agreed.

Three days later the mystery was solved when Detective Sergeant MacGregor came clumping down into the basement of Miss Donaldson's Tearooms in Gordon Street where Rosie took lunch.

Miss Donaldson's, all chintz, embroidered tablecloths and painted china, was one of the few restaurants in town where single women felt thoroughly at home. Sometimes Rosie was joined by Pam, a legal secretary, or Marion, under-manager of a shoe shop. On that afternoon, however, she happened to be alone at a table near the stairs when a pair of size twelves came hesitantly into view. She spotted the intruder fully a minute before he spotted her. The advent of a handsome young chap caused a stir among the ladies. Chatter dwindled to indignant muttering and every eye at every table fell upon the gentleman who, on reaching the foot of the stairs, seemed dismayed to discover that he was the only male in the place.

Smiling to herself, Rosie let Sergeant MacGregor stew for a moment or two before she called out, 'Hoy, here I am,' in a voice that gained in bravado what it lacked in sophistication. The sergeant swung round and glowered at her from under his curly thatch. Patting one of the vacant chairs, Rosie said loudly, 'You will be a great deal less conspicuous, Mr MacGregor, if you sit yourself down.'

Gathering his coat about him he hauled out the chair and sat down, almost knocking over the cruet and the water jug in the process. Rosie resisted the temptation to tidy her hair and, ignoring the hubbub that had risen around her again, said, 'My, My! Is this not a bizarre coincidence?'

Sergeant MacGregor glanced this way and that then, leaning across the table, mumbled, 'I didn't realise this place was only for women.'

'Oh, it isn't.' Rosie enunciated as correctly as she

could under the circumstances. 'I mean, men aren't barred. They just do not seem to want to come here at the lunch hour.'

'I'm not surprised,' said Kenny MacGregor. 'For a minute there I thought they were about to attack me.'

'Some of them would, if you gave them half a chance. Do not tell me that you are intim-a-dated by a bunch o' lassies, a big stalwart officer of the law like you?' Rosie said. 'Are you going to buy me lunch?'

'What? Well . . .'

'Is that not what you are doing here?'

'Well, I . . .'

'If you want to ask me questions,' Rosie said, 'then you are going to have to fork out for my answers. I do not come cheap, Sergeant MacGregor.'

He had regained his composure. He wasn't a CID officer for nothing. Presumably he had faced up to situations even more dangerous than this. He adjusted the position of his chair, plucked a menu from behind the water jug and studied it.

'Mac-a-roni cheese,' said Rosie. 'And a jel-ly pud-ding. Please.'

'Now I'm here,' Sergeant MacGregor said, 'I suppose I could go a bit of dinner myself.'

'Lunch.'

'Oh, all right then,' he conceded. 'Lunch.'

'You can put it on ex-pen-ses.'

'Heck I can,' said Sergeant MacGregor, and grinned.

He looked much more human when he smiled. Rosie suffered a sudden silly urge to pat his light brown heathery curls, and didn't trust herself to speak for a moment or two. She followed the movement of the sergeant's lips as he addressed the middle-aged waitress who, as if she too were a policeman, jotted down the order on her pad. When the waitress left for the kitchens, Kenny lifted his head.

'Is it always this crowded at dinner – at lunch time?'

Rosie nodded.

'Do you come here every day?'

Rosie nodded.

'Can you – I hope I'm not being – I mean, can you hear me okay?'

Rosie nodded.

'I mean *hear* me?'

Rosie shook her head.

'How then do you – I mean, you lip-read, is that it?'

'Tha's it,' Rosie got out.

'Am I easy to read?'

'Yuh.'

'You're very good at it.'

'I huh – *have* had a lot of practice.'

'Have you been deaf since birth?' His interest was genuine, his questions tentative. He didn't want to offend her before he got to the point, though she was well aware that he was only softening her up.

She found her voice again. 'I had a fever when I

was very small. It affected my hearing. I've been deaf for about twenty years.'

'Can you hear anything at all?'

'Some sounds.'

'Voices?'

'Only on the wireless, only su-um.'

'You don't have to be nervous, Rosie.'

'I am not nuh-nervous.'

'You've no reason to be nervous just because I'm a policeman.'

'Why did you not tell me you were a policeman?' Rosie said. 'Did you think you would truh-trap me into saying something about my brother-in-law?'

'How did Manone react when you told him I'd been to the shop?'

'Huh-how did who react?'

'Manone. Dominic.'

'He did not react at all for the simple reason that I did not tell him.'

'Oh!'

'The book, the *Hours*, that was just a ruh-ooo . . .' She could not get the word out. She gave a little groan of impatience with her disobedient tongue then went on, 'You borrowed that book from the University library, didn't you?'

He looked down at the tablecloth. 'How did you find out?'

'You are not the only one who knows how to be a detective,' Rosie said.

'It wasn't my idea.'

'Whose idea was it?'

He took a deep breath. 'I thought you'd be sure to tell Manone.'

'Tell him what?' said Rosie. 'Tell him that a daft copper brought in a book for valuation? Dominic isn't interested in books.'

'I didn't think it would work,' Kenny MacGregor said.

'Is that why you followed me here,' said Rosie, 'so I could tell you how my brother-in-law ruh – reacted? Sorry to disappoint you. If you must know, I don't see much of Dominic. What he does is not my concern.'

'You do know what he does, though?'

'I was brought up in the Gorbals,' said Rosie. 'I have probably seen more monkey business than you have. I know what my brother-in-law used to do but since he married my sister he has gone on to the straight and narrow. He buys and sells imported goods and has a warehouse in Govan, all perfectly above board.'

Kenny pressed his lips together and frowned. 'That's just not true, Miss Conway, not true at all.'

'Prove it,' she said. 'Go ahead then, prove it.'

Kenny reached into his jacket pocket, brought out a photograph and placed it on the tablecloth. 'Have you ever seen this woman before?'

The head-and-shoulders snapshot was faded but quite clear. The woman was young, hardly more than a girl. She had a slender neck, high cheekbones and long eyelashes, and looked, Rosie thought, like a film star.

'Who is she?'

'That's immaterial. Have you ever seen her before? At your brother-in-law's house maybe?'

'Nuh.'

'Is that No?'

'I have never seen her before.'

'Are you telling me the truth?'

'I am.'

The sergeant cupped his hand over the photograph and put it back into his pocket. 'Fine,' he said. 'Now, tell me about yourself.'

'I thought there would be no more questions.'

'That isn't a question. Well yes, I suppose it is.'

'Oh-kay,' said Rosie. 'Let me ask you one first.'

'I can't answer any questions about the girl in the photograph.'

'It's not about her.'

'What then?'

'Sergeant MacGregor, are you married?'

'No, I'm not. And the name, by the way, is Kenneth.'

'Well, my name is Rosalind,' said Rosie. 'I am very pleased to meet you.'

And they shook hands as if everything that had passed between them was forgotten and, as Kenny and Rosie, they were about to begin again.

★　　★　　★

Tony hadn't been sorry when Dominic had sold the bookmaking business along with most of the other rackets that had provided Dom's father with the basis of the family fortune. He had wearied of violence and the toll it took on your nerves and did not want to return to the old days or to the old ways of settling disputes and stamping your authority on the community.

Once, long ago, his father had been Carlo Manone's bodyguard and they had fought side by side for control of the Genoa fish market and when things got too hot for them in Italy his father had been one of the *tempestosi* who had escaped with Carlo to set up business in Scotland. Dominic and Tony had been boys together in spite of the fact that the Lombardis were staunch Catholics and Carlo Manone had renounced all forms of Papal domination. Tony had heard tales about how young Carlo and the priest in one of the hill towns had been at loggerheads over a girl and how the girl had finally killed herself and the priest had called down the wrath of God on Carlo and his brother Guido and how the boys had burned down the chapel of Santa Esta and the priest's house and the farm that the priest's brother owned, and had fled to Genoa not into the arms of the law but into the waiting arms of the Protestant church.

Tony wasn't sure he believed all his papa's stories but at least he had an inkling where his coldness came from.

So far he hadn't murdered anyone, though. He'd

ordered men killed, watched men killed, had disposed of bodies and covered up afterwards but he'd never had to draw the knife and do the deed himself. For that small mercy he was thankful now, for conscience was the key to success in his line of work, conscience and control. If you could keep one separate from the other then you could do your job and sleep sound at night; if not, then you were in trouble and not God or the Virgin or even Dominic Manone could protect you from the consequences. He had always accepted that fact even while he was falling in love with Dominic's wife.

He would never forget the night when he'd first kissed Polly, thrusting her against the panelling in the hallway in the half dark in Dominic's house in Manor Park Avenue: how she'd cried out in a low, hungry voice and to his astonishment hadn't pushed him off: how she'd put her hand down and touched him between the legs: how he'd lifted her skirts, slipped inside her panties and entered her: how by that hot, wet, trembling act he had sacrificed his ability to separate conscience and control, and how, soon perhaps, he'd have to pay the price.

God knows it had been difficult enough to manage an affair with Polly under Dominic's eagle eye but now that Dom had taken a mistress and had put him in charge of her welfare everything was bound to become more complicated.

There had been frost in the night, a sifting white frost that had compacted the mud in the fields around Blackstone and turned the building site into an obstacle course. Bonskeet's trucks were slithering on the gradient up to the brick-piles when Tony, driving cautiously, came past. On the eight or ten big villas that were already shrouded in scaffolding he could see slaters clinging to the roof ridges. He had never had to work like that, in all weathers, with dirty hands, and the rackets had given him a hundred times more than dog labour ever could.

He had picked the Weston girl up in Glasgow, on the corner of Woodside and St George's Road. Even muffled in a swagger greatcoat and a hat like a guardsman's busby she'd attracted more than her fair share of attention. She'd slid into the Dolomite almost before it came to rest and once inside she'd twisted round and peered through the rear window as he'd steered down Woodside Road then, satisfied that they were not being followed, she'd given him a little slap on the arm and said, 'Tony, how are you?' as if they were old friends.

He had been leery of her that night in the road-house at Rutherford when Dominic had introduced them, for Penny Weston was arrogant and challenging in a way that Polly was not. He had resisted the temptation to try to question her, to tease from her some of the things that Dominic hadn't told him, how she'd travelled to Glasgow, for instance, and why Dom was hiding her away on the city's north-western fringe. Tony was uncomfortable north of the river. His stamping ground was among the tenements and bars that nuzzled behind the Govan shipyards. In new garden suburbs there were few pubs and no closes or dark alleyways where a man could do business out of sight.

He said nothing about any of that and let the girl do the talking.

Penny Weston was no Garbo, not the silent type. She interrogated him about where they were going, what these buildings were and how one road linked to another. She'd taken off her fur hat and had run a comb through her hair – which Tony knew wasn't a ladylike thing to do – and she'd opened her overcoat to show off her tight white sweater and her pointed breasts.

He answered her questions curtly, concentrated on finding his way.

Eventually they reached the turn-off to Blackstone Farm. Tony was relieved that he'd manage to find the place first time. He coaxed the car along the rutted track into a cobbled yard flanked by sheds as clean as farm sheds ever could be. He drew up in front of the handsome stone-built farmhouse.

'I want to look around,' the girl told him: her accent was more apparent this morning: 'I *vaunt* to look *arrr-ound*.'

Tony got out of the car, opened the boot, took out a pair of rubberised ankle-boots and fitted them over his shoes. He carried a second pair to the passenger door and held them out to her. 'You'll need these if you're going for a walk.'

'Ah, you have thought of everything.'

He had thought of everything or, rather, Dominic had thought of everything. In the boot was a basket of cooked chicken pieces, bread rolls, flasks containing hot tea and soup, bowls, forks and spoons wrapped in a chequered cloth. He lit a cigarette and waited for Penny to emerge from the car. In his overcoat pocket were the five keys locked on a ring that Dom had brought to his flat last night. Dom had told him that he wanted the girl treated well and that anything she required Tony was to supply. Couple of years ago he would have quizzed Dominic or made a joke out of it: 'Hey, this girl, you didn't bring *her* in from Italy,' but he couldn't joke with Dominic about the girl now, for the ironies were too obvious to ignore.

The girl swung round on the car seat, stretched out her long legs and stamped her feet into the boots.

'What is it you call these things?' she asked.

'Galoshettes.'

'How funny!'

'Don't you like them?'

'I like them because they are useful.'

The greatcoat was wide open, showing off her figure. Even in the grim November light her hair gleamed like polished metal.

'Do you want me to open the house?' Tony said.

Hands on hips, she surveyed the horizon's bare beech trees and blackthorn hedges, looked up at the sky as if she were looking for stars, Tony thought, or aircraft, then she said, 'We will inspect the barn first of all.'

He took the key ring from his pocket but she had gone ahead of him. The door to the largest building was apparently unlocked. She threw it open and vanished into the gloom.

Tony followed as far as the threshold. Cold came up through his feet and the taste of the farmyard was musty on his lips. Inside the building were beams, high wooden partitions, a stone floor with a drainage channel, but no rats, no hay or mouldering straw.

'Stables,' Penny said. 'Can you not smell the horses?

'Wouldn't know what a farm horse smells like,' Tony said.

He remained in the doorway while she walked down the length of the stables and back up again, back and past him and out into the daylight.

'Very well, now I will go inside the house,' she said.

It had never occurred to him that Dom would betray Polly and the kids. He wondered if this was revenge, if Dom had manacled him to this imperious bitch just to teach him a lesson.

He unlocked the main door and, stepping back, let the girl enter the farmhouse before him.

'Are you not coming too?' she asked.

'Sure I am', Tony answered.

And flipping away the cigarette, he followed her indoors.

Soon after marriage, and before she became pregnant with Stuart, Polly had joined the Sicilian Circle, a group of second and third generation Italian women who had hired a *professore* to improve their knowledge of the old language.

Few if any were from Sicily; the majority came originally from Lucca or Siena or the hill towns round about. They met one afternoon a week in the hall of St Francis' church. Sometimes Father Giorgio would pop in and tell them about Barga and Picinisco, Cassino and Atina, where some of them had family connections, and it didn't take Polly long to realise that learning a few Italian phrases wouldn't make her an Italian or allow her to share the sense of *campanilismo* that united students, teacher and priest. She would always be an outsider, not just an outsider but an outlaw, despised and envied for being Dominic Manone's wife but without power or identity of her own.

'*Signora, Signora Manone,*' the smiling, full-lipped Italian matrons would say, 'Is your husband well? Are your children well?'

They never asked about her, about Polly née Conway, who didn't have an aunt in Barga or a cousin in Cassino or a brother who had thrown everything up to go home and farm in the old country. What she had and what she held on to was Tony Lombardi who was worth more than all the decrepit *contadini* in the Province of Lucca put together. If only she could have informed the Italian wives what she had made of herself once she had abandoned the Sicilian Circle, how she had learned a language that no *professore* could possibly teach and no priest condone.

Tony was everything that Dominic was not, a rough and urgent lover who took her as he willed.

On the rare occasions when they found an opportunity to lie together in bed, he thrust into her with such force that she felt as if she would split apart. Afterwards, though, he would he take her in his arms, kiss her breasts and shoulders, tell her that she was the best he'd ever had, that he loved her and would never let her go. Then suddenly Tony was no longer there. The regular schedule of shopping and school and dropping by the house in Manor Park Avenue ceased abruptly and with it the opportunities for lovemaking. Tony had been summoned back to Dominic by Dominic – and she hated him for it.

'Where's Tony? I want him to drive me into Glasgow?'

'He has other things to do,' Dominic told her. 'I'll find someone else to drive you to town. What day would be suitable?'

'I want to go now. Today. Who else can drive me?'

'Charley Fraser, perhaps.'

'I'd prefer to catch a tram than be driven anywhere

by Charley Fraser,' Polly said. 'Where is Tony? What have you done with him?'

'He'll be back eventually.'

'Is he out of town?'

'He has work to do.'

'What's going on, Dominic?'

He smiled, patted her hand. 'Nothing is going on.'

'Why won't you talk to me?'

'I am talking to you.'

'No you're not. You're not giving me answers.'

'I told you, Tony is . . .'

'Are you having trouble with Flint?' Polly said.

'Flint? Why would I have be having trouble with Flint?'

'I don't know,' said Polly. 'Suppose you tell me.'

'I've no truck with Flint now. We move in different circles.'

'Different circles!' Polly said scathingly. 'You mean, he doesn't have to pay you off any more, therefore you don't have to fight with him?'

'Fight with him? What the devil are you talking about?'

'I haven't forgotten what happened to Tommy Bonnar.'

'Perhaps it's time you did,' said Dominic.

They were alone in the oblong dining-room at the back of the house. Patricia was sitting late with the children. Ishbel had been nursing a head cold and was out of sorts. Stuart and Ishbel had separate bedrooms now, for the boy, a troubled sleeper, was prone to nightmares.

Dominic had been delayed at the warehouse. He had arrived at ten minutes to eight and had asked Cook to serve supper at once. He'd hurried upstairs to kiss his son and daughter and talk to them for a little while or, rather, to let them prattle on about their day at school. Polly had been cast in the role of firm hand to Dominic's conciliator. He was never bored by their childish fears or enthusiasms and seldom lectured them. Sometimes when she saw her husband kneeling on the playroom carpet or seated on the end of one of the children's beds she resented his patience not only with the kids but with her too.

'I don't like not knowing where Tony is. Stuart's been asking after him.'

'Really?'

'Is he chasing after that girl?'

'Girl? What girl?'

'The blonde, the girl at the track?'

'Ah, so that's it.' Dominic shrugged. 'I doubt it.'

'Who is she? What's her name?'

'I have no idea.'

'She waved to you.'

'Did she? She's probably one of Flint's girls.'

'Not one of yours?'

'I don't trade in girls. You know that, Polly.'

'I don't know what you're up to these days, Dominic. I resent being kept at arm's length.'

She expected him to placate her with meaningless

endearments and was surprised when he said, 'You're not in any danger.'

'Danger? Who said anything about danger?'

'You don't need Tony any more.'

'I damned well do.'

'He's too valuable to be a chauffeur. If you require a driver I'll find you one. One I can trust.' He paused. Fright prickled Polly's spine at what might come next. 'We've come in off the street now, all of us, even Tony. You need not be afraid that anyone will do anything to you or the children. I did as you asked, sold the book, sold the collection agency. Now we've moved on to bigger things and I must have Tony's help in the matter.'

'In what matter?'

He shook his head.

Once she'd interpreted his implacability as ruthlessness but she had been too young then to appreciate the quality of independence that she'd inherited from her mother. Besides, she was no longer the girl she'd been in her mother's house: she was the woman that Dominic had made.

'Have you packed him off to Italy?' she said.

'Italy?' Dominic said. 'Why in God's name would I send Tony to Italy?'

'To talk to *Il Duce*.'

He laughed. '*Il Duce* has more to do with his time than talk to business men from Scotland. Who put that daft idea into your head, darling? Don't tell me Bernard . . .'

'I just thought that you might be contributing.'

'To what? A war?'

'Don't say that, please.'

'There's one thing about a war that seldom gets into the history books, Polly. Wars make money,' Dominic told her. 'If you choose the right side and keep quiet about it, yes, there's lots of money to be made from a good-going war.'

'Is that what you're up to, Dominic, making ready for a war? Is that why you've taken Tony away?'

'I haven't taken Tony away. He's just too busy to be your bodyguard. Anyhow, you don't need a bodyguard. You might need a gas-mask and a tin helmet pretty soon but a bodyguard – no, no.'

'So it's only business that's keeping Tony away?' Polly said.

'Yes,' Dominic said. 'Only business.'

Dennis Hallop's wife was a fusspot who gave her poor man no peace. No sooner would Dennis arrive home from a hard day's graft at the garage than she would hand him a paint pot or a screwdriver and demand that he do something about the house. What Gloria needed, Jackie said, were three or four kids running around to take her mind off her damned wallpaper and her bathroom tiles. In spite of appearances, however, Gloria was not fertile. She was a dumpy, big-chested brunette with pouty lips and huge dark eyes whose mothering instinct had been diverted – perverted,

Jackie called it – into turning her brand-new bungalow into an ideal home.

Sunday visits to Gloria's were an ordeal. Gloria
was jealous of Babs and the children but wouldn't
admit it. She took out her frustration by showing off
her house and would drag Babs round the bungalow
pointing out this new rug, that new table and, of
course, the repapered hallway or repainted kitchen.
Dennis would shuffle glumly in her wake as she
whipped open cupboards or knelt on the lino and
criticised his shoddy workmanship which, of course,
was not shoddy at all.

Gloria's house-proudness weighed heavily on the
little Hallops. Even Baby April was castigated for spill-
ing milk on the brand-new Axminster. Only Angus
seemed to have his aunt's measure. He knew precisely how to render a maximum amount of damage
with a minimum amount of risk. When the polished
dressing-table in the bedroom suddenly developed
scars or the floral-patterned wallpaper in the lounge
sprouted inky stains and Auntie Gloria screamed,
'Who done that? Who done that? Angus, wuz that
you?' Angus would look astonished and let his eyes
fill with crocodile tears, and Uncle Dennis would
mutter, 'Ach, Gloria, leave the wee chap alone. I'll
fix everything when they've gone.'

Dennis was exceptionally adept at fixing things.
He could erect a bookcase or re-wire a dining-room
just as efficiently as he could strip a stolen motorcar
of its parts, install the stolen parts into perfectly legal

and legitimate vehicles and place the perfectly legal and legitimate parts that he'd removed on the shelves of the Motoring Salon, a simple enough ruse that fooled clients and coppers alike. Dennis's only hobby, apart from drinking, was reconstructing 'Beezers'. He would tweak the engines of the lightweight BSA three-wheelers until they could top a hundred and, given favourable road conditions, take off like gliders. Gloria had no notion that her husband was so talented, for his passivity had deceived her into believing that he had no character at all.

Babs knew better, however. Babs was all too well aware that without Dennis her husband would be rolling in something less sweet-smelling than clover and that if Dennis ever chose to strike out on his own Jackie would probably wind up in bankruptcy court, if not the jail. When trouble crept into her life it was Dennis to whom Babs turned for advice.

In the dank afternoon air, Babs and Dennis strolled up and down the path that bisected the lawn, puffing away on the cigarettes that Gloria did not care to have smoked in the house. Through the French doors Babs could hear Gloria yelling, 'Angus, Angus, put that down,' and the thin piping wail of Baby April left temporarily in Daddy's custody. Only the girls were silent for they, Babs suspected, had drifted into Auntie Gloria's bedroom to experiment with the powder bowl, lipsticks and perfume spray.

'Dennis,' Babs said, 'has he been back?'

'Who? The copper?'

'Aye, the copper.'

'Nope.'

'What did he do?'

'Who? The copper?'

'Aye, the copper.'

'Didn't Jackie tell you?'

'You know Jackie,' Babs said, 'talks a lot, says nothin'.'

Dennis pinched the Gold Flake between forefinger and thumb and glanced at Babs warily. Drink had already begun to affect him but he had a long way to go before he reached the state of permanent bewilderment in which his father dwelled.

'Come on, Den,' Babs wheedled. 'What *did* the copper want?'

'He wasn't after us.'

'Who then? Dominic?'

'Maybe.'

'Did you tell Dominic about the copper?'

'Nope.'

'This copper was a detective, wasn't he?'

'Yep.'

'Dennis, for God's sake talk to me.'

'He looked at the shelves, never touched nothin'. Never asked t' see the books. He was just tryin' to scare Jackie.'

'What d' you mean – scare Jackie?'

'He thought Jackie'd go trottin' off to Dominic.'

'Why would the copper want Jackie t' do that?' Babs said.

'To confirm the connection between us an' him,' Dennis answered.

They had reached the end of the garden, a red-brick wall scrolled with withered clematis, and had turned their backs on Gloria's little treasure chest crammed with the brand-new furniture that the Hallops' criminal endeavours had purchased. Crime was a word never uttered in the Hallop household; the boys had been at the game for so long that it simply didn't occur to them that the manner in which they made a living was legally or morally wrong.

'It's no secret Dominic put up the money to get us started,' Babs said.

'Nope,' Dennis hesitated, 'but it sure is a secret how much he takes out.'

'How much *does* he take out?'

'Ask Jackie.'

'I'm askin' you, Dennis.'

'Twenty per cent, give or take.'

*'Twenty per cent!'* Babs exclaimed. 'How much is that in shillin's an' pence?'

'A lot,' said Dennis. 'An awful lot.'

She drew closer, laid a hand on his arm.

'It would matter if it dried up then?' she said.

'If what dried up?'

'The monthly pay-out.'

'You mean if we stopped payin' Dominic his whack.' Dennis raised an eyebrow. 'Jeeze, Babs, what would we do that for?'

'Dominic must've made his profit by now,' Babs

said. 'I mean, he must've collected interest on his investment ten times over.'

'It's his due, Babs,' said Dennis. 'Come on, you know how dues work?'

'Takin' dues from your own brother-in-law doesn't seem fair to me.'

'It's the system,' Dennis said.

'It's a lousy system.'

'Don't *say* that.'

'Well, it is.' Babs pinched the coal from her cigarette and dropped it to the ground. 'If the coppers *are* on to Dominic maybe they're on to us too.'

'Don't worry about it,' Dennis said.

'I do worry about it.'

'Everythin'll be fine.'

'Says who?'

'Says Dominic.'

'Says Dominic,' Babs repeated sarcastically. 'Aye, but it's not Dominic who'll go up the river, is it? I mean, it's not bloody Dominic who'll do the time.'

'Nobody's gonna do time.'

'Tell that to the coppers.'

'Got you jumpy, hasn't it?'

''Course it has.'

'We've been turned over before,' Dennis reminded her.

'Aye, but only by uniforms, not the flamin' CID.'

'He was only sniffin' round,' said Dennis. 'Showin' off to his sister.'

'Dennis, you're not tellin' me the truth.'

'It's the war,' Dennis said. 'Everybody's wettin'' themselves about the war.'

'What's the war got t' do with us?'

'Spies.'

'Spies?' Babs set one sturdy leg before the other and shook a little on her half-heels. 'God, I never thought o' that. Of course, our Dominic's an Eye-tie.'

'Got it in one,' said Dennis.

'Is that why the coppers are makin' a fuss?'

'Could be.'

She brought her feet together, gave a little hop. 'If Dominic did get lifted,' she said, 'what would happen to the firm?'

'Somebody else would have to operate it until he got released again.'

'Somebody who wasn't Italian, presumably?'

'Yep,' said Dennis. 'Presumably.'

'You've thought about this, haven't you?'

'Yep.'

'An' Jackie, has he thought about it too?'

'Yep.'

'Who do you reckon would be in the best position t' take over?' Babs said. 'It'd have to be somebody in the family, somebody who wasn't Italian, somebody Dom knew he could depend on, wouldn't it?'

'Could be,' said Dennis.

'And you *know* who it would *have* to be, Dennis, don't you?'

'Uh-huh,' said Dennis, nodding at last. 'Us.'

# Chapter Five

After two weeks Dominic still hadn't shown up at the farmhouse. In fact he appeared so disinterested in Penny Weston's welfare that Tony was beginning to wonder if Dom really had shipped in the girl just to keep him away from Polly. He'd telephoned Polly three times from a call-box in Breslin but had got the nanny on the line on each occasion and had hung up without uttering a word.

Last Monday he'd dropped in early at the Central Warehouse. Dominic had already been in a meeting in the top-floor office with two guys Tony had never seen before and Dominic had steered him hastily into the outer office and, after a word or two, had more or less sent him packing. On Friday he'd called at the warehouse again to pick up some household items for the girl. Dominic had been in the ground-floor stockroom with Sammy McGinn, the foreman, and the moment he'd appeared Dom had snapped, 'What do you want, Tony? Can't you see I'm busy,' and turned on his heel and left without another word. Fifteen years of doing Dom's dirty work, of being Dom's confidante and counsellor entitled him to more consideration than that, he reckoned. If he was being sidelined there could only be one reason for it: Dominic had found out about the affair.

It was almost eleven o'clock before Tony arrived at the farm.

Rain obscured the hills, the wipers clicked infuriatingly, the windscreen was clouded with condensation and he could hear nothing but rain, hard country rain drumming on the car roof. The track was a quagmire, the yard awash. The girl was framed in the farmhouse doorway, looking out for him. She wore the yellow oilskins and sou'wester he'd bought for her yesterday, ankle-length rubber boots, green woollen stockings. Her knees were bare beneath the hem of the oilskin and for an unguarded moment Tony wondered if she was naked beneath the coat.

'You are late,' she said before he even got out of the car.

'Yeah!'

'Are the roadways flooded?'

'The roads are fine.'

'Well, you are here now, so we will get on with it.'

He leaned across the passenger seat and spoke to her through the half open window. Raindrops like steel bayonets struck the slates of the roof and cobbles of the yard. He had to shout to make himself heard above the drumming of the rain.

'Get on with what?'

'They said they would come today.'

'Who did?'

'Dominic did not tell you?'

'I haven't seen much of Dominic lately.'

'Do you want coffee?' she asked. 'We have time for coffee.'

He got out of the car and splashed across the cobbles into the house.

The girl did not close the front door behind him but remained in the doorway, peering out into the rain. For all her aplomb she couldn't disguise her anxiety but when she turned and caught him staring at her she gave him one of her cheesy Americanised smiles.

In the big, stone-flagged kitchen there was no evidence that Dominic had spent the night, no little clues or tell-tales. The kitchen floor had been scrubbed. Shiny new saucepans were arranged on the shelves, the new rug on the floor, the new plaid throw draped over an ancient armchair by the hearth. She had even filled the new brass coal bucket from the coal pile in the byre. Whatever else Penny Weston might be, she was certainly no slattern.

On the marble-topped dresser the new coffee-maker chugged and steamed. She had insisted that he find her a proper Italian coffee-maker. He'd collected it grudgingly from the warehouse on Friday. He could see sense in her request now, though. The machine was the most homely thing in the farmhouse and the aroma of coffee spiced with vanilla certainly made the atmosphere more welcoming.

She came into the kitchen and took off the oilskin hat but not the coat. She tapped coffee from the machine into a cup and gave it to him, poured another cup for herself. She held the cup in both hands and sipped from it, looking up at him through the fragrant steam.

'What has he been saying about me?' she asked.

'Practically nothing since that night in Rutherford when neither of you were giving away a damned thing.'

'Is that why you do not like me?'

'Who says I don't like you?'

'Perhaps it is because you like me too much that you are nasty to me.'

'I'm doing my job,' Tony said. 'If you think I'm not doing it well enough then complain to Dominic.'

She gave him the smile again, then laughed. When she laughed she did something with her body that he had never seen any other woman do, a lithe, wriggling lift of the shoulders that made her look like a naughty schoolgirl. 'Oh, Anthony, you are not jealous of *him*, you are jealous of *me*.'

'I'm not jealous of either of you,' Tony said. 'I just don't know what the hell's going on or what I'm expected to do.'

'You have done it all already.'

He never lost his temper, not with women. He had been reared in a house with three sisters and had learned the hard way how illogical women can be. His sisters had clamoured for admiration not for what they did but for what they were, God's little gifts to mankind. Penny Weston didn't demand admiration, though; she sneaked it from you, in spite of yourself. He reminded himself that he had patience, lots and lots of patience. He could break her down with his patience the way he'd broken down Polly. He felt a sudden warm surge like a soft orgasm in the pit of his stomach at the thought of how he would get the better of this girl in the long run and what he would do to her then.

'Look, kid,' he said, 'I don't much care what fate has in store for you. I've put up with more boring stuff than this.' He didn't break stride. 'Who's coming today. Tell me, or don't tell me. I really don't give a toss either way.'

'Soon you will be back collecting payments from the unions?'

'Is that what you think I do?' Tony said.

'It is what all the Manones do, is it not?'

She had made an error, one little slip. He felt good about catching her out. If she thought that trade union manipulation was a viable racket in Scotland then she had been sadly misinformed. If she imagined that the tommy-gun would ever replace the broken bottle as a Scotsman's weapon of choice then she was naïve.

There were precious few guns on the streets here. Premeditated murder was a rarity, so rare in fact that it stayed in the mind like a great dark ink blot and nobody bragged about it afterwards. Compared to Chicago or Detroit or even Philadelphia this was Hicksville.

For a split second it occurred to Tony that because she didn't know these things she might be an impostor. But no, he was the impostor, Dominic and he and all the other tuppenny-ha'penny hard men, whether they were Micks or Jews or Eye-ties or just plain bread-and-butter Jocks. It had been four years since he'd had to use any muscle at all to enforce a payment. He was a reasonable man, just as reasonable as Dominic. All the clients knew it, knew he'd negotiate if he had to, protect when he had to, bring down the big fist only as a last resort.

'Did Carlo really send you over here?' he said.

She nodded. 'Sure.'

'How is the old buzzard?'

'He keeps good health,' Penny said. 'For his age.'

'My old man will be pleased to hear it.'

'You must not tell your father about me.'

Tony finished the coffee, took the cup to the sink.

Over his shoulder he said, 'I wouldn't know what to tell him even if I did feel inclined. Listen, kid . . .'

'Do not call me "kid". I am not a kid.'

She was annoyed now. He might have got something out of her right there and then if she hadn't gone to the window and then to the door. He stood behind her in the doorway and watched the truck slither down the track.

It was a ten-tonner with a saturated tarpaulin lashed across the flat-bed behind the cab. He could make out two men in the cab. When the truck entered the yard he saw a third man perched miserably on top of the tarp.

'Is this who we're waiting for, Penny?' he said. 'Builders?'

'They are carpenters.'

'Are they here to repair the house?'

'No, the stables.'

'Really?' Tony said. 'Are you going into the riding business then?'

'No, we are going into the business of making money.'

'Making money? How?'

'By printing it,' she told him.

And at that moment Tony realised that it might be rather a long time before Polly and he ever got together again.

In the initial weeks of his courtship of Rosie Conway, Sergeant MacGregor loitered about Mandeville Square and tried to appear as inconspicuous as possible, which was a tall order for a six-foot-two Highlander with curly fair hair. In addition, he had a way of rocking back and forth with his hands clasped behind his back like a pantomime simpleton and even the canny pigeons that strutted on the ledges above Shelby's windows were amused by the daft big boy and would peep down at him, heads cocked, and *crroo-crroo* advice in mock Gaelic.

Eventually Mr Robert took pity on the love-struck lump, yanked open the door and hissed, 'For God sake, Sergeant, at least wait for her inside.'

Gannon, of course, was less sympathetic. Never having had a copper at his mercy before he was determined to make the most of it. 'Hoy, *Sergeant*,' he'd chirp from the doorway, '*Detective* Sergeant. Miss Rosalind's gettin' ready for to be searched. She'll be with yah in just a moment. She's just takin' her knickers off, like you requested,' to which piece of insolence the officer only nodded and looked glum.

Kenny wasn't the only one who'd fallen foul of Cupid's dart, of course.

Rosie spent half the morning bobbing up from her chair, surveying the two great squares of street-coloured daylight and the anonymous faces that flowed past, watching anxiously for Kenny. When Kenny did at last appear her heart beat faster and there was a sound in her ears like rushing water.

He would wait tentatively by the door and she would walk down the centre aisle. Customers skulking among the bookcases would glance up and observe the moment when the deaf girl and the Highland copper met. He would say shyly, 'Fancy a bite to eat then?' and she would shyly answer, 'That would be very nice, thank you,' as if it were all very off-the-cuff and not at all romantic.

The work of the Criminal Investigation Department didn't grind to a halt because Kenny MacGregor was falling in love. On days when he failed to appear, Rosie would assure herself that he had been called away on business or that his shift had been changed without warning. Even so she suffered dreadful doubts, wondering if he had grown tired of her already and had thrown her over for some other girl, one who wasn't deaf.

'I'm sorry, Rosie, really I am,' Kenny would say next time they met. 'I was sent out of town. I couldn't even get to a telephone to let you know.'

She longed to ask him where he had been and what crime he had investigated but she was well aware that she was Dominic Manone's sister-in-law and that any questions on her part might easily be misconstrued. She stepped so warily around such thorny issues that it was only after eight café lunches that she learned that Kenny was thirty-four years old, shared a flat in Cowcaddens with his sister, and that his father and mother were tenant farmers on the Isle of Islay.

'What does your sister do? Is she a teacher?' Rosie asked.

'What makes you think that?'

'I don't know. I just thought she might be.'

'She *was* a teacher, as a matter of fact, a teacher of languages. She works in police headquarters now in a civilian capacity. She translates foreign documents.'

'Is there much call for that in Glasgow?'

'More than you might think,' said Kenny.

'I have heard,' said Rosie, 'that preparations are being made for a war. I do not just mean talk about it, I mean practical stuff.'

'It's true,' Kenny said. 'Special departments and volunteer services are being set up all over the place. The Chief Constable's in his element. You don't happen to drive a motorcar, by any chance?'

'I'm afraid I do not,' said Rosie.

'We're looking for ladies who have a licence to drive.'

'Drive what?'

'Ambulances, tramcars, anything. Women'll need to take over basic services when the rest of us are called up.'

'The rest of you?'

'Those of us fit to fight,' said Kenny.

Rosie experienced a sudden icy pang. It hadn't dawned on her that men like Kenny, like Dennis and Jackie Hallop, might be called upon to fight and possibly die as her father and Bernard's brothers had done twenty years ago. She'd glanced at the casualty lists from the civil war in Spain from time to time but the brigades there were made up of volunteers not conscripts and, rather heartlessly, she felt somehow that they deserved whatever was coming to them.

'Hey, don't look so solemn,' Kenny said. 'I'm not packing my kitbag yet.'

'I cannot help it,' Rosie said. 'I do not want you to be killed.'

'Heck,' said Kenny, 'I've more chance of being killed at a Rangers – Celtic football match than by one of Adolf's snipers. Sorry, I didn't mean to scare you.'

'You just took me aback,' said Rosie. 'I mean, my stepfather . . .'

'That's Bernard, isn't it?'

'Yes – Bernard says that a war is still some way off.'

'Your father, your real father, he was lost in the Great War, wasn't he?'

'How do you know that?'

'I think you mentioned it.'

'No, I did not.'

'Mr Shelby must have let it slip then. Anyhow, your father went missing in action, didn't he? Missing presumed killed. Why didn't your mother claim a widow's pension?'

'They wouldn't give her one,' Rosie said. 'She couldn't prove that my father had joined up. He wasn't using his own name so there was no record, you see.' She paused. 'Are you opening a file on me at the CID? Look, if there's anything you want to know about my family all you have to do is ask. I cannot discuss Dominic Manone, though, because I do not know much about him and I'm certainly not going to pump my sisters for information.'

'Whoa, whoa!' Kenny put a finger to his lips. 'I'm not fishing for information about Manone. I'm just curious how your Mam managed to raise three daughters without any financial assistance.'

'Simple,' Rosie said. 'For ten or twelve years she worked her fingers to the bone. After my sister Polly left school and got a job things became a bit easier. Those years were no picnic, Kenny, especially since I needed special schooling. That is why I resent your implication that my Mam has done anything wrong. It's not her fault that my sister Polly happened to fall in love with an Italian. Anyway, you may think what you like about Dominic but he is a good husband and a good father and takes good care of the family.'

'Not you, though, Rosie. Don't you take care of yourself?'

'I – yes, I suppose I do.'

'I'd like to take care of you some day.'

'Are you proposing to me, Kenny?'

'No, no. Oh, no, no.'

'I thought not,' Rosie said.

He hadn't even kissed her yet, though he had held her hand once or twice. They weren't lovers, never would be lovers, perhaps, not if the war came. Besides, she doubted if the CID would be too happy at one of their officers marrying Dominic Manone's sister-in-law.

'My job,' Kenny said, 'is not just an ordinary job,

you know. It involves long hours and awkward shifts. A copper's wife has a lot to put up with.'

'How long have you been in the Force?'

'I joined when I was eighteen, took the sergeant's exam-inations when I was thirty and applied for a vacancy in the CID. I was backed for promotion by the Chief Constable, Mr Sillitoe.'

'Is he your boss?'

'Not directly, no.'

'Who is your boss?'

'Inspector Winstock. We call him "Wetsock". He's okay, really.'

'Have you caught any murderers?'

'I've been on several cases in which fatality was involved.'

'Don't you have nightmares – about bodies and things?'

'I'm used to it now,' Kenny said. 'I didn't like it much at first. Nobody does. Fishing corpses out of the river, collecting body parts off the railway line. Grisly stuff, Rosie.'

'Folk who have been burned to death in house fires?' Rosie said.

'Yes, that too.'

'Children suffocated by smoke and fumes?'

Kenny frowned and seemed about to ask her to explain herself but thought better of pursuing that line of inquiry.

He said, 'Have you ever been to a pantomime, Rosie?'

'What?'

'Pan-toe-mime: have you ever . . . ?'

'I heard you the first time. No, I've never been to a pantomime.'

'Because you can't hear the music?'

'Yes.'

'Come with me to the King's. They're doing *Mother Goose* this Christmas. It's very lively and there's dancers to look at and I'll tell you what the actors are saying. Would you like that?'

'I'm not sure.'

'Why not?'

'Because if I accept I'll have to tell my mother that you're a copper. I won't lie to her, you know.'

'I wouldn't expect you to,' Kenny said. 'It's Christmas, Rosie. Perhaps she won't mind because it's Christmas. Will you think about it?'

'I'll think about it,' Rosie said. '*Mother Goose*, is it?'

'At the King's,' said Kenny.


'A copper?' Bernard said. 'What sort of a copper?'

'He is a sergeant.'

'What division?'

'He is a detective,' Rosie said. 'CID, St Andrew's Street.'

'Christ!' Bernard said, and shook his head. 'How long have you known this chap and how did you meet him?'

'What's wrong with you, Bernard?' Lizzie said. 'She's twenty-four years old. Isn't it about time she got out and about a bit?'

'Oh, certainly,' Bernard said, 'but this isn't just any old chap, Lizzie. She's contemplating going out with a policeman.'

'Look,' Rosie said, 'I do not need to ask your permission. I can go out with any chap I want to. Look at me, look at me: do you think I'm a prize?' She opened her mouth and pointed her forefinger at her tongue. 'I have never been out with a man in my life and I am not passing up the chance. God, it is only a night out at the pantomime, Bernard. He is not whipping me off to the casbah.'

'The what?' said Bernard, suspiciously.

'If she isn't going to be safe with a policeman,' Lizzie said, 'then who, I ask you, is she going to be safe with?'

'Does he know who you are?'

'Of course he knows who I am,' said Rosie, angrily.

'So how long has this been going on?' said Bernard.

'Going on?' Rosie shouted. 'Going on?'

Bernard cleared his throat, folded his arms. 'All right, keep your hair on, Rosalind. I'm your father, I'm entitled . . .'

'You are not my fah-fah-father.'

'Bernard only has your best interests at heart, dear,' Lizzie said. 'What's the cop— the young man's name?'

'Kenny.'

'Is he nice, is he a big chap?'

'Bigger than him.' Rosie gestured disparagingly at Bernard. 'Six feet if he is an inch. Fair hair. He lives with his sister in Cowcaddens. She is a translator of fah-fah-foreign languages.'

'We'll have to meet him,' Lizzie said. 'If it's gettin' serious, I mean.'

'Serious?' said Bernard. 'It's serious enough for him to ask her on a date.'

'Mah-mah-Mother Gah-goose,' Rosie got out. 'At the Kah-King's.'

Her tongue was tied in knots even though she'd known that Bernard would take it badly. She'd always been sure of his love but the comfort it brought her had diminished over the past weeks and he had begun to seem selfish and possessive. Look at him now, seated in the chair with a ghastly expression on his face as if she'd announced that she was expecting a baby to Kenny MacGregor and not just going out to the theatre with him.

'Thursday,' she said. 'Kenny has already bought tickets.'

'That,' said Lizzie, 'will be lovely.'

'You won't be able to hear a thing,' Bernard said.

'Oh, thuh-thank you,' Rosie spat out. 'Thuh-thank you for reminding me.'

'How does he know what you're saying?' said Bernard.

'He KNOWS,' Rosie shouted. 'He KNOWS.'

'Listen to you now,' Bernard said. 'Shouting.'

'Bernard, stop taunting her,' Lizzie snapped. 'You should be pleased that a nice young chap has asked her out.'

'He can't be all that young, not if he's a detective sergeant,' Bernard said.

'Thirty-FOUR. Thirty-FOUR – if you MUST KNOW.'

Bernard hunched his shoulders and tucked his hands into his armpits. He had turned a strange grey shade and his features seemed suddenly gaunt. She had not expected his reaction to be quite so extreme. She almost felt sorry for him. Then she thought of Kenny, the beautiful warm lift in her heart when he entered the shop, the firm clasp of his hand, the gentle touch of his fingers on her cheek. Bernard hugged her, Bernard took her hand, Bernard accepted her kiss every morning – but Bernard never made her feel the way Kenny MacGregor did.

Bernard tapped her arm and signed, almost frantically, to get her full attention. She watched his lips shape the question.

'Does he know that you are related to Dominic Manone?'

'WHAH – WHAT does that huh-have to do with anything?'

'Does he, Rosie?'

'YES. YES, HE DOES.'

'I thought as much,' and Bernard. 'Oh, dear God! I thought as much.'

And, to Rosie's astonishment, rocked forward in his chair and covered his face with his hands.

Their lovemaking was noisy and rumbustious. Babs always had a sneaky feeling that her daughters were lying wide awake, fully aware of what was going on in the bedroom at the end of the corridor.

When it was over and Jackie had clambered off her, therefore, she got up at once and tiptoed into the children's rooms, found the girls fast asleep and Angus snoring away like a piggy. Relieved, she hurried into the bathroom as soon as Jackie had vacated it and was back in bed beside him three minutes later.

She accepted a cigarette and lay back against the pillows, the quilt tucked under her armpits.

'Good, eh?' said Jackie.

'Good,' Babs dutifully agreed.

Good enough, she supposed. Satisfactory. She had matched his enthusiasm and responded without pretence. Now, though, was the best time with Jackie calm and drowsy. She glanced at him. By the light of the bedside lamp he had a raffish sort of handsomeness that wasn't usually apparent.

He tapped ash into the metal bowl on his chest, blew another smug circlet of smoke, slid his left hand down between her thighs and patted that part of her that was his and his alone. Babs did not resent his casual familiarity.

She said, 'Have you been talkin' to Dennis lately?'

'Sure, I talk to him all the time.'

'I mean lately?'

'About what in particular?' Jackie said.

'Dominic.'

He glanced at her out of the corner of his eye, smoked another half-inch of the cigarette before he asked, 'What about Dominic?'

'Has it occurred t' you that Dom's an Italian.'

''Course it's occurred to me. Everybody knows he's a bloody Eye-tie. I don't need Dennis t' tell me that, for God's sake.'

'What if there's a war?'

'What the hell're you goin' on about now, Babs?'

'If there is a war an' Mussolini sides with Hitler . . .'

'Politics! Jeeze, when did you get interested in politics?'

'They won't let Dominic run a business if there's a war on,' Babs said. 'That ain't politics, Jackie, that's common sense.'

He stubbed out the cigarette, put aside the ashtray and rolled on to an elbow. 'They won't let me run my business neither,' he said. 'Don't you go worryin' about Dom when you should be worryin' about us.'

'What d' you mean?'

'Four kids ain't gonna protect me,' Jackie said.

'From what?'

'Bein' called up.'

She sat up abruptly. 'They won't call you up, will they?'

'Not if I can bloody help it,' Jackie said. 'But what

they definitely will do is drag me away from the garage an' stick me in some bloody dead-end job.'

'Like what?'

'Send me down the pit or into a factory or the ambulance service.'

'What'll happen to the garage?'

'Dunno.'

'What'll we live on?' Babs said.

'Bread an' bloody water, I expect.'

'Dennis – Dennis an' Billy, will they . . . ?'

'Soldier boys for sure.'

'I never thought o' that,' Babs said.

'There's politics for yah,' Jackie said. 'They can do what they bloody like wi' us when there's a war on.'

He leaned against her and put an arm about her, folding it over her breast. He smelled of tobacco smoke and perspiration and she loved him for it and felt the soft stirring of desire again.

She wondered what it would be like not to have Jackie, not to have things as they were now and what would become of her children if Jackie and Dennis were far away or, come to think of it, dead. Her mind had been filled with calculations, a greedy anticipation of changes that would better her lot.

Now she saw how wrong she'd been, how stupid.

For once she closed her eyes when he kissed her.

'We're not gone yet, none o' us,' he murmured.

'Anyhow, bloody Adolf's got more sense than t' fight the British. I mean, Jeeze, we'd scuttle the bastard in a bloody fortnight, he tries his tricks on us.'

'Is that true, Jackie?'

'Sure, it's true. Everybody knows we got the best army, the best navy in the world an' Jerry can't stand up t' us for long.' He kissed her again, cuddled her while she held the cigarette at arm's length and watched smoke crawl over the rampart of the bed-head. 'You wanna 'nother one, honey?'

'No, dearest,' Babs said. 'I just want you t' hug me for a while.'

'Suit yourself,' he said and, without rancour, drew her against his chest.

The Wolseley was ten years old. It had been stolen in Sheffield, lifted in dead of night from the garage of a certain Lord Throgsten on a country-house estate on the edge of the city. It had passed through several hands before it wound up in the Hallops' yard in Govan where Dennis and Billy stripped it, replaced most of the components and repainted it a handsome jade green colour that, as it happened, matched the registration details on another 1928 Wolseley tourer that had been come by honestly but had subsequently disappeared.

The Throgsten version was now a safe commodity. There was no previous record of sale to give the police a clue to its origins. Necessary paperwork was done at the salon, the car re-registered in Jackie's name and duly sold by private bargain, cash down, to his brother-in-law Dominic Manone.

The Wolseley was less ostentatious than a new model van or estate car, given the sort of vehicles that were turning up on the roads these days; Dominic declared himself well pleased with the big 8-cylinder tourer, complete with all-weather equipment and, most important of all, a huge, detachable rear-mounted trunk that was ideal for the transportation of heavy goods.

A week before Christmas he collected the car from the salon and drove across the river and out to the farm.

He hadn't been at Blackstone since the day he'd inspected the place with Bernard, nor had he had met Edgar Harker or the girl again. He had deliberately kept his distance, let Tony and Bernard take care of the arrangements. He regretted the necessity for keeping Tony in the dark but didn't dare take Tony – or anyone for that matter – into his confidence until he had mastered the scheme's intricacies and weighed up its dangers. The truth was that he enjoyed deviousness and secrecy, the return of a rapacious arrogance that had been all but smothered by marriage.

It was a clear day, the sky arctic blue, as he came up past Bonskeet's site. Though he had invested heavily in Bonskeet's he had little to do with day-to-day management. Nevertheless, he was gratified to see villas rising up against the horizon and general activity along the rim of the site where thirty-two trim little bungalows were being erected.

Smiling to himself, he tooled the Wolseley past the site and a mile further on steered it through the field gate that gave access to Blackstone Farm.

The Dolomite was parked outside the main building. The house door lay open. In the buildings to the right of the yard there was evidence of construction, a pile of fresh yellow sawdust and four big timber beams that had not been removed. He must phone Bernard and tell him to have the place cleaned up before the machinery arrived.

He parked the Wolseley next to the Dolomite and got out.

He expected Tony to be on top of him, the girl to come running out of the farmhouse to greet him and was irked when no one appeared. If Tony had taken the girl to shop in Breslin or Glasgow surely the house would be locked and the Dolomite wouldn't be sitting in the front yard.

'About time you got here, man,' Tony said.

Dominic swung round, looking towards the stables.

'Been waiting for you to show up for weeks.'

'Where the hell . . .'

'Up here.'

Dominic stepped back and looked up at the farmhouse roof. The skylight was propped open and in the opening were two faces. Tony and the girl. Tony had a telescope, the girl a rifle. The rifle, a

.22 rabbit gun, was pointed at him. Resting on a tiny tripod, the telescope appeared to be trained on him too and seemed more threatening than the gun. Dominic slid behind the body of the car, rested an elbow on the soft-top, tipped back his hat, and stared up at the window in the slates.

'Trespassers,' the girl announced, 'must be shot.'

'Cut it out,' Dominic said. 'Come down. I want to talk to you.'

'State your business,' the girl said. 'And repeat the password.'

'For God's sake!'

'Better do as she says, Dom,' Tony advised. 'She's lethal with that popgun at short range.'

'What do you want me to do?' Dominic said.

'Repeat the password,' the girl told him.

They looked, he thought, like a couple of over-grown kids. Tony wore a heavy cable-knit sweater, the girl a pink blouse and an embroidered silk bolero that barely covered her breasts. They seemed ridiculously jolly and he knew then – or thought he did – that Tony had been to bed with her.

'I do not think he knows the password,' Penny Weston said.

'Nope, I guess he doesn't,' Tony said.

'Shall I shoot him?'

'Wing him,' Tony said, 'to teach him a lesson?'

'I will pick off his hat, yes.'

'Sure,' Tony said. 'Why not? He's got plenty of hats at home.'

'What the hell's got into you, Tony?' Dominic said. 'Come down from there at once. I've got business to discuss and I haven't got all day to waste.'

'Business?' Tony said. 'I thought I'd been retired.'

'Oh, so that's it,' Dominic said. 'You're making a fool of yourself to teach me a lesson. For God's sake, don't be so childish!'

The rifle went off with a light crisp crack that sent echoes reverberating around the yard. Dominic ducked behind the Wolseley and shouted, 'Bitch! You stupid bitch,' and heard the girl's laughter.

A moment later Tony appeared in the doorway.

'She's a bitch all right,' Tony said. 'Is this the kid you're going into business with, Dom? Is this the kid who's gonna front a counterfeit operation worth a million quid?'

'So she told you, did she?'

'She didn't have to tell me. Soon as the chippies rolled up and started laying a floor in the hay-loft I figured you were getting ready to store something heavy. She let just enough of it slip for me to guess the rest.'

'In bed?'

Tony had folded the legs of the telescope and carried it over his shoulder like small field mortar. 'Hell, no!' he retorted. 'Penny might be gorgeous, Dom, but she ain't my type. Anyhow, like you said yourself, this is business. Big business. You gonna tell me about it now?'

'Where is she?'

'In the toilet, putting on her face.'

'What was all that stuff on the roof about?'

'I'm keeping her amused, that's all. We were playing soldiers.'

'Where did she get the rabbit gun?'

'I bought it for her in Glasgow. She's a crack shot, you know. You should see her on targets. Deadly. She tells me she learned to shoot in the Vienna woods by knocking off woodpigeon. True or false? God knows! This kid lies like a trooper. Hey, I like the motorcar. Jackie do it up for you?'

'Yes.'

He was disturbed by Tony's sudden loss of discretion. Perhaps he had been wrong to put Tony in charge of the girl, but how could he have predicted that Tony would be so affected by her. Had the long-legged blonde bewitched him or was this some ill-advised strategy that Tony had devised to punish him for his neglect? There had been no such insubordination in the old days when there had been no women around to mess things up. He remembered why he had elected not to run girls and understood why even John Flint had pulled out of pimping: you brought in women, you dealt with women, everything went haywire.

'She might be a fruitcake,' Tony said, 'but she *can* take care of herself. Come on in, Dominic. It's your love-nest, not mine.'

'Love-nest?'

'Forget it.'

'Did she tell you . . .'

'You want her, you're welcome.'

'I don't want her.'

'That's good to hear.' Tony patted the Wolseley's soft-top and ran his hand down the side panel. 'Dennis made a nice job of this one? How does it handle?'

'Quick but solid.'

'Good for a fast getaway,' Tony said and, laughing, ushered Dominic into the farmhouse before him.


Meetings of the Special Protection Unit convened at half-past ten o'clock on the third Monday in every month. They were hardly formal gatherings for the office was downstairs in the basement in St Andrew's Street and the walls were lined with dusty boxes of evidence of crimes long solved or long forgotten. There was a desk, five or six wooden chairs, a gas-ring, a kettle, a teapot, an array of chipped cups and a battered biscuit tin within which lurked a selection of stale cookies that not even Inspector Winstock's hungry hunters would touch with a barge pole. Now and then Fiona MacGregor would bring in a batch of scones and a pat of butter in greaseproof paper and old Wetsock, before helping himself to a scone or two, would remind everyone that police work was not supposed to be a picnic.

Gareth Winstock had a small moustache – a butter-curler, Fiona called it – ferocious eyebrows and the sort of haggard features that seemed to be standard issue for senior detectives. He also had bad teeth and a stomach ulcer, not helped by his fondness for an off-duty dram. He was, and always had been, a worried man. He worried about his cases, his staff, his promotion prospects, whether he would live long enough to collect his pension and what he would do when retirement eventually caught up with him. His anxieties had increased with the arrival of the 'New Broom', Chief Constable Percy Sillitoe, who had dragged the City of Glasgow police force into the twentieth century by streamlining the divisions and sacking ranking officers right, left and centre.

Gareth Winstock had survived only because he was good at his job and, dare one say it, because he was a Brother in the Barns o' Clyde Lodge where, off duty, he did most of his drinking out of reach of his wife. In recent months his nervousness had been expanded by a brief so vague that he had no idea whether his appointment to the Special Protection Unit signified a career move up, down or sideways, or what would happen to him if war with Germany did not materialise.

Fiona MacGregor was the only woman present, and the only civilian. She had prepared translations of articles from several of the foreign newspapers, mainly German and Italian, which landed on her desk every morning, random items that Winstock and the SPU's three other detectives would try to fit into the big picture and relate to their current investigation of Dominic Manone and the caucus of Fascist sympathisers that he had gathered around him.

'What *are* they up to?' Gareth Winstock began. 'What the devil are they doing that they haven't been doing behind our backs for years. Any ideas, Stone?'

Detective Constable Stone shook his head. 'Don't know, sir.'

'Galbraith?'

Constable Galbraith also gave a negative response.

'What about you, MacGregor? Are you getting anywhere with that girl?'

'I doubt if the girl knows much, sir, really.'

Fiona pursed her lips but did not contradict her brother. She was a redhead – auburn not ginger – with a milky complexion and a manner that was at best aloof and at worst hostile.

Five years of language study and six months residence in Germany had erased the sweetness of her native Gaelic and her voice now was as clipped and 'snecky' as the sound of the old Underwood typewriter upon which she produced her reports. She did not regard herself as inferior to the uniforms with whom she rubbed shoulders and in fact considered *them* rather beneath *her*. It was generally agreed that she must have been a holy terror as a teacher.

'I take it you're still in contact with Miss Conway?' Winstock said.

'I am, sir,' Kenny answered.

'So the bookshop thing did pay off?'

'Not exactly, sir. I mean, she saw straight through it.'

'She hasn't held the deception against you, though?'

'No, sir. I can't say she has.'

'What has she told you about Manone?'

'Not much, I'm afraid,' Kenny said.

Fiona gave a little grunt and lowered her auburn lashes.

The tasks allocated to Stone and Galbraith were more mundane than those given out to Kenny. They'd been out and about on the streets of Govan putting the arm-lock on small fry and fishing for information on John Flint, trying unsuccessfully to connect him to Manone. Even so, the list of Manone's associates was growing longer week by week; Italian importers, restaurant owners, proprietors of cafés and fish-and-chip shops, the innocent distributors of religious statues. Names were dropped, names hinted. Gradually the links between Manone and certain respected citizens were becoming clearer.

Charges were possible even at this early stage, but Mr Winstock wasn't after petty thieves, smash-and-grab merchants or pedlars of stolen goods. He could have yanked in the Hallops, for instance, and made them sweat but he'd laid hands on a few of Manone's minions in the past and had suffered the humiliation of watching them walk free from court, thanks to the ingenuity of lawyer Carfin Hughes. Manone was a prime target now, though. Faceless men in dank offices in Whitehall were interested in Manone, which suggested that it had become a matter of national security, and he, a humble detective inspector in Glasgow CID, had a chance to make a name for himself by putting the fear of God in every traitor, every smart-arsed criminal who hoped to back the Fascist axis for gain and glory.

'I'm taking her to the panto,' Kenny MacGregor said.

'Pardon?'

'Mother Goose, at the King's.'

'Who? This girl?'

'Rosie, yes.'

Fiona grunted again, a gruff sound from the back of her throat.

'At your own expense, I trust?' Winstock said.

'Oh, aye, Mr Winstock, at my own expense.'

'Do you think a bit of music or a drink at the bar at the interval will loosen her tongue, then?'

'I don't know, sir. It might.'

'How do you talk to her? Can you do the hokey-pokey?'

'The what, sir?'

Inspector Winstock waggled his fingers in the air, scatter-ing crumbs. 'The hokey-pokey. Sign language. She's deaf, isn't she?'

'She can read lips and makes out what I say pretty well.'

'When it suits her,' Fiona put in.

'What else do you have for me?' Winstock said. 'Have you been through the company registers again?

Have you found out how large a slice of Bonskeet's Manone really owns?'

Kenny said. 'He has a thirty-two per cent holding.'

'Legitimate?'

'Nothing to prevent it, sir,' said Kenny. 'It's my guess that if we obtained warrants and combed through every account book Manone keeps at Central Warehouse we'd find nothing. However,' he paused, 'Rosie's stepfather works for the estate agency that Manone bought last year. And that, I think, is quite interesting and possibly significant.'

'Why?'

'Because Bernard Peabody appears to be an honest chap. Fine army record, no black marks against him.'

The inspector sat forward, arms on the desk. 'If Peabody is honest then he's definitely one to work on. Have you interviewed him yet?'

'Not yet,' said Kenny. 'I'm working up to it.'

'Well, be as quick as you can.'

'I don't want to alarm that branch of the family.'

'No, you're right. It's one thing to let Manone know he's under observation but we shouldn't antagonise the rest of them at this stage. Do you think you can get the girl to talk?'

'I can probably persuade her to introduce me to Peabody.'

'That's a start, I suppose,' Winstock said. 'Now, Fiona, what do you have for us this week? Anything we can sink our teeth into?'

Fiona shuffled a bundle of typewritten pages, pulled one out and passed it to her boss. 'Only this, Mr Winstock.'

'What is it?'

'It's a reply from the Immigration Department in answer to the letter I wrote them on your behalf six weeks ago.'

'When did it arrive?'

'By this morning's post, sir.'

Winstock scanned the letter and scowled at the officers as if it was their fault that the information had been so long in arriving.

'Harker?' Winstock said. 'Who is this chap Harker and what's he doing in Glasgow, sucking up to Manone?'

'He arrived in Liverpool off the *Caronia* from New York on the thirteenth of November,' Fiona said. 'I've a copy of the passenger list if you need it. He didn't come alone. He travelled with a woman.'

'What woman?' Winstock said. 'The woman in our photograph?'

'That's what we haven't been able to establish yet,' said Kenny MacGregor.

'The woman Harker travelled with was, apparently, his wife.' Fiona said. 'At least they registered as a married couple and shared a cabin. Constable Stone has picked up on Harker since then, I believe.'

'But not the woman?'

'No, sir, not the woman.' Stone consulted a battered notebook. 'On the nineteenth of November

Harker called on Johnny Flint at Flint's office in the Paisley Road. That's where I first saw him, Harker I mean. But I didn't know who he was then. He had wheels at his disposal and I was on foot so I couldn't follow him. However, five days later, on the twenty-fourth, Flint left the office and drove into Glasgow. This time I had the van and I was able to tail him. He went to the Athena Hotel in Glasgow in the late forenoon and spent two and a half hours up in one of the rooms with Harker.'

'How do you know it was Harker?'

'I checked at the desk, sir. He'd registered under his own name.'

'Well, he's either stupid or has ba . . . nerve,' Winstock said. 'The woman, the wife, was she there with him?'

'No sign of her, Inspector. At least I didn't see her.'

'Are you sure she was ever there at all?'

'No, sir, I can even be sure of that.'

'So none of you have actually seen the woman Harker travelled with?' All three officers shook their heads. Winstock regarded them balefully before he went on, 'Harker, known to be one of Carlo Manone's cronies from Philadelphia, steps off a transatlantic liner travelling on an open passport with his wife. What does that suggest?'

'That he intends to stay in Britain for a while,' Galbraith offered.

'And he's not shy about advertising his presence,' Winstock said. 'At a guess I'd say the action's elsewhere.'

'With the wife?'

'Possibly.'

Galbraith said, 'I think I'll trot round to the Athena this afternoon and find out if Harker's checked out and if he has, who paid his bill.'

'Take Kenny along,' Winstock said. 'Show the desk clerks, waiters and chambermaids the photograph. See if we can find out exactly who this woman is and give her a name. I don't suppose there's even the remote possibility that she *is* Harker's wife, but you never know, do you? So what's our first priority?'

'Find the wife,' said Kenny.

'That's it,' the Inspector said. 'Wherever Harker's lady is hiding, I want her located as soon as possible.'

'And watched, sir?'

'Oh, yes,' Inspector Winstock said. 'And watched.'

# Chapter Six

Mechanisation hadn't ruined the printing industry after all and any paid-up member of the Scottish Typographical Association should have been able to find work with one of the many publishing houses that flourished north of the Border.

Drink, however, had rendered master-printer Dougie Giffard unemployable. Now and then he would be taken on for a spell by a jobbing printer to whom cost-cutting was second nature and who hoped to coax from the bleary-eyed craftsman a little of his expertise. Charity was not involved, a fact of which Giffard in his lucid moments was very well aware, but occasional short-term jobs earned him just enough to pay rent on a single-end in a tenement in Waldorf Street, buy booze and cigarettes and, when he remembered, a couple of eggs and a rasher of bacon to nourish his skinny frame.

He was still several years short of fifty but drink

had reduced him to a wispy, grey-haired wreck without relative or friend in the world, give or take the odd publican.

Giffard had once been an upstanding citizen, sought by fine-press publishers for his ability to design and set their flagship productions. In the course of eight days in the winter of 1932, however, his wife and two half-grown sons had fallen victims to influenza. Back in 1918 he had lost his mother and sister to the same virulent disease but in those days he'd been too caught up in making money to grieve for long. Losing his wife and sons had pitched him into black despair, however. There was no redemption from that sad condition and soon he had little else to live for but his next mouthful of whisky.

The stink of the close in Waldorf Street made Tony catch his breath and Penny snatch her scarf up over her nose. Foul air hung against the light from the shattered windows of the landing and the girl was careful not to touch the walls or bannisters as she picked her way between broken glass and the river of filth that flowed from the ground-floor lavatory.

Dominic led the way. Tony followed behind Penny, his gaze fixed on her polished black half-boots and the brand-new leather attaché case that bumped against her calf. She'd refused to relinquish the case even for a moment, had sat in the rear seat of the Wolseley with her long arms wrapped around it as if it were a delicate child. He knew that the case contained the engravings from which Dominic's team hoped to produce a million pounds in counterfeit English banknotes, even more if the product stood up to inspection and viable channels of distribution could be established and maintained. He was dazed by the scale of the operation, more scared than excited, but he was part of it now whether he liked it or not, and was relieved that Dominic still trusted him and that his affair with Polly had not been uncovered.

They climbed past a third-floor lavatory that had no door at all.

In the closet, knickers around her ankles, a small girl perched precariously on the overflowing bowl. She watched them pass without embarrassment.

'Oh God!' Penny murmured. 'How can people live like this?'

'Because they've no choice.' Dominic's voice sounded strange, screeching a little like chalk on slate in the dank tenement stairwell. 'You may say that they do have a choice, Penny, but I can tell you that they do not. Have you nothing to match this in Vienna?'

'Vienna?' she said. 'No, nothing like this in Vienna.'

'Or Philadelphia?' Tony asked.

Penny did not answer.

They lingered on the half landing to listen to the rat-like scutter of the child's bare feet, heard a woman's shout, savage as a battle-cry, a slap, a shriek and a door slam. In silence they climbed up to the fourth floor where Dominic knocked on one of the peeling doors.

The letter-box had no lid. Through the opening Tony could make out a patch of worn linoleum covered with old newspapers. He could smell gas and the stench of a burnt frying pan and other odours, the old, undying breath of stark and inescapable poverty that he'd almost forgotten existed since he'd stopped collecting protection money in the backland tenements of Gorbals and Govan.

'Is that you?' said a voice from behind the letter-box.

Trousers, stained and soiled. Dangling from a claw-like hand was a half-pint bottle of Old Highland Dew, the cheapest whisky on the market.

'Yes, Douglas, it's me,' Dominic said. 'I told you we'd be today.'

'Have ye brung the stuff?'

'I've brought the stuff, yes.'

'Who's that wi' ye?'

'Tony Lombard. And a friend, a lady. Are you decent, Douglas?'

'Aye, ah'm decent.'

The door opened abruptly, releasing a rush of sodden air.

'Come on, come in,' said Dougie Giffard, 'afore y' catch your death.'

It had been a dozen years or more, Tony reckoned, since the kitchen had been properly scrubbed. The woodwork was layered with grease, the old-fashioned iron fireplace draped with vests, stockings and shirts as damp as the room itself. There was no fire in the grate, only a heap of cold cinders that spilled on to the newspapers on the floor. Curled on the cinder heap was a fat ash-grey cat. It opened one sleepy eye, surveyed them for a moment then leapt up and scurried under the bed in the alcove.

'Frobisher,' Dougie Giffard informed them. 'I was settin' a full eight-volume edition o' Frobisher's Travels for Mackenzie-Clark at the time I got her. She shouldn't have a man's name, I suppose, but the boys fair liked it. They ca'ed her "Frobe". She slept on the foot o' their bed. Not here, though. We was at a better place down near the Cross in them days.' He knelt stiffly and scratched his nails on the carpet of newspapers. 'Come on out, Frobe, say hullo t' wur visitors.'

But the cat would have none of it and remained hidden under the bed.

Giffard lurched to his feet, and held up the bottle.

'Fancy a wee snifter then?' he offered.

'No,' Penny said. 'Thank you.'

'Ah've a cup somewhere.'

'No. No, really.'

'She your sweetheart, Mr Manone?'

'I'm afraid not, Douglas. She's the lady I told you about.'

'Penny?' Giffard said. 'Aye, well, is that not most appropriate?'

Why had Dominic chosen to reveal his secrets to this grimy wee man, Tony wondered, and what role, if any, would he play in the deal that Dominic was putting together?

'Nobody is going to drink with you, Douglas,' Dominic said. 'Put that damned bottle away. You can plaster yourself out of sight later if you wish but right now you've a piece of business to do for me and you'd better keep your head clear. How much have you had today?'

'Half, just the half bottle.'

'How much is that compared to a normal day?'

'Half again,' Giffard said. 'I can stop any time I like, ye know.'

'And the band played "Believe if it you like",' said Dominic.

Giffard wore flannel trousers and a collarless shirt adorned with egg yolk and cat's fur. There was no evidence of food in the kitchen, though, save for a frying pan half-submerged in a sinkful of water under the window and a chipped soup bowl filled with a lumpy white substance that may have been haddock-in-milk. The position of the bowl on the floor indicated that Frobisher at least was well fed.

'I can do it, Mr Manone. I've done it afore, remember.'

'Things were different in those days,' Dominic said.

'I done it for your old man. We never got caught neither.'

'I know,' Dominic said gently. 'Put the bottle away, Douglas.'

Tony watched the claw tighten on the whisky bottle, then Penny pushed the scarf from her mouth and held out her hand.

'Give it to me, Mr Giffard. I will keep it safe for you.'

'You're a Jew, aren't ye, lass?' Giffard held out the bottle. 'I done a Talmud once, y' know. Set in Hebrew characters. Two rabbi leanin' over me for weeks just t' make sure it was right. By God, they were educated men. Fussy, though, so fussy I thought I'd never get done. Quarto page size on hand-made paper wi' hand-cut capitals. Grand job when it was finished. The rabbis were fair pleased wi' it.'

'Are you a Jew, Mr Giffard?' Penny said.

'Not me.'

She placed the bottle on the table behind her.

'How can you tell that I am Jewish?'

Giffard tapped his nose. 'You might be a woman but you've the same clever look about ye that yon rabbis had. Okay, you've taken mah bottle an' you're carryin' the case so sling it up here on the table an' show me what you've brought.'

Penny glanced at Dominic.

He nodded.

She lifted the attaché case, braced it against the table's edge, and opened it.

Tony looked to the window. The glass was so clouded that he could barely make out the adjacent tenements. No one could possibly see into the kitchen even if they were perched on the roof.

He stepped closer as Penny lifted out the plates.

She held the blocks, one in each hand, for Giffard to study.

The printer's vagueness vanished. He put a hand on Penny's sleeve.

'Who done these?' he said. 'Nobody from round here, I'll bet.'

'They were engraved abroad,' Dominic said. 'That's all you need to know.'

'I'm not just standin' here for the good o' mah health,' Giffard said. 'If I'm expected t' manage the printin' then I'll need t' have a closer look at those.'

'Give them to him, Penny,' Dominic said.

Penny slid the blocks on to Giffard's grubby palms.

Some residue of professional pride stirred in the man. The agitated trembling in his hands ceased as soon as he touched the plates. He carried them to the draining board by the sink under the window and put them down. He opened a cupboard beneath the sink and fished out an old cardboard box, opened it and dug out a rectangular reading glass. He rubbed the glass on the sleeve of his shirt, sighted against the light from the window, rubbed again.

It was so still in the kitchen that Tony could make out the clang of a shunting engine from the goods yard a half-mile away. He felt excitement tighten the muscles of his stomach as he watched Giffard go to work. All that had gone before, plus all the stuff he hadn't been told about, hinged on the printer's judgement. He had already guessed that Giffard was a forger who had done work of this kind for Carlo Manone. He wondered if it was Giffard's efforts that had furnished Carlo with the stake he needed to buy his way into the American rackets.

Giffard examined the face plate minutely through the reading glass. His thoroughness was reassuring. Tony noticed that the cat had come out from hiding and was squatting among the ashes, watching too.

'Bloody Britannia!' Giffard let out a wheezy chuckle. 'By God, whoever done this got bloody Britannia right. I'll need a lot more magnification t' be certain but so far it looks prime. I'll have it up to twenty-fold enlargement t' compare against the genuine article but it seems t' be a model engravin' so far.' He turned. 'No one man done this. It's a team effort. What's your connection wi' the team, lass, an' why did they trust you wi' somethin' so valuable?'

'I am only the courier,' Penny said.

'Did *you* know it was a workshop job, Mr Manone?' Giffard said. 'There's a deal o' money invested in producin' a plate of this quality. Will that kinda money be invested in the printin' too?'

'What do you mean, Douglas?' Dominic asked.

'An accurate engravin's only the start,' Giffard said. 'The plates'll have t' be doctored for mass-production. Paper an' ink must be dead right too.'

'I haven't seen the paper yet,' Dominic admitted.

'British notes're printed on paper manufactured from Turkish flax,' Giffard said. 'But it's used flax, rags in other words. It's bleached an' washed for paper-makin' an' that's what gives such a funny tint to the finished product. It's bloody hard to replicate, believe me.'

'What else will we need to do?'

'Add chemicals to the ink. In circulated notes oil from the ink seeps into the paper, so we'll need a suitable chemical to release the oil to give the forged notes the right look of age. It can't be done mechanically.'

He held the plate balanced on the tips of his fingers. His nails, Tony noticed, had been bitten to the quick and the fingers looked blunt and clumsy. Considerable dexterity would be required to alter the plates and hand-set the num-bers. Numbering, he reckoned, would be a major problem if the print runs were going to be large enough to be profit-able.

He said, 'What will you do about the serial numbers?'

Giffard said, 'Cut slots in the face plate an' set the serial numbers in moveable type. Bulk runs'll need several different sequences. We'll need to cut a second slot for the Chief Cashier's signature too, for it can be changed overnight. I take it, Mr Manone, this isn't a tuppence-ha'penny exercise, like last time?'

'No,' Dominic said. 'We intend to leak at least half a million notes into circulation over the next couple of years.'

'Tall order,' Giffard said. 'Will you sell the notes

through the black market or push them on the international exchanges?'

'Both,' Dominic said.

'Then we'll definitely need a perfect type face for the serial numbers.'

'Do you know what that type face is and where it can be obtained?'

'Aye, I think ah do,' Giffard said. 'If it can't be got easily then I'll cast it myself – if you'll supply the equipment an' a quiet place t' work.'

'How long will all this take?' said Penny.

'Longer than ten minutes,' Giffard said.

'Can we have marketable notes by Easter, do you think?'

'Not a hope's Hades, lass,' Giffard said and with an apologetic little shrug, handed her back the plates.

The Wolseley, like the girl, had a mind of its own. Steering was heavy, the gear lever imprecise. Tony concentrated on maintaining a steady speed on the drive back to Breslin. Slumped in the broad rear seat, Dominic seemed half asleep. The girl, up front, knelt with her back to the windscreen, her arms on the seat back so that she could look directly at Dominic while she challenged him, bitching, Tony thought, like any wee Glasgow sweetie-wife with a grievance against the world.

'You promised me you would be in production by Easter,' she said.

'I didn't promise you anything of the sort,' Dominic murmured.

'Why do you want to employ that filthy little fellow? He will be drunk all of the time. I will not have him in my house.'

'It isn't your house,' Dominic reminded her.

'He will bring the cat with him.'

'Well, he isn't gonna leave the cat behind,' Tony said.

'That filthy man, that filthy cat.'

'Don't you ever listen?' Dominic said. 'Didn't you hear what he told us?'

'Is he the best you can find?'

'He's the best there is,' Dominic said. 'He made over a hundred grand for my father just after the war. A single fast production run off plates that weren't up to scratch. If you want an expert forger, Giffard's your man.'

'It is the past, you are delving into the past.'

'That's probably true,' said Dominic.

The light was fading fast now the sun had gone down. The distant hills had lost the pale rose glow that defined their contours. Trees and hedgerows were etched black against the skyline and the bungalows along the road to Breslin seemed more isolated in the wintry dusk.

Through the steering wheel Tony could feel the road come up at him in harsh gulps. The girl rocked beside him, knees digging into the leather. He heard the scratch of a match, smelled cigar smoke, saw the glow of Dominic's cigar in the overhead mirror, Dominic's lips and cheek illuminated.

'You are the wrong person,' the girl stated.

'For what?' said Dominic.

'To manage this thing.'

'Well, maybe I am,' Dominic said. 'On the other hand, who else are you going to get that will put up with you.'

'Me?'

'Grow up, kid,' Tony said. 'This is the best deal you're gonna get on this side of the English Channel. Maybe you're used to big wheels moving every time you shake your tail back in Vienna, but this is the deal Carlo Manone set up and this is the deal you're stuck with.'

'I am not living with that drunkard,' the girl said. 'I am not staying alone with him out there at Blackstone. There is no telling what he may do to me.'

Tony laughed. 'I don't know Dougie Giffard from Adam but I reckon he's about as interested in you as you are in Father Christmas.'

'You won't be alone with Giffard,' Dominic said.

'You will be there?'

'Of course I won't be there,' Dominic said. 'Tony will.'

The wheel gulped up at him. He dug his elbows into his hips to hold the big car steady. It had already crossed his mind that he might be put in as supervisor, his stint as nursemaid extended. He thought regretfully of his quiet, comfortable apartment, of the routine he'd evolved across the river that had allowed stolen acts of lovemaking with Polly.

'Permanently?' Tony said.

'Yes, I think it better if you move out there,' Dominic said.

'When?'

'As soon as you can.'

'Before Christmas?' Tony said. 'I promised my father I'd . . .'

'Do what you have to, Tony,' Dominic said. 'But I want Giffard installed and the machines up and running as soon as possible.'

The girl turned her head and Tony knew that she was watching him, appeased by the irony of the situation. He should never have allowed her to draw him out of his shell. He felt a sudden surge of panic as he contemplated how uncomfortable it would be to live with one woman while he remained in love with another. He wanted to ask, 'What about Polly?' but horse sense told him that the question had no relevance now.

'Tell me what Giffard needs,' Dominic said, 'and I'll get it for you.'

'And me?' Penny said. 'What about me?'

Dominic drew in a mouthful of smoke. 'From now on you'll do exactly as you're told, Penny.'

'And if I do not?' Penny said.

'Then you won't get paid.'

'It is not you who will pay me,' the girl said.

'Yes, it is,' said Dominic. 'From now on you depend on me for everything.'

'How much will you give me?' Penny said.

'Your fair share,' said Dominic.

'How much is that?'

'More than you deserve,' said Dominic.

And to Tony's surprise, the girl laughed.

As soon as the orchestra filed in from the hatch beneath the stage Rosie knew that her deafness would not ruin the evening.

It was her first time in a theatre. She was enchanted by the ornate décor, the steep plush seats, by the smell of perfume and fur coats and the whole dense, gilded atmosphere of the dress circle where, close to the front row, Kenny and she were seated. Breathless with excitement she watched the pit orchestra tune up. Saw the slither of a trombone slide, the tightening of violin strings, the tamping of the drummer as he adjusted the tension of his skins.

She clung tightly to Kenny's hand and leaned against him.

'Is this what they call tuning up?' she asked.

'Yes, but you're not missing much. It sounds like a cats' convention.'

'What?'

He pulled back a little, faced her. 'Cats' con-ven-shun.'

'Ah!' Rosie said, enraptured. 'Ah! I see.'

In hanging boxes to the sides of the stage gentlemen in dinner suits were pandering to ladies in
full-length gowns. Children too, children in party
frocks with bows in their hair.

Rosie watched the ushers close the exit doors and,
curling her programme in her hand, stared at the flat
cork-like board as it soared up to expose a shimmering
crimson curtain. She felt a lift of expectation in the
audience and, glancing round, saw that the people
about her were settling down. Some had miniature
binoculars trained upon the stage, others were scanning their programmes or fiddling with the wrappings
of chocolate boxes, one or two were laughing as if the
entertainment had already begun.

Kenny tugged her hand and nodded towards
the stage.

Down in the orchestra pit the conductor raised
his baton and looked up at the curtain. He was very
tall and had a shock of grey hair that seemed silvery
in the glow of the footlights.

She watched him tap the baton on the stand again,
saw the drummer's arms rise and fall, the cheeks of the
trumpet players puff out, and deep, deep inside her
head imagined that she could hear the muffled musical
notes of the fanfare as the huge, soft-winged curtains
parted and scenery and chorus were revealed.

'Oh!' she gasped. 'Oh! Oh, Kenneth!' and pressed
herself back against the curve of the seat as light and
colour and gaiety flooded out upon her and, like a
whisper, she thought she could make out the heels

of the dancers tapping on stage and the voice of the chorus raised in song.

Twelve rows behind Rosie and off to her left Inspector Winstock lowered his rented opera glasses, folded his arms, and muttered to the woman seated next to him, 'Is that her, do you think, the deaf girl?'

'Who else could it be?' Fiona MacGregor said.

'Is Kenny pretending to be her boyfriend?'

'Actually, I don't think he's pretending, sir.'

'Really?' Winstock said. 'I wonder what on earth he sees in her?'

And Fiona answered sourly, 'God knows!'

Polly was in bed before Dominic returned home. She had more sense than to ask where he had been but she had consumed just enough gin to be vaguely amorous and wearing her new nightgown was conspicuously propped up on the pillows.

She'd purchased the nightgown from Daudet's, the most expensive shop in Buchanan Street, together with a crochet brassiere and a pair of triangular knickers decorated with needle-run lace, had bought the garments not for the pleasure that wearing them would give her but for the pleasure they would give Tony. She had eaten dinner alone in the dining-room and as soon as the children were asleep had gone up to the master bedroom, locked the door and tried on her purchases in front of the full-length mirror. The light of the bedside lamp softened the angles of her body, made her feel frothy and diaphanous as if she might float into Tony's arms just as she was. It was close to midnight before she heard the front door open and close, by which time she was weary of pointless self-indulgence and imaginings.

She scrambled into bed and lay back, listening to Dominic padding about downstairs. She felt faintly foolish playing the tart – but spiteful too, so spiteful she was even tempted to practise on Dominic some of the wicked tricks she had learned from Tony. She waited, eager and apprehensive, for her husband to come upstairs. He would look in on the children first, of course, to be sure they were asleep. She assumed that the servants were asleep too, though it hardly mattered if they were awake for she was never noisy with Dominic whose lovemaking was too measured and deliberate to make her cry out.

He entered the bedroom stealthily, shoes in one hand, and didn't seem to notice her at first. He put the shoes under the polished wooden valet, seated himself on a chair, hitched up his trouser legs, unclipped his suspenders, peeled off his stockings and massaged his feet. Then he padded across the carpet to the wicker basket by the side of the wardrobe, opened it and dropped the stockings inside.

'I thought you would be asleep by now,' he said.

'Well, I'm not,' Polly said. 'I'm here, wide awake.'

He unbuttoned his trousers and braces, drew his shirt and undervest over his head, put shirt and vest into the basket and the trousers into a mahogany trouser press. He smoothed the creases with the flat of his hand, screwed down the press's butterfly nuts, then placed his watch, cuff-links and loose change in a bowl on the dressing-table. He stepped methodically out of his undershorts.

'Where are my pyjamas?'

'Under the pillow.'

'What are they doing there?'

'I don't know,' Polly said.

'Why aren't they in the usual place?'

'They're under the pillow, damn it.'

He padded round the foot of the bed and slid his hand under the pillow.

'No, under my pillow,' Polly said.

'For God's sake, Polly!'

She pushed herself forward, her breasts visible under the expensive night-gown. He reached behind her, groping beneath her pillow. She touched him, not tenderly.

'Have you been drinking?' he said. 'You have. I can smell it.'

'One gin,' she said. 'Well, one and half. Pink.'

He did not pull away. He kept one hand under the pillow, the other braced against the bed-head while she stroked him.

'I'm not in the mood for this, Polly,' he said. 'Where are my pyjamas?'

'You'll have to find them, darling. I'll give you a clue. They're somewhere nice and warm.'

'You're drunk, aren't you?'

'Merry,' she said. 'Werry, werry merry.'

He was warm, his flesh warm, but he was not aroused.

He drew back a little, took her wrist between finger and thumb and in the same methodical manner in which he had screwed down the butterfly nuts broke her hold on him.

'Aren't you up to it?' Polly said. 'Won't you even try?'

'Not when you're drunk.'

'I'm not drunk.'

'I say you are,' Dominic told her.

'I'm seconds, aren't I? That's it, I'm seconds.'

He seated himself on the bed.

'Polly,' he said, 'you've really got to stop this.'

'Stop what?'

'Spoiling everything.'

'Spoiling – *I'm* spoiling – what am I supposed to be spoiling?'

'All right,' he said. 'I admit it isn't entirely your fault. I'm busy, that's all. There's something in the pipeline that demands all my attention.'

'What? What's in the pipeline?'

'Tony – I told you about Tony.'

'You told me nothing of the kind.'

'It's important business, Polly, very important.'

'Will it make us rich?'

'Yes.'

'I thought we were rich,' Polly said.

He looked smooth and rather plump in the lamplight. Soft, she thought, too soft to be wholesome. The hair that downed his chest and thighs had a washed look, as if he had bathed recently. She felt again an anxious little rage of desire beating against the fact of his rejection.

He said, 'Do you want me to make love to you?'

'Yes.'

'All right.'

He put out his hand and cupped her breast. He hadn't noticed the night-gown, hadn't even remarked on it. If it had been made of platinum laced with pure gold it would have made no difference. He had failed to realise that she had made herself pretty for his sake, that she needed love as well as lovemaking.

'All right?' Polly said, shrilly.

He rubbed his palm gently over her breast. 'Sorry if I've been neglecting you. My fault, my fault entirely.'

He leaned forward to kiss her.

And down in the hallway at the foot of the stairs the telephone rang.

And rang.

'Look, Dominic,' Bernard said. 'I know it's late but I had to wait until Lizzie was asleep before I could get out of the house.'

'Where are you?'

'In a phone box at Anniesland Cross.'

'Why don't you call me from the office tomorrow morning?'

'It's something you may not want Allan Shakespeare to know about.'

Dominic drew the dressing-gown about his thighs and leaned against the panelled wall. He had switched on the lamp on the hall table but the rest of the ground floor was in darkness.

'What is it, Bernard? What's so urgent that it can't wait until morning?'

'Rosie – our Rosie – is being courted by a policeman.'

'Good for her,' said Dominic.

'He took her to the pantomime.'

'Did she enjoy it?'

'Yes, but that isn't the point.'

'What is the point, Bernard?'

'He's been asking questions about us.'

'If he's falling for her then naturally he'll want to know about her folks.'

'Specifically, 'Bernard said, 'about you.'

Dominic heard Bernard fumble for change then the tinny rattle of coins falling into the box. 'Still there?'

'Yes, I'm still here,' said Bernard.

'This policeman, what is he? A beat copper, a flat-foot?'

'He's a detective sergeant.'

'Really? From what division?'

'St Andrew's Street.'

'He's CID, is he?'

'Yes.'

'Did Rosie volunteer this information?'

'No.' Bernard paused long enough to suggest that he might be lying. 'He's been seeing her for weeks apparently but she was so elated when she got home from the theatre that she blurted it all out.'

'Did he bring her home?'

'No, he put her into a taxi.'

'A taxi? On a sergeant's pay?' said Dominic.

'That's what I reckoned,' Bernard said. 'Official expenses, maybe?'

'Possibly. Do you know what sort of questions he's been asking her?'

'Not in any great detail, no.'

'But he does know who Rosie is? Who I am?'

'Oh, yes,' said Bernard.

'Are you sure about that?'

'Positive.'

'Perhaps it's just an unfortunate coincidence.'

'I don't think so,' Bernard said.

'Why couldn't it be?'

'Because of what's going on at Blackstone Farm.'

Dominic hesitated. 'What *is* going on at Blackstone Farm?'

'Heck, I don't know,' said Bernard. 'And I don't want to know. But I do know you've got something cooking up there. You didn't have me organise a crew of carpenters just to redecorate your lady-friend's bedroom.'

'She isn't my lady-friend,' Dominic said.

'And I gather Tony Lombard's billeted there more or less permanently.'

'Tony is . . .'

'I don't want to know. I don't want to know,' Bernard repeated. 'What you're up to is your affair, Dominic. I just thought I'd pass on the information for what it's worth.' Another coin tumbled into the box. 'I wouldn't go saying anything to Polly, though, just in case it gets back to Rosie.'

'Polly knows nothing about my affairs, nothing.'

'Even so we'll have to be extra careful at the Christmas get-together.'

'You're still on for Christmas, I take it?' Dominic said.

'If you think it's wise,' said Bernard.

'It would be difficult to invent a credible reason for cancelling,' said Dominic. 'We always get together at this time of year.'

'Yes,' said Bernard. 'And Lizzie's really looking forward to it. Listen, I've got to go. I'm running out of change.'

'Last question,' Dominic said. 'This detective, what's his name?'

'MacGregor. Kenneth MacGregor.'

'Thanks, Bernard. You did the right thing in letting me know.'

'What do you want me to do now?'

'Nothing. I'll handle it.'

'Rosie won't come to any harm, will she?' Bernard said. 'I don't want Rosie hurt because of something I've said or done.'

'Rosie won't come to any harm,' Dominic promised.

'If she does . . .' Bernard began, but his threat was lost in pips and clicks and the long drone of the line going dead.

She had a burning sensation just under her breastbone and the taste of gin in the back of her throat, all desire dissipated as she crouched in the darkness at the top of the stairs listening to Dominic talk on the telephone.

It wasn't what she had done with Tony that terrified her but what would happen if Dominic discovered what she had done with Tony, how everything could be destroyed and Tony lost as a result of an incautious word or, as now, a single late-night telephone call.

As soon as she realised that the call was from her stepfather she assumed that Bernard had somehow found out about Tony and she and, outraged, had called Dominic. It took only a moment of eavesdropping, however, for her fears to be replaced by bewilderment.

When Dominic put down the receiver she stole swiftly back up to bed.

She thumped her head into the pillow, pulled the sheet up over her ears. Heard him come into the bedroom. Did not move. In the glow of the bedside lamp through the weave of the sheet, she saw his shadow pass and a split second later the light went out. He slid in beside her on a little billow of cold air. She waited tensely for his cold hand to cup her breast or slide between her thighs but heard him sigh, felt him turned on to his back and sink into the pillows, hands behind his head.

She swallowed, said, 'Who was it?'

'No one of any consequence.'

'Was it Tony?'

'No, it wasn't Tony.'

As if she had lost all interest in the telephone call, she inched away from him.

'Polly,' Dominic said, 'if you still want me to make love . . .'

'No,' she said, 'No, darling. I think I'll pass: all right?'

And Dominic said, 'All right.'


Frost still stained the sheltered corners of the yard when the chippies arrived to bag the sawdust and remove the old tim-bers; three cheerful young men who had no inkling as to the purpose of the platform they had been sent to construct.

Penny made them coffee and meat-paste sandwiches and kept them chatting for half an hour. They readily swallowed her inventive little lies and thanked her profusely, almost obsequiously, before they clambered on to the truck and drove off back to the building site.

After the young men had gone the yard seemed oddly empty in the thin winter sunlight with nothing on the horizon but faint smudges of smoke. She went indoors, washed and dried the cups and plates. Then she put on the warm tweed jacket that Tony had bought for her, went back out to the stables and climbed the ladder to the platform that jutted out over the stalls.

She switched on the current that fed the light bulbs, played with the switches, flicking them on and off; then she began to dance, whirling and pirouetting and stamping her feet so that fine lines of sawdust welled up from the joints and a beige dust sifted into the shaft of sunlight in the doorway.

For lunch she would serve mutton chops and fresh vegetables, the best selection that Tony could find in Breslin's greengrocer's. She had also told him to reserve one of the turkeys that hung plucked and naked on hooks in the butcher's window. She would roast it with a simple stuffing of bacon, breadcrumbs and sausage-meat for there were no chestnuts to be had in Breslin, none of the herbs that her mother had favoured, and certainly no cranberries.

Eventually she stopped prancing about, seated herself on the floor and slumped disconsolately against the wall.

She could not stop her mind whirling, filling up with thoughts of what she would be missing – the noisy cocktail parties, glittering balls and concerts, dinner tables set for forty or fifty guests. And snow, snow cloaking the brown spires and factory chimneys while the lights of luxury stores winked in the dusk and the harsh lines of the city were temporarily softened by the Christmas season.

Christmas at home: she longed to be there again, the toast, the talk of the town, boys stepping up to salute her, poor besotted boys so manly in their uniforms, so disciplined, passionate and intense. Mature, sagacious men too, in tuxedos and bow-ties, smoke from their cigarettes drifting across the dinner table, their fingertips brushing her bare shoulders as if to convince themselves that she was real and not some artificial image created by the light. All that choice, all those opportunities and, out of boredom and a weary sense of obligation, she had finally given herself to Edgar Harker, a blunt, broad-buttocked nobody.

When she heard the approach of the car she jumped to her feet, wiped away her tears and, putting on a false smile, hurried out into the yard.

She had hoped that it would be the big Wolseley: Dominic. She was already attracted to the sullen little Italian with his slumbering eyes and brusque manner. The fact that he was married mattered not a jot. He would not be the first married man whom she had twisted around her finger. She had asked Tony about 'the wife' but Tony had gone cold and had stubbornly refused to discuss her.

The Dolomite rumbled into the yard and came to a halt. Tony got out. She could not truthfully say that she was displeased to see him. He was like Dominic in some ways, though not so distinctly Italian. Eddie had told her about the bond between Carlo Manone and Papa Lombardi. Had also told her why Dominic had been left behind in Scotland to run the business that Carlo had established before the Great War began. She felt no genuine affinity with either Tony or Dominic for she dared not share her own wild and quarrelsome history with them just yet or tell them of the gigantic error that she had made in coming to Scotland at all.

Tony seemed unusually rattled.

He flung open the door of the Dolomite, snapped, 'Okay, Dougie, hop to it.'

The printer emerged cautiously with the cat cradled in his arms. His head appeared over the roof of the motorcar and he stared at Penny as if he had never seen her before. The cat squirmed a little, dug her claws into the shoulder of the new overcoat and hung on for dear life, her green eyes narrow and unblinking.

'Present for you,' Tony said. 'He's all yours, Penny.'

'Mine?' she said. 'I understood that you were to be his keeper.'

'Nope. I'm your keeper. You're his keeper.'

'Nobody's mah bloody keeper.' Dougie lowered the tabby to the cobbles and watched her strut away towards the farmhouse. 'Is this the place ah'm stayin'?'

'Yeah,' Tony said. 'This is it, Doug. Shangri-La.'

'Remote enough, ain't it?'

'Not a pub for miles, Dougie, if that's what you mean.'

He was different, the printer; younger. Not only had Tony supplied him with a new wardrobe but he had also had a haircut and a shave and, Penny suspected, a bath. His hair was plastered down with Brylcreem, shaped to an elegant skull with a domed forehead and close set ears. He reminded her of a whippet her father had once owned and from which he had bred a line of aristocratic pups that had been sold for substantial sums – not, she told herself, that Giffard was worth much for, a shapely skull notwithstanding, he was still just a scruffy little mongrel.

'New and much improved, don't you reckon?' Tony said. 'It's amazing what twenty minutes in a public bath-house can do for a guy.'

'Did you accompany him into the bath-house?'

'Unfortunately, yeah,' Tony said. 'I even had to scrub his back.'

Indifferent to their sarcasm, Dougie leaned on the car and observed the tabby sniff at the doorpost and then, still sniffing, slip into the kitchen.

'Got any spare grub in there, lass?' he asked.

'Yes, I will make us lunch in due course,' Penny told him.

'Not if Frobe gets there afore you, you won't,' Dougie Giffard said and grinned as the girl rushed shrieking into the house.

# Chapter Seven

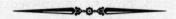

Looking back, it seemed to Polly that Dominic had known that this would be the family's last Christmas together and for that reason had pulled out all the stops. He had always been lavish with gifts and hospitality, a benefactor not just to kith and kin but to all the charities and institutions to which he lent support.

In the week preceding Christmas he had been invited to lunch at the Exchange, had dined at the Union as well as the Cassia, and had presided from the wings at the Jewish pipe-band's annual bun-fight, for which he picked up the bill. There was no evidence of enjoyment in him, though, no beaming smiles or expansive gestures of goodwill. He did not sings carols, tell risqué jokes or perform conjuring tricks; he just signed the cheques and left the celebrating to others.

Polly could not be sure if his dourness had to do with the imminent threat of war or with the state of the business. She had never been able to read her husband's moods accurately and, lately, he had become as opaque as a blown mirror. In this respect he was not alone. Many men and women were reluctant to decide whether they were pessimists or optimists and were content to bob like corks on the tide of press opinion as news from Europe ebbed and flowed.

She didn't even know what Tony thought of the current crisis, how he interpreted the Munich Agreement or the shop-worn non-aggression pact with Poland – or if he even cared. She had seen nothing of him, heard nothing from him. Her anger, like fear of war, swung first one way then the other.

In compensation she threw herself into Christmas shopping, purchasing ridiculously expensive gifts for everyone she could think of, including Cook, Leah and Patricia, spending Dominic's money hand-over-fist. She took the children into town by taxi-cab – riding out with Charley Fraser was just too demeaning – and trailed them round the department stores, buying clothes that would not fit them for two or three years, buying for herself the most expensive garments she could find, useless jackets and little dresses, silk suits that she would have few, if any, opportunities to wear. Stuart and Ishbel soon got over their initial excitement of being in town with Mummy. They began to droop and whine and had to be fed cream cakes and lemonade in a tea-room to keep them going. All in all even Polly found it rather too hectic and depressing and, laden with packages, was glad to sink into a taxi-cab, light a cigarette and ride home again.

Cook had been consulted over the menu and grocery lists were compiled in advance. Dominic did most of the ordering straight from the warehouse and throughout Christmas week crates and hampers and boxes turned up at Manor Park Avenue almost hourly. Mrs O'Shea and Patricia had agreed to forego time off until New Year, which was, in any case, the traditional holiday for servants, and Leah had been persuaded to come in on Christmas Day to help lay table and serve.

Polly pretended that she was taking the occasion in her stride. But this year she felt curiously cut off from the rich and vivid pleasures of the festive season. She was trapped in swirling little eddies of anxiety, anger and fear that stemmed, of course, from Tony's absence.

By Christmas Eve she was near to breaking point, to screaming aloud in frustration. Only a stealthy stream of cocktails saw her through the afternoon while down in the kitchen and up in the playroom other women competently took care of 'her party', and her children.

A fir tree had been put up in the living-room. Dominic had taken the children out in the huge ungainly motorcar he had acquired from Jackie and had returned an hour later with the tree stowed in the cavernous boot and Stuart and Ishbel chattering about their adventure in 'the forest'.

Later that evening, the twenty-third of the month, Dom and the children opened boxes of ornaments and after securing the tree in a tub of earth decorated it prettily while Polly, *sans* cocktail glass, drifted in and out of the room, feigning enthusiasm for the children's sake, approving this touch and vetoing that, as if she were an arbiter of taste and the only person whose opinion mattered.

In spite of her tension she was pleased to see her children happy and went upstairs and sat with them for a half-hour after supper while Dom put through three or four telephone calls.

The tree, Polly had to agree, was pretty, almost a work of art. It occupied the space behind Dom's long brown sofa, tall and upright like a green guardsman and on the afternoon of Christmas Eve, when she found herself alone in the living-room – Patricia had taken the children to a matinee – she brushed it with the rim of her glass just for the pleasure of watching the boughs tremble and the baubles nod. She was just about to touch it again when she saw the Dolomite appear out of the gloaming and draw to a halt in the driveway.

She met him at the door before he could ring the bell.

Laden with parcels, he stood on the step big and awkward as a bear.

'For me, Mr El?' Polly said.

'Only one of them, Mrs Em,' said Tony.

'Which one?'

He juggled the parcels, fished in his overcoat pocket, brought out a small oblong packet wrapped not in brown paper but in tissue tied with silk thread.

'This one,' he said. 'It's not to be opened 'til tomorrow, though.'

'In mixed company?'

'Maybe not,' said Tony. 'No, definitely not.'

Polly glanced round, saw no one in the hall or on the stairs. She moved suddenly against him, kissed him on the mouth and whispered: 'Oh, God! I was beginning to think I'd never see you again.' She held the cocktail glass out to one side and, pressing her breasts against the parcels, kissed him again. 'Dominic's not here. I don't know where he is.'

'I do,' Tony said.

'Where?'

'He won't be back for hours,' Tony said.

'For sure?'

'Yeah, for sure.'

'Come in then, oh please, do come in.'

'Better yet, if you can slip out for an hour why don't we go to my place?'

'Yes,' Polly said, 'Oh God, darling! Yes!'


He had less respect for the plates than seemed quite proper and Penny had to remind herself of Tony's warning that Douglas Giffard might seem like an unwholesome drunkard but that she would do well not to underestimate his intelligence. When the printer annoyed her, therefore, she bit not on the bullet but on a sugared almond from the jar that Tony had given her just before he announced that he was going away for a while.

'How long?' she asked.

'I'll be back first thing tomorrow.'

'Does Dominic know that you intend to abandon me?'

'It's Christmas Eve. I'm taking my folks to Mass,' Tony said.

'What if I want to go to Mass?'

'You're not a Catholic, though, are you?'

She remembered how Giffard glanced up from the armchair by the hearth and gave her such a sly, quizzical look that she had been quite shaken by it and had realised at that moment that Tony's warning was not without substance.

She said, 'I think you are going to meet your girlfriend.'

'No girlfriend,' Tony said.

'Your lover then.'

'I'm taking my parents to Mass, Penny, that's all. I'll eat with them beforehand, them and my sisters, because I won't be around tomorrow, Christmas, like I usually am.'

'Where will you be tomorrow?'

'Here,' he told her, flatly. 'Tomorrow I'm moving in.'

'On Dominic's orders.'

'Yeah, on Dominic's orders.'

There were four bedrooms in the farmhouse, two on the floor above the kitchen, two others tucked under the sloping roof. The attics each had a skylight and a quaint little iron fireplace and were furnished with an iron cot, a corner what not with a basin and jug and a rush-bottomed chair that reminded Penny of a painting. There were no azure skies or giddy patchwork quilts for Mr Giffard, though. He had to settle for rain on the roof and a brown army blanket, not that the printer seemed to mind. He was concerned only about his cat and his whisky, and Penny had already negotiated a truce with the tabby and held the key to the cupboard where the whisky was kept.

She had that element of power over Giffard, control of his whisky ration.

One half bottle per day, delivered at noon.

She had expected him to plead, to keen and nag and humiliate himself but in that respect she was disappointed. He might be twitching inside but outwardly he was calm, though he would eye the clock with baleful eagerness as noon approached or smoke one cigarette after another and go for a toddle about the yard with the tabby clinging to his shoulder. Most of the rest of the time he occupied himself with newspaper crossword puzzles or by poring over the engraved plates under the light that hung above the long deal table in the kitchen. He had requested drawing materials and Tony had brought him big sheets of glazed card, black Indian ink, a selection of fine-nibbed pens, and a penknife with a sharp heart-shaped blade that were stored with the plates in a drawer lined with clean newspapers.

A watchmaker's glass screwed into one eye, Dougie would sit for hours studying the surface of the face plate, peering at it until his eyes began to water and his hand shake. Only then would he reach for the glass and bottle, measure himself an inch of Haig's and knock it back to restore and revive his concentration.

Tony left soon after lunch. Penny was sorry to see him go. She was excited at the prospect of having him sleep at the farm from now on, though, and spent the best part of the afternoon airing the bedroom adjacent to hers. She laid clean sheets for the bed, fine woollen blankets and a quilt with a sun-burst pattern that cheered the room up enormously. She put an ashtray on the bedside table and filled the water carafe, did all the things that a nice, new conscientious wife might do for a husband, while downstairs Dougie and the cat dozed in the armchair by the fire.

He looked peaceful in that pose, almost grand-fatherly, Penny thought when she returned to the kitchen, almost as if he had been born and bred on the farm. He was no shabbier than the average shepherd or pig-breeder and the manner in which he had disciplined his craving for drink roused a sneaking respect.

She moved so quietly about the kitchen that

the cat, curled on Giffard's lap, did not even raise its head.

Outside it was almost dark, the weather grey and still, not ominous. She leaned on the edge of the sink and looked from the window, thinking of nothing much, nothing too serious – of Dominic, of Dominic and Tony, Tony and Dominic, a loose little *pas de deux* in which she danced first with one and then the other in an empty ballroom with the lights turned low.

'Homesick?' Giffard said.

She started, turned swiftly, almost guiltily.

He was exactly as he had been a moment ago, the cat still asleep on his lap, his stockinged feet stretched out to the fire. But now his eyes were open and he was studying her as intently if she were Britannia engraved on a metal plate.

'Pardon?'

'I asked if you was homesick?' Dougie said.

She shook her head and came away from the window, walked across the kitchen with the table between her and the man in the chair by the fire. The half bottle of Haig whisky was on the table together with a clean shot glass. He had taken a nip after lunch but that was all. She smiled at him cheesily and lifted the bottle.

'Shall I pour one for you?'

'Nah, not yet, lass,' Giffard said. 'What would you be doin' now if you was at home? Gettin' dolled up for a cocktail party?'

She was surprised that he had even heard of

cocktails, this inveterate consumer of neat whisky: again Tony's little warning bell sounded in her head. She plucked a floral apron from a hook on the larder door and tied it about her waist. Preparations for Christmas dinner were well in hand. And she had made a cheese and potato pie for supper that evening that required only an hour of slow cooking. An orange trifle was setting nicely on a high shelf in the back of the larder where Frobe couldn't get at it. There was nothing to do, nothing with which to occupy her hands. She felt more confident with the apron on, though.

'Are you sure that you do not wish to drink?' she said, brightly. 'I think that since it is the Christmas season you might be permitted a little extra.'

He shifted the cat gingerly and sat forward. He reached for his cigarette packet, tapped one out, lit it with a match, blew smoke away from the drowsy tabby.

He said, 'It'll be snowin' where you come from, I expect?'

'Yes.'

'In the mountains?'

'Yes, in the mountains.'

'The Alps?'

'It always snows at this time of the year,' Penny said, 'in the Alps.'

'Ah've never been t' the Alps.' For some reason Penny felt relieved at his confession. 'Ah've never been anywhere, hardly.' He looked a her, blew smoke, grinned. 'Always had a fancy for t' climb the Hummelstreek an' look down on the Vienna woods. I'm too old for those capers now, though.'

'How old are you?'

'Forty-eight.'

'Did you not fight in the war?'

'Bad eyes kept me out o' that nasty business.'

'You are not blind?'

'Nah, but it's amazin' what damage a few wee drops o' menthol can do before a medical inspection – provided y' know what you're doin'.' He stirred again and this time the tabby awoke, lolloped lazily down from his lap, curled up on the floor under the armchair and promptly went back to sleep. 'That's the secret in this life, lass, always to know what you're doin'.'

He glanced at her from under greying brows, let his gaze linger, studying her with what seemed like calculation – but not cockily like Edgar Harker, not the way young men in uniform had studied her, their eyes swimming with longing. She could not define the manner in which Giffard looked at her or what image of her he saw, the fantasy or the reality.

She tugged nervously at the hem of her apron then, clearing her throat, said, 'If you are not going to drink your whisky, will I make you tea instead?'

'Aye, lass,' Giffard said. 'Tea will do fine for me, thanks', and to her relief picked up his newspaper and busied himself with the crossword again.

\*　　\*　　\*

She lay back across the bed as he pulled away from her. She was wetter than she had ever been, all that part of her between her stockings and underskirt, wet and cold after lovemaking. She wasn't satisfied, though, and still felt twitchy and needed him back upon her, pressing down, warming her in the limp, exhausted lulls between orgasms, to be joined to him, rocking rhythmically to his will.

But Tony had gone. Turning her head, she saw him bulked against the uncurtained window and the faint light of the street lamps below. She lifted herself from the quilt, her head spinning. She spread her arms and hoisted herself into a sitting position. The full, dull ache in her loins closed about the only part of her that still seemed congnisant. She could not bring herself to move and remained braced on her elbows. Her knees and feet stretched out, vague and disembodied in the gloom.

'Polly,' Tony said thickly. 'We'd better get going.'

'Going?'

'Home,' he said, 'get you home.'

'Why?'

'Because it's late.'

'Late? How late?'

'After six,' he said.

He had put on his trousers and buttoned his shirt. He sat on the bed and stooped over to find his shoes. When he reached out to switch on the light, Polly said. 'Please don't.'

'Are you all right?'

'Yes.' She rested her cheek against his back. 'I don't want to go home.'

'You have to.'

'I know.'

He stroked her hair then lifted her, took her in his arms and kissed her. She leaned her head against his chest. 'I missed you, darling,' she said. 'God, you've no idea how much I missed you.'

She heard him laugh. 'I kinda got that impression,' he said. 'I missed you too – in case you hadn't noticed.'

He did not hurry her. After a moment, though, Polly released him, put both feet on the floor and tried to stand up.

'Do you remember where it is?' Tony said.

'What?'

'The bathroom.'

'Yes, I . . .'

'Let me put on the light.'

'No.'

He supported her as she groped on the carpet for her panties and suspender belt. Her handbag and shoes were where she had thrown them in her haste to be with him an hour – no, two hours ago. The children would be home by now. Dominic too perhaps. She tried to devise a credible lie to tell Dominic but couldn't bear to think of Dominic while Tony was with her.

Holding on to his hand, she stood upright. Clutching her clothes and handbag, she made her way to the bathroom and switched on the overhead light. She was blinded by its brightness, startled by the visage that blinked at her from the circular mirror above the wash-basin – a thin, pinched face, foxy and furtive, hair mussed, lips bruised, eyes dark and anxious.

She turned her back to the mirror and fumbled with the hooks and rubber knobs of the garter belt. She washed, applied make-up, repaired her hair and only when she felt stronger and more in control did she return to the bedroom.

Tony had switched on the light.

'Better now?' he asked.

'Hmm.'

He had remade the bed and closed the curtain. He was fully dressed, his scarf, overcoat and hat lying on the bedspread. On the bed too was a large brown-leather valise. He offered her his cigarette case. She took a cigarette, leaned into him while he lit it for her, dabbed the back of his hand with her fingertips, a stupid little gesture, far too flirtatious in the circumstances.

The living-room was still in darkness. She could see nothing in the light from the bedroom save a rectangle of burnt-pink carpet and a shell-shaped standard lamp. She wanted to sit on the bed but the silk spread was too smooth to disturb. The pillows had been neatly tucked away, all house-proud and shipshape. At any moment Tony would pick up the valise, take her arm, lead her through the darkened living-room, down the cement staircase, out into the courtyard and into the motorcar to return her to her children and her husband.

'Why haven't you called me?'

'I tried,' Tony said. 'Believe me, Polly, I tried.'

'Where have you been? I mean, where are going with your case all packed?'

'I'm having supper with my folks, then Mass at . . .'

'And tomorrow? Will I see you tomorrow?'

'No, Poll. I won't be around for a while.'

'I should have guessed that much, shouldn't I?'

'Please,' he said. 'Don't.'

'Am I not entitled to ask?'

'I can't tell you anything.'

'Can't you? What am I to think then? That I'm just a bit on the side, a sort of interlude to something or someone else?'

'That isn't true, and you know it.'

'Why won't you tell me? I won't blame you. Just tell me.'

'I'll be gone for a couple of months.'

'Where?'

'Not far away,' he said. 'But . . .'

She walked away from him, clipped over to the window and lifted a corner of the curtain. She looked down into the court, at puddles of pastel-coloured light on the macadam, the misty bloom around the lamps, at the motorcar waiting below. She gave him time to complete the sentence, to help her understand.

He said nothing.

Cigarette between her fingers, an elbow cupped with her hand, she swung round: 'Are the police after you? Are you hiding out?'

His surprise was genuine. 'Hell, no! What makes . . .'

'Where *are* you, Tony. I just want to know where you are.'

He stubbed out his cigarette in the steel ashtray on the bedside table and did not look at her.

'Breslin,' he said.

'What?'

'I'm camped over in Breslin.'

'With Bernard?'

'Bernard? No, not with Bernard.'

'It's the girl, isn't it? Tell me. I won't be angry. Is it that girl, that blonde? Are you having an affair, Tony? Are you living with her? It's got nothing to do with Dominic at all, has it?'

'Nope, that's not true.'

'What is true, then?'

'I tried to call you. Three times. I got that damned girl, Patricia. I didn't want to . . . Look, it *is* the girl, the blonde, but she's only part of it. I'm not . . . Oh, Christ! *She*'s the one who's hiding out, not me. I'm her damned nursemaid, Polly, not her lover.'

'Is it Dominic?'

'*No.*' He closed his eyes for a moment before he told her. 'It's not Dominic either,' he said. 'She's hiding out on a farm near Breslin. We're looking after her. If you want the truth, Polly, I can't stand her. It's worse than you can imagine being cooped up with her all day long, day after bloody day.'

'Is it really?'

'Yeah, it is,' Tony said. 'Living with her and thinking about you. All the time, thinking about you, wishing I was with you, wishing . . .'

'Are you trying to tell me that you're in love with me?'

'Yeah,' he told her. 'Yeah, I am.'

He made no attempt to take her in his arms and Polly, satisfied at last, did not press herself upon him. She wafted her hand to disperse the smoke that hung in the bedroom, then nodded. 'All right, Tony' she said. 'I'll take your word for it. Now perhaps we really ought to go.'

'Polly, I love you.'

'Hush,' she said, gently. 'Hush, darling.'

'I mean it, for God's sake.'

'Yes,' Polly said. 'I know you do.'

'My, but it fair stinks in here,' Lizzie said. 'Now, remind me how I do it.'

'Put out some money,' Rosie said. 'Four pennies.'

She watched her mother fumble with the scuffed purse, thumb the brass clips that even after twenty years of constant use were still stiff enough to break the edges of your fingernails. Mammy stuck her nose into it, fished in the squirrel-store of old tram tickets and out-dated receipts and found four coins. She glanced at her daughter helplessly.

'Put them on the ledge on top of the box,' Rosie instructed.

'Right.'

'Insert two pennies into the slot. That slot.'

'Right.'

'Hold the receiver . . .'

'The what?'

'This bit, hold it to your ear and when you have dialled – here, never mind, I will dial the number for you.'

'I wisht you would,' Lizzie said, gratefully.

She stood back, jamming herself into a corner of the telephone kiosk as if the act of turning the silver dial would result in an explosion. It wasn't the substance of the call that made her mother nervous Rosie realised but the mechanics. Lord knows, it had taken her long enough to persuade Mammy to make the call in the first place. She'd used all her wiles, all her charm, had even shed tears at one point until Mammy had crumbled, as Rosie had known she would.

She dialled the number, adjusted the earpiece against her mother's ear, instructed her where to put the pennies when she heard an answering voice. Rosie was nervous too, well aware that there might be repercussions. Love had made her careless, though, and she was dying to see her sisters' faces when she walked in with a tall, handsome man on her arm, a man of her own at last.

Her mother stiffened, nodded.

Rosie pressed the silver button.

'P-Polly, is that you?' Mammy said. 'Can you hear me? I can hear you fine.'

Cursing her weakness, Rosie watched her mother's lips move.

'What is she saying, Mammy?'

'*Ssshhh*.' Mammy spoke into the telephone again. 'It's Rosie. I've Rosie here with me. She wants to know if she can bring a friend to the Christmas party?' Rosie bit her lip, clenched her fists. Mammy went on. 'Aye, a boyfriend.'

Rosie watched her mother's plump cheeks quiver, the worried expression fade. She wondered what Polly had said, what particular remark had tickled her mother and relaxed her. She longed to snatch the speaking-piece from her mother's grasp and shout into it. Useless, of course. She wouldn't be able to decipher a word of Polly's answer, not a blessed word.

'Aye, it's a sweetheart. We think it's serious.' Mammy chuckled. 'One more won't make much difference to you, will it, Polly? He's on his own. Comes from the islands. We want to see what he's like, Bernard an' me.' She nodded, listened, nodded once more. 'Aye, I suppose we are just bein' nosy.'

'Tell her that Kenny is a policeman,' Rosie said.

Mammy held up a hand for silence. The ear-piece was pressed into her hair, her hat askew. She was pleased to have mastered the intricacies of the telephone system, relieved that the miracle of communication had worked for her.

Rosie plucked at her sleeve. 'Tell Polly that Kenny is . . .'

Mammy hunched and turned away and as she'd done so often in the past engaged in close conversation with Polly, her favourite.

Rosie opened her mouth to protest but found that she could not utter a sound. An answer had been given, apparently. They would be talking about the children now, about Stuart and Ishbel, about Babs too perhaps, what Babs was up to, not about the most important thing, the only thing that mattered, getting her together with Kenny on Christmas Day and showing him off to her sisters.

Rearing a little, Mammy shook the receiver. 'Polly's not there. She's gone. I was just goin' to . . .'

'What did she say?' Rosie shouted. 'Did Polly say that it would be all right for Kenny to come to the party?'

Mammy nodded. 'Aye, of course she did.'

Rosie closed her eyes and sank back against the glass, almost overcome with relief that her Christmas would be complete after all. When she opened her eyes again she found that Mammy had scooped up the unused pennies and snapped them away in her purse.

'Are you pleased?' Mammy mouthed.

'I am. Yes, thank you, I really am,' said Rosie.

And Mammy said, 'Now all we have t' do is tell Bernard.'

★　　★　　★

Dougie had never seen the like before, a great tray of piping hot mince pies dusted with fine sugar. The aroma from the baking tray filled the house and, mingled with the fragrance of coffee, seemed to represent the rich, exotic life that he might soon be entitled to share – if, that is, he could keep himself off the booze.

He was more sober than he had been in years. And not suffering. Why wasn't he suffering? No nightmares, no uncontrollable fits of shaking, no clouding of the mind and, astonishingly, no great upsurge of grief. To his chagrin he found that he thought of Emma hardly at all, or of his dead sons. They seemed like phantoms now, like characters out of a storybook he had read when he was very young. Had Dominic Manone known that this would happen? Was that why Dominic had continued to feed him a bit of cash now and then, or had he been just too valuable all those years back to be allowed to rot away?

When she poured brandy into large glass globes and handed him one, Dougie thought that he had died and gone to heaven.

'What time is it now?' the girl asked, in spite of the fact that the clock on the wall, which he'd wound for her that very morning, showed three minutes to midnight. 'Is it Christmas yet?'

'Nah, not yet,' Dougie told her.

The door was open and the cat had gone out. It didn't matter to the tabby what day it was, Dougie thought, though Frobe would have her share of turkey tomorrow, and her share of cream.

He carried the brandy glass out into the yard.

The midnight clear? Hardly. But the sky was calm, almost serene, and through the clouds that sauntered over the vault of heaven he detected the odd star. God, it's Sunday, he thought. Christmas falls on Sunday, and that's why the mills and shipyards are closed, the steam hammers stilled. There would be no bells, no sirens or hooters to signal midnight as there would be on Hogmanay. The Scots were a backward people who still favoured the pagan ceremonies of New Year, all drink and family sentiment, over a celebration of the Saviour's birth.

Dougie walked on, the glass in his hand untouched.

The girl would be pining for her people, for Christmas at home. It would be unnatural if she were not. He was grateful to her for putting up with him and to Dominic Manone for digging him out of his shell. He felt elated, almost exalted, by the strangeness of the experience, by being sober and sharp in his senses, by having a clean bed to sleep in and someone to cook his food, someone to remind him of the good things he had left behind, screened by a whisky haze.

He imagined that he was alone out there at the end of the yard, staring at the curve of the field and the sky but the girl was just behind him, staring up at the sky too, expecting – what? A sign, a signal that Christmas had come down upon them, even if it was just a siren or a blast from a factory hooter? No, no, dear, he felt like telling her, not in Scotland.

She expected something, though, and he turned as she closed on him.

Behind her he could see the cobbles scribbled with warm light, the farmhouse door wide open, Frobisher sitting on the step like a picture in a book.

'Is it Christmas?' the girl asked, soft-voiced as a child.

'Aye, lass,' Dougie told her. 'I reckon it must be by now.'

She stood by him, touching his shoulder, looking out at the fields.

She had a brandy globe in her hand and tears in her eyes. He could see them glistening in the light from the farmhouse door.

He nodded and raised his glass.

'*Zum Wohl, Fraulein,*' he said. '*Frohe Weihnachten!*'

And Penny, without pausing, answered him:

'*Zum Wohl, Mein Herr. Zum Wohl!*'

# Chapter Eight

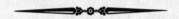

It was just after two o'clock when Jackie arrived in a spanking new Austin four-door to pick them up and convey them across the river to Manor Park. He was even more garrulous than usual for he had been as excited as a child at the English-style Christmas morning ritual that Babs had adopted soon after their marriage.

There were baubles, balloons and paper chains all over the bungalow – though Babs had drawn the line at having a tree – and Angus and his sisters had been awake since five a.m. and at five-thirty had been let loose on the presents that Santa Claus had piled up around the fireplace, a brand-new two-wheel bicycle for Angus and a huge doll's house filled with miniature furniture for May and June prominent among them. Baby April, of course, had not been forgotten but she seemed less interested in cuddly toys than in wrapping paper and cavorted among it like a little puppy until giggling made her sick.

By half-past seven Jackie had been out with the lad and the bicycle, steering his son along cold grey pavements, having almost as much fun as the boy. The rest of the morning, however, had been anticlimactic if all out war can be called an anticlimax. Angus had squabbled with the girls and the girls, very unusually, had squabbled with each other. April had reacted by howling and Babs had had to fight all the way to bathe and dress her little darlings, bathe and dress herself while Jackie, already sporting a hand–cut pale blue three-piece suit and pure silk necktie, had tried vainly to calm the kiddies down by reading from a big colour-plate storybook in which none of the little monsters had any interest at all.

At one-thirty he loaded them all into the Austin, whizzed round to Manor Park Avenue, dropped off his family and a great stack of presents at Dominic's house and headed back through Glasgow and across the bridge and out by the round route to Knightswood. He was still buzzing with the thrill of being Daddy Christmas, still searching optimistically for the missing ingredient – peace, perhaps, or goodwill – and had high hopes of finding it with Bernard's bunch.

But no. No. No. Bernard's bunch were sullen and sulky and Jackie would have had more chance of uncovering the spirit of Christmas in a Sally-Ann hostel than in the bosom of this branch of the family.

Bernard was done up in a black suit and overcoat and, of all things, a bowler hat. If it hadn't been for his red-striped tie he might have been going to a funeral instead of a Christmas party. Rosie was no better. She looked, Jackie thought, good enough to eat in a sort of tea-gown thing with a fur-trimmed cape over her shoulders and a natty little hat, not unlike Bernard's bowler, perched on top of her curls. But his big, smacking kiss of seasonal greeting was met with a shove and something akin to a snarl. Even Lizzie, his comfortable, consoling mother-in-law, wore a face like thunder as she sank down in the back seat and folded her arms over the parcels she had carried out from the house.

'Give me those.'

'No.'

'Suit yourself. Who's sitting in the back?'

'Me.'

'Where's Rosie sitting?'

'Here, with me.'

'You in?'

'Aye.'

Bernard dumped himself into the front seat, slammed the door. Jackie swung the Austin away from the terrace, executed a three-point turn and headed out on to Anniesland Road.

'Merry Christmas everybody, eh?' he shouted cheerily.

Nobody returned his greeting. Nobody uttered a word.

'What's wrong wi' you lot then?' he asked.

'Nothing,' Bernard told him snappishly. 'Just shut up and drive.'

Bernard was first out of the car, first to the door. He was not usually so lacking in courtesy but today he left Lizzie to extricate herself from the narrow seat unaided. He darted across the gravel, arrived at the front door just as Dominic opened it, clasped his boss by the elbow and drew him down the hallway.

'Is he here yet?' Bernard hissed. 'Has he arrived?'

'He's drinking punch in the living-room.'

Bernard pulled Dominic to him, not quite by the lapels. 'It had nothing to do with me. I knew nothing about it. God, if I had known what they were up to I'd have put my foot down. Who did they talk to? Polly? Was it Polly? They told me Polly said it was okay. Doesn't she know . . .'

'Bernard, Bernard, calm down.' Dominic said. 'It isn't your fault.'

'Didn't Polly know Rosie was bein' courted by a copper?'

'Today he isn't a copper. He is Rosie's young man.'

'Are you nuts?'

'No, Bernard, I'm pleased to welcome him to my house. That's all there is to it.' Dominic glanced down the hallway at Lizzie, Rosie and Jackie who were divesting themselves of their coats. 'Go and introduce yourself. He's eager to meet you, I gather. And,' Dominic smiled, 'of course he can't wait for Rosie to arrive.'

'I'm sorry. I really am,' Bernard said. 'He's goin' to ruin the party.'

'Oh no, he isn't,' Dominic said. 'In fact, it is going to be fun.'

Then he turned away to greet his mother-in-law and left Bernard to make his own way into the living-room.

The feeding of children, not just babies, was woman's work and at half-past six o'clock Lizzie and her daughters repaired upstairs, shepherding the youngsters before them. A table had been set up in the playroom and a great gooey spread laid out, complete with sausage rolls and dainty sandwiches, jellies and trifles and cream cakes. There was a bowl of fruit punch − non-alcoholic − just like the grown-ups' and a variety of milk shakes selected from a menu ornamented with pictures of robins, holly and cows.

For the girls, who were already studying to be ladies, there was clear fizzy lemonade poured from a genuine champagne bottle into champagne glasses, an imaginative touch that made the day for May and June. And for the lads, for afterwards, a box of chocolate cigars, perfect in every detail right down to the gold-paper bands. There were also presents, dolls and guns and games and books that had been handed out in the living-room in the afternoon, all of which treasures were lugged up to the playroom as if the children doubted the honesty of their fathers. Angus had even brought along his new bicycle, insisted on it being carried upstairs, and propped where he could see it while he stuffed his cheeks with pies and puddings and made disgusting noises with his milk-shake straw.

For an hour or more the children were the stars of the show, waited on hand and foot by Gran and Mum and Auntie Rosie and were allowed – within limits – to wreak havoc on the party table and in so doing discover that harmony and co-operation could be almost as much fun as bullying, badgering and squabbling among themselves.

Dressing-gowns, pyjamas and nightdresses were duly produced, however, and aroused howls of protest even from the girls. But Dominic had one more trick up his sleeve and as soon as the table was cleared appeared in the playroom with an interesting black box under his arm and a long roll of stiff white cloth.

Curiosity soon got the better of petulance, and protest died.

Even Angus allowed himself to be led meekly into the bathroom to have his face washed and teeth brushed. When he came scampering back into the playroom he found that the black box had opened out into a thing like a camera and the cloth had been pinned to the wall and his sisters and cousins, snug in dressing-gowns, were seated cross-legged before the screen while Dad and Patricia fiddled with knobs and switches.

Then, right there on the wall of the playroom, the cheerful face of Mickey Mouse appeared, projected on a shaft of brilliant white light; Mickey Mouse in a Santa hat under letters covered in snow:

A MERRY CHRISTMAS, GIRLS AND BOYS.

'A merry Christmas, Mickey,' rose the delighted response.

Leaving the rest to Patricia, Dominic slipped quietly away and went downstairs to dine.


Baby April, in the bath, was too sleepy to splash. She leaned back against her mother's arm, nodding like a fat pink doll, while Babs gently worked the sponge over her and crooned the tune of a carol the words of which she could not quite recall. Her dress was protected by an apron that Mrs O'Shea had found for her, a breast-high garment of coarse canvas not unlike the ones her mother had worn in her days as a drudge in the hospital laundry. Babs wasn't thinking of her mother at that moment, however, and wasn't surprised when the bathroom door opened and Polly slipped in, Polly with a glass in one hand and a cigarette in the other.

'Well, that went off pretty good,' Babs said. 'Whose idea was the slide show?'

'Dominic's.'

'Trust him!'

Polly seated herself on the toilet seat, sipped from the glass, blew a little plume of smoke upward towards the light fitting.

'So what do you make of him?' she asked.

'Big and cuddly, like a teddy bear.'

'Oh, for God's sake, Babs!'

'The kiddies seem to take to him.'

'Rosie dotes on him; that much is apparent.'

'Well, it's the first time she's had a man after her,' Babs said. 'I don't blame her for hangin' on to him. Bit of a shock findin' him in your living-room, though. I mean, Jackie turned pure white when he saw him. He's the copper who came . . .

'I know,' said Polly.

'How long's he been courtin' our Rosie.'

'Five or six weeks, I gather,' Polly said. 'Do you think he actually likes her?'

'Oh yeah, sure, you can see he thinks she's the cat's pyjamas.'

'I think it's an act,' said Polly.

'If it is, it's a damned good one.' Babs glanced round at her sister who sipped again from the glass. 'How much of that stuff've you had?'

'Not enough,' said Polly.

Babs folded a hand towel, put it on her lap and lifted April out of the water. Seated on the edge of the bath she wrapped her daughter in a large towel and began to dry her. The baby girned sleepily. Babs soothed her with another little tune.

'He's a lot older than she is?' Polly said at length.

'What? Eight or nine years?' Babs said. 'That's nothin'. Look at Mammy and Bernard. That worked out okay, didn't it?' She paused in her baby-work, drew her daughter's head to her breast and scowled at her sister. 'It's just because he's a copper. If this was some ordinary guy off the street you'd be happy for Rosie, wouldn't you?'

'Oh yes, certainly,' Polly said. 'Dom would find him a job in the warehouse, lay a few extra quid on him and he'd become one of the family in no time.'

'But that can't happen because Kenny MacGregor's a cop.'

Polly finished her drink and put the glass into the wash-basin. 'That might be less of a problem than you imagine. Kenny MacGregor wouldn't be the first copper to wind up on the Manones' payroll.'

'You're kiddin',' said Babs.

'I'm not,' said Polly. 'How do you suppose Dominic got away with running an illegal book out of the Rowing Club all these years?'

'Jackie never mentioned that.'

'Jackie may not know,' said Polly. 'Anyhow, it's immaterial. The point is that Sergeant MacGregor is sitting in our living-room talking to our husbands at this very moment and may have no more interest in Rosie than fly in the air.'

'In – in – what's the word I'm lookin' for?' Babs said.

'Infiltration,' Polly told her.

'Yeah,' Babs said. 'He's infiltratin' our family. It'll be spies again.'

'Spies?'

'Because Dom's an Italian.'

'Because Dom's a crook.' Polly shrugged. 'What's more, he's up to something dangerous and the police have somehow got wind of it.'

'Dangerous?' said Babs. 'Like what?'

'I have no idea,' and Polly, 'but I do intend to find out.'

'How?' Babs gave a dry laugh. 'By asking Rosie's boyfriend?'

Polly got to her feet, dropped the cigarette into the toilet bowl and flushed it away. 'Now that,' she said, smiling, 'is not a bad idea.'


Cooked to perfection, the bird had seemed far too large even for a table of eight, so large in fact that Mrs O'Shea could not carry it and Bernard and Jackie between them had lugged it up from the kitchen on a silver platter.

An hour later nothing remained of the turkey but skin and bone and a few greasy flecks of dark meat that nobody, not even Jackie, seemed to want – and a breathing pause ensued while Leah changed the plates and cutlery and brushed the cloth free of crumbs.

Dominic replenished the glasses while Babs and Lizzie seized the opportunity to steal upstairs and check on the children who, flushed and innocent, were all fast asleep. Patricia was dozing in the nursery chair. Neither Babs nor Lizzie had the heart to disturb her and seated themselves in the small side room one on each side of April's makeshift cot and set about discussing the character of the policeman and his suitability as a husband for Rosie.

In the dining-room, Dominic lit a cigarette and settled back in the chair at the head of the table. He seemed pleased with himself, as well he might be, and radiated a benign sort of bonhomie.

'So,' he began, 'you're a policeman, are you, Kenneth?'

It had only been a matter of time before her husband set about bating the young man, Polly reckoned, but the Highland copper had put himself into this position and deserved all that was coming to him. She puffed on her cigarette and sat forward, eager to see how well Rosie's sweetheart would defend himself and if his air of naïvety was after all a pose.

'I am, sir.'

'Oh, come now, you don't have to call me "sir". You know my name well enough I'm sure. No need to stand on ceremony with us. Is there Bernard?'

'No, no, of course not.'

'Well then,' Kenny said. 'Well, Dominic, yes I am a policeman.'

'Kenny's a sergeant,' Rosie put in.

She had been clinging to him all evening, touching him whenever she had the chance and he, Polly noticed, was curiously protective of Rosie as if she and not he were the intruder.

'A detective sergeant, I believe,' said Dominic.

'That's right,' said Kenny.

He inched his chair towards Rosie, close enough for her to lean on him. Polly suspected that they were holding hands under the table. She was relieved that Dominic had waited until Mammy was out of the room before he began probing, for Mammy obviously approved of Kenny MacGregor. They'd had a long chat that afternoon, chuckling together as if the situation in which they found themselves was not to be taken seriously. Her mother was adept at ferreting for information, however, and Polly was sure that she already knew more about Sergeant MacGregor than any of them.

Dominic pushed on: 'St Andrew's Street?'

'Yes.'

'I used to be acquainted with a sergeant there, several in fact.'

'I work under Inspector Winstock.'

'Ah!' Dominic said. 'Old Wetsock. Well, well! What a small world.'

No one, not even Rosie, had any inclination to join in the conversation and they sat, faintly embarrassed, with ears twitching.

'Not that small, Mr Manone – Dominic,' Kenny said.

'Oh, really! Are you telling me that it wasn't chance that brought you and Rosie together?'

'Of course it wasn't,' Kenny said.

Bernard looked up sharply.

Jackie coughed behind his hand, stuck a cigarette between his teeth and lit it.

'What was it then?' said Dominic.

'I met Rosie at Shelby's in the process of conducting an inquiry.'

'Into what – stolen books?' said Dominic.

'Well, no,' said Kenny. 'I was making inquiries about you, Mr Manone.'

'Me?'

'I think you're aware of that,' said the sergeant. 'I didn't know what Rosie was like then, of course, or . . .'

'Or you wouldn't have become involved with her?' Polly heard herself say.

'I was ordered to become involved with her,' Kenny said. 'I was supposed to become involved with her so that she'd come back and tell you, Dominic. But I'm glad now that she didn't.'

'Why are you glad that she didn't?' Dominic asked.

His soft dark eyes had become brittle, his alertness tinged with caution; the sergeant's candour had thoroughly disconcerted him. Polly chalked up a point to Kenny, who was – or appeared to be – telling the truth. She watched as he turned to Rosie and quite openly and without a trace of shyness took her hand in his. She found it hard to believe that he was a policeman. Most coppers she'd encountered were rough, gruff and as inscrutable as Chinese mandarins and would drop dead before they'd hold a girl's hand in public.

'Rosie knows why,' Kenny said. 'That's all that matters to me.'

'It isn't all that matters to us, son,' Bernard said.

'Let it go, Bernard,' Jackie said. 'For God's sake, let it go.'

'How can we?' Bernard said. 'I mean, son, you're a professional snoop and we're – well, hell, you know what we are.'

'You're Rosie's stepfather,' Kenny said.

'No, that won't wash,' said Bernard. 'You'll be telling us next that your intentions are nothing but honourable.'

'I'm sure they are,' Dominic put in.

'As far as Rosie's concerned, maybe, but . . .' Bernard said.

'Kenny has a job to do,' Dominic said. 'We mustn't hold that against him.'

Polly laughed. She couldn't help herself. The tactic was too clumsy to fool anyone. There were tears in Rosie's eyes but whether they were tears of joy or sorrow she could not tell. She wasn't laughing at Rosie but at Dominic who thought he was being so smart and urbane when all the time he was simply making a difficult situation worse.

'Yah, right!' said Jackie. 'Unless his job's puttin' us all behind bars.'

'Inspector Winstock isn't interested in you,' Kenny

said. 'Frankly, Inspector Winstock could have you and your brothers hauled up in court any time he fancies.'

'Gerroff!' said Jackie. 'We run a straight business. You got nothin' on us.'

'No?' Kenny let the question hang for an instant. 'What's going to happen to you, Mr Hallop, when your yard in Govan is requisitioned?'

'Rek-wee – what?'

'Is that liable to happen?' Dominic asked.

'I've heard rumours,' Kenny said.

'What other rumours have you heard?' said Dominic.

'None that would interest you, sir.'

'I wouldn't be too sure of that,' said Dominic. 'Have you heard rumours concerning my warehouse? Is it also a target for a government takeover?'

'You'd have to ask my superiors that question,' Kenny said.

'Winstock, do you mean,' said Dominic, 'or Percy Sillitoe?'

'My superiors in London,' said Kenny.

'London!' Jackie shouted. 'What the bloody hell've we done for t' get London's back up?'

'Jackie, please, there's no need to raise your voice,' Dominic said. On the surface he was still benign, still in control. 'It's Christmas and this is a family party and if we're fortunate then Sergeant MacGregor will become one of the family in due course. Isn't that what you're hoping for, Kenny?'

'If you mean marriage . . .' Kenny began.

Then Rosie tugged at his sleeve, brought him round to face her so that she could read his lips. She had been clinging to more than his hand, Polly realised, for the conversation had been swirling about her deaf sister like smoke. Surely it wasn't on the cards that after a six-week courtship the sergeant was about to blurt out a marriage proposal. Whatever else he might be, and however smitten by Rosie, he didn't strike Polly as the impulsive type. Would he go so far as to marry Rosie just to infiltrate and undermine Dominic's little empire? It seemed like a mad idea, far too extreme, but there were madder and more extreme things happening these days.

'He can't marry our Rosie, for Christ's sake,' said Jackie.

'Why not?' said Bernard.

Polly observed her sister's confusion with sudden sympathy; saw the darting motion of her head as she tried to fathom what was being said. Rosie looked to Kenny, not Bernard, for reassurance, and missed Jackie's shout: ''Cause he's a bloody snoop, that's why.'

Polly slapped the tablecloth to catch Rosie's attention.

'Rosie,' she mouthed, 'please go downstairs and ask Leah to bring up the Christmas pudding. Kenny, will you go up to the playroom and tell my sister and my mother to stop gossiping and come down and join the party.'

'*I'll* bloody do it,' Jackie snapped, scraping back his chair.

Bernard thumped a forearm across the young man's chest. 'No, you won't.'

'You want rid of me, is that it?' Rosie said.

'Both of you,' Polly said, nodding. 'For just one little minute.'

Rosie nodded too, a faint smile on her lips. They were sisters, would always be sisters. She trusted Polly implicitly. She got up from the table, held out her hand.

'Come along, Kenny,' she said.

He hesitated, seemed reluctant to leave the men at the table, to break off the discussion just as it was turning quarrel-some – and interesting. At that moment Polly realised that in spite of his apparent frankness Sergeant MacGregor was just as big a rogue as her husband, just as devious and cunning, and that in him she had found an accomplice.

'Please,' she said sweetly. 'For me.'

And Kenny answered, 'Of course.'


Fiona said, 'And then what happened?'

'Nothing much.'

'You kissed her under the mistletoe, I imagine?'

'What if I did?'

'And clean forgot what you were supposed to be doing there?'

'Nope.' Kenny uncapped the sauce bottle and

poured a squiggle of brown sauce on to his ham and eggs. 'Duty was always uppermost in my mind.'

Noon now, Monday, Boxing Day: he was on duty at two o'clock and would be expected to deliver his report to Inspector Winstock first thing tomorrow morning. Fiona had also been called in that afternoon on the two to ten shift. With luck he might be able to persuade his sister to type to his dictation so that his report would look formal and substantial even if its content was thin.

'Do you want another slice of ham?' Fiona asked.

'No thanks.'

'After all you ate last night I'm surprised you can face breakfast at all.'

He grinned. 'I'm a growing boy, don't you know?'

'Did she tell you that?' Fiona said.

'No, her mother did.'

'Oh, yes, you're well in there, I see.'

'I could be even better in if I was that way inclined.'

'I hope that doesn't mean what I think it does,' Fiona said.

'It means I could marry Rosie, give up the Force, take a well-paid job with Manone – and live happily ever after.'

'Kenny, you wouldn't!'

'No, I wouldn't,' he said. 'Might marry Rosie, though.'

'In which case you'd have to resign.'

'If I'm still there, yes,' Kenny said.

'Where else would you be?'

'In the army,' Kenny said, 'like everyone else.'

Fiona was dressed for the office; navy blue pleated skirt, white blouse, starched collar fastened with a cameo brooch that had once belonged to her grandmother. What would their old granny say if she knew that her treasure was gracing the throat of a civilian assistant to a police inspector, Kenny wondered? He covered a fried egg with a slice of ham, lifted it carefully on his fork and put the lot into his mouth while Fiona seated herself at the narrow kitchen table and poured herself tea.

'Is that your plan, Kenneth?' she said, soberly.

'Hmm?'

'To leave the Force, join the army, and marry this deaf girl?'

'It's a thought,' Kenny said.

'Be serious, please.'

'I am being serious. I think I'm in love with her.'

'How depressing,' Fiona said. 'How really and truly depressing.'

He ate again, cleaning the breakfast plate, then he said, 'I thought you wanted to hear what happened last night?'

'I do.'

'She told us off – Polly, Manone's wife. Gave us a good earful and warned us not to start arguing again in front of her mother.'

'Lizzie Peabody?'

'Aye, they're very protective of the big woman.'

'*Mater familias,*' Fiona said.

'Come again?'

'Head of the household, elder of the tribe.'

'She's not head of the household. Manone's head of the household,' Kenny said. 'But they certainly do look after her.'

'Why shouldn't they?' said Fiona. 'She raised them, didn't she?'

'Fiona, they're crooks. They're all crooks, all except Rosie. The mother was married to a crook at one time and she let her daughters . . .'

'Yes, yes,' Fiona said. 'Never mind the anthropology. Get on with it.'

'Not much else to tell,' Kenny said. 'Except that all is not quite what it seems in the Manone family.'

'Elucidate, please.'

'The wife, Polly, she nabbed me in the hallway just as we were leaving. About one o'clock in the morning it was. She'd been drinking quite a lot. Manone was mad at her for drinking so much. He kept it quiet but you could see how angry he was. She's not a happy lady, our Mrs Manone.'

'What, did she make a pass at you?'

'God, no! She wasn't *that* tiddly,' Kenny said. 'Just as I was putting on my overcoat to go out and look for a taxi, she slipped me this.'

He fished in the pocket of his shirt and brought out a visiting-card, passed it to his sister who studied the printed name and address as intently as if it were code.

'Other side,' said Kenny.

Fiona turned the card over and read out the message scribbled in pencil on the back: *'My house is your house. Call me.'* Puzzled she looked up at her brother. 'My house is your house: what the devil does she mean by that?'

'Search me,' said Kenny, 'but the other bit's plain enough.'

Fiona said. 'I take it that you will call her?'

'You bet,' said Kenny.

'When?'

'Soon, but not immediately.'

'Inspector Winstock will expect you to establish contact at once.'

'Ah, but old Wetsock won't know about it, not just yet.'

'Kenny!' said Fiona, warningly.

'I think we may have found what we're looking for,' Kenny said, 'but I want to be dead sure before I take it to Winstock.'

'Found what?' Fiona asked.

'The family's weakest link,' said Kenny.

'The wife, you mean?'

'Oh, no,' Kenny said. 'I mean the mother.'

# Chapter Nine

Polly did not know why she became breathless when she heard the sergeant's voice. She had no designs on him, none at all. Even if he hadn't been Rosie's boyfriend she wouldn't have fancied him: Kenny MacGregor was emphatically not her type.

Leah held out the telephone.

'It's a man for you. He's asking for you.'

Polly took the receiver and spoke into the mouthpiece.

'Polly Manone.'

'Sergeant MacGregor. Kenny.'

'Ah, yes. Good of you to call.'

Leaning on the handle of the Hoover Leah eavesdropped with unabashed interest. Her hair, like Polly's, was tucked into a dust-cap. Like Polly she wore a floral housecoat and an apron. The air in the hallway was defined by a fine haze of dust and the smell of Mansion polish mingled with the faint burnt-toast odour that the Hoover gave off when it was used for long periods. From the stairs that led to the kitchen came the sound of Mrs O'Shea banging pots and pans and singing away to herself, not some quaint Irish ditty but a chorus of 'If I Had a Talking Picture of You'. Patricia had taken the children to school. She had been given a list of groceries to hand in to Lipton's on her way home. She would dawdle in the shop, Polly reckoned, for a young man there had his eye on her and Patricia was well aware of it. There were worse things to be up to on a blustery Monday morning in January Polly reckoned, than flirting with a grocer's assistant.

'One moment, please,' Polly said, mimicking an operator.

She held the phone away from her ear and frowned at Leah who, after ten or fifteen seconds, took the hint and with a sigh, unplugged the vacuum cleaner and wheeled it away, cord trailing, into the living-room.

'Yes,' Polly said into the telephone. 'I'm here.'

'I'm not disturbing you, I hope.'

'Housework, that's all.'

'I won't keep you then,' said Kenny. 'I was hoping we could meet somewhere, at your convenience.'

Polly was reminded of a rude music hall joke but it hadn't struck her as funny first time she'd heard it and she did not wish to embarrass Sergeant MacGregor by repeating it now. He sounded distinctly Highland on the phone. She wondered where he was: CID headquarters in St Andrew's Street most likely, with his boss breathing down his neck.

Unconsciously Polly rounded out her vowels and shaped her consonants properly as if she were speaking to Rosie.

'Why would I want to meet with you, Sergeant?'

'You – you gave me your card.'

'I was only being polite.'

'Oh!' a pause. 'Sorry.'

Polly glanced up and down the hallway.

The living-room door was closed and even if Leah did have her ear pressed to the woodwork she wouldn't be able to hear anything. Down in the kitchen, Mrs O'Shea was still trilling away.

Polly's heart beat a shade faster under the housecoat as the prospect of a long drab day of house-cleaning and grocery shopping slid away.

She said, 'Where are you? Right now, I mean.'

'In – in Glasgow.'

'Are you taking Rosie to lunch?'

'If I can find time.'

'You don't have a date with her then?'

'Open, it's open,' said Kenny. 'She understands.'

'What? About us?'

'No, she – no, there's nothing to understand about us. Is there?'

'I'm teasing,' Polly said.

'I see,' said the sergeant.

'As a matter of fact I would rather like to have a word with you,' Polly said.

'May I ask what about?'

'Not Rosie,' Polly said. 'Something else.'

'I see,' Kenny MacGregor said again.

'Perhaps you'd care to take me to lunch instead of my sister.'

A hesitation, a careful pause: 'Yes, that would be very nice.'

'Today. Twelve-thirty.'

'Fine. Where?'

'The Ramshorn in Ingram Street. Do you know it?'

'I know where it is,' Kenny said. 'Is it maybe not a bit . . .'

'Public?' said Polly. 'What harm if we're seen together? You're courting my sister so naturally I'm interested in getting to know you better. If you're worried about my husband, he's gone off down the coast.'

'Twelve-thirty it is then, Mrs Manone.'

'At The Ramshorn,' said Polly.


If she had known that Dominic would bring the next consignment of machinery in person she would have spent more time on her appearance. Since Christmas she had become careless and had allowed herself to slip into a routine that left little or no time to fuss with her hair, paint her nails or apply make-up. Indeed, she barely managed to keep herself clean, for little Dougie Giffard had discovered the pleasures of the tub and would soak for hours in the bath in the bathroom adjacent to the laundry-room. He did not, thank God, sing, but his silences seemed more sinister than song and Tony was concerned that Dougie had found a means of buying drink and was tapping into a secret stash of whisky and would sink into a state of paralytic collapse before the printing equipment was fully installed.

Penny considered the accusation unfair. There were no signs that Dougie was back-sliding. He still enjoyed his daily ration of spirits but she'd noticed that the half bottle was no longer empty at the witching of noon when Tony or she unlocked the cupboard and brought out a replacement.

Tony remained agitated, however, and would beat upon the bathroom door and shout, 'What the hell are you doing in there, old man?' And Dougie's gruff reply would drift out damply, 'The crossword, man, the bloody crossword.'

Tony was agitated about everything these days, of course. He was also drinking more than Dougie now, not just the flavoured coffee that the girl brewed in her fancy Italian percolator. He would punctuate long hours of nurse-maiding, when he had nothing to do but watch the girl at work, with grumpy little trips to the whisky cupboard.

It wasn't much of a life stuck out on a farm

for a man who was used to a different sort of idleness, Dougie supposed. Personally he loved it here, and Frobe was in his element. Even the girl seemed content, especially after the equipment began to arrive and he took her under his wing and showed her how to do things with it while he adapted the rotary type multigraph that Dominic had found for him and which he intended to link to a flat-bed press.

He had no idea where Dominic had raked up the machinery but he had seldom worked with such fine equipment. Big lenses, shaded spotlights, even a reflector camera with which to enlarge the plates for detailed scrutiny. He crammed the camera on to a table in his bedroom and had Tony rig up lights from a power box on the ground floor, for the attic was warmer than the stable and he needed to be comfortable to concentrate while he worked on perfecting the signature of the Bank of England's current Cashier, Kenneth Oswald Peppiat.

Kenneth Oswald Peppiat was driving him crazy, though. The *K* bore more than a passing resemblance to an *H* and the nib the chap had used for the original copy-plate had reduced the final *T*-cross to a fat left-to-right slash. In addition Mr Peppiat had popped in two full stops slightly, just slightly, out of alignment. Practice and enlargement, copying and checking would do the trick, however, and before long he would be ready to engrave a separate block for the signature.

Dominic had picked up a tray of type which would exactly duplicate the serial numbers and all Dougie required now was a routing machine and he'd be ready to undertake the delicate process of cutting into and building up the block.

'When?' the girl would ask. 'When, Dougie, when?'

'When I can, lass,' he would tell her. 'It's somethin' I can't rush.'

'Are not the plates good enough?'

'Aye, the plates are grand,' Dougie would say, 'but I've only got one pair o' hands, in case ye hadn't noticed.'

Penny was more patient than Dougie gave her credit for.

She ran the household with ease and efficiency, cooking and cleaning and attending to the laundry-bags in a manner that would have made her mother proud. Blackstone had already begun to feel like home. Only the oddity of the sleeping arrangements, and Tony Lombard's hostility, prevented her being happier than she'd been in many months. She pressed Dougie for answers not because she wanted this phase to end but because she knew that war was imminent and she must get out of the country before it did or risk being stuck here until the Panzer army came growling over the hill and Scotland became just another outpost of the Reich.

The Wolseley drew up in the yard, and Dominic got out.

For once he was less than immaculate. He wore a bulky woollen sweater, a pair of corduroys and a knitted cap that made him look like a stevedore.

There was no one else in the motorcar but a wooden crate was propped in the rear seat and, in the luggage trunk, three large flat parcels.

'Where is Giffard?' Dominic asked.

'Upstairs.'

'Is he sober?'

'He is never not sober,' Penny answered. 'He is working, I think.'

She ran her hands down her flanks, smoothing her rumpled skirt.

The day was blustery, the wind veering from the north, chilly rather than cold. She watched the breeze flirt with Dominic's dark hair. He was clearly in no mood to be teased today, however, and she put on her serious face.

'Tony?'

'I think he is in the toilet. I will fetch him if you wish.'

'No.' Dominic placed himself in front of her, so close that she could see perspiration on his upper lip, a strange dry sort of sweat. 'You lied to me, Penny. I want to know why you lied to me.'

'I did not lie to you,' she said. 'I do not tell lies.'

'Ballocks!' he said.

She was not offended by the dirty word, only by the manner of its utterance. She had never seen him like this before, his veneer of cool courtesy rubbed away, anger and aggression showing through. He seemed now like what he was, perhaps, not a well-educated Scottish businessman but the son of a violent Italian peasant. She was shocked and thrilled at one and the same time and wondered fleetingly if he had a gun on his person or a revolver hidden in the car and if it came to it – if he ever discovered just how many lies she had told him – he would have the nerve to use it. She arched her back, spread her hands, spoke loudly:

'What lies have I told you? What is it that I have said?'

'You told me the paper was coming in from Verona.'

'And is it not?'

'You told me my uncle Guido was handling that end of it.'

'So?' she said.

'My uncle Guide is dead.' He dug into the hip pocket of the corduroy trousers and brought out a cablegram, the yellow-tinted form crushed and crumpled. He snapped it between his fingers and waved it at her. 'He's been dead for over a week. And he wasn't in Verona. He was nowhere near Verona. He died in a hospital in Genoa.'

'Perhaps he was taken suddenly,' Penny said.

'He'd been in the hospital for months, for all I know,' Dominic said. 'Guido was never part of this deal, was he?'

'I did not tell you that he was. Edgar said that . . .'

'Sod Edgar!' Dominic said. 'I'm not interested in Harker. I want *you* to tell me what's going on and where the first delivery of paper really came from.'

'I do not know.'

'It arrived by carrier from Hull. Hired carrier from the docks at Hull. Dumped on my damned doorstep like the morning milk,' Dominic said. 'How many other guys are working on this deal and, more to the point, who's paying them?'

'I do not know. Honestly. I will cross my heart if I am telling . . .'

'Who sent you to me?'

'Your father.'

'Liar!'

'Where did the cable come from?' Penny asked.

'What?'

'Who was it who sent you news of your uncle?'

The question stopped him in his tracks.

She knew perfectly well that the old man in Italy had not been involved. She could not imagine why Eddie Harker had told her to support that particular lie. God knows, there were lies enough in the air, lies and deceptions stretching endlessly to the horizon, without adding one more. She could see no reason for it, not now, not in hindsight. But then much of what was done seemed to be based on reasoning so twisted that it was not just stupid but perverse.

'Who?' she insisted. 'Was it your aunt?'

'Teresa? No, she – I don't know where she is, or what will become of her.'

'Carlo will take care of her,' Penny said. 'Perhaps he will bring her to America, out of Italy.'

'If he can,' Dominic said.

'Tell me,' she spoke quietly, not backing away. 'Who sent you the cable?'

'Pappy,' Dominic said. 'My father.'

'Then it was he who lied to you, lied to Edgar – and to me.'

'Don't try to put the blame—'

She placed a forefinger on his chest and brought her mouth close to his, close enough to kiss. 'There is no blame,' she said. 'Do we not have the paper?'

'Yes.'

'Is it the right paper? Is it good paper for our purposes?'

'I don't know. Giffard will have to take a look at it.'

'If it is good paper, the right paper,' Penny said, 'does it matter that it does not come from your uncle in Verona?'

'I suppose not,' Dominic said. 'I just don't like being lied to.'

She spread her hand, laid it very lightly against his chest. 'I am sorry that your uncle is dead. Truly.'

'Thank you.'

'He was like a father to you, no?'

'He looked after me, he and Aunt Teresa,' Dominic said.

'Cared for you?'

'Probably.'

'I am sorry you have lost someone who was dear to you. I am sincere.'

'Yes,' Dominic said, softening. 'I know you are.'

She was tempted to kiss him, to taste the perspiration that anger had brought out on his lips. She resisted, though, did not play on her advantage.

Dominic said, 'I still want to know where the damned paper came from.'

'There are docks in Hull, no?'

'Of course there are docks in Hull. But where did the package come from, where did it originate?' Dominic said. 'There were no packing notes, no customs stamps, nothing to give me a clue. Obviously this is only the first batch and there will be more on the way if we approve this stuff. So where's it coming from, that's what I want to know, Penny?'

'Perhaps Eddie sent it.'

'And where did Eddie get it from?'

Penny shook her head.

Dominic said, 'Italy? Maybe even Germany?'

'Why do you worry so much where it comes from?'

'Because I don't want to be caught trading with Germany,' Dominic said. 'God knows, I'm having trouble enough keeping my warehouse stocked with goods from Italy right now, legitimate goods. My manufacturers are being squeezed by government regulations and import restrictions.'

'It is not against the law to import from Italy,' Penny said.

'No, not officially,' Dominic said. 'But I already have the coppers breathing down my neck.'

'What is it you say?'

'Nothing, nothing,' Dominic said. 'I'd just like to be sure that your friend Harker has the route covered.'

'Perhaps,' Penny said, 'it's all here already, stored in a warehouse in Hull.'

'Is that what Harker told you?'

'I haven't seen Eddie in weeks. I do not even know where he is.'

'Well, this damned paper didn't come from Woolworth's,' Dominic said. 'It was manufactured especially for us and I'd like to find out where.'

'Maybe it is not the right paper,' Penny suggested.

'Well,' Dominic said, just as Tony emerged from the farmhouse, 'there's only one sure way to find out. We'll lug the packages into the stables and have Giffard examine the contents sheet by sheet. Go get the little beggar, please, Penny. We'll need his help to lift that box out of the back seat.'

'Which is,' said Tony, 'what exactly?'

'Giffard's routing machine.'

'Yeah, he will be pleased,' said Tony.

Dominic opened the passenger door and reached

into the car. He backed out again, three square cardboard boxes suspended from each hand by thick cord slings. 'And these,' he said. 'I brought these for you.'

'What are they?' Tony said.

'Gas-masks.'

'Gas-masks!' Penny exclaimed.

'You're supposed to report to a local centre to be fitted but I brought six so you can find one that more or less fits you. Giffard too.'

'How did you get six of them?' said Penny.

'He bought them from people who don't believe there's going to be a war,' Tony said. 'Right, Dominic?'

'Quite right,' Dominic answered and leaving Penny by the car took Tony by the arm and led him off a little way to break the bad news about Guido.

The Ramshorn had quite a history to it, a history that seemed to adhere to the wood-panelled walls and to hang in the air like ectoplasm. To Polly though history smelled of grilled chops, strong ale and tobacco smoke, for the restaurant in Ingram Street had been, and still was, a haunt of city traders.

It was crowded, loud and bustling. Kenny and she were lucky to find a table away from the door, tucked under the beams at the rear of the long, low ground-floor room. She doubted if any of Dominic's cronies would be here but if they were, if they recognised her and snitched to her husband then she would tell him the truth, or the most obvious and undeniable part of it, that she had asked Kenny MacGregor to lunch simply to discover more about him. It was, after all, the least a sister could do.

The sergeant was more at ease than she had expected him to be. In the first quarter hour of casual conversation she even detected a faint trace of condescension towards her, not patronage so much as dislike, as if he had already sized her up and, in comparison to her little sister, had found her wanting.

Imagination! Polly told herself: he's merely being guarded because he doesn't know what I want from him and what he might receive in return.

She hadn't forgotten how Kenny had knocked her husband off balance at Christmas, and Dominic was a more astute and experienced negotiator than she would ever be. She found herself putting on an air of almost girlish eagerness, as if to convince the sergeant that Rosie and she were not so very different after all.

'Rosie tells me your father was killed in the war.'

'He walked out on us in nineteen-seventeen and vanished into thin air,' Polly said.

'And you assume he died in the trenches?'

'That's what we've always been led to believe.'

'By whom?' said Kenny.

'The family, my mother and her sister.'

'Her sister?'

'My aunt Janet.'

'And where is she?'

'Does it matter?' Polly said. 'She can't help you.'

'Help me do what?' said Kenny.

'Build a case against my husband.'

'Is that what you think I'm doing?' said Kenny.

'You said as much yourself.'

'Your father worked for Carlo Manone, didn't he?'

'He was a runner. He ran a book, and did other things too.'

'The bad old days,' said Kenny, smiling.

'In some ways not so bad as they are now,' said Polly.

'Do you remember him?'

'No, not at all.'

She was disconcerted by his line of questioning. Much of what she had learned about her family history, her father's disappearance in particular, had come from biased sources. Until she'd met and married Bernard Peabody, Mammy had clung to the notion that one day Frank Conway might turn up on her doorstep again: Aunt Janet too had kept a torch alight and, as far as Polly knew, still did.

'Have you seen the sandbags?' Kenny asked.

'Sandbags? Where?'

'In George Square,' Kenny said.

'No,' said Polly. 'Really? Why are we sand-bagging the Square. I thought we'd appeased Herr Hitler and the threat of invasion had gone away.'

'Gas-masks, air-raid precautions, Civil Defence exercises,' Kenny said. 'It's a mad panic in the regional stations, I can tell you. The man in the street might choose to believe Hitler's gone soft but those in the know – well, they know better. What does your husband think will happen?'

'Do you mean whose side is he on?' Polly said. 'I can't give you an answer, I'm afraid. In spite of the fact that I'm his wife I've no idea where Dominic's sympathies lie. I imagine he regards himself as much more Scottish than Italian, however, and will do what he can for the country.'

Kenny nodded. 'That's good. We'll need all the patriots we can get when the balloon goes up.' He paused, reached into his jacket pocket. 'Speaking of patriots, have you ever seen either of these two before?'

She took the photographs, tilted them to the light. Even in the gloom of the restaurant she recognised them at once: the blonde girl, younger, fresher, more innocent, but the blonde girl none the less: the other – the squat, bull-like little man with the huge moustache.

She handed back the photographs.

'Who are they?' Polly said. 'Are they suspected of a crime?'

'We're anxious to trace their whereabouts, that's all.'

'I can't help you, sorry,' Polly said.

She wondered what he would do now: bully her,

threaten her, or cajole? Would he be too frightened of putting himself out of favour with Rosie, perhaps, to do anything at all?

He broke bread into his soup and ate.

The photographs lay on the tablecloth by his left hand.

At length Polly said, 'The girl, is she connected with my husband in some way? I mean, Kenneth, are you easing your-self into blackmailing me?'

He glanced up in alarm. 'Certainly not.'

'Where are they, these people?'

'I wish we knew.'

'Have you been – what's the word – have you been tailing my husband?'

'This isn't America, Mrs Manone. We're not G-men.'

'Or Tony: tailing Tony?'

'Tony Lombard? No.'

'Could you really put Jackie Hallop in prison if you wished to?'

'I think we probably could.'

'What department *do* you work for, Kenneth?'

'Criminal Investigation.'

'Isn't my brother-in-law, isn't Jackie a criminal?'

'We're not concerned with the Hallops right now.'

'Ah!' Polly said quietly. 'So you're after bigger fish.'

'That's it in a nutshell, Mrs Manone.'

'I do wish you'd call me Polly,' Polly said. 'If

we're going to do business together at least we should try to pretend that we're on friendly terms.'

'Are we going to do business together?' Kenny said.

'Exchange information,' Polly said.

'Information about what exactly?'

'About the blonde girl in the photograph.'

'You do know her then?'

'Not her name, not who she is. I've seen her, though. Once.'

'Where?'

'At the races at Ravenspark last November.'

'Did you speak with her?' Kenny asked.

Polly gave a scornful little 'huh' at his naïvety. 'My husband did.'

'Not you?'

'No.'

'And the man, the chap with the moustache?'

'He was with her. They were together.'

'Have you seen them since?'

'No.'

'Have you any idea where either of them might be right now?'

'I think,' Polly said, evasively, 'that they're friends of John Flint.'

'Can you find out where either of them is right now?'

'Find out,' said Polly. 'How?'

'By asking your husband maybe.'

'Don't be silly,' Polly said. 'My husband tells me

next to nothing. If he does have this young blonde girl put away somewhere, do you suppose for one moment that he's going to tell me, tell his wife?'

Kenny nodded and tried, without success, to look understanding.

Polly went on, 'I'm not turning informer, you know.'

'I realise that.'

'And I'm not giving away information for free.'

'Surely you don't want paid?'

'Money is the last thing I need,' Polly said. 'Answer me a question: you do care for my sister, don't you?'

'I thought that was pretty obvious.'

'Don't be glib with me, Kenneth. Tell me honestly that you care for my sister and that you aren't just using her to worm your way in our family?'

'I'm in love with Rosie.'

'Will you marry her?'

'It's not the right time to think about marriage.'

'Why not?'

'The war – that sort of thing.'

'Rosie knows nothing,' Polly said. 'Nothing about anything except books. She's very good on the printed word. Besides, deafness is not a sterling attribute in an eavesdropper, is it? What I mean is this – I don't want to see Rosie suffer. If you must ask questions, ask them of me not her. If we settle that point right here and now I'll give you what little help I can.'

'If you don't mind me saying so, Polly, you're not being very consistent,' Kenny said. 'In one breath you're telling me you're not an informer and in the next you're promising to help me.'

'This is very difficult for me, you understand,' Polly said. 'I owe a great deal to my husband, everything in fact. And I've my children to consider. What you're asking me to do is help bring him down.'

'I'm not asking you to do anything, Polly; you volun-teered.'

She was about to argue, to let her tension show, then thought better of it. He was right, of course. She had given him the lead and she couldn't blame him for pressing her now. They had reached the nub of the conversation. One more step, one more word and she would be committed to betrayal. She might pretend that she was doing it for Rosie, for Mammy, to keep them safe but she wasn't. She was doing it for herself – and for Tony.

'That,' she said, 'is true.'

'Do you know where they are, the girl and the man?'

'No,' Polly said. 'But I'll make every effort to find out.'

'By asking Dominic?'

'By asking someone else,' Polly said. 'I do want something in exchange, however. I want to know what you have on this girl, and who she is?'

'Can't tell you that,' said Kenny.

'Because it's top secret. Because the Home Office is barking at your heels?'

'Because we don't really know,' Kenny said. 'Honestly.'

'In that case there's nothing I can . . .'

'All right,' Kenny said. 'I'll tell you who she is, at least who we think she is.' He pushed his plate to one side and lifted the photographs again, one in each hand. He held them towards her, faces uppermost.

'The man is Edgar Harker,' Kenny said. 'The girl is his wife.'

'His wife, not his daughter?'

'Man and wife on the passport that brought them into Britain.'

'Are you sure?'

'As sure as we can be at this stage.'

'Well, well!' said Polly. 'Well, well, well!'

'Doesn't Dominic know that Harker's her husband?'

'I'll bet he doesn't,' Polly said.

And laughed.


They were gathered on the platform above the stalls. Tony had knocked up eight or ten planks, padded with several bales of straw purchased from the Breslin riding academy. He had told the owner, a woman, that he needed straw to fill camp mattresses for a Civil Defence training weekend, and she had swallowed his tale and taken his cash without a qualm.

The bales gave Dougie a little protection from chill draughts and screened the machinery from plain sight, though any competent constable or air raid warden could find it just by climbing the stairs. The fact that the machinery wasn't hidden meant that its presence in the stables could be plausibly explained. As an added precaution Dougie would run off a batch of cheap-paper pamphlets cribbed from government handouts and leave them bundled on the floor as any small jobbing printer might do. So far no one had come near the farmhouse. The local ARP wardens were not well organised and the threat of bombs falling from the skies had receded since the signing of the Munich agreement.

Tony leaned against the bales and watched Dougie slit open a package with a penknife, peel away the waterproof outer layer and expose the dense weight of paper that the package contained.

Kneeling, Dougie slipped the knife blade under the top sheet and separated it cleanly from the ream. He got to his feet again and, holding the sheet high, let it unfurl down the length of his body. He peered at the sheet for half a minute then, frowning, carried it to the guillotine, attached it to a roller and just like a washerwife with a mangle, cranked a handle that fed the paper under the blade. He tugged another handle and the blade dropped, making a single clean cut along the top edge of the sheet. He extracted the cutting, removed the original sheet, adjusted the scale on the side of the guillotine precisely, fed the cutting

through the roller and brought the blade down again
– once, twice, three times – slicing the cut sheet into
four banknote-sized pieces.

The girl leaned against Dominic, their shoulders
touching.

Tony had the impression that she would have
liked him to hold her hand.

From under his pullover Dougie produced a
genuine Bank of England fiver. He snapped it several
times, rubbed it flat between his palms and compared
it with one of the blanks fresh from the guillotine.

'Uh!' he grunted. 'Uh-huh!'

'Is there something wrong, Douglas?' the girl
asked.

Her breath hung in the cold air of the stables, the
question contained in a white cloud, like something
inside a glass paperweight.

Dougie did not answer. He fingered the genuine
note, then the blank. Then he picked up the three
remaining blanks from the tray, slipped the genuine
note between them and fanned them out like a hand
of cards.

'Feels like money,' Dougie said. 'Feels like real
money.'

'So it's okay, is it?' Dominic said.

'I'll need t' examine it under an ultra-violet
light,' Dougie said, 'but so far it looks damn-near
perfect.'

'You'll have to check the whole consignment,'
Dominic said.

'You bet I will,' said Dougie. 'Every bloody sheet.'

'And then what will happen?' Tony asked.

'We wait for some kind person to send us a supply of ink,' Dominic said.

'Like who?' said Tony.

But Dominic didn't answer.

'Does Jackie know what you're up to?' Dennis Hallop said.

'Nope.'

'How did you get outta the house?'

'Told him I was goin' to the pictures,' Babs said. 'The kiddies are in bed an' he's had his face fed so he didn't kick up much of a fuss. What did you tell Gloria?'

'Pub.'

'She wouldn't be too pleased.'

'She's never too pleased,' said Dennis. 'Are you ready for this?'

'Yeah,' Babs said. 'Let's get on with it.'

It was dark at the end of the cul-de-sac and she was nervous, more nervous than she had been in years. Last time she'd been this nervous was when they'd wheeled her out of the bungalow and banged her down the steps into the ambulance, when she'd panicked and thought she was losing Angus. Losing Angus: what a hope! She couldn't have lost Angus if she'd jumped off the Kingston

Bridge without a parachute. Six weeks after her panic attack the doctors had induced labour and Angus had come hurtling out into the world yelling *Brrrrroooooommmmmm-Brrrrroooooommmmmm* or some equally unintelligible infant gibberish, and she'd never had a minute's peace since.

She was nervous again now, though, seated behind the wheel of the Beezer that Dennis had brought out of the yard — and a view of the blank brick wall at the back of the shipyard didn't help soothe her.

Dennis said, 'Do you know what that is, Babs?'

'Aye, it's a bloody wall.'

'Naw, naw: this.'

'Steering wheel.'

'Good. An' this?'

'Gear lever.'

'What about this?'

'Handbrake.'

'Fine. Stick your legs out.'

'Dennis, I'm not sure I . . .'

He put out his big, reliable hand, stuffed it between her knees and thrust them apart. 'Three pedals down there. Feel 'em.'

'Yeah — yep.'

He was almost on top of her, squeezed into the narrow leather seat that groaned and creaked every time he shifted his weight. She did not know why but she was nervous of Dennis too. Being crowded into the narrow BSA three-wheeler with him was — well, sexy.

She took a deep breath and said, 'Are we gonna move, or what?'

'Not 'til you switch on the engine.'

'Dennis, in case you haven't noticed we're facin' a brick wall.'

'Aye,' Dennis said.

'Is that, you know, wise?'

'A Beezer,' Dennis said, 'isn't an ideal vehicle for to learn to drive in, Babs. Also, it's not a good idea for you to be takin' your first lesson in the dark.'

'It's a surprise,' Babs said. 'I want Jackie t' be surprised.'

'He'll be surprised all right,' said Dennis. 'Hands on the wheel, please.'

She did as bidden. 'Okay?'

'Elbows down, grip it light, don't cock your thumbs, feet on the pedals, right foot on the far pedal, that's for to make it go, accelerate, right foot brake too, middle pedal, clutch for the left foot, just the left foot. Got all that?'

'Yep.'

'Left hand off the wheel, find the key, the key next the big switch. Don't fumble, Babs, straight to it. Got it?'

'Yep,' she said. 'Will I turn it on?'

'Why are you doin' this, Babs?' Dennis said. 'Women don't hafta drive.'

'I just wanna be prepared.'

He said nothing, gave no instruction for a full half-minute. He sat as stiffly as Dennis ever could, head pressed down a little by the arching roof, motionless, gazing out into the darkness, brooding on the word that remained unspoken, contemplating a war that might never take place.

'The trouble wi' Beezers,' he said, 'is you can never get them t' stop.'

'Is that why we're facin' a brick wall?'

'Yeah.'

'An' is that why you've got your hand on my leg.'

'Yeah.'

'Is that the only reason?'

'Oh, yeah,' said Dennis.

'Will I switch on now?' Babs asked.

And Dennis said, 'Why not?'

The house was difficult to find. The new council estate sprawled behind tall, old-fashioned tenements, hemmed in by chemical works and the great smoking stacks of the steel works. Rough-cast and black slate, scruffy privet hedges and gardens without growth all served to reduce the development into a confusion of identical roads and avenues.

When he'd tracked down the woman's address from the files it hadn't occurred to him that she'd be living in a new scheme. He had imagined her in a clean-cut Gorbals tenement refurbished for spinsters and widows and safely removed from noisy thoroughfares and the cut-throat pubs of the Calcutta

Road. He didn't know the south side of the river well, of course. As a young constable his beat had been Anderston, which wasn't exactly the Garden of Eden but as far as slums went wasn't a patch on Gorbals or the over-crowded acres of Laurieston.

The council project of semi-detached, two-storey houses confused him for it had already assumed a chafed and shoddy appearance as if the fabric of the social cloth had been stretched too tight for the tenants' comfort. There wasn't a pub this side of Jewel Street or a tramcar short of the Westbrae. The streets were strangely deserted even at this comparatively early hour and there was no one about from whom he could ask directions.

At length he discovered a dented metal sign – Primrose Avenue – and walked along the pavement, counting out numbers. He turned into a gateless opening, walked up a little path and knocked on a green-painted door.

Light glimmered faintly behind an orange curtain in the front-room window: darkness upstairs. When he saw the curtain flick, quick and furtive, he knocked on the door again.

'Who is it?' the voice had a rasp to it, thin as a fret-saw blade.

Kenny didn't want to alarm the woman. He had always been considerate – perhaps too considerate – of the finer feelings of the citizens with whom he came in contact.

'Miss McKerlie?' he said.

'Yes.'

'I wonder if I might have a word with you, please.'

'What're you sellin'?'

'I'm not a salesman. I – I'm from the Civil Defence.'

She opened the door an inch.

At first he thought it was the smell of the house but when she eased the door back a little more he realised that the odour came from the woman herself. She did not smell musty or unclean, but she did smell of milk, the faint moist acidic undertone of curdled whey.

'Is it the garden? Are you wantin' t' dig up the garden?'

'No,' Kenny said cautiously. 'It's not the garden, Miss McKerlie.'

He took out his card and held it up to what light there was.

He could see nothing of the interior of the house, only the implacable green door and the woman leaning around it, shorn off at the waist like a glove-puppet.

She did not see the card, or perhaps deliberately ignored it.

'I've told them they're not diggin' up my garden. They've been at me before, them and their like. They can dig up Jimmy Dunn's garden but they're not diggin' up mine, not for all the bombs we're goin' to have fallin' on us. Is it gas-masks you're sellin'? I've got mine already.' When she made to close the door Kenny put out his hand, closed it into a fist, stuck it against the jamb. The woman swayed back, grizzling: 'Have you come for me as well? Have you come for t' take me away too?'

'Please, Miss McKerlie, look at my card. I'm a policeman. I just require to ask you one or two questions about . . .'

'No uniform, no helmet?'

He wondered if the few sparse details he had garnered about her had somehow lacked the salient fact that she was nuts. She certainly looked nothing like her sister and had not one shred of Lizzie Peabody's affability. She was small, shrivelled and waspish, and her hair was dyed bright red.

Kenny planted one foot on the top step and kept his fist where it was.

'Ten minutes of your time, Miss McKerlie. That's all I ask.'

'Did *she* send you?'

'She? Who?'

'Her, my sister.'

'Your sister,' Kenny fibbed. 'I didn't even know you had a sister.'

She took the card at last and squinted at it briefly. She had, he guessed, already made up her mind that he was trustworthy. She gave him back the card, opened the door, popped her head out and glanced up and down the deserted avenue as if afraid that someone would see her admitting a man to her spinster's domain and think the worst.

Kenny stepped into the hall.

There was a small antique table with cloth flowers in a Chinese vase upon it. A door led to the bathroom, another to the kitchenette, and stairs disappeared into darkness on his left. The aroma of pine-scented wax polish absorbed the woman's sour odour completely. He followed her into the ground-floor living-room.

It too was nicely furnished, not cluttered. The dining-table was covered with an embroidered cloth and a whatnot in the corner displayed a modest collection of cheap china bric-à-brac. The armchair in front of the coal fire was upright and had wooden arms but had no mate on the other side of the hearth. On the rug by the side of the chair was a sewing basket, open to show needles and bobbins of thread. There were, he noticed, no photographs or prints and nothing on the mantelshelf except a clock and a pair of empty brass candlesticks.

'I'm not givin' you tea,' Janet McKerlie said.

'I didn't ask for tea,' Kenny said, though after his journey out from the city by tramcar and his long walk he would have been glad of a cup. 'You're obviously busy, Miss McKerlie, so I'll come right to the . . .'

'How did you get my name?'

'Pardon?'

'How do you know who I am?'

'Ah – em – it came up in the course of enquiries.'

'Enquiries? What enquiries?' the woman said.

She was as small as her sister was large, had the same sort of build as Polly, the same shape of face as Rosie. He wondered if this is what Rosie would look like when she reached her fifties. He sincerely hoped not.

Kenny said, 'I've a couple of snapshots I'd like you to look at in case you recognise either of the . . .'

'Snapshots, is it?' She put one skinny hand into the pocket of her sewing apron, folded the other arm cross her bosom and clasped the side of her neck. Her pose was aggressive, proud. 'I don't know anythin' about snapshots.'

'Please, just look at them.'

'Are they murderers?'

'No, no, nothing like that.'

'Are they Manone's boys?'

He hesitated: he hadn't expected her to drop Dominic's name without prompting. He was tempted to chase the lead and a queer feeling of anticipation stole over him at the realisation that Janet McKerlie probably knew a great deal about Carlo Manone's activities before the Great War.

If his hunch was correct Janet McKerlie may also have been connected with Manone's mob, may even have cut herself off from the family because she disapproved of Polly's marriage to Carlo's son. He reminded himself sternly not to invent, not to pre-judge the volume or quality of information that this woman might be able to divulge – even if she was a nut.

He said, 'No, they are just two people that we're interested in, that's all.'

She unwrapped her arm from across her chest and held out her hand.

'Show me,' she said, 'an' get it over with.'

He gave her the photographs one at a time.

She dipped into her apron pocket and produced a pair of spectacles, stuck them on her nose and studied the snapshot of the girl.

'Is she a tart?'

'No, I don't think so,' Kenny said.

'She looks like a tart to me. What's that she's wearin'?' Janet McKerlie peered more closely at the photo. 'Is that shot silk?'

'I really couldn't say. Do you recognise her, Miss McKerlie?'

'No, I do not.' She flung the photograph back at him. 'Never seen her in my life before. Never want to, a tart like that. Huh!'

'How about this chap?' Kenny said.

He passed her the shot of Edgar Harker.

She held the photograph at arm's length, brought it closer, blinked, held it almost against her nose, then let out a long, whimpering cry.

'What is it, Miss McKerlie? What's wrong?'

She reached behind her, groping for support, staggered and might have fallen if Kenny hadn't caught her arm. He eased her into the armchair by the fire.

'Is it the snap? Do you recognise him?' Kenny asked urgently.

'It's him,' she said. 'Oh, God! Oh my good God! It's Frank.'

'Frank?'

'Frank Conway. My Frank. He's come back for me at last.'

# Chapter Ten

Tony was lying in bed reading a Peter Cheyney novel he'd purchased in Glasgow while picking up supplies. Ten or a dozen books were stacked on the narrow shelf in the smaller of the two first-floor bedrooms; reading kept his mind off Polly, particularly at this late hour of the night.

He was fatigued but not sleepy. His shoulders ached from hefting the routing machine upstairs to the attic. It had not been an easy task, even with Dominic to help him. Giffard was useless when it came to heavy labour and the girl, though willing, wasn't strong enough. The paper had also been unloaded and stored under a tarpaulin in the stables for there was no room for it in Giffard's attic where every inch of space was taken up with equipment of one sort or another.

Soon after Dominic had left, the printer had filled a mug with coffee, cadged a packet of cigarettes from

Tony and had gone upstairs to install the routing machine and check the paper quality. Penny had accompanied him. Seated on the cot, the cat in her lap, she had been content to watch Giffard at work and Tony had seized the opportunity to drive into Breslin to telephone Polly.

Polly had not been at home, however, and just to get away from the farm for a while he had driven on into Glasgow.

The weather was neutral, neither cold nor warm and there was no wind to whistle in the empty fireplace. The tasselled shade of the bedside lamp was tilted to throw light on the page but Tony hardly took in the words. He was thinking of Polly after all. He could not put her out of his mind. Talking sense to himself didn't help. He was plagued by a restless yearning that he couldn't smother and daren't encourage. He tossed the book away, rolled on to his elbow and poured himself a dram from the half bottle of whisky he'd filched from Giffard's supply. He propped himself up on the pillow, sighed, drank a mouthful of the stinging liquid, lit a cigarette, lay back and stared at the ceiling.

There was no noise from the attic. Presumably Giffard had quit fiddling with his new toys and had finally gone to bed.

Then, 'Tony, are you still awake?'

'What do you want, Penny?'

He felt as guilty as if it were his mother tapping on the door and he was a boy again, stealthily

experimenting with nicotine and alcohol – sex too –
in the imperfect privacy of his bedroom.

'I want to show you something,' Penny said.

'What?' Tony said, thickly.

She opened the door – no lock or latch on any of
the doors upstairs – and slipped into the bedroom. She
wore clinging coral-pink pyjamas. And a gas-mask.

'*Blooh!*' she said, the word all fat and blubbery.
'*Blooh!*'

'Oh, for Christ's sake, Penny!'

She raised her arms and advanced upon him like
a ghoul.

'*Blooh, blooh, blaaah!*'

The flanges of the rubber mask palpitated and
the ugly tin pig-snout thrust out towards him, the
eye-piece clouded with vapour.

'*Glumme a kluss. Glow on, glumme a kluss.*'

She leaned over him, nuzzling the metal snout
down into his face.

He swung the whisky glass and cigarette away
and tried to push her off. She was playful, frenetically
mischievous, but he was in no mood to be teased.
Breasts pointing up the fabric of the pyjama jacket, the
curve of her stomach dipping down into her thighs,
she bent one long leg like a hurdler and climbed on
to the bed. He could hear the monstrous suck and
slobber of her mouth taking in air as she struggled to
pin him down and press the snout of the gas-mask
against his lips.

Still juggling glass and cigarette, he defended

himself with his forearm. She was lithe and angular, stronger than he had supposed her to be. She forced herself upon him, then collapsed, laughing, hot and wet and breathless within the mask. He reached across her and dropped the glass on to the table, the cigarette into an ashtray. He snared her waist and lifted her up. She was suddenly no longer playful and mischievous but tense with expectation.

He held her rigidly above him with the respirator only inches from his face. He fumbled with the buttons of the jacket. He flicked the jacket open and pinned it under her arms. She lowered herself to meet him. He opened his mouth and sucked her breast, put his hand beneath her breast, raising it so that he could take more of it into his mouth. He curled his tongue over her nipple, felt her stiffen and shudder. He slid his hand down the curve of her stomach under the waistband of her pyjamas, going on until his fingertips touched hair. She lifted her hips to give him room, arched her back. He felt gone from himself, apart. He said nothing. He had nothing to say. He pushed her on to her feet and flung back the bedclothes.

She glared at him through the clouded eye-piece, lifted her hands to peel off the mask. He said loudly, 'No.' Swinging out of bed he tugged down her pyjamas, sliding them down her long legs and saw how beautiful she was, the angular hipbones rounded, the belly smooth and rounded, her thighs sleek. She stepped out of the pyjamas and stood before him wearing nothing but the rubber gas-mask. She was, at that moment, both grotesquely ugly and grotesquely beautiful.

Once more she tried to loosen the mask but he rose, almost lunging, from the bed, and carried her before him. She staggered, staggered again. He caught her, not gently, his arms about her waist. He backed her against the door and thrust himself against her. She opened her legs and yielded to him, seemed somehow to absorb him so that he was no longer apart but had become enveloped in a strange hard fusion that had no meaning but conquest.

She pushed the snout of the respirator over his shoulder, let him lift and carry her and lay her across the bed, let him drive into her as if she were nothing but a sleek, ugly, faceless object. She cried out, choking, and struggled to reach the clasps of the mask, to strip it away but he would not allow it. He smothered her with his body, pinned her hands with his forearms and drove on until she reached a suffocating climax. Then he withdrew.

She tore off the gas-mask, gasping like a fish, gasped and panted and sank back against the pillow, red-faced and dewed with perspiration.

He stood by the bed looking down on her.

She sighed and smiled, and said, 'Am I good, Tony? Am I not good?'

'The best,' he answered sourly, and went downstairs to wash.

*　　*　　*

'Never mind Winstock,' Kenny said, 'just think of the position this puts me in.'

'It's entirely your own fault,' Fiona said, 'you shouldn't have gone charging off on your own, following your own leads.'

'It was pure chance, just a hunch,' Kenny said. 'How was I to know she'd recognise the bloke? My God, Fiona, it's over twenty years since she saw him last and look at him – big moustache, a scarred lip. It didn't seem to make a whit of difference. She took one look at the photograph and nailed him straight away. I even tried to convince her that it *wasn't* Frank Conway, that it couldn't *possibly* be Frank Conway, but she was adamant, absolutely adamant. It didn't even occur to her that it might be an old photograph.'

'Well, it isn't an old photograph so it's obvious that he isn't dead.'

'Heck, do you think I don't know that? That's the problem.'

'Seems to me,' Fiona said, crisply, 'that he escaped the war all in one piece, changed his identity and went to work for Carlo Manone in America. That seems logical, doesn't it?'

'You mean he's been in Philadelphia all this time without once trying to contact his wife and children?'

'These people,' Fiona said, 'are not like you and me, Kenneth.'

'I'm not going to take the McKerlie woman's word for it.'

'Then what are you going to do?'

'I don't know.'

'Winstock will insist that you hand over the lead to him, you know.'

'I'm not doing that,' Kenny said. 'I'll have to find another way of confirming Janet McKerlie's identification.'

'Show the photograph to Lizzie Peabody. If his wife doesn't recognise him, even with that stupid moustache and the scar, then . . .'

'His wife: yes, precisely.'

'Ah, I didn't quite think of that,' Fiona admitted. 'Of course, she's married again. If her first husband turns out to be still alive that may cast doubt on the validity of her present marriage. A court would straighten it out, I imagine, and find her innocent of any charge of bigamy.'

'A court? Do you honestly believe I'd bring this to court for a decision? God, it would be all over the newspapers. See the problem? How am I going to tell Rosie that I've found her father, that he's a crook and possibly a traitor and that we're hell-bent on laying him by the heels so we can send him to clink?'

'Won't the McKerlie woman tell her sister even if you don't?'

'Not her,' Kenny said. 'She thinks – wait until you hear this – she thinks that Frank Conway has come back for her.'

'What do you mean?'

'Apparently she was in love with him all those years ago.'

'You mean he was her lover?'

Kenny shrugged. 'She didn't go quite that far, but I think it's probable. On the other hand perhaps she just imagined it and he's forgotten she even existed. He certainly hasn't tried to make contact with her, with any of them, that we know of.'

'Except Dominic Manone.'

'I wonder,' Kenny asked, 'if Dominic knows who Harker really is?'

'That's an interesting question,' Fiona said.

'What a devious, scheming rat he'd be to keep it from Polly.'

'Perhaps, like you, he's afraid to tell her the truth. Does the McKerlie woman have any idea where Conway, alias Harker, is at the present moment?'

'Of course not. She's waiting for me to produce him like a rabbit out of a hat and deliver him on to her doorstep.'

'You *could* tell her that he's dead.'

'She'd never believe me, not now.'

'Convince her.'

'Fiona, she isn't open to reason. Even if I brought her his head on a platter she'd suspect me of trickery. I've given her the one thing in life that's kept her going, a nonsensical belief that Frank Conway would come back from the dead.'

'That's insane.'

'Do I not know it,' said Kenny.

'Well, what *are* you going to do?'

'Find him myself,' Kenny said.

'And then?'

'Get rid of him pretty damned quick.'

Dominic spent longer than usual saying goodnight to the children. Stuart had been nursing one of his interminable colds, nothing too serious, not bad enough to keep him from school, just a stuffy nose and tickling cough that rendered him pale and listless. Even Polly had taken pity on him, had brought him down to the back parlour after supper and had played several hands of Old Maid with him before bath and bedtime while Ishbel, for once, had Patricia all to herself.

It was after ten o'clock before Dominic returned to the living-room by which time Polly had fortified herself with a couple of Manhattans and was seated on the sofa smoking a cigarette and sipping coffee.

'He doesn't look well to me,' Dominic said.

'He's fine.'

'Perhaps we should keep him in bed for a day or two.'

'If he runs any sort of a temperature,' Polly said, 'I will.'

Dominic poured black coffee from the urn on the sideboard and brought it to the fire. He didn't sit by her but sank into the deep leather armchair that faced the curtains. He lit a cigar, crossed his legs, sipped coffee too.

'Has Patricia shown him how to put on his gas-mask?'

'Of course. Besides,' Polly said, 'they have lessons – drills at school.'

'With that chest of his a whiff of poison gas would kill him.'

'Now you're just being morbid,' Polly said. 'Hitler won't attack without warning. In addition to which we're not even at war with Germany.'

'If it comes to it,' Dominic said, 'we'll move them to the country.'

'Move who?'

'The children – and you.'

'I don't want to go to the country. I might consider the seaside.'

'The coast won't be much safer than the city.'

'Is that where you were today? Surveying bolt-holes in Ayrshire?'

'The entire Clyde basin will be a target for air attacks,' Dominic said. 'And they're already assembling boom defences to keep submarines out of the Firth.'

'Didn't you tell me just a few weeks ago that there would be no war.'

'I've altered my opinion.'

'Will you serve?'

'Serve?'

'Your country,' Polly said. 'Join up.'

'If they'll have me, of course.'

'You won't be conscripted?'

'No, not initially. Young men will be first to go, then those without wives and children then, if necessary, anyone who can carry a rifle.'

'Just like the last time.'

'Yes' Dominic said. 'Only this one will be much, much worse.'

'What will they make of you, Dominic?' Polly said. 'Will you be a quartermaster, or a bombardier, or a naval officer?'

'I've no idea.'

'You must have thought about it.'

'I've too many other things on my mind to worry about that.'

'What other things?' said Polly. 'The business?'

'Yes.'

'Tell me, what sort of stock do we have in the warehouse right now?'

'You've been in the warehouse.'

'Only once, a long time ago,' Polly said. 'So tell me, Dominic, is everything in the warehouse bona fide?'

'Bona fide?'

'Legal and legitimate,' Polly said.

'Never been anything else,' Dominic said. 'We're wholesalers, darling, importers, not receivers of stolen goods. We can produce receipts and licences for every cup and vase and effigy on our shelves.' He glanced at her out of his solemn jet black eyes to make sure that she was convinced. 'Eighty per cent of our imports are from Italy, however, and if the war comes that trade will cease immediately and the warehouse will probably be requisitioned by the Ministry of Defence.'

'What will we do for income then?'

'We – you won't starve.'

'We could go abroad, you know. I'm sure your father would take us in.'

'No,' Dominic said, sharply, 'that isn't an option, Polly.'

'All your other irons, are they liable to melt away too?'

'Some will, inevitably.'

'But not all?'

'No, not all.'

She carried his empty coffee cup to the sideboard, refilled it and brought it back to him. He had almost finished his cigar. He inhaled a final mouthful of smoke and threw the stub into the fire. He accepted the coffee cup, cradled it on his palm. He had fine soft hands, a little plump now. She couldn't imagine him ever having hit anyone, having ever struck out in anger or with cruelty.

'Won't you tell me where our money comes from?' Polly said. 'Better yet, Dominic, why don't you show me how our businesses operate?'

'No.'

'If you do have to go off to serve King and country . . .'

'If I do, then it won't matter,' he said. 'It'll all be going to hell and no one will be able to salvage anything.'

'I'm not sure I believe you.'

He placed the little cup and saucer on a side table, reached out and took her hands in his. He rubbed the ball of his thumb on her wedding-ring as if it were a good-luck charm.

'Whatever happens,' he said, 'you and the children will be taken care of.'

'By whom?' Polly said. 'By Tony?'

'If I go,' Dominic said, 'Tony will go too. But you won't want for money, I promise you that. Even in a state of war – especially in a state of war – money can buy almost anything.'

'If you know how to use it properly,' Polly said. 'I know nothing, Dominic. I know as little about what you own and where your income comes from as I did the day I married you: less, in fact, because at least I understood how bookmaking worked and – what did you call it? – street insurance. Now it's all partnerships, seats on the board of this and that, deals written out on paper.'

'Safer,' Dominic said. 'Cleaner and more profitable. I thought that's how you wanted it?'

'Tell me, Dominic. Show me. Teach me.'

He released her hands abruptly and sat back in the leather chair.

'Please,' Polly said.

But Dominic, frowning again, refused.

\*     \*     \*

Bernard was staffing the office while Allan Shakespeare escorted a young married couple out to the site at Blackstone to view one of the modestly priced bungalows. There wasn't much to see, a half-built framework of bricks and mortar rising from a sea of mud. The site reminded Bernard of a little French township near Bovet that had been bombarded for weeks by heavy artillery and when he passed the foundation trenches on his way up Blackstone Hill he almost expected to see corpses huddled in the mud.

The villas had sold well – apparently there was still money floating about looking, literally, for a home – but the bungalows were 'sticky', and the Bard had not been in the best of moods since Christmas, counting out daily not what he had gained but what he had lost in commission because of the threat of war; a war, incidentally, that he did not believe would ever come to pass.

The other thing Bernard hated about going out to the Blackstone site was that it took him close to the farmhouse where Dominic had installed his mistress. In spite of Dominic's denials, Bernard was still inclined to believe that the beautiful, long-legged blonde whom he had met on two or three occasions was sleeping with his stepson-in-law. Stepson-in-law: he found it almost impossible to think of Dominic Manone as a relative. There was something too sharp and sophisticated about Manone, a quality that he, plain Bernard Peabody, could not relate to. Between them – yes, Polly too – the couple evinced a mendacity that was absent in Babs and Rosie and that Lizzie, for all her experience of the streets, could not even recognise as being there at all. He was condemned to remain silent when talk turned to Dom and Polly. He could no longer confide in Rosie, his lovely Rosie, who was so wrapped up in romance that she wouldn't have known what he was talking about. Never had Bernard been so depressed, not even in the dark, dead days just after the Great War – which he was now beginning to think of as 'the last war' – when his mother was grieving for her lost sons and he was shrouded in guilt just because he had managed to survive.

If it hadn't been for love of Lizzie he would have gone under before now. The girls might assume stepping up in the world had changed him, that the responsibility of managing an estate office instead of merely collecting rents had altered his character, but Bernard could have told them differently. It was Lizzie, soft and plump and, in her charming way, naïve who had changed him; his unflagging love of Lizzie, his desire to protect her from harm. He could have done it too, could have kept her secure, even with war threatening, if it hadn't been for the girls and the men the girls had married. And, it seemed, the appearance on the scene of the man that the last of the three sisters would marry, the crafty copper from St Andrew's Street, so that war and all the drastic changes that war would bring began to seem to poor Bernard like the easy way out.

Sergeant MacGregor's visit to Breslin was close to being the last straw and from that day on Bernard was a man on a knife's edge who, for two pins, would have abandoned everyone, even Lizzie, and gone off to join the army.

Sandra, the agency's part-time clerk, was looking after the front office when the detective arrived. Bernard had retired to the glass-walled cubicle at the rear of the office to brood in peace. He was slumped in Allan Shakespeare's chair smoking a cigarette when Sandra popped her head around the door and told him that he was wanted. In his present frame of mind the word 'wanted' had so many negative connotations that Bernard groaned inwardly and, like an arthritic old veteran, forced himself out of the chair. He had no appetite for work, no interest in bonuses and commissions and was unable to raise even the ghost of a smile when he opened the door of the cubicle and saw Detective Sergeant Kenneth MacGregor, Rosie's sweetheart, loitering shyly by the outer office counter.

'Ah, Mr Peabody, may I have a word with you?' the sergeant said.

'Do I have a choice?' said Bernard.

'Won't take long.'

'When did Breslin become your beat?'

'I don't have a beat, Mr Peabody.'

'Is this call personal or professional?'

'Bit of both,' Kenny told him.

'You'd better step inside,' said Bernard.

Babs said, 'I'm taking lessons in how to drive.'

'Drive what?' said Polly, who had been thinking of other things.

'Motorcars,' Babs said. 'Dennis is teachin' me.'

'Dennis? Why not Jackie?'

'I don't want Jackie to know what I'm doin',' Babs said. 'He'd only scoff. You know what he's like about motorcars.'

'I know what he's like about women,' Polly said. 'Is it fun?'

'Aye, once you get used to it,' Babs said. 'You should try it some time.'

'Not interested.'

'All right for you, I suppose,' Babs said, 'havin' Tony Lombard to drive you about all over the place. We don't have that kinda money.'

'I don't have Tony Lombard, not any more.'

'Really!' Babs said, as if the absence of the handsome Italian in her sister's life had totally escaped her notice. 'Who does for you now?'

They were taking one of their rare outings together, not in Bellahouston Park which had been given over to the Empire Exhibition, but on a small area of grassland that everyone called The Round.

The trees were not in bud but snowdrops had struggled out and here and there, where the boys

271

hadn't trodden on them, daffodil pods were beginning to break through the dank, impacted turf. The Round was claustrophobic, in spite of struggling signs of spring, for the old tenements of Macklin Street and St Patrick's Road crowded upon it, ugly, not handsome dwellings that reminded the girls – Polly at least – of where Babs and she had come from and what they had left behind.

The tyres of April's perambulator hissed on the hard-packed gravel path that followed the park's perimeter and Babs, ever energetic, thrust into the swan-necked handle as if she and her sister were going somewhere. The baby was fast asleep, flushed by raw January air, and dribbling into her angora wool cap.

Polly didn't answer Babs's question.

She was here only under sufferance, to fulfil the intermin-able obligations that family bonds put upon her, bonds that she didn't have the temerity to shake off. She had loved Babs once, loved her sister with the intense animosity of rivals. She did not love Babs any more, however, did not love Rosie – there was only pity and protection left of that old fondness – and loved her mother with a patronising condescension that even Polly recognised as wrong.

She had lost herself in love with Dominic Manone and when that love had faded had turned instead to Tony Lombard. She could not help but align herself with handsome, confident males, and the sacrifices she'd made to satisfy her selfish needs hadn't much bothered her – until now.

'Where is Tony anyway?' Babs said.

'I told you at Christmas, I don't know.'

'You told me at Christmas you were gonna find out.'

'Well, I haven't.'

The pram lurched on worn ground. Babs adjusted her course.

'Have you tried?' she asked.

Polly was out of breath and put a hand on the pram handle to slow it down.

She had no compelling need to confide in Babs, to confess that she had taken Tony Lombard as a lover. In recent years Babs's loyalty to Jackie Hallop had made her stuffy and curiously moralistic. She would not approve of adultery, would not regard it as a romantic adventure, not now.

Polly had a sneaking feeling that Babs was right, that what she believed to be love was nothing but a shabby substitute for children who bored her and a husband who kept her at arm's length.

'Yes,' Polly answered. 'I did have lunch with MacGregor.'

'I hope you're not gonna nick him from Rosie.'

'How dare you say that! As if I would.'

'Oh, yeah, you would,' said Babs. 'If it suited you, you would.'

'You don't have much of an opinion of me, do you, Babs?'

'You're my sister: I'm stuck with you,' Babs said, shrugging lightly. 'What did MacGregor tell you?'

'Not much. He's looking for two suspects.'

'I thought the CID would have enough suspects to be goin' on with.'

'Don't play the fool, Babs. Two specific suspects.'

'What're they suspected of?'

'He wouldn't say.'

'Did he tell you who they were?'

'One of them's a girl.'

'Hah!'

'What's that supposed to mean?' said Polly.

'Is that who Tony's with right now?'

'You're jumping to conclusions awfully damned quickly, aren't you?'

'It's Tony Lombard you're really worried about, isn't it, not Dominic?'

'I – I'm worried about the future.'

'Well, sis, you ain't the only one,' said Babs. 'Why d' you think I'm learning to drive? It's in case this bloody war does come an' we're left holdin' the baby.' Babs checked the charge of the perambulator, applied the footbrake and, head cocked, contemplated her sister. 'We're not flirty wee girls any more, Poll. We're not Mammy's little rays of sunshine. I got four kids an' a bungalow in Raines Drive. You – you've got a pearl in every oyster, plus two kids an' a husband who can make money fall down outta the sky. Look at us, for God sake! None of this is gonna last. Funny thing is, I don't think it even *deserves* to last. You got me?'

'No, I'm afraid I haven't got you.'

Babs sighed. 'Whether it does or doesn't, I'm not gonna let any of it go without a fight.' She took a step towards her sister and planted her hands on her hips as if the conversation had suddenly become a quarrel. 'They're closin' in from all sides, Polly. I don't mean the damned Jerries. I mean the law. They're after your Dominic an' that means they'll get my Jackie in the process – unless we do somethin' about it.'

'What *can* we do about it?' said Polly.

She spoke wearily, not warily. She didn't resent being dressed down by her young sister for Babs's selfishness had point and whatever she decided to do would benefit her husband and children. Mammy all over again: Mammy's struggle writ large. For an instant Polly felt shame, then a grey, annealing weariness stole over her once more, a pervasive sense that time had stopped and there was nothing she could do to make it start up again.

'Be ready to take over,' Babs said.

'Take over?'

'What the hell's wrong with you, Polly Conway? Is the gin gettin' to your brain at last? Listen. Listen to me: we're married to crooks, to criminals. There's no good blinkin' that fact. Hell's bells, I'm no more honest at heart than our Jackie, though I hope I do know where t' draw the line.' Babs folded her arms across her bosom and though there was no one else in The Round at that early hour in the afternoon, lowered her voice to a near whisper.

'Rosie's detective is sure on to somethin' an' it's not somethin' small either. There's money bein' made, or about to be made, an' it's *real* money this time.'

In spite of herself, Polly nodded agreement.

'This isn't a wad o' banknotes stuffed into a cocoa tin,' Babs went on. 'This is sackfuls o' the stuff – an' that's not countin' what you could realise by liquidatin' Dominic's assets.'

'Is it Jackie who's put you up to this?' Polly said.

'Jackie! God, Jackie wouldn't know an asset if he sat on one,' Babs said. 'I mean, he still doesn't know what an asset I am an' I've been with him for ten years. Listen. Listen to me, Polly: have you forgotten what went on wi' Mammy all those years ago, all that rubbish about her bein' in the Manones' debt?'

'That was a mistake, a misunderstanding.'

'Was it hell!'

'In any case, it's water under the bridge,' said Polly.

She still felt grey and detached but in Babs's vehemence she recognised some of the anger that had been in her too over the past months, a strange sourceless anger that found no focus of expression, none, that is, except the betrayal of her marriage vows. She felt the muscles at the back of her calves tremble slightly, her mouth become dry. What had she done? She had allowed Tony Lombard to become her lover without knowing whether or not he loved her. She had made promises not to Tony but to a stranger, promises that for all their shambolic confusion had more to do with her family than the Manones.

Now Babs was standing up to her. Babs was telling her that there were debts to collect as well as debts to pay and that she must be prepared to call them in.

'They won't be here much longer, you know,' Babs said. 'They'll go the way Daddy went all those years ago, leavin you an' me an' six kiddies to fend for ourselves. Haven't you thought about that, Polly?'

'Yes,' Polly said. 'God, yes, of course I have.'

'So what are you gonna do about it?'

'What do you suggest?' Polly said.

'Sell out,' said Babs. 'As soon as the boys are gone, sell out.'

'Sell out what, though?'

'Everything we can lay our hands on, you an' me together.'

'Sell out to whom? I mean, who'd buy from us on a buyer's market?'

'I've thought of that too,' said Babs.

'Who then?'

'John Flint.'

And Polly, wide awake, said, 'Yes.'

'I have reason to believe,' said Kenny, 'that your wife's first husband is still alive.'

Bernard felt his heart lurch and a wave of nausea rise from the region of his stomach. He had been seated in Shakespeare's chair, trying to pretend that he was entirely unruffled by the sergeant's arrival. He'd expected questions, of course, questions about the operation of Lyons & Lloyd's and Dominic's other business interests, perhaps about Rosie, Rosie's past, Rosie's infirmity, but he hadn't expected this sudden shattering blow. He put his hand to his mouth, clenched his fist, and gawked, bug-eyed, at the Highlander.

'Not only still alive, Mr Peabody, but actually back in this country.'

'How – how . . .'

'How do we know?'

Bernard managed to nod.

'Are you all right, sir,' Kenny said. 'You look terrible.'

Bernard managed to nod again.

'I shouldn't have come right out with it, should I?' Kenny said. 'I didn't know what else to do, you see, who else to turn to.'

'G-go on,' Bernard whispered. 'Tell me what you've f-found out.'

'Well, I haven't located the gentleman in question,' said Kenny.

'Then h-how can you be sure it is Frank Conway?'

'Can't,' said Kenny. 'That's why I'm here.'

Bernard slid his arms on to the desk. In the office outside one of the telephones was ringing, distant and detached. Sandra would fend off the caller for, like most girls of her class, she had inordinate respect for the forces of law and order and would ensure that he and the policeman were not disturbed. The thought glided past almost unnoticed as he slumped across the desk, heart thumping and a hand still clamped to his mouth. Kenny shifted uncomfortably in an upright chair, embarrassed by his victim's distress.

Bernard tried to collect himself, to square up to the possibility that the detective was in effect a sadist, that there was no substance to the rumour that Frank Conway had returned from the dead.

'I take it you don't have Conway under arrest?' Bernard said.

'I wish we did.' Shaking his head, Kenny revised his statement. 'No, that's not true. It's probably just as well that we haven't caught him yet. If and when we do lay hands on him we'll need positive identification and that'll mean approaching Mrs Con – Mrs Peabody, I mean.'

Bernard lifted his head a little. 'You want me to break the news, is that it?'

'Lord, no,' Kenny said. 'I don't want anyone to break the news to – well, to anyone.'

'Least of all to Rosie?' Bernard sat up. 'Is that why you've come to me first?'

'Yes,' Kenny said. 'I don't want Rosie blaming me for her father's arrest.'

'What's he supposed to have done?' Bernard said.

Kenny glanced down at his hands folded in his lap. 'I thought you might be in a position to tell me.'

'Well, I'm not,' said Bernard.

'Did you know him?'

'Nope, never met the man in my life. He was long gone before I encountered Lizzie and her girls.'

'So you wouldn't recognise him if you saw him?'

'Wouldn't know him from Adam.' Bernard was breathing more easily now and his heart had returned to its normal rhythm. 'Are you absolutely certain the chap you're chasing is Frank Conway?'

'Almost certain.'

'Who gave you the lead? Who recognised him?'

Kenny hesitated. 'Janet McKerlie.'

'Janet! She hasn't been in touch for years. Wanted nothing to do with us after her mother died. How in God's name did Janet get mixed up in all this?'

'We're more thorough in the CID than you give us credit for,' Kenny said. 'Perhaps you've met Conway without knowing it. I'll show you a photograph, see what you make of it.'

The photograph was produced, examined, returned.

'Sorry,' Bernard said. 'Never met him. That's the truth.'

'What about this lady?'

Kenny placed the photograph of the girl on the desk.

Bernard didn't have the inbred shutter-like defence that the Italians had perfected. He could not help but blink. He knew the policeman was watching him closely and did his level best to remain inscrutable – but it was too late.

Kenny said, 'You do know her, don't you, Bernard?'

'I – I don't know her name.'

'Do you know where we can find her?'

'What's she got to do with Conway?'

'We've reason to believe that she's his wife.'

'*What!*'

'Hmmm,' Kenny said. 'Complicated, isn't it?'

'God in Heaven!' Bernard said. 'Complicated isn't the word for it. Are you telling me that Frank Conway got married again. If he's still in the land of the living he's still officially married to my Lizzie. It was assumed he'd joined the army and had been killed in the war. Lizzie couldn't prove it, though, for there was no record of him with any of the regiments.' Bernard reached for the snapshot. 'Is that moustache genuine?'

'We believe it might be.'

'You don't seem exactly sure of anything, do you? I mean, it's all "we believe this, we believe that". Just how much do you have on Conway? And what's he doing back in Scotland? If this young filly is Conway's wife then I doubt very much if he's come back to reclaim Lizzie.'

'Where did you meet the girl?' Kenny asked.

'I only saw her once.'

'When?'

'Week or two before Christmas.'

'With Dominic?'

He was cornered. He had to decide very quickly what would wash with the facts that MacGregor already had in his possession. He couldn't put Rosie

and Lizzie out of his mind, though, the dreadful effect
that the news would have upon them. He had never
doubted that Lizzie loved him, didn't doubt that she
would continue to love him, but if Frank Conway
wasn't dead, if Frank Conway was liable to stroll into
their lives at any moment . . .

'Yes, with Dominic,' Bernard heard himself say.

'Where did this meeting take place?'

'He brought her here, a week or two before
Christmas.'

'Why?'

'I don't know. He just did.'

'How did he introduce her?' Kenny said.

'He didn't. He just said that she was a friend.'

'Did he have any conversation with Mr Shakespeare?'

'No, Allan was out at the time.'

'I see,' Kenny said. 'Dominic arrived here with
the girl, brought her into the office, didn't introduce
you, and left again?'

'Yes, that's exactly what happened.'

'How did he travel to Breslin?'

'By – by motorcar,' Bernard said. 'I think.'

'Did you see the motorcar?'

'No.'

'So you don't know if anyone else was with them
in the car?'

'No.'

'Tony Lombard, say?'

Bernard shook his head.

Kenny said, 'What did Manone really want? A house, a property? Did you find one for him, Bernard? Did you offer him one off the books?'

'No,' Bernard said. 'No, no.'

'I'm sorry,' Kenny said, 'but I don't think you're telling the truth.'

'I am, I am,' said Bernard. 'What reason have I got to lie?'

'Plenty of reason. For one thing, you work for Dominic Manone.'

'Hold on, hold on,' Bernard said. 'I mean, for God's sake, you come waltzin' in here, tell me my marriage is liable to go up in smoke and Rosie is liable to find out she's got a crook for a father . . .'

'She's already got a crook for a brother-in-law,' Kenny put in.

'No,' Bernard said. 'No, no, no, no. I know where my loyalties lie. If it comes to protecting Lizzie and her girls or Dominic Manone then there's no question, no question at all, which way I'll go.' He sat up straight, palms pressed down on the desk. 'I'm not the only one in a cleft stick, am I? I think that's why you've come here to see me on your own. You haven't told your bosses in the CID about Conway yet, have you, Kenny?'

'He calls himself Harker now.'

'Harker, huh!'

'Edgar Harker,' Kenny said. 'He's been one of Carlo Manone's henchmen in Philadelphia for years. Whether he fought in the war or whether he didn't is something we haven't discovered. We've asked the Philadelphia police department and the Federal Bureau in Washington to post us anything they may have on Harker. We'll know more about him when the information arrives, probably.'

'Rosie will hate you for doing this to her.'

'I know,' Kenny said. 'You're right, Bernard. I haven't told anyone in the office who Harker really is. If – and it's a long shot – if I can get him out of Scotland, have him arrested elsewhere, then none of it may come out. Trouble is that Harker and Dominic Manone are working hand in glove and our department's under terrible pressure to put a stop to their activities.'

'I don't know anything about that,' Bernard said.

'It isn't a local matter,' Kenny said. 'It's a Home Office issue.'

'Home Office?'

'A matter of security.'

'I don't follow you,' Bernard said.

'We have reason to believe – sorry, but we do – that Dominic's working for or with the man who used to be Frank Conway.'

'And who's Conway working for?'

'Hitler,' Kenny said.

'Hitler?' Bernard said. 'Come on!'

'Or one of his Nazi cohorts,' Kenny said. 'Now do you see my problem?'

'Oh, aye,' said Bernard. 'I do.'

*  *  *

Over the curve of the field just where it ran into moorland a band of cornflower-blue sky had opened up in the cloud cover. Later in the evening there would be a sunset worth watching, one of those brooding, melancholy explosions of crimson and orange that might lead you to suppose that Arran's dormant volcanoes had surged awake to spew lava into the Firth and shoot great gouts of fiery trash into the heavens above Clydebank. From the attic skylight Tony would look out at the spectacle, would wonder if Polly was watching too or if, as she often did, she'd had the maid close the curtains early.

He walked out with Penny only because he didn't trust her, not when she had the .22 tucked under her arm and her trousers stuffed into the tops of a pair of his woollen stockings and galoshettes flapping on her big, inelegant feet.

She was, he reckoned, such an eccentric sight that any nosy official from the Civil Defence squadron in Hardgate who happened to be wandering in the area wouldn't forget her in a hurry or be inclined to swallow whatever tale she told him to explain what she was doing on Blackstone Farm.

He accompanied her over the cobbles of the yard, through the gate and into the wet, empty pasture, walking not by but behind her. Only when they were out of range of the farmhouse did she break step and, loitering, wait for him to catch up and, as he had feared she would, held out her hand.

The gun butt was pressed against her breast, stock cradled in her right hand. In that pose she looked every inch a hunter. He could just imagine her out with the menfolk in search of wild goats or boar in the wooded country north of Barga that his old man had told him about.

'Do you not want to take my hand, Tony?'

'Not when you're waving that gun about.'

'I am not waving it about. Take my hand.'

He felt like a fool, a cheat, but took her hand none the less.

She wore mittens, clumsy hand-knitted things that covered her palms and wrists but left her fingers bare. She took his hand firmly and when she had it in her grasp, crooked her forefinger and tickled his palm, scratched the ball at the base of his thumb with her fingernail. She leaned against him, rubbed against him like a cat, like Frobisher when Giffard put out the food bowl.

'What is wrong? Why are you so tense, darling?'

'I'm tired, that's all.'

'Did you not enjoy me?' Penny asked, still rubbing.

He didn't have the gall to answer her honestly. He was afraid of her or, rather, he was afraid of the effect that she had on him. He wanted to explore that sleek, elongated body, to make her writhe and beg him to stop, to prove who was master. But he could never be Penny Weston's master, not when he was in love with Polly Manone. He knew now that the urgent lovemaking to which he had subjected Polly was only an apology for love and that Polly had touched him in a way that this girl, any girl, no matter how sleek and beautiful and willing, could not.

'I made a mistake,' Tony said. 'Last night was a mistake.'

He tried to pull away but she held on tightly.

'I am a mistake? What happened was a mistake?'

'Yeah.'

She pouted for an instant, then laughed.

'Are you saying to me that it will not happen again?'

'Yeah, I am.'

'Is it because you are not in love with me you think what we did was wrong?'

'I didn't say it was wrong, just . . .'

'The mask, you liked it with the mask, did you not?'

He tugged his hand from hers. 'Listen,' he said. 'We've a job to do here, both of us. I can't cope with distractions.'

'Hoh! Am I a distraction now? I've never been called a distraction before.'

Four strands of wire separated the pasture from a strip of ploughed ground. The acreage, turned in the autumn, had been left to weather and the furrows, marled by rain and frost, swooped down into a plantation of young firs that gave protection from the biting east winds. Above the tree line the sky was waxing, the cornflower-blue patch expanding.

'You do not love me.' Penny pouted again.

'Of course I don't bloody love you.'

'I will put on my mask for gas and then you will love me?'

'No,' Tony said.

She adjusted the rifle, arched her back a little, offered her cheek. 'Not even one small kiss for me, here, where no one can see us?'

'I told you. It was a mistake.'

'I will catch you out.' She pivoted on the rubber heels and leaned all her weight against the sagging fence, careful with the gun, though, always careful with the gun. 'If I come to you tonight, when you are dreaming of someone else, will I not catch you out?'

'Be careful, Penny,' Tony said.

'There is someone else, am I not right?'

'None of your damned business. Just because we . . .'

'What? What do you call it? What name do you have for what we did together?'

'You've got more names for it than I have, I reckon,' Tony said.

He was tense: Penny was right about that. Being with her in open country with nothing but the rooftops of the farm building showing, he felt more vulnerable than ever. As a rule he was relaxed with women – except in the bedroom. He had never been casual about his performance in the bedroom, had never left a woman wanting more, never left them in tears. He might be more man than gentleman but he had never deliberately hurt a woman in his life.

Now *he* was hurting, hurting bad. He wanted Polly, to see her smile, hear her laugh, feel her slender arms about him, her small hard breasts pressing against him; not to use her, not to prove himself, not to count out her climaxes like loose change, but just to hold and protect her, assure her that he'd be there when she wakened in the darkness and needed him to keep her safe.

'I know all sorts of names for it,' Penny said. 'Love is not one of them.'

'I didn't figure it would be,' Tony said.

'I doesn't matter,' the girl said. 'I do not mind if you do not love me.'

'No, but I do.'

She smiled, a sly, secretive sort of smile.

'You are in love with someone else,' she said. 'I think you are in love with Dominic's wife.'

'You've got some imagination, kid,' Tony told her.

She bounced a little on wire, making the strands whirr and sing between the rotting posts. 'Does Dominic know?'

'It would never cross his mind,' Tony said, 'because there's nothing to it.'

'I am guessing,' the girl said. 'I guess that he would kill you if he found out that you were in love with his wife? He is Italian and you are Italian so he would feel entitled to kill you for betraying him. It is just like the opera, is it not, with all that loving and killing?'

'You're nuts, Penny, do you know that?'

'So I can ask him, can I? Ask Dominic about his wife? What will he tell me? That she is faithful, that she adores him, that she is the mother of his three lovely children and would never betray him with another man?'

'Two,' Tony said, 'just two children. And I wouldn't do that, if I were you.'

'I would like some of that,' the girl said.

'What? Children?'

'To be loved – just a little bit, to be loved,' Penny said. 'Perhaps I will ask Dominic to tell you to love me the way you love his wife. You will do as he tells you to do, will you not, darling? It will make me happy just to pretend.'

'Won't going back home with forty or fifty thousand dollars in your luggage make you happy?'

'Oh, I will have that too,' Penny said. She moved closer, sliding along the wire until she was almost beneath him. 'Maybe I will not have to ask Dominic for the other thing. Maybe you will give it to me without asking.'

'And maybe I won't,' said Tony.

She pushed herself upright, adjusting the angle of the rifle once more.

Even in the scruffy outfit and ugly rubber boots, she had a unique, dangerous quality that in the filament of sunlight appeared almost wicked; then

Tony realised that she was no longer looking at him. She was looking past him. Swinging round, he saw the hare limping across the crown of the pasture, just as the girl raised the rifle and fired. He heard the shot ring out, ring away into the distance, its echoes muffled by the trees.

The hare rose on its hind legs, sleek and slender ears cocked, fore paws bunched daintily at its breast; close enough for Tony to read its startled expression, one sad eye rolling as it caught the scent of its own impending death.

He heard her fire again.

She was rock steady, disciplined, light and smiling.

The hare swivelled in the air, flopped and lay struggling on its back, its long body bowed, its paws kicking ineffectually.

Penny ran towards it, reloading.

Tony followed as a dog might, lumberingly obedient. He imagined he knew what he would find but it was not what he expected, not bloody, not heavy, not a dead thing at all but a thing still alive. Its neck hairs glistened in the rays of the sun, neck twisted and head raised and in the little soft black curve of the mouth were two perfect prominent teeth, so pathetic, so beseeching that he felt as if the bullet had entered his belly and the sticky star of blood on the fur was his blood too.

The girl planted the heel of her boot on the hare's

hind legs and, leaning back to find an angle, fired a final shot into the head.

She shouldered the rifle and knelt, lifted the corpse by the ears.

'One for the pot,' she said. 'Big fellow too, a fine big buck by the look of it.'

Tony didn't answer. He was already walking rapidly towards the farmhouse, hands in pockets, shoulders hunched, his back turned towards the sunset and the cornflower-blue gap in the cloud.

# Chapter Eleven

In a more fanciful world there would have been a hidden entrance to John James Flint's headquarters above the Stadium Cinema. The cinema belonged to a company in which 'Flinty' Flint was a major shareholder and the construction of a sliding panel in the lavatory or a secret staircase sneaking up from the stalls would have been easy to arrange.

Johnny Flint didn't run that kind of organisation, however, and admission to the top-floor offices was via a grand wishbone-shaped staircase that cascaded down into a wide open yard behind the picture house. The stairs were topped by a beautiful wrought-iron railing against which John James Flint would lean while he sipped his mid-morning coffee or after-noon tea and surveyed the wall of a coal-merchants' dump and the towering edifice of the Paisley & District Flour Mill, as if the atmosphere of black dust and white was both aesthetically pleasing and a suitable symbol for the sporting empire over which he presided.

Flint had Dominic Manone to thank for his exalted position in the great grey netherworld of almost bloodless crime. It was on Manone's instruction that Flinty's boss, Charley – Chick – McGuire had met a sticky end some eight or nine years ago, a fact of which only four or five men had sure knowledge, and the police no knowledge at all. John Flint had not been one to waste a golden opportunity, however, and as soon as Chick had turned up dead in an alleyway on the other side of the river he had assumed control of the illegal book and the handful of other rackets by which Chick had turned a dishonest buck, and in the years that followed had spread his interests into the entertainment business, melding legal and illegal activities in a manner that bamboozled even the most diligent investigators.

He had purchased the Ferryhead Rowing Club from Dominic and had turned it into a billiard hall. He had paid fair money for the remnants of Manone's protection racket and the right to infiltrate the rich, feudal lands of Govan and Ibrox as far to the east as Gorbals. He was, and always would be, a street crook, however, for he had none of Dominic's panache when it came to socialising with stockbrokers and big-city businessmen. John Flint's contacts were limited to crooked councilmen, a handful of on-the-payroll policemen and an accountant who could make numbers dance like angels on the head of a pin.

He was sharp, natty, affable and unflappable. He had a shock of steely grey hair that was coifed by a professional barber three or four times a month, and the sort of vulpine good looks that maturity had only improved. Women thought he was wonderful. Even his new young wife, Natalie, was so hypnotised by his awful charm that she turned a blind eye to his outrageous philandering and never asked him to explain himself or demanded to be told what he was up to or where he had spent the night; she was, in fact, just grateful that he deigned to come home at all.

Flint was standing on the balcony sipping coffee when Dominic drove the Wolseley into the parking lot behind the cinema. There were few car owners in the vicinity of Paisley Road West and the quarter acre of asphalted ground behind the Stadium provided no cover for nosy coppers. For the most part it lay empty, save for Johnny's private transport and a couple of small delivery vans.

'Dom,' he called out. 'By God, you're a sight for sore eyes. Come up, for God's sake, man, come on up and let me take a look at you.'

They hugged at the top of the staircase and moved out of the damp January air through the big double-door that gave access to the offices.

Although it was still early afternoon the cinema had commenced its matinee performance and a mutter of gun-fire and thundering hooves and the ebb and flow of panic-stricken music filtered up into the office's carpeted corridor. In dockets and alcoves clerkesses were busy at typewriters and smart, Brylcreemed young men were hammering away on comptometers. In a shuttered office just outside Flint's private suite two well-groomed young women were managing a teleprinter, and the overall impression was one of clean-cut commercial endeavour, though who or what shady connections lurked at the end of the telephone wires was anyone's guess.

Still carrying his coffee cup, Flint ushered Dominic into the suite.

A far cry from Dominic's office in Central Warehouse, it was decorated more like a lounge bar or nightclub than a place of work. A massive walnut wood cocktail cabinet occupied half a wall, glasses and bottles glinting. Framed, signed photographs of football players, jockeys, and less-than-leading lights from theatre and film crammed every available inch of space. Pride of place was accorded to an enormous painting in the Landseer tradition of a greyhound – *Half Way Home* – posed on a rock at the top of a misty mountain, though what the animal might be seeking at that altitude Dominic could not imagine.

Flint's desk, a great flying wing fashioned from exotic hardwoods, seemed to come at you out of the light from the window, a glazed and tinted masterpiece that must have cost Flint more than a Clydeside riveter could earn in a lifetime. Standing behind the desk, as if he, not Flint, owned the place, was Edgar Harker, looking implacably American in a black alpaca overcoat and a suit with stripes so broad that you could have driven a tramcar along them.

There was, Dominic realised, a disturbing similarity between Harker and Flint, not so much in appearance as demeanour; a cocky, arrogant, superior manner that Johnny managed to make work for him but that Eddie Harker could not. He felt himself bristle at the sight of the little man who, like a pantomime villain, was stroking his moustache, and grinning.

'Surprise!' Edgar Harker said. 'Surprise, eh what?'

'You know Eddie, of course?' John Flint said.

'Of course,' said Dominic. 'I thought this was to be a private meeting, John?'

'No secrets from Eddie,' Flint said. 'Right, m'boy?'

'Right you are,' said Harker. 'I've just arrived myself, in fact.'

Dominic tossed his hat on to a padded banquette that filled a corner under the big painting. He took out and lit a small cigar, blew smoke, while Flint made the long trip around the desk and seated himself in an armchair.

Harker remained positioned at Flint's right hand.

'Where have you just arrived from?' Dominic said. 'Hull, by any chance?'

'Don't be so bloody sniffy, Dom,' said Harker. 'You got all I promised you.'

'Why didn't you tell me about Guido?'

'Didn't know about Guido.'

'What's happened to my aunt?'

'Teresa?' Harker said. 'She's gone to stay with Benedetta.'

'Who the hell is Benedetta?'

'Her younger sister. Surprised you didn't know that. She'll be safe as houses with Benedetta,' Harker said. 'Benny's boys are both army officers.'

'Where?'

'In Roma.'

'I didn't even know Teresa had a sister in Rome.'

'Lots of things you don't know, son,' Harker said. 'Lots of thing you really should try t' catch up on. Pronto, pronto.'

'I hate to interrupt this family reunion' Flint said, 'but time's money an' it's money we've come here to discuss. Dom, did you bring me a sample?'

'A sample of what?'

'The counterfeit notes you want me to put through the system.'

Dominic studied the end of his cigar and shifted his weight from one foot to the other, not awkwardly but in the manner of a boxer who might be called upon to weave and duck defensively.

At length he said, 'Just how much *has* friend Harker told you?'

'Pretty well everything,' Johnny Flint answered.

'Pretty well everything,' Dominic said. 'Then that's pretty well more than he's told me. How come you got involved before I did, Johnny? It was presented to me as an open and shut job – and my show.'

'Nope, it was never your job to handle distribution, Dominic,' Harker said. 'You print the goddamn things and we channel them through the system. That was the deal your old man laid out for you, wasn't it?'

'Who's "we"?' Dominic said. 'And what "system" are we talking about?'

'That don't concern you,' Edgar Harker said.

'Hang on,' Dominic said. 'The agreement was that I would manage the production of the notes for twenty-five per cent of market value. My old man told me I'd be expected to finance the management *and* distribution and . . .'

'Not distribution,' Harker said. 'That's always gonna be our pigeon.'

'So how do I get paid, on what reckoning?' Dominic said. 'Face value?'

'Hell no!' Harker said. 'That'd be far too much. You'll get what you were promised, son, which is twenty-five per cent of sale value of each run.'

'And you'll tell me what each run has fetched?' said Dominic.

'Prices are gonna vary,' Harker said. 'I mean, that's obvious. We sell down through a friend like Johnny here an' the price will be lower than if we trade through the foreign exchanges.'

'Trade in what currency?' Dominic said. 'Lira, dollars, Deutschmarks?'

'Who the hell cares?' Harker said. 'Rubles or kronen or even bloody pesetas if the rate is advantageous enough. The plates you were given were top-notch. A lot of sweat an' blood went into gettin' you the right paper an' the right inks. Your old man told me you had the best contact in creation for managin' the printing. Was he wrong? Ain't you an' your guy up to it?'

'Oh, we're up to it,' Dominic said. 'I just want to know where the materials came from, where they originated?'

'Does that really matter, Dom?' John Flint put in.

'Of course it matters,' Dominic said. 'We'll be running off a hundred thousand face value a month by Easter and the way it was explained to me we're expected to keep the run going at that rate of production for six or eight months.'

'Longer,' Harker said. 'Much longer.'

'So what do I do when the paper supply dries up.'

'We ship you another batch,' said Harker. 'Same quality.'

'If it's coming in from abroad, from Italy,' Dominic paused, 'or Germany . . .'

'It ain't comin' in from anywhere,' said Harker. 'It's here, a ton of it, all you'll ever need. Signed in and stored away in a nice, dry, rodent-proof warehouse. You think your old man would risk having an expensive cargo of manufactured paper confiscated at the ports or, worse, turned back like an Italian coal ship?'

'So,' Dominic said, 'I make, you distribute.'

'Yeah, that's it.'

'Where do I deliver?'

'You don't,' Flint said. 'I collect.'

'*You* collect.'

'Sure,' Edgar Harker said. 'Sweet, ain't it?'

'I don't see what's so damned sweet about it,' Dominic said. 'You expect me to stand back and watch a hundred thousand pounds in doctored fivers sail away in the back of one of Flint's vans every month, then hang around waiting for you to tell me how much – or how little – I'm going get for it. I'm already out twenty-eight hundred in basic expenses.'

'Take it off the top then,' Flint said.

'Is that what you've been promised?' Dominic said. 'A cut off the top?'

'Naw, that ain't what Johnny's been promised,' Harker said, a faint threatening snarl in his voice. 'We hand you a goddamn money-mill, son, an' you have the bloody gall to bicker about twenty-eight hundred.'

Dominic held up a hand placatingly.

'All right,' he said. 'All right.'

Harker stroked his moustache with bridged fingers and smiled broadly, showing the twisted scar and worn teeth. 'Aye, you're Carlo's boy, sure enough,' he said. 'I thought you'd no balls at all but I should've known better.' He chuckled, shook his head. 'I figured you'd quibble when it came to it, though, so I'm gonna make you a better offer.'

'Like what?' said Dominic.

'Five per cent face value on every cargo.'

'Five thousand a month ain't hay, Dominic,' Johnny Flint reminded him.

'You gear up to a higher production rate,' Edgar Harker said, 'we can cope with that. You make it, we take it, you get more moolah.'

'Why wasn't I offered those terms in the first place?'

'I thought you were,' Edgar Harker said, shrugging. 'Must've been a breakdown in communications somewhere along the line. Happens.'

'All right,' said Dominic again. 'Five per cent of face value is . . .'

'Generous, Dom, generous,' Johnny Flint put in.

'. . . acceptable,' Dominic said. 'Tell me, who pays the girl?'

'I do,' Edgar Harker said.

'She's thinks I'm her paymaster,' Dominic said.

'She can think what she bloody-well likes,' Edgar Harker said. 'She'll get her rake-off from me. Nobody else.'

'Is that all she'll get from you?' Dominic said.

'None of your goddamned business, son,' said Edgar Harker. 'Five thousand pounds clean cash money in your hot wee hand every calendar month, *that*'s your business. That's the offer I'm empowered to make. Now, no more stupid questions, Have we got a deal, or haven't we?'

'Yes, we've got a deal,' said Dominic and, sliding

on a satisfactory smile, shook Harker's outstretched hand.

It was long after Lizzie's usual time to sleep, but she could not shut an eye. She was worried about Bernard who had been so morose and uncommunicative these past few days that she felt alienated from his affections, though she couldn't for the life of her imagine what she'd done to offend him.

'It is not you, Mammy,' Rosie assured her. 'Bernard is mad at me for falling for a policeman. But I am not going to stop seeing Kenny, no matter how much Bernard sulks.'

Her daughter's explanation did seem logical, particularly as Bernard and Rosie no longer walked to the railway station together and one or other would contrive an excuse for leaving early. They barely spoke now and at meal times it was left to Lizzie to scrape the bones of conversations that died in vexatious little grunts or stone-cold silences.

The situation had become worse in the past couple of days. Bernard hadn't come home until after nine o'clock and had smelled of drink.

'Did you go for a dram with Mr Shakespeare, dearest?'

'No.'

'I just thought I smelled . . .'

'If I want to go for a dram with Shakespeare then I will.'

'Bernard, what's wrong?'

'Nothing's wrong. Nothing.'

Lizzie had no wish to turn into a nag and did not press him further. When he pushed away most of his dinner and refused his pudding, however, she began to fear that he was ill with some dreadful disease that he was keeping from her. Convinced that she had uncovered the truth, she lay awake in bed at night, listening intently to the sound of his breathing, waiting, really, for it to stop.

When she tried to hug him he pretended to be asleep and lay stiff as an ironing-board beside her or uttered a painful groan and rolled away from her, so far away that he was left hanging half out of the bed.

Alone in the house during the day, Lizzie frequently dissolved in tears.

She was even tempted to make the long journey across the city to call on Polly or on Babs but it wasn't just the river that separated her from her daughters now; the style in which they lived, their sophisticated acceptance of things that frightened her made it difficult for her to confide in them. She didn't want them to think that Mammy had turned soft in her old age. Besides, what did she really have to complain about; that Bernard was sulking; that Bernard might be ill? How daft those reasons seemed, how feeble. She had no proof that he was ill, only a paralysing anxiety that her silly hunch might actually turn out to be accurate.

Nights were the worst. He and she lay side by

side, not daring to hug and cuddle, jerking away when a knee brushed a hip or toes touched as if any sort of contact between them might prove to be contagious.

Lizzie crouched on her side, a pillow stuffed under her shoulder so that her head was raised up enough to allow her to look at the darkened ceiling instead of the darkened wall; the house so quiet that she could hear ash falling in the grate and now and then the hum of a late-night bus speeding past on the Anniesland Road.

She listened anxiously to Bernard's breathing, heard him sigh, then, shockingly, sob: one sob, like a raindrop, falling into the silence, then another and, loudly now, another. Suddenly her man, her tower of strength, was sobbing fit to burst. She rolled towards him at the same moment as he turned to her. Their arms tangled under the bedclothes and she found him, gathered him, shaking, into her embrace and pressed his lean body against her breasts to absorb his misery.

'Bernard,' Lizzie said, beginning to cry too. 'Oh, Bernard, Bernard, will you not tell me what ails you?'

'I'm frightened, Lizzie. I'm so frightened.'

'Oh dear, oh dearest, please tell me what you're frightened of?'

'Everything,' Bernard said.

She was overwhelmed by relief that she was not the reason for her husband's tears and believed she understood: he was worn out, poor lamb, tormented by worry about the possibility of war: that must be it, and that must be all.

Sighing, Lizzie drew him closer, almost enveloping him. She kissed and patted and hugged him, his head upon her breast, soothing him as if he were a child to whom the world meant nothing, nothing but a mother's love:

Until, exhausted by her many attentions, poor Bernard fell asleep.


The shop was busy that brusque early spring afternoon and even Albert had been routed from his bunker in the alcove to attend to casual customers. Mr McAdam and Mr Robert had gone off to a house sale in Jefferstone where there were many lots in the library and not much time to price up the catalogue. There had been problems in the packing department and an unusually heavy lunch-time post had come down from the secretary's office upstairs and Rosie had been co-opted to type out letters of quotation.

She was more than up to the task, of course, and had been distracted from her own concerns by a beautiful three-volume edition of Ackerman's *Microcosm of London,* with all one hundred and four coloured plates intact, which Brentano's had expressed an interest in buying.

She had lunched in that day, nibbling a sausage roll and drinking tea in the bleak little staff room in the basement while the packing department lads squabbled and swore and pranced in and out just to annoy her. She had eaten in yesterday and the day before too. It had been over a week since Kenny had appeared at the shop, over a week since they had shared a plate of macaroni-and-cheese in the Lido Café, over a week since she had heard a word from him.

Common sense told her that Kenny was busy, just busy, that awkward shifts and a full card of crimes had taken him away from her. Common sense also indicated that things between them were not as they had been before Christmas, however, and that now Kenny was practically her fiancé she deserved a little more consideration in the shape of a telephone call or a letter of explanation or apology. She was both annoyed and deeply concerned, panic-stricken in fact, at the prospect of never seeing Kenny again.

Common sense, a quisling virtue at the best of times, finally betrayed her. She was filled with not unrealistic imaginings that Kenny had decided to give her up rather than risk the wrath of his superiors in St Andrew's Street and that this was his cowardly way of waving bye-bye: or that he had discovered just how closely her sisters were involved in unimaginable crimes: or that he had finally realised that her deafness was an impediment that he didn't want to live with for the rest of his life, signing and stammering and being embarrassed by her shouting out in public, and that he didn't have the heart to tell her so face to face.

Even while she typed letters of quotation she felt helpless and abandoned and filled with self-pity, so much so that she didn't see Albert pad back into the alcove and pick up his pipe from the ashtray and almost jumped out of her skin when he put his hand on her shoulder.

'If,' Albert said, 'you're going to start cryin' lass, I think it might be an idea not to do it all over the Rowlandson plates.'

He fished in his breast pocket and found a clean if crumpled handkerchief, handed it to her, watched her blow her nose. He gave her a little pat on the shoulder and drawing his chair closer, seated himself by her side.

'Is it him? Have you heard from him?'

'Nuh-no, I huh-have not heard from him. Tha-ut's the trouble.'

'Bit early for a broken heart, though,' Albert said.

'Yuh-you don't understand.'

'Strange to relate, Rosie, I've had my share o' broken hearts,' Albert said. 'Long years ago, admittedly, but I can still remember how it hurt. When did you see him last?'

'Nine days ago.'

'Did you quarrel?'

'Nuh-nothing like that.'

'Then he's just busy.'

'He should have let me know. He should have been in touch.'

'Possibly,' Albert said. 'Think on this, though: the tramlines run both ways.'

'Pa'din?'

'You haven't been in touch with him, have you?' Albert said. Rosie wiped her cheeks with her knuckle, blew her nose once more and offered the handker-chief back to Albert. He shook his head. 'Keep it. I've another one at home. Now, answer my question, Rosalind? Have you let him know?'

'Whuh-what?'

'That you miss him. Why haven't you written to him?'

'It's not up to me. I'm a girl.'

'So what?' said Albert.

'Albert! I'm surprised at you!' Rosie said, more cheerfully. 'I thought you were still opposed to women having the vote. The fact of the matter is that I do not have Kenny's address.'

Albert smote his forehead with his palm forcefully enough to create a resounding smack that Rosie, of course, could not hear. She could read his expression, however, and exasperation was evident in his gesture.

'Call yourself a researcher,' Albert said. 'By gum, if Kenny was a copy of *First Principles* you'd find him fast enough, wouldn't you?'

'But I do not know where to begin?'

'Try the Post Office Directory,' said Albert.

*　　*　　*

There had been a special assembly in the police Gymnasium that afternoon which all ranks had been ordered to attend. The meeting had been addressed by no less a person than the Surgeon General, Sir James Wilkie, who had travelled from London to deliver a series of illustrated lectures on the organisation of air raid casualty services. Coloured slides depicted the effects of gas attack and the emergency treatment of victims in such grisly detail that several young constables were swaying in their seats and even Kenny, who had seen more than his fair share of charred and dismembered corpses, had had to lower his gaze a couple of times.

Among the civilian personnel only Fiona remained unfazed. Her blue eyes never left the screen for she found the graphic horrors more fascinating than shocking and couldn't wait to leap into a Civil Defence Volunteer uniform and begin saving lives.

At the end of the two-hour ordeal off-shift officers sidled away to wait for the pubs opening and those on-shift galloped along to the canteen for a reviving cuppa before reassembling in the muster room. Kenny would have prefered to leave with Fiona, for the lecture had depressed him. He had been summoned to Inspector Winstock's office to explain his recent failure to pull his weight, however, and trudged gloomily up the stone staircase and into the long corridor where the cupboard-sized offices of senior inspectors rubbed shoulders with the registration and licensing departments.

Winstock was already slumped in a wooden chair, smoking furiously.

He looked rumpled, his complexion ashen. Tell-tale stains of milky fluid at the corner of his mouth indicated that he had been tippling from a bottle of stomach medicine. His tongue, when he opened his mouth to speak, was pure white.

'What did you think of that then?'

'Interesting,' Kenny answered.

'Interesting?'

'Well, disturbing might be a better way of putting it, sir.'

'How did your sister take it?'

'She loved it.'

'Aye, she would,' Inspector Winstock said. 'I expect she'll be off as soon as the whistle blows, off like all the rest of you, and I'll be left here high an' dry with a bunch of old men and cripples. Will you stay on in the Force when the war comes?'

'I don't know, Mr Winstock.'

'Not you, Kenny,' the inspector said. 'You'll go leaping into the cannon's mouth first chance you get. God knows, son, you're a Highlander and Highlanders are always spoiling for a fight. The real battle won't be out there in Flanders, though. The real battle will be right here on our streets.'

'Yes, Mr Winstock.'

'I mean it.' He flicked a finger over the corner of his lips and removed the tell-tale stain. 'There will be fire raining down from the skies and the dead piled up on the streets like rats.' Kenny's depression was no match for the inspector's apocalyptic vision. 'Anyway,' Winstock went on, 'the Chief Constable wants to know what we're doing down in the basement, and since it's my head on the block, it's your head on the block too.'

'Manone hasn't turned up at the Athena again, sir.'

'God Almighty! I know Manone hasn't turned up at the Athena. Stone's been squatting in the damned lobby for weeks, ogling the tarts and having a high old time. I've taken him out of there and put him in a radio van across the street from Tony Lombardi's flat. And, guess what, Tony Lombardi's also done a bunk, vamoosed, vanished into thin air.'

'What about Dominic?'

'Oh, aye, your friend Dominic,' Inspector Winstock said. 'Why don't you tell me about your friend Dominic?'

'Haven't you read my report, sir?'

'This?' Winstock lifted a cardboard folder and shook it. 'This is toilet paper, Sergeant. What's more, you damned well know it's toilet paper. If you don't come through with something more valuable that this very soon then you'll find yourself interrogating the Irish and running up closes in the Gorbals searching for detonators.'

'I've been occupied with other cases.'

'Ballocks! Half a dozen domestics. I've checked the log. Where's Manone?'

'At home, at the warehouse.'

'Where's Lombardi then? Where's the blonde girl? Where's bloody Edgar Harker who, incidentally, has a file as long as your arm with the Philadelphia police department? A file as long as your arm.'

'Convictions?'

'One assault charge three years ago. Dismissed.'

'Is that all?'

'Yes, Sergeant, that's all.'

Kenny tried to control his mounting panic. He was not intimidated by the inspector's threats, though he knew his performance had been disappointing and that he deserved more than a verbal reprimand. He had been a good constable, an efficient and conscientious sergeant, had carved out a promising career as a detective. Now, at this moment, he was on the point of throwing it all away to satisfy an aspect of his character that he had never known existed.

He had felt pity for the urchins in the streets, compassion for some women and men who were regarded as the dregs of society, but that was a general thing, finite and individual. What he felt for Rosie Conway was quite different.

There was nothing in his experience to compare with it. If only his sister had been more − what? − human, perhaps, then he would have been able to ask her what to do about his troubled heart. But Fiona would only scoff at what she perceived as weakness. She had supported his unprofessional behaviour so far only because she was unclear precisely what or who the department was pursuing and because, he supposed, she loved him in her cold, clinical way. That situation wouldn't last much longer. He had detected a look in her eye today, a passionate enthusiasm for engagement, for a war in which she could participate and not merely translate. He couldn't depend on Fiona keeping quiet much longer.

What he should do, right here and now, was inform Inspector Winstock that he had discovered Edgar Harker's identity, then he would shine again. He would also be ordered to interrogate Lizzie Conway Peabody, however, and to put pressure on Bernard. Perhaps he would even be pulled off the investigation altogether, and it would all be up for Rosie and him.

He had avoided Rosie for nine long, unendurable days. He wasn't so naïve as to imagine that he could avoid her forever, though, or that the feelings inside him would lessen, that the pining in his heart would diminish. He was in danger of putting his career in jeopardy for the sake of a girl who might be a whole lot less innocent and vulnerable than he imagined her to be.

'You're not going to tell me anything, are you?' Inspector Winstock said.

'I'm sorry, sir, but so far I've drawn a blank.'

'What about the weak links you spoke of, what about them?'

'Who's that, Mr Winstock?'

'The mother, Peabody's wife, for a start.'

'She knows nothing.'

'Have you interrogated her?'

'Yes.'

'When?' Winstock said.

Kenny fabricated and answer: 'The weekend, at her house at the weekend.'

'It's not in your report. It's not even recorded in the log.'

'I did it on my own time, sir.'

'That's no damned excuse.'

'She knows nothing,' Kenny said again.

'Are you lying to me, son? Are you keeping something back?'

'No, Mr Winstock, I'm not.'

'If I didn't know you better, Kenny, I might even begin to suspect that you've drifted away from the straight and narrow and that Dominic Manone has been making you tempting offers.'

'Not true, sir. In fact, I resent the implication.'

'Did you really interrogate Lizzie Conway?'

'Yes, sir, and . . .'

'She's pure as the driven snow, I suppose.'

'Neither she nor her husband seem to know anything about what Manone's up to these days.'

'Either that or they're pulling the wool over your eyes.'

Kenny laid the tip of his tongue on his dry nether lip and licked it. It had grown dark outside and the rampage of traffic heading for the bridges indicated that the evening rush hour had already begun. Above the clash of tramcars and the rumble of horse-drawn carts he could make out the piercing cry of a corner newsvendor calling out the headlines from the evening edition.

'Are you still seeing the girl, the dummy?' Winstock said.

'She isn't a dummy, sir. She's deaf, that's all.'

'You've a big heart, son, taking on a dummy,' Winstock said, 'and a helluva cheek getting tangled up with a relation of Manone's.'

'I think I know what I'm doing, sir.'

'I wonder,' Winstock said. 'I really do wonder.'

'If you're not happy with my performance, Inspector Winstock, or if you suspect my integrity you can always have me transferred.'

'No, I'm not gonna do that,' Winstock said. 'I'm gonna give you a week, Sergeant MacGregor. One week. Seven days to bring me something concrete on Harker or the girl or, for that matter, on Manone. I'm sick to death of working in the dark. I need to know just what the Eye-tie is up to and since you seem to be closer to him than anybody else it's up to you to find out. Do I make myself clear, Sergeant?'

'As crystal, sir,' said Kenny.


The tenement was quite swanky, at least by Rosie's lights. There were no lavatories to stink up the landings and ornamental tiles gleamed on the walls. There was still that damp-dungeon smell, though, that every tenement close in the city, posh or poverty-stricken, shared to some degree.

On the second floor an engraved brass plate told her that the apartment of K. R. & R. F. MacGregor was precisely where the Post Office Directory had indicated it would be. Beneath the rectangular plate was a smaller circular plate with an ivory button in the centre and the words *Push Me* scrolled around it, an instruction that brought *Alice in Wonderland* popping into Rosie's head. She would not have been entirely surprised if the Duchess had opened the door to her, or even the White Rabbit, for such bookish little fantasies calmed her in times of stress.

She thumbed the button, rang the bell, stepped back.

The door opened as swiftly as if the woman had been waiting for her. No Duchess, no White Rabbit, and certainly no Kenny; the woman, though not tall, had a severe and imposing presence that made Rosie want to turn on her heel and run.

She was difficult to read, mouth firm, lips compressed, the obvious vowel almost invisible.

'Yes?'

Losing control, Rosie bellowed, 'I am looking for Suh-sergeant Mack-Gregor, Suh-sergeant Kuh-kenneth Mack-Gregor.'

'All right, all right, no need to shout. I'm not dea . . . Ah, but you are!'

The frown brought form to the woman's face, made it less classically austere, more human. The blue eyes were hard, though, when she pursed her lips she had the look of a nun about her, one of the stern teachers at the School for the Deaf. A stiff, laced-collared white blouse and pleated black skirt fostered that daunting impression.

'Is Suh-sergeant Mack-Gregor at home?'

'No, he's on duty. You're Rosie, are you not?'

'Pa'din?'

'Kenny's on duty. Are you Rosie?'

'Yes.'

The woman's frown did not yield to a smile but at least she had the decency to shape her words more clearly.

'Come in,' she said. 'Yes, come in. It's high time I had a word with you.'

And Rosie, not quite trembling, stepped into Fiona's lair.


Kenny was stuck, desperately stuck. He had lost the thread of the investigation entirely or, more accurately, had never picked it up in the first place. There were none of the usual leads to follow, no battered corpse, no bloodstains, no fingerprints, no shattered shop front or blown safe, no footprints, tyre tracks or witnesses to the event. There had been no event, in fact, no episode or incident from which Inspector Winstock's little band could trace their way back through motive and opportunity to collar a murderer, embezzler, or thief. So far no crime had been committed, certainly no crime of sufficient magnitude to attract the attention of the Home Office.

Dominic Manone had been up to his ears in shady dealings for years, of course, and, like his father before him, had sailed so close to the wind on occasions that only luck and a skilful lawyer had kept him out of the dock. He had never had any truck with Glasgow's notorious gangsters and, though he had employed some thick-eared louts in his day, had never been personally involved in acts of violence. No one had ever turned King's against him, which suggested loyalty bought and paid for rather than loyalty induced by fear.

Kenny had no doubt that Dominic Manone had locked on to something big this time, something that the gentlemen in London had got wind of. With war looming and Fascist spies under every bed, Percy Sillitoe's boys in blue were expected to put a stop to it before it even happened which, given the Glasgow CID's limited resources, was a tall order indeed.

Kenny went down to the basement office which, at that hour of the evening, was deserted. He had bought himself a sausage sandwich from the canteen and, with a mug of luke-warm coffee and ten Player's Weights, settled himself at the table under the lamp to do a bit of brooding before he signed off for the night.

He hauled out his sister's typed reports together with bulky files of clippings and translations that she had compiled over the past half-year and spread them out on the table. He munched the sandwich, sipped coffee, and treated himself to one of the little cigarettes to aid his concentration – but there was nothing to concentrate on and no sudden flash of inspiration, no blinding insight came to him.

At ten to eight he replaced the files, dusted crumbs off the table, switched out the lamp, climbed back up to street level and signed off at the desk. The main doors batted open and shut as officers in and out of uniform came and went and the smell of Glasgow on a dank weekday night came drifting in to the hall. Kenny put on his overcoat, stuck his hat on his head, stepped out into St Andrew's Street, turned right and set off towards the Trongate to catch a tram home.

She was standing outside one of the closes, not leaning on the wall but upright, arms folded across her stomach, handbag clutched in both fists. She did not have the appearance of a prostitute or even a beggar and, given her posture, certainly wasn't drunk.

Kenny barely glanced at her and would have gone on by if she hadn't stepped in front of him and caused him to execute a deft soft-shoe shuffle to avoid collision. Next thing he knew her hand was fixed on his sleeve like a claw.

He gave an involuntary little shake, then a wrench, but she clung to him and brought him round to face her before she said his name: 'Sergeant MacGregor.'

He peered at her in the streetlamp light.

'Miss McKerlie?'

'Aye, it's me.'

'What on earth are you doing here?'

'I've been waitin' for you.'

'But how did you know where to find me?'

'Headquarters,' Janet McKerlie said, nodding. 'Detectives live there.'

'I could have been anywhere, though, or not on duty.'

'I waited last night too.'

'Good God!'

'An' the night before. I knew you'd show up eventually.'

'Look . . .'

'Where is he? Where's Frank?'

'I don't know.'

'Have you not found him?' Janet McKerlie said.

'Not – no, not yet. It takes time. I mean, for all we know he may not be in Glasgow. May have gone elsewhere, moved along.'

She continued to hold on to his sleeve with her little grasping claw. One good swipe with the handbag would have knocked Kenny for six. He raised his arm a little to protect himself just as a clerk from the licensing office came up behind him, touched him on the shoulder, muttered, 'Aye, aye, bit on the old side for you, Sergeant,' and went on towards Glasgow Cross without a backward glance.

'You took his photo,' Janet said. 'Frank's photo.'

By the light of the street lamps he saw that her face was grotesquely daubed with powder, rouge and lipstick. Her hair had been dyed and waved and dangled from beneath her cup-shaped hat in doughy russet coils. The overcoat, if not brand new, had been cleaned, the fox-fur collar brushed.

He was tempted to break free, run down to Glasgow Cross, hop a tramcar, leap on to a bus, anything to get away from this woman, this parody who, he couldn't help but recall, was Rosalind's aunt.

'No,' he heard himself say. 'No, Miss McKerlie. I didn't take his photo. It's an old photograph, an old likeness. It came off the file. I honestly don't know where he is right now.'

A brace of constables came tramping along the pavement. They knew perfectly well who Kenny was but paused none the less to ask Janet if the gentleman was giving her trouble. She answered that he was not and the constables, chuckling at their little joke, went on around the corner into St Andrew's Street.

Kenny said, 'Have you had your tea?'

'I came straight from the dairy.'

'Is that where you work?'

'Aye. Sloan's.'

'Well,' Kenny said, 'you must be ready for your tea.'

'I'm not carin' about my tea. You promised you'd bring Frank to see me.'

'I promised nothing of the kind,' Kenny said.

It occurred to him that Inspector Winstock might not have a 'lodge meeting' that evening and might at any moment appear around the corner; and old

Wetsock would not be so readily put off or so easily amused as the constables.

'Come on,' Kenny said. 'I'll stand you a bite.'

'A what?'

'A bite. Something to eat.'

'I'm not needin' you for t' feed me.'

'For God's sake,' Kenny snapped, and without further argument linked her arm to his and dragged off towards the Trongate where he knew there was a fish and chip shop with a sitting-room at the rear.

Fiona had always hoped that her brother would marry a girl of some intellectual capacity and when she first clapped eyes on Rosie Conway she was disappointed and couldn't quite fathom what Kenny saw in her, apart from an obvious vulnerability that her big, soft-hearted brother probably found appealing.

After a few minutes of casual conversation, however, Fiona began to detect something of herself in Rosie Conway, just a trace of the innocent girl-child who had come down to Glasgow from the isles and who, until then, had shown no aptitude for anything much except teasing Kenny and making mischief on the farm. A year at language school had matured Fiona, though, and she had gone off without a qualm to the University of Wurzburg for two terms of special training. Her father had had to scrape the barrel to pay her fees and Kenny, still in constable's uniform, had added a few pounds from his meagre wage, but neither Daddy nor Kenny could have possibly foreseen just what sort of instruction she would receive in the shadow of Marienberg Castle on the banks of the Main.

In retrospect it seemed incredible that a man like Max von Helder and a farmer's daughter from Islay should have met at all, particularly in an old Bavarian town ringed with Baroque prince-bishop's palaces, Gothic churches and rococo gardens. Max was an officer in the Luftwaffe and had been posted from Ulm to Wurzburg to polish up his English for reasons that he could or would not explain. He was everything that Fiona had imagined a German would be: tall, slim-waisted, blond, blue-eyed, well-mannered and charming. Every girl in the Universität was intrigued by him but he, by his own choice, was Fiona's friend; just her friend, not her sweetheart, not her beau, not – not then – her lover.

He took her under his wing and showed her all the sights; the Tiepolo frescoes in the Residenz, the cathedral, the sarcophagus of the Irish monk St Kilian, Apostle of the Franks, with whom Max wrongly supposed she would have an affinity. He taught her to enjoy wine, the best Franconian vintages, to fall in love with the views from the Furstengarten, and asked her questions, endless questions, about 'her country' which one day he hoped to visit.

He spoke of the war, of the depression in Germany, of the political necessity of being rid of von

Hindenburg from the Reichstag, spoke too of the vigour of the National Socialist Party whose ranks were already swelling with young idealists who wanted no truck with Marxists or the Wise Men of Zion, and to whom the notion of *Gleichschaltung* – co-operation – was not anathema but tonic. He talked quietly, sometimes in English, sometimes in German, talked charmingly, almost convincingly, of the future of Germany and of England's past, but he did not attempt to kiss her or to put an arm around her waist, not once in all the time they were together down in quaint old Gothic Wurzburg.

Max left six weeks before Fiona's second term was up. He wrote to her from Ulm, from Northeim and from Hanover. He sent her pamphlets and snippets from local newspapers and, finally, an invitation to join him for five days sightseeing in Berlin just before she sailed for England.

Fiona knew by then that she was not in love with Max von Helder.

In fact, she disliked the shabbiness of his ideals, but two terms at the Universität would probably be the great adventure of her life for she would have no opportunity, or money, to travel abroad again. She was no longer a naïve island girl-child, and had Max von Helder to thank for that, at least in part. She understood only too well what Max wanted and that if she went to Berlin she would give it to him and that he would be too arrogant to realise that she, not he, had set the terms for their love-making.

He put her up in a fifth-floor room in a modern hotel close to the corner of the Friedrichstrasse and Unter den Linden. He took her for lunch at the Hotel Baur, for coffee at Kranzier's, and to a mass meeting of the NSDA, three or four thousand strong, in one of the squares. There she heard for the first time, and possibly the last, the persuasive voice of one of the party's twelve deputies, Joseph Goebbels, and observed, with satisfaction and some excitement, the brawling that went on in the side streets outside the railings.

That night she put on a new cotton nightgown, lay upon the huge bed in the fifth-floor bedroom and invited Max to make love to her.

He was cautious at first, then lascivious, then triumphant at having taken the virginity of an English girl. Fiona hadn't the heart to tell him that she was Scottish and had been willing, and no victim at all.

On parting Max promised to write, to visit her in England if he could. She was under no illusions that he would do so and did not expect to hear from him ever again. He'd had what he wanted from her. She in turn had taken what she wanted from both Max and Germany. She had no guilt about the matter, only concern that she might become pregnant and she had endured a month of anxiety on that score, a nervous, snappish time that Kenny put down to misery at being back home in dear old dowdy Glasgow.

'Why did you come here tonight? Fiona said. 'I'm

sure Kenny didn't invite you or he'd have made a point of being here.'

'I have not seen him for over a week,' Rosie said.

'A week? A whole week?'

'I – I thought he might be avoiding me.'

'He's very busy. It's quite chaotic down at police headquarters.'

'So he – he has not given me up?'

'I doubt it,' Fiona said. 'What makes you think he might give you up?'

'Because of who I am.'

They were seated knee to knee in the parlour that adjoined the kitchen.

Fiona crossed her legs and braced an elbow on the drop-leaf dining-table and said, 'Because you're deaf, you mean?'

'Because of who my sister is married to,' Rosie said.

The girl was not ingenuous enough to assume that Kenny had kept anything back from her, Fiona realised, and was grateful for her candour. It was one thing for a daft wee factory lassie to fall like a ton of bricks for an unsuitable male but quite another for an intelligent girl like Rosie Conway to admit to having given her heart away.

'So it's a question of loyalties, is it?' Fiona said.

'Yes. I know what Kenny stands to lose.'

'I'm not even going to ask if you're in love with him.'

'I would not be here if I was not.'

'Oh, you might,' said Fiona. 'You might be here because your brother-in-law suggested you keep in with Kenny.'

'No. I never see Dominic, hardly ever, and I really do not know anything about what he—'

'Yes, yes,' said Fiona. 'But you do see your sister, and your mother.'

'I live with my mother. What does my mother have to do with it?'

'She's the hub of the family circle,' Fiona said. 'Where would my brother fit into a family circle like yours, I wonder? Have you given that any thought, Rosalind?'

'I've thought of hardly anything else for weeks,' Rosie said.

'And what's your answer?'

'I do not have one.'

There was something pleasantly intense about the deaf girl; her need to lip-read and the concentration it entailed would be at the root of it, of course. But there was more, a soberness, a fierce, rather chilling need to have her say. She was no milksop, no yielder. Fiona chose her words with care.

'Sooner or later,' she said, 'there's going to a war with Germany. I take it you are aware of that probability, Rosalind?'

'All too aware.'

'And when that happens everything will change.'

'Yes, my father has explained it to me.'

'Your father?'

'My stepfather, Bernard. Kenny met him at Christmas.'

'Oh, yes, your stepfather, of course,' Fiona said. 'Has your stepfather told you that if there is a war with Italy your brother-in-law is most likely to be arrested?'

'Dominic is Scottish. He's a British citizen.'

'Even so.' Fiona said, shrugging. 'Everyone who isn't a British national will fall under suspicion.'

'What does this have to do with Kenny and me?'

'Rather a lot,' said Fiona. 'If your brother-in-law, Dominic Manone, is removed from the equation then there's absolutely no impediment to you and Kenny getting married – if that's what you want to do.'

'Has Kenny mentioned marriage?' Rosie asked.

'It's safe to say it's been on his mind, yes.'

The girl smiled. She looked quite different when she smiled. There was something about her, Fiona realised, that made you want to please her; a dangerous characteristic.

'Why did you never get married?' Rosie asked.

Fiona cleared her throat, and said, 'No one ever asked me.'

'That is a shame.'

'It isn't the be-all and end-all for women, marriage,' said Fiona, testily.

'Wouldn't you like to get married?'

'I have a job, a career, and if there's a war . . .' Fiona shrugged again.

'Will you join up?'

'I might. Yes, I expect I will,' Fiona said.

She wasn't quite sure how the conversation had swung on to her problems or if the deaf girl had turned it deliberately.

'I don't know what I will do,' Rosie said. 'I would not be much use as an air raid warden, would I?' She laughed. 'I want to marry. I want to marry Kenny.'

'And have children?'

'Perhaps.'

'And perhaps this is not the best time to be bringing children into the world.'

'If Kenny left the police force, if he joined the army instead . . .'

'Ah!' Fiona said. 'So that's your little scheme, is it?'

Rosie looked puzzled. 'Scheme? I am not scheming.'

'My brother might be forced to stay on in the police.'

'Forced?'

'As soon as a war is declared, perhaps even before then, a little thing called the Emergency Powers Act will be brought to bear and we won't be able to call our souls our own,' Fiona said. 'Do you hear what I'm saying, Rosalind?'

'Yes, I hear you.'

'Firemen and policemen and shipwrights and steel

workers and, oh, a host of other trades will become crucial to the war effort and some younger men will have to be left at home to staff these trades and services.'

'You sound just like my teacher, Mr Feldman.'

'I am a teacher; at least I was,' Fiona said. 'I apologise if I've been lecturing you but you don't seem to understand the gravity of the situation.'

'I do not remember the last war but Bernard has told me about it. Do you remember the last war?'

'I was a child, a child on a farm on an island called Islay.'

But she did remember the last war, how her father had tried to enlist and how he had been turned down for service because he was weak in one arm, an arm almost torn off by a bull at the Dalmally market in the year that Kenny had been born. It seemed that a man who could work a team of plough horses or shear a flock of sheep could not necessarily fire a rifle or load a howitzer. Her father had not been dismayed at being rejected and, as the war had dragged on, he had often expressed relief that he had been permitted to stay safe at home. He was too down-to-earth a person, her father, to brand himself a coward for not dying in the trenches like many of the young men from the island. She thought, in the same breath, as it were, of Max again, of the vicious nature of his patriotism, his thirst for conquest, and wondered vaguely if he were even now flying bombing missions in Spain, rehearsing for a greater conflict to come.

Rosie got to her feet suddenly. 'I am sorry. I should not be asking these impertinent questions. I only came here to see if Kenny was – was all right.'

'He's fine,' said Fiona.

She would have liked the Conway girl to stay, to talk, to provide her with company until Kenny came home but she was wary of any relationship that involved even a modicum of surrender. It was as if she had used it all up eight years ago in Germany, in that hotel room in Berlin, with Max.

She got to her feet too. 'I will tell him you called.'

'Will you tell him, please, that I miss him.'

And Fiona said, not sternly, 'Of course I will, my dear.'

# Chapter Twelve

It was one of those dull, cold, depressing February spells when all signs of an early spring had been crushed by hoar-frost and heavy, snow-laden cloud but Penny had done her level best to prevent Tony slipping into black, snarling moods and Dougie from freezing to death in the stables where he spent long hours matching up the printing machines.

Even Frobe seemed mournful and would trail in from hunting expeditions mewing plaintively, head first to the food bowl and then to the hearth where she would stretch out before the grate and ignore all Tony's efforts to get her to move.

Penny cleaned and cooked, drank coffee – and ate too much.

She'd gained pounds since coming to Blackstone and her clothes pinched in all the wrong places. She'd tried to discipline herself to go for a walk every afternoon but the weather was awful and Tony refused to let her stray further from the house than the end of the pasture. She'd also tried limbering with the rhythmic exercises she'd been taught in League camp some years ago but she was no longer a nimble teenager and soon became breathless and disheartened. She was turning into a frumpy *hausfrau* whether she liked it or not, a wife without the consolation of a man to share her bed. Several times she'd tried to persuade Tony to make love to her again for she felt that if she could please him in that way he would stop despising her and perhaps even abandon his passion for Dominic's wife.

Meanwhile, they read books and magazines, attempted crossword puzzles, completed intricate jig-saws, drank too much, ate too much, and talked as little as possible in the tedious hours between meals.

Penny didn't even have the pleasure of shopping for groceries now, for Tony had forbidden her to accompany him into Breslin which, according to Tony, was crawling with tin-pot officials all far too nosy for their own or anyone else's good.

Then one afternoon Tony informed her that he was going away for a day, possibly two, warned her not to wander far from the farm and told Giffard to keep out of sight if a Civil Defence volunteer or local copper showed and started asking awkward questions. Penny watched him drive away in the Dolomite, certain that he was going off to meet his lover, Polly Manone.

It was wearing on towards dark before Dougie

came in from the stables with the cat hanging on his shoulder. He stroked the animal gently, tickled her ears and crooned to her before he set her down on the kitchen floor by the food bowl to scoff the mutton scraps that Penny had put out after lunch.

Penny was baking. Breslin was not short of cake shops but beating sponge mixture was good exercise and an excellent way of passing the time. She wore an apron over a blue twill skirt and had her hair bound up in a bandanna.

Dougie said, 'Tell me, Penny, who does your hair?'

'I do it myself,' Penny said, glancing up from the bowl. 'Why is it you ask?'

'I could do with a trim, if you've got the time.'

'You wish me to cut your hair?'

'It's clean. I had a bath this mornin'.'

Penny pushed the bowl away. She was pleased by the diversion but not at all sure that Giffard wasn't flirting with her.

As if reading her thoughts, Dougie teazed his greying locks and said, 'Tony won't take me down to the barber in Hardgate an' I'm beginnin' t' feel like the wild man o' Borneo.

Penny laughed. 'Oh, very well. Place a chair under the light and I will find my scissors and make you respectable.'

'I doubt that,' Dougie said. 'Tidy'll do.'

She washed sponge mixture from her hands and went upstairs and brought down her special make-up bag, took out a pair of long-bladed scissors, a little pair of clippers and a miniature razor with a sharp, fixed blade. She found a bath towel on the rack in the laundry room, swept it around Dougie's neck and tucked it under his collar.

'Sit,' she said.

Obediently he seated himself on the upright chair directly under the light.

She moved behind him, lifted a comb and the long scissors and touched his hair lightly, flicking the comb and scissors through it. She had never touched Giffard before and she was surprised at how pleasant and consoling the intimacy was. She lifted a tuft of hair with the back edge of the comb and snipped it off.

'Ah'm no' wantin' a Barlinnie special, remember,' Dougie said.

'What is that?'

'A prison haircut, a baldie.'

Penny laughed again.

It was almost dark outside and she had a strange feeling that it might snow tonight. She found that prospect exciting. Behind her, almost at her heels, Frobe stretched out in front of the fire, purring loudly. She ran her fingers through Giffard's hair and with her thumb tweaked down his right ear, snipped carefully, snipped again. He sat patiently under the bath towel, moving his head only when she told him. She pressed her breasts against his shoulder blades and lifted the fringe of thinning hair over his brow: snipped.

Dougie said, 'Has he gone off for t' be with his girlfriend?'

'I expect that may be so,' said Penny.

'An all-nighter?'

'Probably, yes.'

Dougie said nothing for a while.

Then, 'You're no Jew, Penny, are you?'

She stopped, scissors poised.

Dougie said, 'An' you've never been in Vienna in your life.'

She worked the comb, lifted hair, trimmed it away.

'How do you know?' she said.

'Hummelstreek,' Dougie said. 'I just made the name up. There's no such mountain that I know of.'

'Oh, I see. It was a trick.'

'Where are you really from? Germany?'

'Yes,' Penny said. 'Berlin.'

'This money we're makin', is it for the Nazis?'

'That is not my concern,' Penny said.

She felt no sense of shame and no panic at being caught in a lie. The story had not been watertight in the first place and the only surprise was that it had taken someone like Dougie Giffard to guess the truth. She bore no animosity towards the little Glaswegian, had no desire to hide from him or invent more lies.

She said, 'Does it concern you who the money is for?'

'Naw, not much,' Dougie said.

'You are wrong about the other thing, however.'

'What's that?'

'It is true that I am not a Jew. I am a half-Jew. My mother is Jewish.'

'So you weren't chased out o' Vienna?'

'Of course I was not,' said Penny. 'I have never been to Vienna.'

'What does your old man do?'

'My old man?'

'Your father? Is he a Nazi?'

'My father is dead.'

She felt Dougie stiffen a little and knew that he would be frowning that deep, steep frown. She ran a forefinger down the nape of his neck and felt him shiver.

'I'm sorry to hear that,' Dougie said.

'You do not have to be sorry. It is nothing to you.'

'Did your father engrave the plates?'

'He was involved in making the plates, yes.'

'So the plates are your inheritance, your legacy?'

Penny laughed softly. 'What a fanciful person you are, Dougie. No, the plates are not my inheritance. My father was not an engraver. He was a banker. The plates were made by a team, a team that was taken over when he died.'

'Taken over by the Nazis, you mean?'

'By the party, a branch of the party.'

'Was your old man murdered?'

'Of course he was not murdered. He died of a disease in the kidneys.'

'Is your mother still in Germany?'

'You are very good at asking questions,' Penny said. 'My mother is in New York now, with her sister in New York. It was through my mother's sister that Carlo Manone became involved in all of this.'

'Why didn't this Nazi "team" you talk about just take over completely,' Dougie said. 'Why did they bother wi' Carlo Manone at all?'

'They required the currency to be manufactured in England.'

'I thought it was just a bit too well organised,' Dougie said. 'I take it you stayed on in Berlin t' make sure your mother gets somethin' out of it?'

'That is correct.' She busied herself with his hair and for several seconds neither of them spoke and there was no sound in the kitchen but the purring of the cat and the rapid clickety-click-click of the little steel blades. Then Penny said, 'Are you going to tell Tony what I have told you?'

'Naw.'

'Will you not tell Dominic?'

'Why would I want t' tell Dominic?'

'Because he pays you. Because he is your boss.'

Dougie gave a wry little grunt. 'I don't know who mah boss is an' I don't care much. There's big money to be made off of this operation an' all I want is a wee share. I owe somethin' to Dominic for keepin' me

339

alive but all Dominic's doin' is payin' off his father's debt. If you ask me, Penny Weston, the bulk o' the profits from the money we manufacture will go t' finance agents.'

'Agents?'

'Nazi sympathisers in Britain. God knows there's enough o' them. There's a new name for them now,' Dougie said. 'It's called a Fifth Column; an army wi' no uniforms or guns, but ready an' willin' t' fight from the inside when the time's ripe.'

'Informers?'

'Informers, saboteurs, spies; they'll all need funds.'

'Counterfeit money?'

'The best counterfeit money that money can buy.' Dougie fumbled under the bath towel and eased out an arm. He flung the towel back like a toga and, without turning, held up his hand. In it was a five-pound banknote. 'Money like this.'

Penny put down the scissors, took the banknote reverently between fingers and thumbs, her blue eyes round as moons.

'*O Gott! O Gott!*' she whispered. 'You have done it. You have truly done it.'

'Aye, I have,' Dougie said. 'What's more, it is damned near perfect.'

'Perfect!' Penny gave a hop of delight. 'I knew that you would make it perfect.' She leaned over the chair-back and kissed the printer on the brow. 'When do you think you can begin the run?'

'Two weeks, maybe three,' Dougie Giffard said.

Leaning over him, breasts brushing his cheek, she held the note out.

'Keep it, lassie, keep it as a souvenir,' Dougie Giffard said. 'Before the summer's over we'll have a hundred thousand more.'

She wore an elongated Rodex country style overcoat and a navy blue hat that rendered her almost invisible against the great mass of the privet hedge.

Tony fisted the steering wheel and slid the motor-car alongside the kerb. She scuttled out of the shadows so furtively that for an instant he was not entirely sure that it was Polly at all. She jerked open the door on the passenger side and flopped in beside him, did not reach for him, did not offer him a kiss: said, 'Drive, Tony, drive away quickly.'

'My place?'

'No. No, around the park, just around the park.'

'Is Dominic . . .'

'For God's sake drive, will you?'

He found gear, pressed the accelerator and shot the Dolomite forward away from the Manones' drive-way. Polly's urgency, her lack of interest in anything but escape hurt him. He had been looking forward to the moment of meeting, to seeing her smile, to having her in his arms. Now he was roaring around the corner with tyres squealing as if this were a getaway and not a lovers' tryst.

'Why did you call me?' Polly said.

'I needed to see you,' Tony said.

'Did you have to leave a message with Leah?'

'You never seem to be at home these days.'

'If you gave me your number . . .'

'I don't have a number,' Tony said. 'There's no phone where I am.'

'I'm not one of your tarts, Tony. You can't just ring me up and expect me to drop everything and come to you because you fancy it.'

She hadn't looked at him yet, hadn't met his eye. She sat with her head down, picking at the stitching of her glove.

He had no notion where they were and turned the steering wheel automatically whenever a corner presented itself: somewhere in the hinterland of Manor Park, on a tree-lined avenue among the mansions: disorienting to be cruising the Glasgow suburbs after weeks cloistered on the farm: strange to be with Polly, not the Polly he had yearned for night after night but someone else, someone different: had she changed, he wondered, had he? He glanced at her again. She turned her head away.

'I hate being treated like a tart,' Polly went on. 'I hate being summoned just when you need a woman. I'm not at your beck and call, Tony. If that's all you want from me then I suggest you find someone else.'

'I'm love in with you, for God's sake.'

'I don't think you are,' Polly said. 'If you were really in love with me you wouldn't treat me like dirt.'

'I'm not treating you like – like anything.'

'Where *are* you, Tony?' She swung round and clutched his forearm. 'God, I don't even know where you are? Why won't you tell me?'

'I did tell you.'

'Breslin! Where in Breslin? What are you doing there?'

'I can't tell you that, Polly.'

'In that case I'm afraid you'll have to choose.'

'Choose?'

'Between Dominic and me,' said Polly.

'You're crazy!'

'No, you're the one who's crazy. You tell me you love me, snap your fingers and expect me to tumble into bed with you but you don't even have enough faith in me, enough trust to tell me where you are and what you're doing.'

'I don't force you, Polly. I've never forced you.'

'I didn't say you had.'

'If you're tryin' to tell me you're not – that you weren't in love with me . . .'

'You don't know the meaning of the word, Tony.' She let out a sigh and, taking her hand from his forearm again, looked pointedly out of the side window. 'Where are we?'

'I thought we might go to my place.'

'No.'

'Half an hour, Polly – just to talk.'

'I've nothing to say to you, Tony.'

'Please,' he said. 'Please, let me try to explain.'

'There's nothing you can say that will change my mind.'

'Is this it? Is it over?'

She did not answer him at once. She leaned her brow against the side window and he knew that she was weeping. Her tears hurt him more than her anger. He eased the pace of the car to a crawl and put an arm about her, holding her tentatively, hoping, still hoping, that she would turn back to him, beg his forgiveness and assure him she understood how it had to be between Dominic and him. She pressed her brow against the glass, sobbing, as unsettled by his tenderness as if this was the first step in their relationship and not, possibly, the last.

'I don't know,' she said, her voice choked. 'I don't know whether it's over or not. It's – it's up to you, darling, very much up to you.'

He turned the wheel gradually, prowling the Dolomite around a left-hand bend, and knew now where he was. He pressed down on the accelerator and put both hands on the wheel. There was a slow suffusion of gratitude within him, nothing so grand as elation, though. He needed her, wanted her – and Polly still needed and wanted him. He was sure of it, sure that he would not have to go through an ordeal of negotiation to prove just how much he loved her.

He drove briskly, swung the car into the sloping courtyard behind the block.

He made a circle and braked smoothly to a halt under the hanging light.

'Come up,' he said. 'Half an hour, Polly, that's all I ask.'

'Is this your answer?' She was angry again, her lips white in the slant of light from lamp. 'Is this your only sort of damned idea of an answer, to drag me upstairs and have sex.'

'Polly, don't talk like that.'

'Is it? Is it?'

'I just need to be with you for a while, that's all.'

'That's all? That's all, is it? You say it as if it were nothing.'

'What the hell more do you want from me?' Tony snapped.

'I need you to let me in.'

'"In", what d' you mean "in"?'

'To confide in me, trust me, share with me. I have to be sure you aren't just using me, darling, for I'm finding it harder and harder to believe that you love me at all, love me properly, I mean.'

He stared out of the windscreen at the almost empty courtyard.

Frost was already sifting down out of the evening sky and the cold would soon become numbing. When the cold eased there would be snow, so Penny had told him, and he thought of her smile, her child-like eagerness for snow.

There were three motorcars and a van parked in the courtyard. Only half of the windows in the apartment block were lighted for the long trail back from businesses in the city had only just begun. He wondered exactly where Dominic was right now, who Dominic was negotiating with and just how much trust there had to be in a relationship to make it function.

He said, 'I'm staying at a farm in the country, not far from Breslin.'

'Why?'

'I have to look after the girl.'

'The blonde?'

'Yeah.'

'And the man, the little guy with the moustache.'

'He isn't there. I don't know where he is.'

'Does Dominic visit?' Polly said.

'Once, that's all, not to visit Penny, for – for something else.'

'Why does the girl need to be looked after?'

'It's money, Polly. Counterfeit money. She owns the printing plates.'

'Oh!' Polly said. For an instant there was fire in her eyes, a sudden flash of the passion that he remembered from their first sexual encounters. 'Oh, I see. Forged notes?'

'Yeah.'

'Banknotes?'

'Yeah.'

'Dominic's printing and distributing them, I suppose?'

'He's heavily involved in managing the scheme.'

'Well!' Polly exclaimed. 'Well, well!'

He was suddenly alarmed at his lack of rectitude, at the ease with which she'd broken him down. She hadn't even threatened him, just turned him around, roasted him in the name of love. He didn't know if it *was* love any more or if it had transformed itself into something infinitely more corrosive.

'Dom had to take it on,' Tony said. 'His old man wouldn't let him refuse.'

'His father? What does Carlo have to do with forged banknotes?'

'I don't know and can't tell you,' Tony said. 'In fact, I've told you too much already. But I wanted you to—'

'To know how much you love me?' Polly said.

'Yeah.'

He felt flat and deflated. In telling her even a small part of the truth, he had betrayed Dominic and tossed away his integrity. At that moment he hated Polly for demanding it of him, for not understanding what honour meant.

He twisted the ignition key and fired the engine.

'I'll take you home,' he said.

'Don't you want to go upstairs?'

'No, I'd better get you back before Dominic arrives home.'

'He won't be home for hours. Never is these days. Now,' Polly said, 'I know why. How much is involved, darling, and will you share in the profits?'

'Yeah, I'll have my cut,' Tony said.

She touched his arm again. 'Then you'll be rich too.'

'Sure I will,' said Tony.

And before she could talk him out of it and into the bed upstairs, he flung the Dolomite into gear, drove past the cars and the van and down the slope that would take Polly back to the mansion in Manor Park and her husband, Dominic Manone.


'In God's name, why didn't you follow him?' Inspector Winstock said.

'I did, sir. I followed him back to Manone's house where he dropped off the woman but after that he lost me.'

'Did he know you were trailing him?' Kenny said.

'No, I don't think so,' Detective Constable Stone replied. 'He just sped away along the Paisley Road, heading for Glasgow.'

'Why didn't you use the wireless to request assistance?' Winstock said.

'I can't drive an' operate the wireless, sir, not at the same time.'

'You were probably out of range of the HQ receiver anyway,' Kenny said.

'Bloody new-fangled things!' Inspector Winstock said. 'More trouble than they're worth. Are you certain the woman was Manone's wife?'

'Positive. I saw her very clearly,' Stone said.

'And they didn't go up to Lombard's flat?' said Winstock.

'No, sir. They just sat in the car an' talked for a while.'

'Did they kiss and cuddle?' Kenny heard himself ask.

'Didn't see none of that,' said Stone. 'They were only there for about five minutes. Drove up, parked in the courtyard, talked, then drove off again.'

'Perhaps she didn't want to play ball,' Winstock said.

'Or he didn't,' said Kenny.

'That's daft,' said Winstock. 'I mean, why the heck would he take her to his flat if it wasn't for a bit of how's-your-father.'

'She is Manone's wife,' said Kenny.

'So what!' said Winstock.

'Lombard would hardly try it on with Manone's wife.'

'It might not be the first time,' Winstock said. 'Are you sure they weren't at it in the car, Stone?'

'I'm certain. I'd a good view from the van. All they did was talk?'

'Did they argue?'

'I'm not sure but I think she might've been crying at one stage.'

Winstock sat back, reached for the glass of stomach medicine which he downed as if it were whisky, then for a cigarette. 'What,' he said, 'were they doing there and what were they talking about? I'd give a week's wages to find out.'

Kenny did not attempt an answer. In the back of his mind was the notion that Polly Manone had been pumping Tony Lombard on his behalf. He would telephone her tomorrow on the off chance that his theory was correct. If only to keep the McKerlie woman at bay he needed to learn a whole lot more about the man who called himself Harker. She had given him a hard time in the fish restaurant and had revealed nothing about Harker alias Conway that had any value.

'After I lost Lombard,' Stone said, 'I went back to the Manone house an' sat outside for a while just in case the woman went out again, or Tony came back.'

'Did he?' Inspector Winstock asked.

'No, sir. Manone arrived home in the big Wolseley about a quarter past eight. He went indoors and didn't come out again. I packed it in about eleven. All the house lights were out by that time.'

'You've logged all these observations, I take it?' said Winstock.

'I have, sir.'

'Dictate your report to Janet and get it on file. Kenny?'

'Sir?'

'How well do you know Manone's wife?'

'I've only met her once, in company.'

'Well, your sweetheart's not liable to know if

her sister's havin' it off with Manone's right-hand man, but if she is that would be a real bonus for us.'

'Would it, sir?' said Stone.

'Sure, it would,' said Winstock. 'Kenny, tell him why.'

'I think we're talking about blackmail,' Kenny said.

Winstock chuckled and issued a stream of cigarette smoke from his nostrils.

'Blackmail,' he said. 'Now wouldn't that be nice.'

Penny had just stepped out of the bath when she heard the motorcar drive into the yard. She was pink and warm and perfumed from the salts she'd dissolved in the water and was looking forward to sliding into bed. She felt more relaxed now that she knew that Dougie was close to churning out money. In five or six months she would have earned enough to leave Scotland and sail back to New York, to pay her mother what was owed her and settle, as it were, the heinous debts that her father's criminal activities had laid upon her.

She had one foot on the rim of the bath-tub, lazily towelling her leg, when the faint, grating noise of a car engine filtered through the steam. She reacted instantly, wrapped the towel around her waist, knotted it like a sarong, grabbed her robe from the hook on the door and wriggled into it then she flung open the door and dashed through the stone-floored laundry room into the kitchen.

Dougie had been dozing in front of the fire, the cat on his lap. He'd heard the motorcar too, however, and was on his feet before Penny entered the kitchen. He snatched the rabbit gun from the corner, the box of shells from the shelf, tossed the gun and then the shells to her. She caught the weapon cross-handed, fielded the box of shells and loaded the gun while Dougie went to the outside door and unlatched it.

'Now,' Penny said.

Dougie yanked the door wide open.

'Who are you? What do you want with us?' Penny shouted.

No answer. Headlamps switched off, the car stood in cold silhouette, darker than the darkness of the yard.

'I have a gun,' Penny cried shrilly.

'I know you have a gun, for God's sake. What you gonna do with it, kid, shoot me for the pot too?'

Tony swaggered into the light, hat tipped back, hands in his overcoat pockets. He was jocular and arrogant, like a man who's succeeded in whatever he'd set out to do: Penny thought she knew what that had been.

'Put the damned popgun away, Penny,' Tony said.

'Why are you back so early?' Penny asked.

'I just couldn't stay away, 'Tony said, 'I missed you both so much.'

Shrugging, Dougie went back into the kitchen. He fished the startled cat from under the table and seated himself in the armchair again, Frobe on his lap. He had taken a half bottle of whisky from the cupboard and had drunk two small nips by way of celebration for a job well done. The bottle, corked, stood on the floor by the side of the chair, the little glass on the mantelshelf.

Tony took off his hat and coat and flung them on a chair at the table. He lifted Dougie's glass from the mantelshelf, rubbed the rim with the heel of his hand, lifted the bottle from the floor and poured himself a dram. Holding the glass carefully between finger and thumb, he guided it to his lips and tossed back the contents. He swallowed, blew out his cheeks, sighed, poured a second shot and, leaning against the edge of the table, looked Penny up and down.

She held the rifle in one hand, barrel pointing to the floor.

Tony said, 'Love the rig-out, kid. I can just about see your belly-button.'

Embarrassed Penny pulled the robe about her stomach and thighs.

He continued to stare at her, a cocky little smile on the corner of his lips.

He said, 'Who're you all perfumed up for, Penny? Are you gonna take old Dougie to bed with you. Gonna give *him* a lesson in love?'

'You have been drinking, have you not?' Penny said.

'I haff indeed been drinking,' Tony said. 'I am dronk as a skonk.'

'You should not have been driving the motor-car.'

'Nag, nag, nag,' Tony said. 'Nag, nag, nag. Hell, I can drive a motorcar with my eyes closed. I can do plenty of other things too – eyes wide open.'

'What other things?' Penny said.

'Plenty of other things, with or without a gas-mask.'

She blinked then glanced at Dougie who shook his head indicating that this was not an opportune moment to show Tony Lombard the brand-new counterfeit banknote and let him share their triumph.

'Well, it's past my bedtime,' Dougie said. 'I'll be goin' upstairs now if nobody's got any objection.'

'How about you, kid,' Tony said, 'you goin' upstairs too?'

'How drunk are you?' Penny asked.

'Not that drunk,' Tony said. 'Just drunk enough.'

'Night-night,' Dougie said and with Frobe clinging to his shoulder made his way out of the kitchen and up the creaking staircase to the attic.

Penny propped the rabbit gun in the corner, took the box of shells from the pocket of her robe and replaced it on a shelf of the dresser. She knew that Tony was watching her, staring boldly and insolently at her legs. The ends of her hair were wet against the nape of her neck and the towel at her waist was slipping, slipping down, damp and bulky against her hips and thighs. She reached under the robe and loosened the knot, drew the towel out and draped it over her shoulder, tightened the sash of the robe and turned to face him.

'You look like a damned cream cake,' Tony said. 'Pink sponge.'

'Do you want me to fetch the mask?'

'Nope, I want you just like you are, sweetheart. Anyhow, the gas-mask was a pretty sick idea, don't you think?'

'I do not know what you want me to think.'

'I don't want you to think at all,' Tony said.

He drank the dregs of the whisky and wiped his lips with the back of his hand. He was less intoxicated than she had supposed. He put the glass on the table and unbuttoned his trousers. He drew out the tail of his shirt, pure white against dark suiting, and pushed down the band of his undershorts.

'I don't want you to think about anything,' he said, 'except me.'

Parting the folds of her bathrobe, he drew her to him.

And later, much later, he took her upstairs to bed.

'My! My!' John Flint said. 'This is a pleasant surprise, a very pleasant surprise. To what do we owe the honour, Mrs Manone – or may I call you Polly?'

'Come off it, Johnny, you've always called me Polly.'

'True, that's true. I remember when you were just a skittery wee lassie in ankle socks and sandals. How's your dear mother, by the way?'

'My dear mother is fine,' Polly said.

'And this lady . . .'

'My sister Barbara.'

'Charmed, I'm sure,' Flint said.

He strode around the enormous desk, kissed Polly on the cheek and Babs on the back of a gloved hand which she had sense enough to offer, wrist arched, as if she had entered a medieval court and not a room above the Stadium Cinema.

'I'm Jackie Hallop's wife, by the way. Maybe you know Jackie?'

'By reputation. Aye, his reputation has preceded him.'

'You can call me Babs.'

'Honoured.'

'Everybody calls me Babs.'

'Still honoured,' Flint, unruffled, said.

'I thought Dominic might be with you,' Polly said.

'Dominic? What would Dom be doing here?'

'Business,' Polly said.

'His business is round at the warehouse,' Flint said. 'Dom and me don't see much of each other these days – not enough anyway. Don't tell me you're chasin' your husband, Polly? Can't give him peace even for a single minute, uh?' He gestured to the banquette in the corner of the office. 'Take a pew. I'll order us up some coffee.'

'Don't bother,' Polly said.

Flint's feigned bonhomie vanished. He cocked his head and studied the sisters, Polly first then Babs. He found Babs sturdy and unpolished and the more attractive of the two. She didn't intimidate him with airs and graces or patronise him with her supercilious intelligence. He'd fancied Polly Manone when she was younger but his taste in women had matured since then. Babs Conway Hallop was more his type, big-breasted, fair-haired, confident but probably none too bright.

'At least take the weight off,' Johnny Flint said. 'Here, these chairs are more comfortable than they look.'

Polly and Babs seated themselves before the desk.

Flint hesitated, unsure quite what the women wanted and how, therefore, to dispose of them before Harker arrived. He didn't dare use the intercom to pass word to Cherry to keep Harker from barging into the office. He would just have to trust to luck that Harker would turn up late.

He strode behind the desk again and sat down in the big chair.

'So,' he said, 'what's up, Polly? What's the news?'

'The war's the news,' Polly said.

'War? What war? Been a war declared that I ain't heard about?'

'Tell him.' Babs leaned towards her sister. 'Go on, Poll, don't beat around the bush. Ask him.'

'Tell me?' Flint said, raising his brows. 'Ask me? What's it to be, ladies? Asking or telling? What's on your mind? You wanna place a bet on something?'

Polly picked at the stitching on her glove and said nothing for a moment. Flint feigned patience. He had no idea what was coming but had a sneaky suspicion that dainty Mrs Manone was about to step into deep water and that he'd better be careful that she didn't drag him along with her.

'In a manner of speaking,' Polly said, at length, 'it is a gamble.'

'Doesn't Dominic know you're here?'

'No,' Polly answered. 'And I'd prefer to keep it that way.'

Flint nodded. 'Confidential?'

'Highly confidential,' Babs put in. 'Tell him, Polly, for God's sake.'

'Do you know what my husband does?' Polly said.

'I know what he doesn't do,' said Flint. 'He doesn't run book and he doesn't dabble in insurance any longer. Don't blame him. Too damned risky for an honest family man.'

'That wasn't the question,' Polly said.

'Well then, the answer's in the negative,' Flint said. 'I don't know what he does these days – just that it seems to be profitable and don't interfere with anythin' going on in my neck of the woods.' He frowned. 'Hey, you don't imagine I'm threatening him, surely? Is that what you meant by war?'

'I meant the real war, the German war; Hitler,' Polly said.

'Tell him,' Babs said again.

The Hallop woman's agitation was palpable, eagerness and guilt all mixed up. Her cheeks were flushed and she breathed high in her chest, her bosom rising and falling in a way that Flint found enticing.

He looked to Polly, though, for answers.

'If,' Polly said, 'war does come and it behoves us . . .'

'Behoves? What kinda a word is that?'

'If it becomes necessary for my sister and me to sell off certain parts of my husband's business, would you be interested in buying them?'

'Necessary?' Flint said. 'Necessary, like in the event of a war?'

'Yes.'

'Okay,' Flint said. 'Cards on the table, Polly. You know there's gonna be a war. Hell's teeth, the car manufacturers are producing aircraft by the thousand and hard-workin' entrepreneurs like me and Dominic are bein' squeezed by extra taxes to pay for defence. War's inevitable.' He rubbed his long chin speculatively. 'What's your worry, Polly – that Dominic will be conscripted? Take it from me, Dom won't be conscripted. How old is he? Thirty-eight, thirty-nine? Married with two young kids. They won't scoop him up for military service until we're fightin' the Jerries hand-to-hand on the beach at Ardrossan.'

'It's not conscription that worries me,' Polly said.

'What does worry you then?'

'Deportation.'

'Deportation? Dom's as Scottish as you an' me.'

'He's not, you know. I think he's registered under dual nationality.'

'What!' Johnny Flint exclaimed. 'You mean he's officially an alien?'

'Possibly,' Polly said.

'Haven't you asked him?'

'If I did he would simply fob me off without an answer.'

'Is that a fact?' Flint said. 'An alien, eh! Well, well!'

'Do you see my predicament?' Polly said.

'Our predicament,' said Babs.

'I do, yeah, I certainly do,' Flint said. 'What about old Tony? Same boat?'

'Same boat,' said Polly.

'You'll just have to hope that *Il Duce* don't sign a pact with Adolf then.'

'If I . . .'

'We,' said Babs.

'Yes, if my sister and I *are* left to fend for ourselves,' said Polly 'we'll need someone we can trust to take over certain parts of the business and pay us our fair share or perhaps even buy us out.'

'Buy what out?'

'The best of it, the parts of it that will still make money.'

'Black market goods?' Flint said. 'Is Dom importing those already?'

'No, I mean special goods,' said Polly. 'Very valuable goods.'

'Like what?' said Flint.

'I'm not a position to tell you just yet,' said Polly. 'All I require from you, Johnny, is an expression of interest in what I – what my sister and I – may have to offer if the worst comes to the worst.'

'An interest in principle,' Flint said, nodding. 'Sure. Sure. I wouldn't see you stuck, Polly, or you – Babs. I'm flattered to be asked. You can trust me to do right by you.'

'Only if it becomes necessary.'

'Pray God,' said Flint, 'it won't. But if it does I'll be there, ready and willing to do whatever I can to keep old Dominic's flag flyin'.'

'Won't you be called up too?' Babs asked.

'Bad heart,' said Flint, grinning. 'Could go at any time,' then, not grinning, said, 'I can take over the collections easy, cream off his share from cafés and restaurants, particularly as we'll most likely be dealin' with inexperienced women. If Dom's deported or interned half the Italians in Scotland will go with him. But the demand will still be there, folks will still want their ice-a-da-creams and fish and chips, places to drink coffee or go dancing.'

'I was thinking of another sort of business, actually,' Polly said.

'What would that be?' said Flint.

'Money,' Polly said. 'Money as a commodity not a service.'

'I don't follow.'

'Perhaps that's just as well,' said Polly.

She got abruptly to her feet.

'No, wait,' Flint said. 'Come on, Polly, don't leave me in suspense. What's all this about raw money? What's your old boy got into that you can't handle?'

'In due course, Johnny,' Polly promised then before Babs could open her mouth, caught her sister by the arm and yanked her to her feet too. 'We've had a nice little preliminary meeting, but that's enough for now. It's comforting to know that we can count on your support in an emergency.'

John Flint rose to his full height. He seemed capable of stretching himself, of gaining inches, and towered over the two young women as he came around the desk again. He had switched off his curiosity and was all avuncular charm. He put an arm about Babs's shoulder, a hand on Polly's arm and escorted them to the door.

'Nobody ever spares a thought for the likes of us, do they?' he said. 'I mean, does anybody have any idea how tough it's gonna be for those of us who don't walk the sunny side of the street when the country's crawlin' with special constables and wardens and every Tom, Dick and Harry who wears a uniform will be ready to pounce on us for every soddin' infringement? Oh, yeah, it's gonna be hard times for the likes of us, Polly, and we'll just hafta stick together and co-operate. Dom will come to appreciate that in due course. Meanwhile, though, we'll keep it strictly to ourselves for a while.'

'I was hoping you'd say that,' said Polly while Flint steered her into the corridor and gave Babs's waist a squeeze. 'I'm relying on your discretion, John.'

'Discretion,' Flint said, 'is my middle name,' then blanched as the outer door opened and Harker stepped into the corridor.

They sat on a bench in George Square in the heart of the city. In summer the square was crowded with office workers eating lunch but in drab and chilly February few citizens cared to occupy the seats between the statues and the pigeons went hungry. The couple were too intent upon their conversation to pay much attention to the birds that flocked about them, begging for crumbs.

The girl was whey-faced with cold and looked younger than her years; the man, hunched and angular and awkward, looked older. There was something pathetic in the way she stared into his face and appeared to hang on his every word. Even the raggle-taggle band of vagrants who inhabited the square at all seasons were leery of the couple for a sixth sense told them that he was a copper and not to be tampered with.

'I don't mean now, Rosie,' Kenny said. 'I don't mean this week or even next month. I mean if there is a war, once it becomes inevitable, will you think about it.'

'You are going to join up, are you nuh-not?'

'I'm giving it serious consideration.'

'Will they not force you to stay in the police?'

'I'm not sure I want to,' Kenny said. 'If I resign now they can't stop me.'

Their contact was not of hands but of feet, legs loosely linked and touching.

Rosie faced him, gloved hands clasped in her lap like an illustration from a Hans Andersen fable. Kenny had his scarf wound round his neck, collar turned up. The bitter little wind that scuffed down Cochrane Street past the City Chambers and the Cenotaph teased his curly brown hair. I must buy him a hat, Rosie thought, a fedora: he will look well in a fedora. He could be married before the registrar in trenchcoat and fedora, more fitting than a uniform. She didn't want to see him in a uniform of any kind, not even policeman's blue.

'What do you want to do, Kenneth?' she asked.

'I want to marry you, Rosie.'

'And then what?'

'I don't know,' he said.

'Do you wuh-want to go to buh-bed with me?'

'Of course I do.'

'Enough to marry me?'

He sighed. 'How can you ask such a question?'

'There are a luh-lot of girls getting married because the war is coming and they do not want to be left on the shelf. They want to have a man make love to them before he . . .'

'Dies?' said Kenny. 'Rosie, dearest, I've no intention of dying.'

She looked down at the pigeons strutting at her feet. There were tears in her eyes, watery little effusions that may have been brought on by the gritty wind.

'Kenny, I hardly know you,' she said.

'I'm just what you see, Rosie – and you've met my sister.'

She glanced up to read his lips. 'What does that have to do with it?'

'I don't need her approval, if that's what you're thinking,' Kenny said. 'But it would be better if you liked her, under the circumstances.'

'Better?'

'When – if I'm away for a while she'll look after you.'

'I do not nuh-need your sister to look after me. I huh-have sisters of my own to look after me,' Rosie told him. 'And my Mammy. And my Daddy.'

'Daddy?'

'Bernard.'

Kenny stared bleakly across the square towards the monument. 'Your brother-in-law too, I suppose.'

'That is the problem, is it not?' Rosie said. 'Dominic Manone?'

'I suppose it is, really,' Kenny admitted.

'You want to separate me from my family. And you can't.'

'It's not going to be safe in Glasgow,' Kenny said. 'The minute we go to war with Germany bombs will start falling. Do you have any idea the amount of damage a single ton of explosive can cause?'

'Stop it,' Rosie said. 'Stop trying to frighten me.'

'I'm sorry,' Kenny said.

Rosie said, 'I will have to get back to work.'

'I know. Yes, I know,' Kenny said. 'I shouldn't have asked, should I?'

'No,' Rosie told him. 'It is too soon. And too difficult.'

'Do you not want to marry me?'

She got up from the bench, stood before him.

'I would marry you tomorrow, Kenneth, if I could.'

'I love you, Rosie. If I want to go to bed with you, I can't help that,' Kenny said. 'It's all so damnably uncertain.' He got up and stood in front of her, sheltering her from the cutting wind. 'But I do love you and I'd do anything to keep you from being hurt.'

'I do not think that is a promise you can keep,' Rosie said, 'not the way things are.'

'Then I'll change the way things are,' said Kenny.

'How can you?'

'You're right, of course,' Kenny said. 'I can't.'

And then, in broad daylight among the pigeons and the tramps, he took her in his arms and kissed her tenderly on the lips.


There was something about him, something that Polly could not put her finger on, something that caused her to step back. Perhaps it was his aggression, the sheer force of his personality, a bullish rather brutal quality apparent in the way he stalked down the corridor between the cubicles. She had no time to examine her feelings, however, before the little man was upon her.

'Harker,' he said, gravel-voiced. 'Edgar Harker. Pleased ta meetcha.'

Flint, nonplussed, stammered, 'This – this – these are . . .'

'I know who they are,' said Harker. 'Couldn't be anybody else.'

'I'm sorry,' Polly said. 'Have we met before?'

Flint had gone an odd colour, not pale but flame red.

'Maybe.' Harker said. 'A long time ago.'

Collecting herself, Polly said, 'I saw you at the racecourse in November.'

'Clever girl.'

'You were talking with my husband in the enclosure.'

'Right on the button.'

'There was a girl with you, a blonde.'

'Sure was, usually is.'

He grinned and his moustache lifted to show brown, tobacco-stained teeth. For an instant Polly supposed that the upper lip had snagged then realised that the grisly smile was a scar, the result of a wound or an injury that had healed badly

She tried not to stare, and said, 'She's not with you today, however?'

'Nope, left her home today.'

'Is she your wife?' Polly asked.

'In a manner of speakin'.'

'Eddie,' Flint found his voice at last. 'Eddie, why don't you toddle down to the office and help yourself to a drink. I'll be with you soon as I see the ladies out.'

'Keepin' them to yourself, are you, Flinty?'

'Come on, Eddie, be nice.'

'Not me, pal. Never been nice in my life. If you're Polly,' Harker said, 'I guess you must be Babs. You look just like her.'

'Like who?' Babs said.

A dry, strident note in her voice indicated that Babs was more annoyed than charmed by Mr Harker's familiarity. It occurred to Polly that perhaps her sister and the stranger shared an unfortunate character-istic – namely, a short fuse – and that the prudent thing to do would be to escape before tempers flared.

'Well, it's been a pleasure meeting you, Mr Harker, but Babs and I . . .'

'Like who?' Babs stood challengingly before the stranger, a hand on her hip. 'If you're referrin' to my Mammy you'd better watch your tongue, Mr Harker.'

'Spiky,' Harker said. 'Very spiky. I like that in a woman.'

'I do believe,' said Flint, taking Polly's arm, 'the ladies have another appointment an' must be on their way.'

'Gimme a break, Johnny,' Harker said. 'I ain't gonna blow it.'

'Blow what?' said Babs. 'An' who are you callin' spiky?'

'Easy, sweetheart, easy,' Harker said. 'Where I come from most gals would take that as a compliment.'

'Where do you come from then?' Babs said. 'Mars?'

'Close enough,' Harker said. 'America.'

'Philadelphia?' Polly heard herself enquire.

Without a moment's hesitation, Harker answered: 'New York.'

The strange proud light in his eyes hadn't diminished. He seemed more amused than irked by Babs's rudeness.

In a loud check overcoat and turkey-red scarf he looked less like a bookie than a variety-hall comic; Polly almost expected him to whip out a water-pistol and a raucous motor-horn and begin squirting and *parping* away.

'Huh!' Babs said. 'You're no more a Yankee than I am.'

'Right you are there, sweetheart. I'm from these 'ere parts originally.'

'So you did know my Mammy?' Babs said.

'Everybody knew Lizzie McKerlie. Fine big thumping woman.'

'An' I'm just like her, am I?'

'The very spit,' said Harker.

Polly felt the question rise into her mouth like water brash.

'My father, did you know my father too?'

Flint fell away from her, a hand to his brow, palm covering his eyes.

'Who was he again?' Harker said.

'Frank, Frank Conway,' Babs said.

'Yeah, old Frank.'

'You knew him?'

'Nope.'

'But if you knew my mother . . .' Babs began.

'I was gone before Frank appeared on the scene, sweetheart, long gone,' Edgar Harker said. 'Whatever happened to him, anyhow?'

Out of a sick, hollow little space in her chest, Polly answered:

'He died in the war.'

'A hero's death then,' Harker said.

'Yes, a hero's death,' said Polly and without even

shaking hands, headed off down the corridor and out on to the balcony at the top of the steps where Babs caught up with her.

'What's wrong with you, Poll? You look like you've seen a ghost.'

'I just – I felt a little faint, that's all.'

'That guy . . .'

'What?' Polly said. 'What about him?'

'I think he fancied me.'

'Oh God!' Polly groaned.

'Maybe 'cause I remind him of Mammy when she was young. I reckon he fancied Mammy, don't you? Anyway, he's old enough t' be my father so he'll get no change out of me.' She placed a hand on Polly's shoulder. 'You okay?'

'Yes, I'm all right. Really, I'm fine.'

They went carefully down the steep steps, arms linked, and walked around a corner of the cinema into Paisley Road West to find a taxi to take them home.

'What d' you think then?' Babs asked as soon as some colour returned to her sister's cheeks. 'Will Flint keep his word when it comes to it?'

'I doubt it,' Polly said.

'How come?' said Barbara. 'I thought you trusted him.'

'I don't trust him. I don't trust anybody these days,' Polly said.

'Not even Tony?'

'Not even Tony,' Polly said, and was startled to realise that she meant it.

# Chapter Thirteen

For the most part Lizzie managed to ignore the pamphlets that eager volunteers shoved through the letter-box.

Bernard, however, read and collected them assiduously.

'What are they askin' us to do now?' Lizzie would enquire.

Bernard, who understood his wife's reluctance to admit that anything was wrong, would answer, 'Nothing much.'

'Nothing much' was not a phrase favoured by Lizzie's neighbours, however. As soon as she set foot out of doors she was beset by wild speculations about just how soon German bombers would appear over Knightswood and how much damage they would do. Suckled on injustice and weaned on protest, the Scots were by no means a stoical race and pessimists outnumbered optimists two to one.

Mrs Kearney, a widow, believed that everyone would die in a cloud of poison gas, and Mr Galbraith and his wife were already hoarding tinned foodstuffs and filling the bath with coal. On the other hand, scatty Mrs Deans, mother of three sons, was convinced that Hitler's army would crumple before the wave of conscripts that would parachute into the heart of Berlin to give that dirty dog what for.

Towards the end of February council carts arrived at the cottage row bearing sheets of corrugated steel and lengths of wood, the rudiments of Anderson shelters. Brick shelters had already been erected in the local park and the rose garden adjacent to the hospital was so pitted with trenches that there was serious danger of subsidence. In council houses on the high ground that gave unparalleled views of the Clyde basin, miles of sticky brown tape had been applied to oriel windows and home-spun sandbags were banked against trellises and garden sheds.

Anderson shelters were a different proposition, though. They had to be buried deep into the ground and turfed over, not just for protection from enemy bombs but to preserve a suburban fondness for neatness. Lizzie, who depended entirely on Bernard to save her from whatever might fall from the skies, was pleased to see the carts arrive for hard physical labour would surely keep her husband from brooding about Rosie and Kenny.

Meanwhile she carried on with cooking, cleaning, scrubbing floors and, stepping over the holes that the menfolk, mole-like, had thrown up in the back green, hung the washing out to dry as usual.

Meetings were convened in the Caldwells' house, meetings that Lizzie did not attend. Expert advice was sought from Civil Defence administrators who knew no more about constructing shelters than coal-merchants or shipwrights and considerably less than Bernard who had personally studied structures under stress and who retained vivid memories of the havoc that shrapnel could wreak on the human body. He kept this information to himself, however, for unlike many of his cohorts, he had no desire to show off.

On the last Sunday in the month Bernard and Lizzie attended morning service at St Margaret's. The church was packed. The organist played a medley of voluntaries and rousing martial hymns. The congregation sang lustily about 'True Valour' and 'Marching as to War'. The minister, Mr Heatley, delivered a quiet sermon for he was as mild-mannered and unmilitary as the new King George. His prayer for peace was heart-felt, however, and the congregation's 'Amen' could be heard halfway down Great Western Road.

As soon as he arrived home from kirk Bernard changed out of his suit into a pair of old dungarees and while Lizzie set the table for lunch went out to the green at the back with a measuring string and a little booklet of instructions to mark the line of the drainage pipes that would make the Peabodys' shelter not only safe but habitable.

Rosie hadn't accompanied her parents to church. She'd had a period that week and a bit of a sniffle and Lizzie hadn't had the heart to dig her daughter out of bed just to join in worship. When Bernard and Lizzie got home at half-past twelve o'clock, Rosie was still in her bedroom. The drone of the wireless filled the closet-like hall, not dance music but the high falsetto of proper English voices pontificating on religious topics. After putting on her apron and lighting the gas under the soup pot Lizzie returned to the hall and listened outside the bedroom door.

She heard nothing but the cadences of the radio, not a sound from her daughter. She didn't knock – Rosie couldn't hear knocking – but opened the door and put her nose around it. Rosie was lying tummy down on the bed, arms by her sides, face buried in the pillow. She had exchanged her nightgown for an old black skirt and blouse and her legs and feet were bare. She lay so still that Lizzie was filled with dread that her lovely wee daughter had suddenly fallen ill. She darted to the bed, grabbed the first thing that came to hand – Rosie's leg – and gave it a tug.

Eyes red, cheeks wet with tears, Rosie shot up at once.

'*What? What do you want?*' she shouted.

'Are you all right, dearest?' Lizzie mouthed.

'*Leave me alone, just leave me alone.*'

Rosie flung herself down and buried her face in the pillow again.

Lizzie had long since learned to distinguish distress

from a tantrum. She switched off the wireless, seated herself on the bed and, refusing to be deterred by her daughter's wriggling, stroked Rosie's hair until the girl rose again, crying, *'Stop that, stop that, Mammy, please.'*

'Are you not well?'

'I am perfectly okay,' Rosie said 'There is nothing wrong with me,' then, sobbing, flung herself into her mother's arms.

Lizzie hugged her, soothed her, let the storm of tears blow itself out.

'Now,' she said at length, 'tell me what's wrong, dear.'

'It is Kuh-Kenny. He wuh-wants to muh-marry me.'

'Oh!' Lizzie studied the tear-stained features while Rosie read her lips. 'Is that all?'

'All? All? Is it not enough?' said Rosie, outraged.

'Has he asked you to marry him?'

'He huh-has suggested it.'

'Suggested? What does that mean?'

'He wants me to marry him before he – before he . . .'

More tears were imminent and Lizzie pushed the conversation on before the flood-gates could open once more. 'Take a deep breath, dearest, an' tell me just what Kenny said that's got you so upset.'

'He says he is going to join up.'

Lizzie experienced a sharp clutching sensation about her heart. Smothering her panic, she said, 'Join the army, you mean?'

'Yuh–yes.'

'But why?'

'To fight the Germans.'

'Does Kenny want to fight the Germans?'

'I duh–don't know, duh–do I?'

'When did he ask you to marry him?'

'Last week,' Rosie said. 'In George Square.'

'What did you tell him?'

'I told him I would have to think about it.'

'Wouldn't you like to be Kenny's wife?' Lizzie asked.

'*Yes,*' Rosie shouted, all control of her vocal chords gone. '*Yes.*'

'What's wrong then? Why all the tears?'

'He wuh–wants to go to bed with me.'

'Ah!' Lizzie said, softly.

'Not now. After we are married.'

'What's wrong with that?' Lizzie said. 'It's perfectly natural for a man to . . .'

'Before he guh–goes off to the army.'

Lizzie uttered a little *tut*, too restrained to be audible. 'Come on now, Rosie, let's sort this out. What are all the tears about? Because you don't want to marry Kenny an' are frightened of going to bed with him, or because he might not come back from the war?'

The war: Lizzie could hardly bring herself to utter those two nasty little words. She had lost her Frank in the Great War – or so she chose to believe. If she had been alone she would have found some simple chore with which to occupy her hands, to take her mind off the bleak, blank future, but now she had Rosie to think of, and Polly and Babs, and their children. She could not shy away from her responsibilities. If a war did come and the men went marching off for months or years on end then her girls would need her more than ever before. She felt herself stiffen, literally stiffen.

She planted both her big soft hands on the bed and raised herself up.

'Rosie, do you love Kenny MacGregor?'

'Yes, Mammy, I do.'

'Then when he's good an' ready, when he needs you enough to take you for his wife, no matter what, you should marry him.'

'What – what if he is killed?'

'Then at least you'll have known what love is an' Kenny will die lovin' you.'

Lizzie had a vague notion that the comforting phase had been cribbed from a magazine story but its banality troubled her not.

'What about Dominic?' Rosie asked.

'Dominic?'

'What will Dominic say if I marry a policeman?'

'Dominic doesn't rule our lives.'

'I think that is why Kenny wants to leave the police and join up, just so he will nuh-not have to arrest Dominic.'

'Is that what he told you?'

Rosie shook her head. 'I could not stand it,

Mammy, if Kenny joined the army and fought and died just so he could muh-marry me.'

'God!' Lizzie said. 'Isn't there enough in your head without dwellin' on morbid thoughts like that.' She sat up straight and looked down on her daughter whose eyes, washed by tears, were no longer solemn but bright and attentive. 'We'll take this one step at a time, Rosie.'

'What do you mean?'

'Marriage isn't just about brides an' grooms and goin' to bed together,' Lizzie said. 'It affects a lot of other people besides the happy couple, that's true, but Dominic Manone isn't one of them. I think you're lucky to have a man who loves you so much he'll put you before his career.'

'Is that what he is doing?' said Rosie. 'Sacrificing himself for my sake?'

'If that's the way you want t' put it, aye.'

'Oh, my!' said Rosie. 'Oh, my goodness!'

Lizzie pushed herself upright then, leaning, kissed her daughter on the brow.

'One step at a time, dearest. We'll have them here for tea, him an' his sister an' thrash things out then.'

'But nuh-not with the family?' Rosie said. 'Not with Polly and Babs?'

'No, not the family, just the three of us,' said Lizzie. 'You, me, and Bernard.'

'Oh, Mammy, when can I invite them?'

'Any time you like,' Lizzie said.

★    ★    ★

It was cold in the stables and the men wore overcoats. It could have been a funeral or a wake, the men in sombre black, the girl, Penny, wrapped in a long grey army-style coat with the busby hat pulled down over her ears.

Outside, though it was only an hour past noon, daylight already seemed to be waning. At Giffard's request Tony had switched on the overhead light. The naked bulb hanging from a dusty cable served only to increase the gloom and it was not until Giffard had finished tinkering with the press and gave Tony the nod to throw the big switch on the power box and run current into the machines that the platform shuddered and came to life.

Dougie had a pair of pliers in his hand and a small screwdriver clenched in his teeth like a pirate's dagger and did not exude confidence.

Now that the machinery was ready to go into operation Dominic saw just how jerry-built it was, how amateur the whole thing had been from the start and that he had erred in expecting Giffard, a one-man-band, to pull it off. The guillotine, flat-bed printer and modified multigraph, linked by screws and bolts, looked like a cartoon and he wouldn't have been surprised to hear a whistle hoot and see little puffs of steam fart out of the ink slots. He stood back against the wall, hands in his pockets while the machine shuddered and growled like an aeroplane revving up.

For several seconds there was no movement apart

from the shudder then, in sequence, the guillotine blade dropped, a feeder bar lifted, a band of paper was grabbed by a rubber roller, dragged over the flat-bed and, caught by the cylinder of the multigraph, passed jerkily into a collecting tray.

'It is working, Dougie,' the girl said.

Dougie removed the screwdriver from his teeth. 'Wait a wee minute, but.'

The band of paper feathered into the tray, followed by another, and another.

'Dear God!' said Tony, and laughed. 'The old devil did it.'

'I haven't done nothin',' Dougie said. 'It ain't right yet.'

'What's wrong with it?' Tony said.

'It'll have t' deliver a bloody sight quicker than that,' Dougie said.

Dominic said. 'What about the printing?'

'Yes,' Penny said. 'How well does it print?'

The machine hesitated, jerked wilfully and fed a wrinkle into the next sheet, and the one after that.

'Switch it off, Tony' Dougie said.

Reaching behind him, Tony snapped off the current.

The four of them moved in to stare at the spoiled sheets of paper in the tray.

Dougie eased the top sheet from the layer, squeezed it like a concertina, crumpled it into a ball and tossed it into a wire basket in which, Dominic noticed,

were umpteen other crumpled balls of paper. Dougie
extracted another sheet, glanced at it, demolished
and dumped it too. Four bands of printed paper
were now left in the long tray. From each band
ten Brittanias looked up out of fussy lines of script
above a prominent hollow-letter *Five*.

'Are they dry?' Dominic said.

'Dry enough,' said Dougie.

'Let me see.'

The printer lifted the sheets and placed them on
a trestle table by the straw bales. Dominic stepped
forward and studied the banknotes carefully. Neither
Tony nor Penny joined him and Dougie, as if he'd
lost interest in the matter, walked around behind the
guillotine and began to fiddle with the blade.

'They don't look new,' Dominic said.

'I added chemicals t' the ink,' said Dougie, shrugging.

'But they do look right,' Dominic said.

The girl whimpered.

'They look very right,' Dominic said. 'Cut me
some.'

Tony threw the switch and a moment later paper
ran beneath the blade. Dougie snapped down the
manual bar with a flick of the wrist and gathered the
notes one by one as they nosed out of the machine.
He tidied them and handed the bundle to Dominic.

'Soft,' Dominic said. 'Too soft.'

'It's the heat,' Dougie said. 'Leave them for half
an hour an' they stiffen up.'

Dominic rolled the little bundle of banknotes in one hand, furling them like cigar leaves. He extracted one, held it up to the bulb, changed position, held it up to filtered daylight. 'You're a month ahead of schedule. When will you be ready for a full run?'

'Not yet.'

'How bad is the wastage?' Dominic asked.

'Three in ten, thereabouts.'

'Can you reduce that figure?' Dominic said.

'Maybe.'

'Dougie, I need an answer.'

'I can't gi'e you an answer,' Dougie said. 'What's the run, anyway?'

'Twenty thousand, perfect, each month.'

'What!' Dougie exclaimed. 'For God's sake, Dominic! This contraption won't stand up t' that kind o' treatment. It's not the Royal Mint. You can't expect treasury production from one man, from me, just me. Who's askin' for twenty?'

'I am,' Dominic said.

'Can't do it.'

'I think you'd better, Dougie,' Dominic said and putting the little roll of counterfeit fivers into his overcoat pocket went downstairs without another word.

They had taken the boy out for a spin in the last of the Beezers that Dennis had stored in the Govan yard. It was Sunday again. The dank weather that had marred the week had eased and sunlight strayed over

Warriston Braes and off to the west the high peaks of Arran were just visible under lifting cloud.

The sandpits at Warriston remained soft, though. The dips and hollows between the miniature hills were puddled so that the three-wheeler snaked down the tracks and churned furiously on the steep up-slopes while Dennis, in the driving seat, thrashed the long gear stick and Angus, seated on his father's knee, yelled delightedly and spurred his uncle on to greater feats of speed and daring. The car was mud-spattered, the windscreen smeared. Sand and shale sprayed up with every braking manoeuvre that flung the little car on to another tack on the circuit that Dennis had chosen for its humps and hillocks to give his little nephew one last thrilling ride.

Tuesday, the Beezer would be sold well below market value: Wednesday, the money would be in the bank: Thursday . . .

'Dennis, for Cripes' sake, take it easy,' Jackie said.

The Beezer hit the base of the hillock nose down and pitched him forward. He slammed a hand against the unpadded dash and clutched Angus to him. The engine shrieked, the pitch of the car changed abruptly and the boy and he were flung back. Mounds of shale seemed to be coming at him through the glass, and Angus let out a *'yeeeeeeeeeeeee'* of pure, unalloyed pleasure, and glanced at his Uncle Dennis who grinned at him and winked.

The car sailed up into the dappled sky and stuck

the track with such force that Jackie felt his teeth crunch. He gasped as Angus's bottom thumped painfully into his stomach, and decided at that moment that he was getting far too old for this caper and that in future he would stick to the bike.

'Again, again, again,' Angus shouted, almost deafening his father.

'One more, last turn.' Dennis swung right and aimed the car straight at the straggling path that led up to the quarry and on to the back road that ambled down into Paisley. 'Hold on to your hat, Gus.'

Though he would never admit it, Jackie envied his brother his skill at the wheel and his cool nerve. He couldn't rouse himself to perform acts of daring without anger or a knot of fear in his stomach the size of a football. Had been a time when he had thought himself smarter than his brother, had regarded Dennis as a dumb ox, but those happy, carefree days were long behind him. He knew now that his big brother had qualities he lacked, that he, not Dennis, was the Hallop who needed looking after.

Jackie crossed his arms over his son's chest and laced his fingers together as Dennis accelerated. Angus was panting with excitement. He'd been this route before, knew what to expect. He stared straight ahead, straight into the rushing landscape, seeing nothing, not hills or sunlight or the parcels of lambing ewes in the pastures, only the track ahead, the ribbon of shale.

Dry-mouthed, Jackie watched the arrow of the speedo climb towards seventy. He felt the hammering of the engine all through his body, the feverish slaving of piston rods and cylinder heads while Dennis stroked the car up to maximum speed to hit the first of the runnels flat out.

The Beezer leapt up and thumped down.

Angus shouted, *'Ow-Ow!'* – a ritual chant – and then again, *'Ow-Ow-Ow!'* and, laughing, flung his little head about. This is what he'll remember when he's my age, Jackie thought, this sky-high point in his life when he is happy without knowing why.

'OW!' Jackie yelled, his voice united with his son's, then again, with Dennis joining in the chorus too: 'OW-OW-OW. OH-OW!'

Then the car was sliding, sliding away broadside to the track, Dennis braking and releasing, hands fast on the wheel, letting it go, letting the car take them round in giddy pirouette. Jackie held on to his son, held his breath, eyes wide open. He saw a bank of coarse grass, a cluster of grey rocks, the sky, then a jumble of burnt heather and a great ashy, pattering cloud of shale as the car rode backside through its own trail and, steadying again, shot off straight as a bullet towards the loading table above the quarry.

Dennis braked, eased down and drew the Beezer to a halt on an area of flat ground close to a stand of birches that were not yet in leaf. He applied the hand-brake, and sat back. He was smiling, smiling with his eyes as well as his mouth as the engine note died and relieved metal creaked back into place.

'Again, again, Uncle Dennis. Again.'

'Sorry, son, but that's it.'

'Again, please.'

'No petrol left,' Jackie said. 'You don't wanna have to walk home, do you?'

Reluctantly Angus answered, 'No.'

Jackie opened the passenger door and Angus slid from his knee out and ran off to lie belly-down on the cliff top and look down at the great bestial machines that stood, tethered and passive, on the quarry floor below.

Jackie stood up, a shade shaky on his pins.

He lit a cigarette and leaned on the roof of the car, watching his son.

Dennis clambered out too. He stretched his arms above his head. He was still smiling, wistfully. He let Jackie scout the boy and looked away towards the haze that even on Sunday hung over the towns that bled gradually into Glasgow.

'Jackie,' he said, 'I'm quitting the garage.'

'You what?' Jackie said, only half listening.

'I'm giving you a week's notice.'

Jackie lifted his head. He took the cigarette from his lips with finger and thumb, and said, 'Don't be daft, Den. You can't quit. You're a bloody partner.'

'I'm enlisting.'

'Enlisting?'

'Joining up. Joining the army.'

'You! A soldier! Don't make me laugh!' Jackie said.

'Six months,' Dennis said, 'a year topper, we'll all

be in the army. Kid yourself not, Jackie, it's definitely gonna happen.' He moved around the bonnet of the car, propped an elbow on the metal roof. 'I'm just gonna get in there first. If I take the plunge now I reckon I'll have a choice.'

'What d' ya mean by a choice?' said Jackie.

'I want to apply for the Royal Engineers.'

'You – an engineer!'

'Sure, why not?' Dennis said. 'By the time they start draggin' Tom, Dick 'n' Harry off the street, I'll have a head start. Be a sergeant in no time.'

'What's Mam gonna say about it?'

'Mam had better get used to it,' Dennis said.

'An' Gloria?'

'Yeah.' Dennis sighed. 'Gloria.'

Jackie flipped away his cigarette. 'Is it Gloria you're runnin' away from?'

'She'll have a big slice o' my army pay, plus' a piece o' anythin' you make from the garage.'

'Salon,' said Jackie, absently.

'Gloria will do okay.'

'You're not comin' back, are ya?'

''Course I'm comin' back,' Dennis said.

'To what?' said Jackie.

'To whatever's left,' Dennis said.

'You're lettin' me down, Den. Christ, how am I gonna run the place wi'out you. Billy? Billy's a joke.'

'Yeah, well, you maybe won't have Billy much longer either.'

'God Almighty! You're serious.'

'I am,' said Dennis.

He came closer, sliding his elbow along the car roof. He'd known that Jackie wouldn't understand the logic of his decision.

He said softly, 'I want you t' look after Babs.'

'Babs?'

'You got a good woman there, Jackie.'

'Babs?' Jackie said again. 'What about Gloria?'

'You daft bugger,' said Dennis. 'You'll never know how lucky you are.'

'Are you tellin' me you fancy my wife?'

'Nope, I'm just tellin' you you've a lot to lose.'

'Yeah, well, I'm losin' you all right,' Jackie said. 'The army, Jesus!'

He stood with arms folded, watching his son crawl on his stomach around the rim of the quarry crater, the rash, slap-dash boy cautious at last. He thought of his brother and the foolish wife he'd chosen for himself, unable to see past her figure, taken in by her simpering smile. Maybe it was as well that Gloria had never given Dennis kids, Jackie thought, not with a war coming, not with everything changing for the absolute worst. He took a step to his right, then, yielding to emotion, clasped Dennis in his arms and hugged him, a big-bear hug like the kind they'd used when they'd wrestled among the middens in back of the tenement in Lavender Court.

'I don't want ya t' leave,' Jackie said.

'Yeah, but I have to,' Dennis said, thickly. 'I really have to.'

'I know,' Jackie said. 'I know.'

He broke away, shouted gruffly to Angus, climbed into the passenger seat and let Dennis herd the boy back to the car. He felt his son's weight descend upon his lap, wriggle, settle. He put his arms about the lad, holding him tightly.

Dennis squeezed into the Beezer and started the engine.

'Dad?' Angus turned. 'Are you cryin'?'

'Not me, son,' Jackie said. 'Not me.'

# Chapter Fourteen

They had arrived a little after five o'clock, dressed up to the nines in Sunday best. Fiona had sense enough to realise that she must make a good impression on the Peabodys, if only for her brother's sake. In the back of her mind, however, was the thought that she might be better placed than Kenny to take advantage of the invitation and unearth some valuable information to pass on to Winstock.

The Peabodys too were all dolled up. Bernard wore a navy blue suit and a shirt with a scratchy collar while Lizzie, apron cast aside, was in a floral dress that fell almost to her ankles. She had raided her jewellery box and was draped with beads and bangles that clicked and jangled every time she moved. She was graceful for such a large woman, though, with a soft, cat-like face that reminded Fiona, rather, of her late-lamented grandmother.

Rosie, the fiancée-to-be, had gone all 'modern'

in a slim blue dress with a long vee collar of cream linen. She wore make-up, a touch on cheeks and lips, a little pencil to accentuate her eyebrows. She seemed pleased to see Fiona again and was, of course, delighted to have Kenny in her home at last.

The first half-hour was awkward but by the time they sat down at table and Lizzie and Rosie served up soup the atmosphere had thawed and Bernard had been lured into talking about the perils and privations of army life, a subject broad enough, Fiona thought, to keep them going through supper.

'A wee bird tells me,' he said, as he carved away at the roast, 'that you're thinkin' of a career in the army.'

'I'd hardly say a career, Mr Peabody,' Kenny answered. 'But it occurred to me that if I'm going to be called up eventually I might as well go now.'

'Now?' said Fiona. 'That's a new one.'

'Soon,' Kenny said.

Bernard slipped slices of hot roast beef on to warm plates and Rosie, smiling, handed them to the guests. Big bowls of boiled potatoes, tinned beans and bright green garden peas were already on the table and Kenny, not standing on ceremony, helped himself. He was rather too relaxed, Fiona thought. Mention of his plans didn't throw him off his stride. He reached eagerly for the gravy boat.

'Won't you be able to stay put?' Bernard said. 'Surely the police will be a reserved occupation.'

'There's been no announcement to that effect,' Kenny said.

'Somebody's got to keep law an' order on the streets, war or no war.'

'What about you, Mr Peabody?' Fiona said, 'Will you stay where you are when war's declared?'

'Maybe there won't be a war,' Lizzie said.

'Oh, yes, there will be a war,' said Fiona. 'Hitler's determined on it. He'll push and push until Chamberlain's left with no option but to take us into conflict. It's the Teutonic cast of mind, you see.'

'The what?' said Lizzie.

'The German press is filled with praise for the Chancellor and, on the whole, supports the precept of conquest rather than conciliation,' Fiona said. 'I was reading just the other day in *Der Tag* that Hitler's about to deliver an ultimatum to Beran . . .'

'Who's he when he's at home?' said Lizzie.

'The Prime Minister,' Bernard said.

'I thought Mr Chamberlain was the Prime Minister.'

'Prime Minister of Czechoslovakia,' said Bernard.

'Oh!' said Lizzie. 'Aye, I didn't hear you the first time.'

Bernard said, 'Where will we make a stand, do you think?'

'Poland,' Fiona answered promptly. She was aware that she was showing off and had lost Lizzie Peabody entirely but was unable to check herself. 'Soon our Foreign Office will make pledges and forge military alliances, after which we'll be committed whether we like it or not.'

'Unless Hitler honours his promises,' said Rosie.

'Hitler doesn't know the meaning of the word "honour".' Fiona paused. 'Franco's got Spain in his pocket. Before you know it there will be a political and military pact between him and Hitler.'

'And Mussolini too?' Bernard said.

'Oh, Mussolini won't want to be left out,' said Fiona. 'He might be wishy-washy when it comes to making decisions and he's worried about what Hitler might want to grab next but . . .'

'Adolf would never invade Italy, would he?' Bernard said.

'Probably not,' said Fiona. 'He'll save Italy for later.'

'Later?' Rosie said.

'After he's grabbed everything else,' said Fiona.

'You're really very well informed, Miss MacGregor,' Bernard said. 'Tell me, why do you take such an interest in what the foreign newspapers have to say?'

Fiona shrugged, a ladylike lift of the shoulders.

'Part of my job.' She gave Bernard a quick, almost flirtatious glance. 'There's a lot more to police work these days than quelling a bit of a rent riot in Gordon Street or keeping traffic moving along the Dumbarton Road.'

'What are you interested in,' Bernard said, 'specifically?'

'Italy, mainly,' Fiona said.

'Not Germany?'

'Italians,' Fiona said. 'Mainly Italians.'

And Kenny said, 'Fiona, for God's sake!'

She sensed that she had overstepped the mark and concentrated on cutting up her beef for a moment or two before she glanced in Bernard's direction once more. Far from being offended the man was smiling. He put down his knife and fork, rested his chin on his hand and stared at her with something akin to admiration.

He said, 'What about Americans?'

'Americans?' Fiona said. 'I don't know what you mean.'

'How about you, Kenny?' Bernard said. 'Do you know what I mean?'

'I've an inkling,' said Kenny, 'just an inkling.'

'So it's not merely the problem of the Italians we have to deal with, is it?' Bernard said. 'One Italian in particular.'

Prudently Fiona said nothing while Kenny chewed and swallowed, put down his knife and fork and said, 'I was going to wait until later to ask you, Bernard, but since you've raised the subject, now's as good a time as any. I'd like to marry Rosie, if she'll have me – and take it from me the Italian need not be a problem.'

'How can you stop him being a problem?' Bernard asked.

'I'll resign from the Force.'

'Drastic, very drastic,' Bernard said. 'What about you, Fiona? Will you stay with the CID and continue to burrow into our family's affairs when your brother becomes part of that family?'

'No,' Fiona said. 'I'll go too.'

'Go where?' said Kenny, surprised.

'Into whatever service will have me,' said Fiona.

'Haven't you discussed this between you?' Bernard said.

'No,' Fiona answered. 'But if Kenny pulls out then I'll have no choice but to do the same. It would be far too awkward otherwise.'

'Isn't it awkward now?' Bernard said.

Lizzie cleared her throat. 'Can this not wait? Your dinners are gettin' cold.'

Bernard raised a hand, not threateningly, to quiet his wife. He said, 'Tell me something, Fiona; how long do you think it will be before we go to war with Adolf?'

'Why ask me?'

'You're the resident prophet,' Bernard said. 'What's your forecast, your estimate — three months, six months, the end of the year?'

'We'll be at war before the year's out,' Fiona stated.

'Yes, that's how all the signs are pointing,' Bernard said. 'If and when it happens I'll also be out of a job and won't be working for the Italian any longer.'

'Bernard!' Lizzie said. 'What d' you mean?'

'Who's going to buy houses when bombs are falling?' Bernard said, 'The housing market'll go into cold storage for as long as the war lasts. Lyons and Lloyd's may as well close its doors for all the business it'll do, an' not even our mutual friend will be able to prevent it.'

'Our mutual – who are you talkin' about?' said Lizzie.

'He means Dominic, Mammy,' said Rosie, quietly.

Bernard said, 'Rosie, do you want to marry this man?'

'I – I – Yuh-yes.'

'There's your answer,' Bernard said.

'It's not so simple as all that,' Fiona put in.

'Aye, but it is,' said Bernard.

'There are,' said Fiona, 'still impediments.'

'Fiona, please,' Kenny said.

'That's up to you, to you and Kenny,' Bernard said. 'If you want to make Rosie happy then it's up to you to get rid of the impediments.'

'I don't know quite what you mean,' Fiona said.

'Kenny does, don't you, son?'

'Yes.' Kenny nodded. 'Are those your terms, Mr Pea – Bernard?'

'Simple terms for a simple solution,' Bernard said. 'Once that impediment's been removed we can fix a date for the wedding and find you a place to live.'

'It is not your wedding, Bernard!' Rosie said. 'Please do not interfere.'

'Your dad's right to interfere,' Kenny said. 'Don't blame him for it.'

'Is this,' said Lizzie, 'an arrangement? I mean, are you engaged now?'

'I do believe we are,' said Rosie.

And at that moment the doorbell rang.

'Janet!' Lizzie swayed. 'My God! Our Janet. What're you doin' here?'

'I've come for to talk t' Frank.'

'What? Who?'

'Frank Conway. Don't try tellin' me you don't know where he is.'

'Frank's dead, Janet. He's been dead for twenty years.'

'Let me in. I need to see for myself.'

'See what, Jan?' Lizzie said. 'Look, I've got people here.'

'You're hidin' somethin' from me,' Janet said. 'I'm comin' in.'

'*Bernard*,' Lizzie shouted.

Too late: Janet brushed her aside, stepped into the tiny hall and bumped into Bernard just as he emerged from the living-room. There was a scuffle as Bernard and his sister-in-law confronted each other. Lizzie, already distraught, tried to drag Janet back. Surprise was on Janet's side. She gave Bernard an almighty shove. When he staggered back, she tore herself from Lizzie's grasp and chased him into the living-room, peered at the three people at the table and then, raising her arm, pointed a finger straight at Kenny and snapped, '*You!*'

Kenny got up so clumsily that the table grated and shook and a fork clattered to the floor.

'I might've known it,' Janet hissed. 'Thick as thieves, the lot o' you. Keepin' Frank from me. Where is he? Is he not here?'

Bernard put a hand on her shoulder but she shook him off with such ferocity that he jerked away as if he'd touched a naked wire. Rosie shrank down in her seat crushed by the angry scene. One eyebrow raised, Fiona watched the strange, shrewish little woman, her brother and Bernard and Lizzie Peabody all begin shouting at once.

'She's gone mad at last. Frank – Frank's been dead for . . .'

'You tell her, Mr Policeman. He's got Frank's picture.'

'What the hell is she talkin' about?'

'Killed in the war, he was.'

'Dead? Not him. He's come back for me at last.'

'What's wrong with her? Bernard, what's this she's sayin'?'

'Ask him, ask him,' Janet continued to point at Kenny. 'Where is he? Have you got him locked away upstairs?'

'There is no upstairs,' Bernard said. 'Frank's not here, Janet. I swear.'

'Frank's still dead,' said Lizzie. 'Isn't he, Bernard?'

Then silence.

Rosie cowered down, chin almost touching the table's edge. She followed the shouting-match as best she could, eyes darting from the frightening figure of her aunt to her stepfather then up at Kenny who had said not a word so far. One thing was clear, her termagant aunt and her fiancé-to-be knew each other: Kenny and Aunt Janet McKerlie weren't strangers.

'Be careful, Janet,' Bernard spoke at length, his voice steady. 'I'm warning you to be very, *very* careful what you say here.'

'Me? What about him? He's Mr Policeman, didn't you know?'

'Yes,' said Bernard, totally calm now. 'We know he's a policeman.'

'An' did you know he's got Frank.'

'I haven't got Frank,' said Kenny. 'I told you, I've no idea where . . .'

'Frank's dead, long dead,' said Lizzie, adamantly 'He died in the trenches.'

'Dearest,' Bernard said, 'that may not be the case after all.'

'You mean Frank's still . . .' Lizzie began.

'Alive, yes,' Janet spat out.

And Lizzie, without any warning, swooned dead away.


Peace reigned in the bungalow in Raines Drive. The children had been fed and bathed but it was too early for bed and they'd been allowed to amuse themselves as best they could. Cross-legged in front of the gas fire in the bedroom, May and June were playing cards, the pack of Happy Families centred on the rug, little fans of cards held neatly in their hands. They were gambling for peppermints and grimly competing with each other for once.

Mellowed by the excitements of the afternoon and with a little bag of liquorice bullets all to himself, Angus lay full-length in front of the coal fire in the lounge, browsing over a copy of *The Dandy,* chortling quietly to himself and wiping black saliva from his chin with the sleeve of his dressing-gown. Almost asleep, April lolled angelically on her mother's knee and uttered no complaints.

Babs stroked her daughter's fine feathery hair with one hand and held a cigarette in the forked fingers of the other, puffing at it now and then as eloquently as a character from 'Private Lives'.

Mummy and Daddy in big moquette-upholstered armchairs on each side of the fireplace, the standard-lamp behind Daddy, shade tilted to keep the light from baby April's eyes: the adults' conversation was restrained, not argumentative but had an undertow, a tiny grating edge of agitation that Angus failed to notice.

Jackie said, 'I dunno what I'm gonna do without him.'

'He's only joinin' the army, Jackie, not vanishin' into thin air.'

'He could be gone for three or four years.'

'Rubbish,' said Babs. 'He'll be back home every weekend.'

'It's Gloria, that bitch Gloria. He's runnin' away from Gloria.'

'I *could* say he's runnin' to meet his destiny,' Babs declared. 'But I won't.'

'What the bloody hell does that mean?'

'Language, Jackie.'

'He can't hear me. He's not listenin'.' Jackie blew out smoke and gazed fondly at his son. 'Know what else Dennis is doin'? He's liquidatin' his assets.'

'Sounds painful,' said Babs.

'Cut it out. It ain't funny.'

'I know it isn't,' Babs said. 'You're not the only one'll miss him.'

'He said somethin' odd this afternoon. Told me t' look after you.'

'That was nice of him.'

'He thinks you're one in a million.'

'Well, I am,' said Babs.

'If you had it all again, Babs, would ya marry Dennis instead o' me?'

'Is that what's botherin' you?'

'Would ya?'

'You picked a fine time to ask, Jackie.' Babs blew smoke towards the hearth. 'Nope, I'd still choose you. There! Is that better?'

'Is it the truth, but?'

'Are you askin' if Dennis an' me . . .'

He glanced at her. She saw not the lazy bewildered sort of expression that she had grown used to over the years but genuine fear. She was tempted to tell him that Dennis was only a man upon whom she depended for advice but she remembered the hours together in the cab of the BSA, how she'd sensed that Dennis wanted her, not just to kiss and caress but to be his wife. There was no envy in Dennis, no malice or scheming. He was too decent for his own good. He would go off into the army without knowing that she wanted him too and that their friendship could so easily have become something more intimate.

'No, no, no,' she said. 'Dennis would never do that to you, Jackie.'

'Would – would you?'

'No.'

Supposin' it was the other way round,' Jackie said, 'supposin' it was me goin' off to join up?'

'The answer would be the same.'

'Supposin' I got killed, would you marry Dennis?'

'Settin' aside the fact that Dennis already has a wife,' said Babs, 'I couldn't marry him 'cause the law wouldn't allow me to marry your brother.'

'He'd look after you better'n me.'

'You look after us just fine, Jackie.'

'Things are a bloody mess, Babs. Without Dennis they'll get even worse.'

'No, they won't,' said Babs. 'I won't let them.'

'What can *you* do about it?'

'Just you wait an' see,' Babs said. 'I'm not a Conway for nothin'.'

The fear faded visibly and instantly and the uncertain little smile that he used to hide his inadequacies appeared at the corner of his mouth.

'What've you got up your sleeve, sweetheart?'

'Plenty,' said Babs.

'Just what are you up to?'

She hesitated then, holding April to her, leaned out and flipped the cigarette into the fire. She hadn't intended to divulge her plans to Jackie – she was unsure just how deep his loyalty to Dominic lay – but Dennis's departure would change things dramatically and she needed Jackie on her side now.

She said, 'How d' you fancy takin' over from Dominic Manone.'

'Are you nuts?'

'Maybe goin' into partnership with somebody who knows the ropes.'

'Like who?'

'Oh, I don't know. Somebody like John Flint, maybe.'

'You are nuts.'

'He's worth a heck of a lotta money, our Dom?'

'Yeah, but it's his money, not ours,' Jackie said.

Babs eased her daughter down across her lap. Her little pink fists opened and closed and her lips made sucking motions. She was asleep, though, fast asleep, only dreaming of the breast.

'What if Dominic ain't around?' said Babs.

'Dom's not daft. He won't join up, not him.'

'No, but he might be sent to prison.'

'You're kiddin'!' said Jackie in alarm. 'Have you heard somethin'? Has that guy Rosie's goin' with told you somethin'?'

'If there's a war an' Italy sides with Hitler, Dom will be sent away.'

'No he won't. He's a Scot, not an Eye-tie.'

'He's a crook, Jackie. Face facts.'

'Nah, he's not. He's just like you an' me really.'

Babs shook her head. 'Jackie, Jackie, Jackie.'

She watched her husband's eyes narrow. He squinted at her with that foxy look that indicated that he had been struck by an idea.

He said, 'You wouldn't shop him, would ya?'

'God, no! 'Course I wouldn't shop him. All I'm sayin' is, if Dom does happen to get lifted an' shipped off for the duration then somebody has to run his business, part of it anyway. By rights that somebody should be us – I mean you.'

'What if I'm called up an all?'

'With four kiddies?'

'Yeah, right,' said Jackie.

He was interested and hadn't recoiled in horror. Babs wished now that her plans had been riper, that she could have told him just what Dominic Manone was worth and what parts of the empire he, Jackie Hallop, was capable of operating and what parts would be sold off, or leased out, to Johnny Flint.

My God, she thought, I'm waiting for Hitler, actually sitting here hoping Adolf will start dropping bombs soon: a thrill of guilt and excitement passed through her and she felt the fine, blonde hairs at the base of her spine stir and rise as if somebody – Jackie – had stroked them.

Jackie said, 'Trouble is, Dom goes, the business falls to Polly, not us.'

'Polly will need a man to help her run it.'

'Tony Lom . . .'

'Another crook, another Italian. He'll be gone too.'

'I don't like the idea o' workin' with Flint.'

Typically, Jackie had accepted the proposition without knowing anything about it. He was relying on her already, taking her word as gospel.

Babs said, 'Flint knows the ropes. He'll still be on the streets when everybody else is in the trenches or behind bars. Johnny ain't gonna serve in anybody's army but his own. There's big money here, Jackie, big, big money. We deserve a piece of it, don't we? God, what do we owe Dominic Manone? He soaked my Mammy for a debt that wasn't her debt in the first place, an' he's rooked you for the best part o' ten years. You think he set you up in the garage . . .'

'Salon.'

'. . . salon then, for your benefit. He did it for profit, his profit.' Babs eased the baby into the crook of her arm and sat back. 'Manone would screw anyone for a few miserable quid. That's how he made his pile. Shouldn't be him livin' in a mansion with nurses an' nannies an' cooks at his beck an' call. Should be us, you an' me. If the coppers do send him up the river, why shouldn't we get what we can out of it?' She paused to gauge the effect of her oratory, then added, 'My God, he isn't really even British.

When the shootin' starts it could be one o' Manone's cousins puts a bullet through our Dennis's head.'

'Babs, for God's sake don't say that.'

'True, though, innit?'

'Maybe. I dunno. Maybe it is.'

She inclined her head towards Angus who was patiently sucking the sugar-coating from a liquorice bullet. 'Think of him, him an' the girls. Don't they deserve the best we can give them, war or no damned war?'

Jackie was convinced, still a shade wary perhaps, but convinced.

'Yeah,' he said. 'You're right. So what d' ya want me to do, Babs?'

'Nothin' just yet,' Babs said.

'When then?'

'I'll tell you when,' said Babs.


Cold water applied via a clean handkerchief soon brought Lizzie to her senses. Kenny and Bernard had lifted her from the floor and placed her in an armchair by the fire, a cushion under her head. In her confusion Rosie had abrogated all responsibility, had allowed Fiona to unbutton her mother's dress and loosen her stays, to hold her plump wrist and check her pulse against the ticking of Bernard's wristwatch. On the plates on the table the wreckage of Sunday night dinner cooled and congealed. In the kitchen an apple sponge bubbled and charred in the gas oven and the kettle on the stove screamed. The living-room seemed packed with bodies, strangers thrown together so that she, Rosie Conway, felt crushed by them. She couldn't find a voice, couldn't ask questions, as if all her training, all her practice, all that she had ever learned had been struck away.

Kenny touched her. She looked up.

'She's all right, Rosie,' Kenny told her. 'It's only shock. She's not hurt.'

'Hurt,' said Janet, though Rosie didn't hear. 'She's not the one who's hurt.'

Lizzie blinked, struggled, held out her arms to Bernard who, stooping eased her into a sitting position. 'Put your head between your legs, dearest.'

'Nuh, I . . .'

'Here I'll help you.'

'Nuh, I . . . What . . . what happened?'

'You fainted, Mrs Peabody,' Fiona said.

'Fainted?'

'Conveniently,' Janet said.

Supporting herself on Bernard's arm Lizzie drew in several deep breaths, then said, 'Turn off the oven.'

'The what?'

'The oven, Bernard, turn off the oven.'

'I'll do it,' Fiona offered and clopped off into the kitchenette.

A moment later the kettle stopped screaming and the strong hot smell of burnt sponge wafted into the living-room.

'I've spoiled your dinner,' Lizzie said. 'I'm – I'm sorry.'

'Just you take it easy, Mrs Peabody,' Kenny said. 'Dinner's not important.'

'Never mind her an' her dinner,' Janet said. 'Where's my Frank? You said you'd find my Frank.'

'I said nothing of the kind,' Kenny told her angrily. 'I don't know where Frank is. All I have is a photograph and your word for it that it is Frank Conway.'

'I knew he couldn't be dead,' Lizzie moaned. 'I knew I should never have got married again. Oh, Bernard, I'm sorry, I'm sorry.'

Then Rosie found her voice, felt it tearing at her lungs, clawing up into her throat. She had no memory of how her voice sounded only sensations in the muscles of her throat. She tucked her legs beneath her and hoisted herself to her feet.

'YOU KNEW,' she shouted. 'KENNETH, YOU KNEW THAT MY FATHER WAS ALIVE AND YOU DID NOT TELL ME.'

'No, Rosie, no. I had – I had a photograph of a man, another name, I didn't have a clue that he was your – was Frank Conway.'

'You liar. You did,' said Janet. 'I told you who he was.'

'YOU USED ME, KUH-KENNY MAC-GREGOR. YOU JUST USED ME.'

'Aye, an' I'll wager you didn't take my word for it,' Janet addressed her niece, not the policeman.

Rosie followed the movement of the thin lips with difficulty. 'I'll wager you asked somebody else too. Who did you ask, Mr Policeman? Him? Bernard Peabody? Did you tell him that Frank was alive?'

'No, of course I didn't tell Bernard,' said Kenny. 'Didn't tell anyone.'

But Rosie saw how Fiona looked away and knew that Kenny was lying.

'HOW COULD YOU DO IT? HOW COULD YOU NOT TELL ME,' she cried, shouting so loudly that she felt the words ring in her deaf ears. 'GET OUT OF OUR HUH-HOUSE. BUH-BOTH OF YOU. GET OUT. GET OUT.'

'Rosie, I didn't mean to . . .'

'Wait, dearest, wait,' Bernard said but when he approached her, she raised not just her arm but her fist to ward him off.

'MY DADDY. WHERE IS MY DADDY?'

'Kenny,' Fiona said, quietly. 'I think we'd better leave.'

'No, I don't want Rosie to think I . . .'

'I NEVER WANT TO SEE YOU AGAIN, KENNETH MACGREGOR. I JUST WANT MY DADDY.'

'Aye,' said Aunt Janet, very clearly, 'but your Daddy doesn't want you.'


They rocked knee-to-knee in the front compart-ment of the tramcar and Kenny chain-smoked one cigarette after another as the almost empty vehicle swayed and rattled back towards the city. He had been shocked by Rosie's rejection and the haste with which Bernard Peabody had bundled them out of the house. The engagement was clearly off and would never be on again. No remission was possible, no appeal.

Fiona felt sorry for the deaf girl but tinting her pity was a faint egotistical satisfaction that she had been right all along and that Kenny, dazed by love, had handled the whole thing badly. She sat primly, solemnly, hands on top of her handbag observing his restless distress, waiting for him to speak. He dropped his third cigarette to the floor of the cabin and trod on it. She looked down at the flattened butt, at his polished shoes, size twelve: policeman's feet, her mother had called them long before Kenny had thought of joining the Force.

'I'll resign. I'll resign tomorrow first thing.'

'Why?' Fiona said.

'If I resign perhaps she'll have me back.'

'Kenneth, I really don't think . . .'

'What else can I do under the circumstances?'

'It wasn't your fault,' Fiona said, though she knew it was. 'That horrid, spiteful little woman did the damage. Did you see her enjoying herself, revelling in the misery she caused her sister?'

'My fault,' said Kenny. 'I brought the McKerlie woman into it. I should never have done that. I should have left well alone.'

'How *could* you leave well alone?' said Fiona, impatiently. 'You had a job to do. Lord knows, you gave her enough, that girl.'

'I thought you liked her?'

'I do. I did, but . . .'

'I love her.'

'Well, she doesn't love you any longer, that much is obvious.'

'No, no, please don't say that.'

'Kenneth, pull yourself together.'

'I can't.'

'Try.'

'I'm going to resign. I'm going back home.'

'Home?' said Fiona.

'To Mam and Dad.'

'Don't be ridiculous. You're not a spotty adolescent, Kenneth. You're thirty-four years old, a grown man, a sergeant in the CID.'

'I wish to God I'd never got involved.'

'What? With Rosie Conway?'

'No, with the Special Investigation Branch.'

'Bit late for regrets now, isn't it?' Fiona said. 'I thought you were going to enlist in the army or the air force, or something. Now you tell me you're sneaking off to Islay to lick your wounds.' She tapped his knee quite forcefully. 'What did you hope to gain by not telling anyone about Harker?'

'I thought I might be able to get rid of him without anyone finding out.'

'Well, that was pretty stupid of you,' Fiona said.

Her lack of sympathy galled him, rendered him less distraught than defensive. She didn't doubt that he would hear the girl's voice clacking in his ear for months to come, that he would waken in the night shaking with the nightmare of rejection. But that, after all, was the stuff of romance, at least in Fiona's book. Hurt, suffering and loss were just part of the price one paid for falling in love and she was glad it had never happened to her for she was pragmatic enough to realise that happy endings were few and far between.

'Where is her father anyway?' Fiona asked.

'I don't know. I wasn't lying. I have no idea where he is.'

'Might it not be sensible to find out.'

'For what?' said Kenny. 'To please that nasty wee woman?'

'Kenneth, he's a criminal.'

'Yes, I suppose he is.'

'Obviously he doesn't care about Rosie or he'd have made some effort to see her by now.'

'Do you think that's why Rosie's so upset?'

Fiona sighed. 'She's upset because she failed to grasp the fact that you've a job to do and have other obligations beside her. Harker and Manone are up to something that threatens our nation's security and it's your duty to stop them.'

'I wondered how long it would take you to mention my "duty".'

'Look,' Fiona said, 'if you insist on resigning from

the SIB at least do something constructive before you go.'

'What?' said Kenny, suspiciously.

'Track down this Harker fellow and hand him over. With luck you might even catch Manone in the same net. Finish the job you've started. After all it can hardly matter to the Conway girl now, can it? You're not doing anything – unfair.'

'I suppose that's true.'

'How reliable are your leads?'

'I've one fairly reliable contact.'

'Then pressure him. Who is it – Lombard?'

'Heck, no.'

'You aren't going to tell me, Kenneth, are you?'

'No.'

'You will use him, though, won't you? It's such a waste otherwise,' Fiona said. 'Such a dreadful waste of all our hard work.'

'I suppose it is,' said Kenny and took refuge from his sister – and his conscience – by lighting another cigarette.


At half-past nine o'clock on Monday morning two gentlemen from the Housing Committee turned up at Lyons & Lloyd's. No longer mere humble borough councillors, they came armed with badges of authority and sheaves of credentials signed on behalf of the Crown by a minion in the Scottish Office. Swollen with new-found importance, they exuded an air of officiousness that Bernard would have found amusing at any other time on any other day.

Bernard, however, was in no mood to be patronised. He had spent a dreadful evening trying to console his wife and stepdaughter and answer their hysterical accusations of disloyalty. He'd also had the thoroughly unpleasant task of ejecting Janet McKerlie from the house and, because courtesy demanded it, walking her to the bus stop. She had gone on at him as if he'd betrayed her trust when the plain fact was that he hardly knew the woman and had never met Frank Conway. He was stewing with rage by the time Janet's bus arrived, and had stalked about the streets of Knightswood for almost an hour before he'd calmed down enough to risk returning home in the fond hope that Lizzie and Rosie would have calmed down by then too. No such luck: the rest of the evening and much of the night had been taken up in consoling his grieving stepdaughter and trying vainly to assure his wife that their marriage remained valid and intact.

Rosie had been too fevered to go to work on Monday morning.

Bernard had promised that he would telephone Shelby's and report that she would not be in that day. He had made his own breakfast and, with Lizzie still closeted in the small side bedroom with Rosie, had gone off to catch an early train without daring to say goodbye.

He was furious at being cast as the villain of the piece, furious that all the love and trust he had built up with Lizzie's daughter had been shattered in a single evening by a malicious old spinster and the machinations of Dominic Manone. *'I hate you, Bernard,'* Rosie had shouted at one point. *'I hate you. I hate you,'* and he had no reason to doubt that she meant it.

He was still seething when he reached Breslin and too overwrought to be diplomatic when the borough councillors swaggered into the estate office. He refused to bow the knee to their badges or the signatures on their request forms, couldn't bring himself to be civil to these petty administrators who would undoubtedly revel in the backstage war and be the first to kowtow to the Nazis if by any chance the war was lost and Scotland fell into the hands of the enemy. He despised their tight shiny suits, their bowler hats, their arrogance, and made no attempt to hide his feelings. He might even have come to blows with the younger of the two if Allan Shakespeare hadn't arrived to smooth the councillors' ruffled feathers, escort them into his office and, with a scowl in Bernard's direction, order up tea and biscuits.

'What was that all about?' Sandra, the typist, enquired as she stuck the kettle on the little gas-ring in the cupboard behind her desk. 'You weren't very nice to them.'

'They're looking for empty properties to requisition.'

'For what?' said the girl.

'Refugees.'

'Refugees? What does that mean?'

'To house folk who've been bombed out.'

'Temporary accommodations, you mean?'

'Temporary or permanent, who knows? Once they get their hands on a property then there's no saying when it'll revert to private ownership again.'

'Bombed out?' Sandra raised a neatly-plucked eyebrow. 'Well, well!'

Bernard stepped into the closet, emerged with his hat jammed on his head and his overcoat tossed over his arm, went to the street door yanked it open.

'Where on earth are you going?' Sandra said.

'Out,' said Bernard and, slamming the door behind him, set off on foot for Blackstone Farm.


'I'll say this for you, Sergeant MacGregor, you've some nerve arriving uninvited at my house at this hour in the morning. What if my husband had been at home?'

'But he isn't, is he?' Kenny said.

'Fortunately for you, no, he isn't.'

'Why is it fortunate?' Kenny said. 'I mean, he's a civil sort of chap if Christmas is anything to go by. I'm sure him and me could have had a nice chat over coffee and cigars.'

'A nice chat about what in particular?' said Polly.

'You,' Kenny said. 'You and Tony Lombard.'

Polly gave a curt little nod as if his reply had merely confirmed her suspicions. She was irked at being caught in a stained skirt and a floral apron which made her feel like the sort of women the detective was used to dealing with. If Leah hadn't been hanging about in the drawing-room with her ears flapping she would have excused herself and gone upstairs to change into something more respectable, though to judge by the stern look on MacGregor's face and his aggressive manner it wouldn't have mattered to him if she'd been clad in clogs and a shawl. She led him out of the hallway into the back parlour, lit the electric fire and offered him tea, an offer he politely refused. Pleasant and pliant Sergeant MacGregor was pleasant and pliant no more.

'It's no use denying it, Mrs Manone,' he said. 'We know how often you've been with Lombard at his flat. We've dates and times recorded in our logs.'

Polly tucked in a curl that had escaped the dust-cap. 'It's no secret that I spend a great deal of time with Tony Lombard – with my husband's knowledge.'

'At Lombard's flat?' Kenny said. 'In Lombard's bed?'

'Be careful, Sergeant, just be careful.'

'I'm not the one who has to be careful,' Kenny said. 'We can prove you've been up there with Lombard, an hour here, an hour there. Did your husband condone those meetings?'

'You think I'm having an affair with Tony Lombard, don't you?'

'Aren't you?' said Kenny MacGregor.

'Of course not. Tony is, or was, my bodyguard.'

'From who or what is he supposed to be protecting you?'

'From John Flint,' said Polly, without hesitation.

'Flint? Why would Flint threaten you? Dominic and he are . . .'

'Oh, they may be friends now,' said Polly, 'but that wasn't always the case. Granted I haven't needed protection for three or four years but Tony proved useful in many other ways. He drove the car for me, took the children to school when our nanny was busy. Looked after us generally, you might say. Now do you honestly suppose I'd have an affair with a man who guarded my children and is my husband's most trusted employee?'

'Yes,' Kenny said. 'I think you might.'

'Has my sister, has Rosie seen this side of you?'

'Rosie and I aren't together any more.'

'Oh, really!' said Polly. 'Too much of a bully for her, were you?'

He wasn't cowed by her sharp tongue. She felt a wriggle of fear at the realisation that she had lost her protection – not Tony but Rosie. Until now she had regarded the sergeant as a bit of a joke and someone who might be useful to her if she played on his love for her sister. But now she saw that he was a copper through and through and realised that she could expect no favours now that he had broken with Rosie.

She said, 'I was under the impression that we had a mutual agreement.'

'Were you?' Kenny said. 'I don't remember any such thing.'

'What do you want from me?'

'I need to know where Lombard's hiding and who he's working with.'

'He works for my husband.'

'Who's he working with right now.'

'I really can't say,' said Polly. 'Why did you fall out with my sister? Was it her deafness? Can't be much fun whispering sweet nothings to a girl who can't hear them. I expect you've lots of other girls on the string.'

'What I have on the string,' Kenny said, 'is your father.'

'Bernard? What does Bernard . . .'

'Your real father,' Kenny said. 'Frank Conway, back from the dead.'

She knew at once that he was speaking the truth – neither Kenny nor his superiors were imaginative enough to have devised such a wicked lie – and a vision of the little man she'd met in at John Flint's office flashed into her mind.

She began to shake.

She sat down on a chair by the French doors and pressed her knees together.

'Where . . .' She cleared her throat. 'Where exactly is he?'

'Oh, he's around.' MacGregor had the upper

hand now. 'Tony probably knows where he is. Your husband certainly does. We'd like to find him before he does any more damage.'

'Has – does my mother . . .'

'Yes, she knows he's alive.'

'Are you sure it is my father?'

'We've obtained a positive identification from someone who knew him well.'

'Janet!' Polly nodded. 'My aunt, Janet McKerlie.'

'Yes, apparently he's passing himself off as Edgar Harker,' Kenny said. 'We know he's in Glasgow and has been in contact with your husband. Didn't Dominic tell you?'

'No.'

'Harker – your father – has been resident in the United States of America for the past umpteen years. He works for Carlo Manone.'

'I see,' said Polly.

She had been prepared to brazen out her affair with Tony and run off with him if it ever came to a showdown but this news was more than she could bear. She struggled to be selfish, to appear unaffected but suffered an urgent desire to be with her Mammy, to comfort Mammy, assure Mammy that Dominic would take care of this matter as efficiently has he had taken care of everything else. But Dominic had lied to her, had kept this astonishing fact from her too. Was it him, she wondered, the bullish wee fellow with the military moustache and scarred lip who had looked at Babs and her without compassion or sentiment and spun a glib fable about a hero's death? She remembered how the meeting had affected her, all without cause or reason, except instinct, the calling of blood to blood.

'Now he's over here in Scotland, working hand in glove with your husband on something that our government's very interested in,' Kenny pushed on remorselessly. 'They're all involved: Flint, Lombard, Harker and, of course, Dominic. It's something too important to be shoved under the carpet and my boss will move heaven and earth to find out what it is and lay the culprits by the heels.'

'Culprits,' Polly heard herself say. 'What a quaint way of putting it.'

'Whatever you choose to do about your father is a matter for the family,' Kenny continued. 'How this will affect your relationship with your husband . . .'

'Just what *do* you want from me?'

'I need to know where Harker is and precisely what he's up to.'

'So that you can arrest him?'

'If charges are brought, yes,' Kenny said.

'Tony too?'

'Tony?' Kenny said, surprised.

Perhaps he had expected her to trade for her father's safety or her husband's but she no longer cared what Kenny MacGregor thought of her.

She said, 'I'll get you all the information you need – on one condition.'

'What's the condition?'

'I want you to give Tony an opportunity to get out.'

'I can't make that sort of promise.'

'Time,' Polly said. 'I require just a little bit of time, Kenny MacGregor. Surely you can manage to delay matters for a week or two.'

'What will you give me in exchange, Mrs Manone?'

'Absolutely everything you need to make an arrest.'

'Including your husband?'

'Including my husband,' said Polly.

# Chapter Fifteen

Bonskeet's builders were pushing on with the bungalows over the hill from Blackstone Farm. The big
villas were already up and subject to the attentions
of plasterers and electricians. The first would be
occupied before Easter, most of the others by June.
Lyons & Lloyd's had taken their percentage as agents.
The rest of the profit would go into Bonskeet's coffers
from which, Bernard supposed, Dominic would duly
extract his share.

The bungalows were proving much more difficult
to shift, however, for the market had gone stone cold
in recent weeks. Allan Shakespeare had suggested that
the properties be advertised as safe havens from German
air raids, which, Bernard knew, was a palpable untruth.
Hardgate, Duntocher, Blackstone and Breslin lay close
to the Clyde and however efficient the Luftwaffe might
be he doubted if German bombardiers would be able to
target the shipyards with precision.

Such thoughts bobbed about in Bernard's head as he tramped up the track from the road and, stepping over a fence, approached the farm.

It was a breezy day, cloudy, more moist than cold, the wind gusting from the east. He heard nothing from the farm until he reached the whitewashed wall behind the stables and picked up the clack of machinery running an interrupted pattern that reminded him of a weaver's loom. He looked up at the roof. There wasn't a pigeon, crow or gull to be seen on the slates, not one hungry sparrow; whatever was going on inside was noisy and constant enough to keep the birds away. He tightened the belt of his overcoat, went around the gable, found a wooden door, opened it and slipped into the building unseen.

Beams overhead, a stone floor, empty horse stalls: he faced a flight of wooden steps that led up to a gallery protected by rails and straw bales. He climbed the steps and looked along the level of the raw wooden boards at the deafening machine. At first he thought there was no one there, only a scowling tabby crouched on the straw above him, Then a chap in a collarless shirt emerged from behind the machine, a screwdriver clenched between his teeth, an oilcan in his hand.

Catching sight of Bernard, he removed the screwdriver from his mouth, and shouted, *'Who the hell're you?'*

'I'm looking for Dominic Manone.'

'What?'

'Dominic Manone, I'm . . .'

The machine cut off abruptly. Dougie set down the oilcan but not the screwdriver. The tabby stirred, arched her back and surveyed Bernard with unnerving indifference.

'Dominic Manone,' Bernard said. 'I'm looking for . . .'

'Never heard o' him.'

'And just who are you?'

'Ah work here.'

'Doing what?' said Bernard.

'Ah work at not answerin' stupid questions.'

'You're printing something, aren't you?' Bernard took a pace forward. 'What are you printing?'

'Posters.'

'Show me.'

'Who the hell *are* you, man? Are you the polis?'

'I told you, I'm looking for Mr Manone.'

'Never heard—'

'Come off it,' Bernard said. 'Don't give me your patter. I lease this place to Dominic Manone. What's that you're hiding?'

'*Tony?*' Dougie shouted. '*Tony?*'

It was hardly a blow at all, certainly not a punch. Bernard caught Dougie's arm and swung him around, let him skip and fall to one knee, crying out. Then he scooped up an armful of the paper from the litter on the floor and selected from the trash a single wrinkled sheet. He studied it for a moment, then grunted.

'Fivers, forged fivers. So that's Dom's game, is it? Dear God, what next!'

'I guess that's up to you, Bernard,' Tony Lombard said from the top of the stairs. 'Yeah, I guess that's up to you.'

'It's a bit of a chortle, really,' John Flint said. 'I mean here she is tryin' to sell me somethin' I already own. I'm disappointed. I thought Polly had more class. Now the other one . . .'

'Babs,' Dominic said.

'Yeah, Babs – now *she* I could believe, but not Polly, not your dearly beloved wife, Dominic, old son.'

'She doesn't know about the money,' Dominic said.

'Then what's her game?' Flint said. 'I mean, hell, does she think I'm gonna shell out for a buncha stocks an' shares that could be worth less than the paper they're written on in six month time? I haven't a clue what you've got tucked away, Dom. It's your business, not mine. But Jesus, when a man's wife tries to sell him out then I've gotta start askin' questions, haven't I?'

'I told you – Polly can't possibly have found out about the money.'

'I only have your word for that,' Johnny Flint said.

'Big Q is, has she found out about me?' Edgar Harker said.

'What about you?' Dominic said.

'Who I am, what I'm doing here.'

'How could she?'

Harker shrugged. 'Same way she found out about the money.'

'For the last and final time,' Dominic said, 'Polly knows nothing about—'

'Okay, okay, keep your shirt on,' Harker said. 'I believe you, though thousands wouldn't.'

'How could she possibly have found out about Blackstone?' Dominic said.

Harker said. 'Somebody told her.'

'Somebody? Like who?' Dominic said.

Harker shrugged again. 'Somebody on the inside. What about this guy Babs is married to? What about him?'

'Hallop? No, no, not Jackie.'

'Why not Jackie?' said Harker.

'Because he's a nobody,' said Flint. 'Right, Dom?'

'He's also your brother-in-law,' Harker said.

'He runs a motoring showroom,' Dom said. 'Jackie Hallop has no connection with what's going on at Blackstone.'

'So,' Harker said, 'it's Polly we hafta worry about.'

Dominic hadn't taken off his hat or overcoat. He stood before the desk, hands stuffed into his pockets, shoulders hunched. He looked dejected, as well he might considering he'd just been told that his wife was planning to sell his business out from under him. However much you might be tempted to admire strength and determination in a woman there were limits to a man's tolerance and Flint reckoned that Dominic Manone was close to that limit now.

No sounds drifted up from the cinema. It was too early for the afternoon show. Cleaners would be moving between the seats, a Gaumont van would soon deliver the weekend reels. In the projection room an assistant would be dusting the lenses. In outer offices telephones rang and teleprinters chattered monotonously but in Flint's suite silence reigned.

At length Dominic said, 'Did Polly mention Blackstone by name?' He spoke as softly as if he were crooning a lullaby.

Flint had heard that tone before and knew it signified not capitulation but threat. He adjusted his position on, not behind the desk, crossed one leg over the other and folded his arms before he answered, 'Nope.'

'Did she say anything about fake money?'

'Matter of fact, no.'

'She asked if you would be prepared to help her run my business if something happened to me, is that correct?' said Dominic.

'Substantially correct, yeah,' Flint said.

'What did Babs contribute to the conversation?'

'Not much. Moral support, I suppose.'

'So you've not one shred of evidence that my wife knows anything at all about Blackstone or counterfeit money.'

'For Christ's sake, son . . .' Harker protested.

Dominic turned on him. He moved more nimbly than any of the boxers John Flint had on his books. A sudden shift of weight and his hands were on Harker's lapels. He pulled the man to him and turned him, snaring his arm and ramming it hard against his back, forcing Harker's face to the wall. He leaned into him and spoke, still softly, into his ear.

'Don't think I don't know who you are, Frank,' Dominic said. 'Don't think I didn't do *my* homework before I agreed to deal with you. You're enjoying this, aren't you? You just love the whole idea of stirring up trouble for Lizzie Conway and her girls, your daughters. I don't know why. I can't figure out your reasons, unless you're just nasty. Yes, I think that's it – nasty.'

'You're hurtin' me.'

'Oh, no,' Dominic said. 'I haven't even begun to hurt you yet.'

Johnny uncrossed his legs and placed both feet on to the floor. It had been ten years or more since he had seen this side of Dominic Manone, the quiet, invidious, efficient use of violence, but he remembered all too clearly what had happened to his boss, the late Chick McGuire.

'How did you recognise me?' Harker said.

'I wasn't a kid when you skipped out,' Dominic said. 'I saw you hanging around the Rowing Club often enough to remember you.'

'Yeah, but you thought I was dead, didn't you?'

'Why didn't my father tell me you were working for him?'

''Cause I asked him not to,' Harker said. 'You think I wanna be here at all? Know what you are, son? You're a hick, a third-rater. Always were, always will be. That's why your old man left you behind in Scotland.' He twisted his head, tried to look back over his shoulder. 'You gonna tell Polly who I am, Polly and Babs? You gonna blow this opportunity just for the sake of a doll from the Gorbals, even if she is my daughter?'

Dominic released him. Harker eased round, massaging his forearm and shoulder, still grinning that ghastly, disabled grin.

'Polly is my concern,' Dominic said.

'Then do somethin' about her,' Harker said, 'before she gets us all sent up the goddamned Swanee.'

Dominic put his hands in his pockets, walked to the front of the desk and contemplated the opaque glass of the big window.

'I sent her,' he said.

'You what? You sent her where?' said Harker.

'To him, to Flint, to test him out.'

'What the hell for?' Johnny blurted out. 'Don't you trust me?'

Dominic gave a little laugh, three chesty spurts of sound. 'I sent the girls round here to dangle the bait, Johnny. Didn't you guess?'

'Well, I – I mean, I did sorta have a—'

'Is this gonna change things?' Harker interrupted.

'No,' Dominic answered. 'It changes nothing.'

'Just as well,' Harker said. 'Otherwise we could

all wind up dead in the water. I mean it, son. I really do mean dead.'

'What?' Johnny said. 'Me an' all?'

Harker had seated himself on one of the red leather banquettes. He did not appear in the least ruffled. Jaunty, self-loving arrogance was so ingrained that no one, not even Dominic Manone, could shake it. He groomed his moustache with his hand, then said, 'You too, Flinty, you an' him an' anybody gets in the way.'

'I take it you've promised the money to an organisation none of us can stand up to?' Dominic said. 'I take it you know what the profits will be used for?'

'I gotta fair idea,' said Harker.

'How did my father get tangled up with the Nazis?'

'They came to him,' Edgar Harker said. 'They had the plates an' the girl. They offered him the whole package. They wanted to set up in England but your old man talked them out of it. Scotland, he said, Scotland's the place, all they think about in Scotland's football an' drink.'

'Who do you rendezvous with over here?' Dominic said.

'Nobody yet.'

'So how do you channel the cash to the agents?'

'Agents?' Johnny said. 'What agents?'

Harker said, 'I don't.'

Dominic said, 'What do you do then?'

'Agents?' Johnny said again. 'You mean, like spies?'

Harker said, 'It's done through a private bank. The account's already been established.'

'Who opened it? You?'

'Me, yeah.'

'When the account has enough in it to make it worthwhile,' Dominic said, 'I assume you'll transfer smaller sums to other accounts in the provinces.'

'I won't, but somebody else will?' Harker shrugged. 'I'll have my whack by that time, your old man'll have his. What do I care where the loot winds up?'

'You could hang for this, Frank,' Dominic said.

'I could hang for a lotta things,' Harker told him.

'Will somebody please tell me what the hell you're talkin' about?'

'It's a secret, Flinty, a dead secret,' Harker said.

'I don't like secrets. Fact, I hate secrets. Look,' Johnny said apologetically, 'what am I gonna do when Polly comes back here?'

'She won't,' Dominic said.

'You sure?'

'I'm sure.'

Harker got to his feet, slapping his hands on his thighs.

'Dominic knew all about it, remember,' he said. 'Sendin' Polly here was all Dominic's idea in the first place. Right?'

'That's right,' said Dominic.

'Dom's got everything under control.'

'That I have,' said Dominic.

'Includin' my daughter, his wife.'

'God Almighty!' Johnny said. 'What a soddin' mess this is turnin' out to be. I don't know if I wanna be part of it any more.'

'Too late now, Flinty,' said Harker.


'Bernard, for God's sake, will you calm down,' Tony Lombard said.

'Calm down!' Bernard shouted. 'Calm bloody down!'

'It's got nothing to do with you.'

'Hasn't it?' Bernard stormed. 'It's got a lot to do with me. I'm the mug arranged the lease on this place. My signature's on the documents.'

'Burn them then,' said Tony. 'Get rid of them.'

'Bit bloody late for that, isn't it?' Bernard would not be placated. 'So this is what it's all about, is it? Coining? Who the hell's he?'

'Mah name's Dougie.'

'He's the printer, I suppose?' Bernard said.

'Look, why don't we get out of here. Go over to the farm an' have coffee.'

'I don't want coffee. I want explanations.'

Dougie plucked the tabby from the straw and held her close against his chest as if he feared that Bernard would do her harm. Penny appeared on the stairs. She had been caught out and had flung on her clothes and a weird-looking turban. She knew who Bernard was but not his position in the Manone hierarchy and consequently let Tony do the talking.

'Is Dominic not here?' Bernard said.

'No, you might be able to catch him at the warehouse.'

'What about Conway, or Harker, or whatever the hell he calls himself?'

'Conway?' Tony said. 'You don't mean Frank Conway?'

'I do mean Frank Conway,' Bernard said. 'The bastard wasn't dead apparently. Now he's back in Glasgow and in cahoots with Dominic and between them they're wrecking my marriage.'

Tony spun round and grabbed Penny before she could retreat down the staircase. 'Is this true? Is Harker Polly's father? Is he really Frank Conway?'

She had known all along that Eddie had another identity. He'd emerged wounded from the trenches – had deserted, in fact – had stolen another man's name before he'd sought refuge with Carlo Manone in Philadelphia. What hold Eddie had over Carlo Manone was just one more mystery.

She said, 'I think it may be so.'

Tony turned to Bernard once more. 'Does Polly know her old man's come back from the dead?'

'Dominic kept it from her, kept it from all of us, in fact.'

'Can't blame him,' Tony Lombard said. 'I'd have done the same.'

'Because you're all tarred with the same brush,' said Bernard.

'What's that supposed to mean?'

'Eye-ties, traitors.'

Tony bristled. 'Hang on just a damned minute . . .'

'Not only traitors – cowards.'

The girl caught Tony's sleeve before he could throw a punch. He wrestled with her and broke her grip but the split second's delay brought his temper under control. He mustn't allow the guy to rile him. He had spent the night in bed with Penny and on hearing Bernard Peabody's voice he'd suffered a massive fit of guilt at betraying Polly. There was something about Peabody that he both feared and admired, like the sanctity of priests or the chastity of nuns.

'Tony, he did not mean it,' Penny Weston said.

'Oh, but I did.' Bernard jerked a thumb. 'Is that who you're making this counterfeit stuff for, the Italians?'

'No, it's just money,' Tony said, 'just business.'

'God, doesn't he have enough? Does Dominic have to risk his neck and Polly's happiness by making even more.' Bernard blew out a long breath. 'Does this contraption actually work?'

'Yep,' Tony answered, warily.

'Can it print anything else besides English fivers?'

'Like what?' said Tony.

'Lira, Deutschmarks, Yankee dollars?'

'Give us a break, mister,' Dougie said.

'Listen,' Tony said, 'if you want in on it, just ask Dominic. There's plenty to go around.'

'I don't want any of his dirty money,' Bernard said. 'I just want to get my hands on Frank Conway. I want rid of him.'

'Rid of him?' the girl said in a strange, shrill voice.

'I want him out of the country before he does any more damage to my girls.'

'I don't care what you do to Harker,' Tony said, 'but leave Polly out of it.'

'I'm not *that* concerned about Polly. It's Rosie I worry about.'

Tony had never understood men like Bernard Peabody, war veterans, hard-working, dependable, modest guys. In his younger days he'd thought of them as mugs and suckers until Dominic had taught him otherwise.

He watched Bernard lift another spoiled sheet from the floor.

It had been careless of him to sleep late, not guard the stable, keep watch on the track. Wardens, special constables and do-gooding patriots were everywhere these days. Only a matter of time before some nosy parker made his way up the track to Blackstone. Careless, he'd been careless. He had Penny to thank – or blame – for that. All he really wanted was Polly, Polly and a little hard cash.

'How good are these?' Bernard asked.

'Good,' Dougie told him. 'As good as the real thing.'

'How did Dominic come by the plates?'

'Bernard,' Tony said, 'the less you know the better.'

'You're right.' Bernard shook the printed sheet from his fingertips. 'I've no desire to get involved in this dirty business.'

'You will tell no one what you have seen here, will you?' Penny said.

Bernard shook his head. 'All I want is Conway, or Harker, or whatever he calls himself now. I just want that bastard out of our hair once and for all.'

'What will the girls have to say to that?' Tony asked.

'They'll thank me for it.'

'You sure?'

'In the long run,' Bernard said, 'I'm certain they will.'


'Are you tellin' me,' said Lizzie, 'you knew he was here in Glasgow?'

Polly shook her head. 'No, Mammy, I had no idea who he was when Babs and I bumped into him.'

'She had a feelin', though,' Babs put in. 'Didn't you, honey?'

'Yes, yes I did.'

'What sort o' feelin'?' said Lizzie.

'Strange, as if we'd met before.'

'Well, you had,' said Lizzie. 'A long, long time ago. He held you in your arms when you were a babby.

Used t' take you round to the Rowing Club to show you off. He was awful proud o' you.'

'Proud, was he?' Babs said. 'Well, he'd a bloody funny way o' showin' it.'

'Don't you remember him at all?' Lizzie asked.

'No, thank God!' said Babs. 'What was I – three or somethin' when he skedaddled? I thought you said he was tall, dark an' handsome.'

'Isn't he?' said Lizzie.

'He's a nyaff,' said Babs. 'An ugly wee nyaff.'

'And he has a moustache,' said Polly. 'A horrible brown moustache.'

'I can see him wi' a moustache,' said Lizzie, wistfully. 'Aye, I always thought a moustache would suit him. Is he on the run?'

'Not as far as I know,' Polly said. 'He's here to do business with Dominic, however, and Kenny MacGregor's got wind of it.'

'Can't think why you want to meet him,' Babs said, 'not after what he done to us, runnin' out an' leaving you with three kids an' in debt to the Manones.'

'Twenty years in Philadelphia and he made no attempt to tell us he was alive,' Polly said. 'He knew how bad things were for us because he worked for Carlo Manone but we could have starved for all the help he offered you.'

'I want to meet him,' Lizzie said.

'*No,*' Polly snapped, and Babs threw up her hands in despair.

Lizzie had reached Raines Drive by bus and tramcar, navigating her way nervously across the city. Before leaving she had telephoned Polly from the box at Anniesland Cross and had asked – no, told – her to meet at Babs's house. She had stubbornly refused to tell Polly what had upset her and had been saved from interrogation by a telephone operator who had conveniently cut her off.

Polly guessed that it had something to do with her father, not Bernard, the other one: that was how she thought of him now, *the other one*. She had sent Patricia round to Babs's house with a message and instructions to bring baby April back with her which the nanny duly did. Pat would look after the child and also collect the Hallops from school, if necessary.

'Rosie wants to meet him,' Lizzie said.

'Well, Rosie can just bloody want,' said Babs.

'Don't you want to meet him?' Lizzie said.

'I've met him already,' Babs said. 'Once was enough.'

'He's your father, your natural father,' Lizzie said.

'He's a bastard,' Babs declared, 'a natural-born bastard that's what he is.'

'Rosie doesn't know that,' said Lizzie.

'Then it's time somebody told her. Time *you* told her,' Babs said.

'There are things have t' be settled,' said Lizzie. 'Legal things.'

Polly said, 'Stop looking for excuses, Mammy. You are *not* going to meet him – and that's flat.'

'Since when did you become the voice o' authority?' said Lizzie.

'Since the day I married Dominic Manone,' Polly told her.

'She's right, Mam,' said Babs. 'As for the legal stuff – heck, I reckon the old bastard'll run a mile if you just breathe the word "divorce". I dunno what he's up to but I'm willin' to bet it's crooked.' She paused, scowling at her mother who sat in a floral-pattern armchair with her hands in her lap and her eyes cast down, not defeated or contrite but quietly obstinate. 'What do you think, Mammy? Do you think he's gonna present himself before the court to settle a matter he settled years ago. He's *dead*, for God's sake! He's been dead for years.'

'It just doesn't feel right,' said Lizzie.

'What doesn't?' said Babs.

'Bein' married to Bernard now.'

'Oh, God! Is *that* it?' Babs exclaimed. 'Suddenly you've got a conscience about poor old Bernard?'

'Under law,' said Polly, 'Bernard is still your husband.'

'Says who?' Lizzie asked.

'Father, my other father, was declared dead.'

'No he wasn't. They wouldn't even give me a pension.'

'That's beside the point,' said Polly. 'Besides . . .' She hesitated. 'Besides, he's married again too.' Her mother's mouth opened and closed like a fish out of water. She uttered a little popping noise and swayed back in the chair. Polly pushed on remorse-lessly. 'Married to a young woman who's with him over here.'

'You're kiddin',' Babs said.

'I'm sorry,' said Polly, 'I'm not.'

'Did Dominic tell you that?' said Lizzie.

'Yes.' Polly felt cheap at having to lie to her mother but the little ache of conscience passed off quickly. 'He told me that Edgar Harker arrived in Scotland accompanied by his wife. I've actually seen her. Young, very young, and very pretty, if you care for that sort of thing.'

'What sort of thing?' Lizzie got out.

'Blondes with big long legs,' said Polly. 'So, Mother, if you came here this morning hoping I'd be able to set up a meeting between you and my other father then you're going to be disappointed.'

Lizzie began to protest. 'But Rosie . . .'

'It doesn't matter what you or Rosie want. Our problem,' Polly said, 'is to get shot of Dad before he does anything drastic. You wouldn't want to inflict a High Court trial on Rosie, would you, Mammy? God, the press would have a field day.'

'Give in, Mammy,' said Babs. 'Forget he ever existed.'

'I can't,' said Lizzie. 'I can't forget him. And I won't forgive him.'

'Forgive him?' said Polly.

'For goin' away or for comin' back?' said Babs.

'For sleepin' with my sister Janet,' Lizzie said.

★ ★ ★

'How long ago did all this happen?' Dominic said.

'An hour,' Tony said. 'I gave Peabody ten minutes to clear the track then hopped in the car and drove straight here. I thought I'd better warn you he's out for blood.'

'Bernard isn't going to harm me,' Dominic said. 'It's Harker he's scared of. When he cools down he'll realise we're on the same side.'

'He knows about the money, though. He saw the machinery.'

'Bernard won't peach. He has too much to lose.'

'Did you know this guy Harker was Polly's father?' Tony asked.

'I found out for sure only two or three days ago.'

'How did you find out?'

'Through a friend, a good friend.'

They were alone in the office on the top floor of the Central Warehouse. Dominic had sent his secretary off to an early lunch and the corridor outside the pebble-glass door was deserted.

'Somebody who knows Harker, you mean?' Tony asked.

'Somebody who knows him only too well.'

'I wish to God you'd let me in on this. I'm sick of being kept in the dark.'

'I have a friend,' Dominic said, 'who has a friend in Whitehall.'

'I thought maybe you'd cabled your old man,' Tony said.

'Dad?' Dominic paused. 'Dad probably had good reason for not telling me and took a chance that I wouldn't remember Frank Conway.'

'Protecting your wife, was he? Protecting Polly?'

'Protecting himself, more like,' said Dominic.

'Is he throwing us to the wolves?' said Tony. 'Is that why the printing's being done over here instead of Philadelphia or New York? I can't believe your old man couldn't shake out a Yankee printer as good as Dougie Giffard.'

Dominic was seated on the edge of the desk, one leg stretched out. He sat very still, remote and distant as if he were thinking of other things entirely.

'What we're involved in,' Dominic said at length, 'is building a network of enemy agents. The plates probably originated in Germany, the paper was manufactured in Italy. Presumably the Nazis have planted a number of agents in strategic positions in this country and have to find a means of paying them. Harker's managing the scheme but I doubt if even he knows who he's working for. By that I mean, he isn't going to be invited to tea at the Germany embassy. He'll filter the counterfeit money through Flint and he's already established an account in a private bank into which he can deposit the profit. Later, that account will be split and certain sums transferred to other accounts in other banks. By that time the money will be virtually untraceable.'

'Where are these agents located?'

'That's something we'll never find out,' Dominic said. 'Coventry, I expect. Portsmouth, Plymouth, here on Clydeside too for all I know. They'll be strategically positioned in munitions factories or aircraft plants, on the boards of companies who have access to government orders. It really wouldn't surprise me if there were one or two in Westminster, perhaps even in Whitehall itself.'

'Nazis,' Tony said. 'We're printing money for the Nazis.'

'Germany may not be the enemy for long,' Dominic said.

'Hey, don't tell me you're going Italian on me?'

Dominic lowered himself from the desk, turned to the window and stared out at the river. 'When the war does come,' he said, 'where will *you* stand, Tony?'

'Where I've always stood,' said Tony, 'with you.'

'No,' Dominic said. 'No, not with me.'

'I don't get it.'

'It won't be safe to stand with me.' He swung round again. 'I want you to marry Penny Weston and get her out of the country.'

Tony felt his blood run cold. He swallowed, spit sticky in his mouth, like glue. 'What – what's she to you, Dominic? What do you care what . . .'

'Listen,' Dominic said, 'I know what's been going on. I want you out of it.' He smiled again. 'She's perfect for you, Tony. She'll keep you in order. She'll make sure you don't stray.'

'Stray?'

'Don't make me say it, Tony.'

He was silent, stunned but still unsure. Polly was in the forefront of his mind, Polly and adultery, Polly and betrayal. Was he being sent away because of his affair with Polly? Was Dom offering him the easy way out?

'Oh, come on, Tony. You'd think it was a death sentence,' Dominic said. 'If it doesn't work out there's always divorce.'

'I'm – I'm a Catholic.'

'So?'

'Please, no, don't ask me to do this.'

'I'm not asking you,' Dominic said. 'I'm telling you.'

'What if Penny don't wanna marry me?'

'She will,' Dominic said. 'She'll marry any man for a second chance.'

'Second chance, what's that supposed to mean?'

'Anyone who'll get her away from Harker.'

'Harker? What does Harker have to do with it?'

'She's Harker's wife,' Dominic said. 'They were married in New York just before the ship sailed.'

'Did your pal in Whitehall tell you that?'

'He didn't have to,' Dominic said.

'If she's married already,' Tony got out, 'she isn't free to marry me?'

'Widows,' Dominic said, 'are always free.'

'Widows?' said Tony. 'You've lost me, Dom. You've left me way behind.'

'I'm afraid that's true, Tony,' Dominic said. 'I'm very much afraid that's true.'

As soon as he entered headquarters Kenny knew something was wrong. Perhaps, he thought, the Irish had struck with another bomb blast in retaliation for recent arrests but there were no signs of agitation in the crowd that gathered in the hallway outside the muster room and he had hardly stepped through the door when DC Galbraith grabbed him by the arm.

'Whoa!' Kenny said. 'What is it? What's happened?'

'It's Wetsock,' Galbraith said. 'He's gone.'

'Gone? What, sacked?'

'Nah, nah,' said Galbraith. 'He collapsed. One minute he was sittin' at his desk talkin' to your sister, next minute he was spewin' blood from every orifice. What a soddin' mess. The cleaners are still moppin' up.'

'Is Fiona all right.'

'Oh, sure. You know her better'n I do,' Galbraith said. 'She had an ambulance at the door within five minutes, before she even reported to a senior officer. No sense o' protocol, your sister.'

'Never mind my sister,' Kenny said. 'How bad is it with Winstock?'

'Bad, so I've heard. Busted ulcer. Suspected peritonitis. He's in the Vickie undergoin' emergency surgery. May not peg out.'

'When did this happen?'

'Ten or half-past this mornin'. Never know the minute, do you?' Galbraith said. 'Wonder what'll happen to us now?'

'Us?'

'The Unit.'

'Oh that!' said Kenny.

'Since we haven't really achieved anything,' Galbraith said, 'maybe they'll close us down. I don't fancy goin' back on regular duties, do you?'

'No option,' Kenny said, 'unless they put some-body else in charge.'

'Like who?' Galbraith said. 'Fiona?'

In spite of the gravity of the situation, Kenny chuckled.

'We could do worse,' he said. 'Perhaps they'll fetch someone up from Scotland Yard? One thing's for sure, even if he does pull through that's the last any of us will see of poor old Wetsock. I hope he's okay.'

'Me too,' Galbraith said. 'What do we do right now, though?'

'Hang about, wait for orders,' Kenny said.

He slipped his hand into his coat pocket and fingered the letter that he'd typed out on Fiona's machine at home. He hadn't told her that he intended to present a letter of resignation to Inspector Winstock at the end of the shift. It wasn't that he had become disillusioned with policing or wished to plunge into army life. He felt guilty about Rosie and honour bound to try to make amends. In spite of everything, he still wanted to marry her. The thought of some other man stealing her away made his stomach hurt. Resignation was the only solution but it was going to take more guts than he possessed to stand before the Deputy Chief Constable and resign when Winstock was fighting for his life in the Victoria Infirmary.

Within an hour Kenny was summoned to the Chief Inspector's room on the third floor. There he found not only Superintendent Rogerson but also Inspectors Caple and McLaren and, occupying the chair behind the desk, no less a person than the Chief Constable, Percy J. Sillitoe.

The interview was brief and succinct.

Kenny was informed that Inspector Winstock would not be returning to duty in the foreseeable future. Apparently the Inspector had been ailing for some time. The lack of satisfactory results in the SPU investigations might be laid therefore at Inspector Winstock's door. A replacement was urgently needed. Would he, Sergeant Kenneth MacGregor be prepared to head the Special Protection Unit on a temporary basis with the assurance that he would receive a promotion to the rank of Detective Inspector if he proved himself worthy of the honour.

Kenny felt the letter in his pocket crumple of its own accord. He gave it a helping hand, stuffing it into the corner of his pocket as if he feared that the basilisk gaze of Chief Constable Sillitoe, scourge of the uncommitted, would penetrate the material and see just how little honour he, Kenny MacGregor, attached to being part of the thin blue line.

'Well, MacGregor, what do you say?' the Chief Constable asked.

'I – I . . .'

'Come on, lad,' growled Rogerson, 'surely you don't have to think about it.'

Kenny swallowed hard. His stomach hurt. His collar was slick with perspiration but the letter of resignation was nothing but a crumpled ball in his coat pocket. 'No, sir,' he said. 'Thank you, sir. I accept.'

'Good man,' Percy Sillitoe said. 'But hear me well, Sergeant, I need results before I get any more flak from the Home Office.'

'Yes, sir. I'll do my best,' said Kenny.

'Your very best,' said Rogerson.

'My very best,' Kenny promised.

# Chapter Sixteen

The cat was not the only creature at Blackstone Farm who had grown plump on Penny's cooking. Dougie too had put on weight and sported a nice little middle-class tummy that swelled his shirt-fronts comfortably. He was no longer dependent on whisky. In fact he had almost lost his taste for the hard stuff and preferred a dish of tea or a glass of cream soda by way of refreshment, particularly when he was working over in the stables which, as April ran out, was most of the time. Penny would trot across the courtyard several times a day bearing trays of tea and scones or fizzy drinks in tall glasses, would stay with Dougie longer than Tony liked, for he had a feeling they were gossiping like a couple of schoolgirls about him. And for once Tony was right.

'Did he bring you them flowers?' Dougie asked.

'Yes, he did,' Penny answered.

'Bouquets.' Dougie sighed. 'Bouquets an' champagne.'

'They are only daffodils,' Penny said.

'Maybe so,' Dougie said. 'But I don't like it, lass. He's bein' far too nice t' you. He's up to somethin'.' Penny no longer had the gall to blush when Dougie added, 'Besides what goes on upstairs, I mean.'

'He is wooing me, I believe,' said Penny.

'Wooin' you? What the heck for?'

'Perhaps he is falling in love with me.'

'That'll be the day!' said Dougie.

Penny was not entirely taken in by Tony's changed attitude towards her. In bed he was ardent, almost too ardent, though there were no more perverse little acts involving gas-masks. She had a feeling, though, that try as he might his heart was not in it any longer. To compensate he brought her flowers and chocolates. She accepted his attentions warmly enough and applied herself enthusiastically to cooking and cleaning as if she felt obliged to prove herself a good *hausfrau* as well as a good lover.

Dougie observed the *pas de deux* with wry amusement. He reminded Penny a little of her grandmother, Oma Keller, who had been her closest friend and confidante. Dougie had a similar air of watchful affection and however much he teased and even criticised her, Penny was sure he would never let her down. In many ways she preferred Dougie to Tony Lombard for Tony Lombard had no wit or sensitivity and cared nothing for the texture of the world.

'I think perhaps he will ask me to marry him,' Penny said.

Dougie snorted. He was smeared with oil, hair mussed, shirt rumpled.

'If he does,' he said, 'what're you goin' to tell him?'

Dougie was looking at her with a sly questioning expression, exactly like Oma Keller's when she'd trailed home late from a dinner party or a ball.

'I do not know what you mean,' Penny said.

'Well, it's either yea or nay, lass.'

'Yea or nay – or perhaps' Penny said.

'If you fancy Tony for a husband,' Dougie said, 'I wouldn't dangle him on the string too long.'

'Why not?'

'Unless I'm much mistook Tony can have his pick o' women.'

'Ah, but not women like me,' said Penny. 'In any case, I did not come to Scotland to find a husband. I came to make money for myself and my mother.'

'Hard cash is always more dependable than a man.'

'Do you believe that to be true?' Penny asked, frowning.

'Naw,' Dougie said, 'but I thought you might.'

'Do not put words into my mouth or thoughts into my head.'

'Aren't you in luh-huve wi' our Tony then?' Dougie said.

'I did not say that I am not.'

'Make up your mind, lass,' Dougie said. 'I've got this blessed contraption just about ready t' roll.

457

When that happens an' the money flows everythin' will change again, not necessarily for the better.'

'Because of Eddie, do you mean?'

'Aye, an' the rest o' them,' Dougie said.

'So,' Penny said, 'you think they will squabble over the money?'

'I'm damned sure they will,' said Dougie.


Polly waited the best part of a week for Dominic to challenge her for she didn't have the strength to confront him and precipitate the inevitable crisis. She had lived in the shadow of her husband's secrets for years but adjusting to new secrets made her nervous, more nervous than she had ever been at the height of her affair with Tony.

All she had to do was square up to Dominic and say, 'Why didn't you tell me that my father's alive,' and he would be on the spot. She could force him to confide in her, expose at a stroke the depth of his deception, his callous indifference to her family, his double standards, his double life. Provided he didn't know about her call on Flint. She wondered if Flint had told Dominic about it or if greed had kept him silent. If she had known then that her father was involved with Flint – that her father was even alive – she wouldn't have let Babs talk her into it. The fact remained that Dominic had known that Frank Conway had returned from the dead and had not had the decency to tell her. If the boot had been on the other foot what a song and dance there would have been, as if only Italians were entitled to have family ties and not the humble Scots who dwelled in tenement towns.

She fretted about Janet, about Kenneth MacGregor, about her mother, most of all about poor Rosie who had been so hurt by Dominic's mendacity. She did not fret for herself, though, for she was almost willing to admit that she had brought calamity upon herself, a victim of her own restlessness, of wanting more without knowing what 'more' meant or what having it might entail.

Dominic hadn't touched her for a week, in bed or out of it. At night he would lie beside her, hands behind his head, so still and silent that she didn't know whether he was asleep or awake: then, on Tuesday, he suddenly said, 'I'm taking you out to lunch tomorrow.'

'Are you?' Her voice sounded rusty. 'Why?'

'Please be ready at ten o'clock. I'll pick you up here in the car.'

'Lunch, at ten o'clock in the morning?'

'I have someone I want you to meet first.'

Oh God! Oh God! My father, he's taking me to meet my father, Polly thought, and experienced a sickening hollowness within her. She parted her lips to cry out, 'Is it my father? Is it my Daddy?' but realised that was exactly how Dominic expected her to react and that by doing so she would give away every last advantage.

She managed to sound calm, almost bored. 'Some-one interesting?'

'I think you'll find them interesting, yes.'

'Ten o'clock, you say?'

'Prompt,' said Dominic.


It was a bright spring day but deceptively chilly. Cart horses still wore their canvases and the women about town had not yet shed their furs.

Polly selected her outfit with care, a tailored suit in box cloth, a swagger coat draped over her shoulders. The hat was simple, almost mannish, one that Dominic had never liked. He said nothing about the hat, however, chatted casually to her about the children, the weather and the war while they drove into the city. He parked the car outside the Baltic Chambers, escorted her to a side entrance and into a passenger lift that hoisted them slowly up to the fifth floor.

Polly's heart was pounding and she had an ache like an unhealed scar just under her breastbone as the lift laboured upward and deposited them in a corridor flanked by offices. Six or eight paces carried them to a door, not glass but oak. Dominic knocked and ushering Polly before him, entered.

There were two men in the room, two faces she recognised, not strangers.

Dominic said, 'I believe you know Mr Shadwell?'

'I do indeed,' said Polly.

Although Victor Shadwell had visited her house many times but she had exchanged hardly a dozen words with him over the years.

'And Mr Hughes?' said Dominic.

The lawyer too had visited Manor Park Avenue, had been locked in the front parlour with Dominic while she had kept tactfully out of sight. He was tall, with hawkish features, and emanated such an effortless air of good breeding that Polly was flattered to have him shake her hand.

The room was part of a suite. A single window looked out over slates and chimneys and the odd decorative iron-work that had been all the rage in roof finishing twenty or thirty years ago. There was no desk, only an oval table, four chairs padded in maroon leather and an array of bookcases packed with calf-bound volumes. On the desk was a bronze ashtray, a carafe of water, four glasses, and a pile of box files and ledgers.

'Well, gentlemen,' Dominic said, drawing out a chair for Polly, 'shall we get down to it?'

The ache in her chest eased. She felt 'floaty', as if she were recovering from an illness. She'd no idea why Dominic had brought her to the lawyer's chambers but it was obvious that her father had no part in it. She seated herself at the table and took off her gloves.

'Dominic,' she said, 'may I ask why you have brought me here?'

'Haven't you told her yet?' Victor Shadwell said.

'Told me what?' said Polly.

'I wanted it to be a surprise,' said Dominic.

Victor shook his head. He was an old man now but age had granted him a dignity that he had not possessed before. He said, 'I was under the impression that Mrs Manone was keen to participate. Haven't you even asked her, man?'

'I didn't have to,' Dominic said.

The men discussed her as if she wasn't there at all. Glancing up, she caught Carfin Hughes's eye and he gave a little shake of the head and arched his brows as if to absolve himself from discourtesy.

He tapped his knuckles on the table to gain Dominic's attention. 'Perhaps,' he said, 'we would do better to lay out the proposition and enquire of Mrs Manone what *she* feels about it and if she *is* willing to participate.'

'Hmmm,' said Dominic. 'Yes.'

The men seated themselves in a semi-circle facing her. Carfin Hughes leaned forward and clasped his hands as if he were about to lead them in prayer. He paused – a courtroom habit, Polly thought – then said, 'Dominic has expressed a wish that you be shown the books: that is, the profit and loss accounts of the holdings to which he has access: that is, a listing or tally of all Manone investments, together with portfolios of company stock.'

Polly said, 'Why are you telling me this, Mr Hughes? Why not Mr Shadwell who, I believe, is our accountant?'

'There are legal implications,' Carfin Hughes said.

'To what?'

'The transfer of shares, stock, bonds and debentures. The Law of Property Act of 1925 did not make the matter of transfer any less complex. I am here to ensure that you comprehend the law, Mrs Manone, and that the transfer or, more properly, transfers are effected without flaw. Dominic also suggests that I assume full power of attorney. I wish to ensure that you are satisfied with such an arrangement and will give me your confidence when I act on your behalf in matters relating to the holdings and transfers thereof.'

In spite of the flowery language and Carfin Hughes's rich, soft drawl, Polly grasped at once what he meant: Dominic was giving her a hand in the business: giving her what she'd always wanted and more, much much more. She felt a stab of apprehension, not just that he should have capitulated with her wishes so completely but that she would not be able to cope with the intricacies of ownership. My God, she thought, I don't even know what 'business' we're talking about.

She lifted her chin and stared haughtily at her husband.

He was toying with an unlit cigar, dabbing it against the table, his attention fixed on the cigar, eyes down. He was smiling, though, that soft, insufferable smile that was sly and sinister and smug all in one. No other man she had ever met smiled like that, expressing so much and revealing so little.

'Why are you doing this, Dominic?' she asked.

He went on dabbing the cigar, manipulating it with forefinger and thumb, turning it over and over and over until it seemed to whirr in the air like a little brown baton. Then he lost it, let it fall. 'It's what you want, Polly, is it not?'

'I never asked – never once did I suggest . . .'

The three of them – Dominic, Hughes and Shadwell – had obviously argued about it and rehearsed what each of them would say, how the proposal could be put to her as a *fait accompli*.

Smoothly, too smoothly, Carfin Hughes took up the running. 'Let's dispense with euphemisms, Mrs Manone, shall we? In the event of a declaration of a war with Germany and preceding any possible pact with Italy, aliens will be stripped of their rights and entitlements.'

'Dominic isn't an alien. He was born and brought up in Scotland.'

'That's true, but your husband,' Hughes paused tactfully, 'has long been a subject of police attention. You must be aware of it, Mrs Manone. By which I mean that you cannot be unaware that he has engaged in the past in activities that in some circles might be considered less than entirely honest.'

The lawyer's explanation made perfect sense. In the event of war Dominic would be classed as an alien and any defence against such an unjust classification that Hughes might put to a hearing would be bound to expose his less than legitimate activities and might lead to criminal charges. She had never been the sort of wife who saw only good in her husband, a good provider, a loving father and loyal son. She had always known what Dominic was and what he did. What he was and what he did had been a huge part of his attraction.

'Thank you, Mr Hughes. I do understand. Dominic?'

'Dearest?'

'Why are you doing this *now*? Is there a special reason for ridding yourself, nominally at least, of control of the company?'

'I prefer you to have control of our affairs under the guidance of men I can trust to deal with you fairly rather than . . .' He lifted his hands, palms open, and did not complete the sentence.

She knew: Flint had told him, Flint, or her father. All the deceptions, lies and betrayals were coming home to roost at last. Dominic was punishing her by giving her exactly what she believed she wanted. She stared at him across the table and experienced not triumph but guilt, guilt at not loving Dominic enough, guilt at loving Tony more.

'It is, however, imperative that you trust me,' Carfin Hughes said. 'In the course of the next few weeks Mr Shadwell will steer you through the financial statements and, with your agreement, your husband will assign a majority of the holdings to you.'

'A majority,' said Polly, 'not all?'

'Some will be sold or traded off,' Hughes said.

'Why?'

'Because,' Dominic told her, 'they'll have no value in wartime.'

'But others will?' said Polly.

'Others certainly will,' said Carfin Hughes.

'What others?'

'That will be explained to you,' Victor Shadwell said. 'If you'll just have a wee bit patience, Mrs Manone, I'll be pleased to take you through the books page by page and show you what's what.'

'Why can't Dominic do it?' Polly asked. 'Why can't you do it, darling?'

'Because,' Dominic said, 'I may not be here.'

'Where in God's name will you be?' Polly said, sharply.

'I wish I knew,' Dominic told her and with that smile and that shaping of the hands again, shrugged off all further questions on that score.

'Is this where you grill suspects?' Bernard said.

'No, this is my office,' Kenny said.

'I didn't know sergeants had offices.'

'My new office,' Kenny said.

He was tempted to brag about his recent promotion to head of the Special Protection Unit but responsibility had already begun to affect him and he was more guarded than he had been a week ago.

'Is it sound-proof?' Bernard asked.

'Pardon?'

'Can anybody outside hear us?'

'Only if you shout,' said Kenny.

'I'm not going to shout.' Bernard lowered his voice to not much more than a whisper. 'I just need a few words with you, if you can spare the time.'

'My time is your time,' Kenny said, then, 'Why aren't you at work, by the way? Half-eleven on a weekday morning, shouldn't you be at the office in Breslin?'

'I'm here,' Bernard put in. 'That's all that concerns you.'

They glowered at each other for five or ten seconds, though neither man was by nature surly and scowling did not come easily.

At length Kenny said, 'Is Rosie okay?'

'No, Rosie is not okay.'

'Is she the reason you're here?'

'Part of it,' Bernard said.

'What,' said Kenny, 'is the other part?'

'I know what's going on.'

'Going on where?'

'What Manone's up to.'

Kenny tried to appear cool. He had been less than a week in the job and had spent much of it doing little except brood on how he could win Rosie Conway back and at the same time fulfil his professional obligations. He hadn't been entirely idle. He had posted Galbraith in the radio van outside Lombard's flat for late evening shifts but so far Lombard hadn't turned up. He'd sent Stone to loiter in the park opposite Manone's house but the comings-and-going there had been very ordinary. So far he had done nothing original or adventurous, however, and hadn't a clue how to progress with the case on his own account. Until now.

'And what might Manone be up to?' Kenny asked.

'I'm not going to tell you,' Bernard said. 'You can't make me tell you.'

'May I remind you, Bernard, you came here of your own free will, so presumably you had a purpose other than telling me that you weren't going to tell me anything.'

'I know a lot of things I didn't know before.'

'Bully,' Kenny said, 'for you.'

Bernard dropped forward over the desk so abruptly that for an instant Kenny wondered if he, like Winstock, had been struck down by illness. He inched back in his chair, waiting for a fountain of blood: none came of course. Bernard beckoned, drew the sergeant closer so that their brows were almost touching, his voice so low and hoarse that it hardly seemed like a human voice at all.

'Between you and me,' Bernard rasped, 'I don't give a damn about Dominic Manone. He's been a bad influence on everybody he's ever come in contact with. I mean, if he wasn't married to my wife's daughter I'd give him over to you right here and now and say good bloody riddance.'

'But?' said Kenny.

'I can't do that.'

'Won't do that, you mean.'

'Aye, that's what I mean,' Bernard said. 'I won't do that until we have some kind of agreement, just between you and me.'

'I can't make deals,' said Kenny.

'Won't, you mean,' said Bernard. 'Who do you answer to upstairs? Sillitoe?'

'He's at the top of the pole, yes,' said Kenny.

'What would he settle for?' Bernard asked.

'I'm not sure I like that question. It smells like a deal to me.'

'Would it be enough to stop them? Would that satisfy you?'

'It's not a question of satisfaction.' Kenny was tired of craning over the desk. He straightened and sat back. 'Nor is it a matter of criminal law, Bernard. To be honest with you, it's gone beyond that.'

Bernard nodded. 'Treason.'

Kenny hesitated. 'Possibly.'

'If what you're investigating is a treasonable offence then you'll have all sorts of special powers at your disposal,' Bernard said.

'I still can't make a deal.'

'Could you make a deal with Manone, perhaps?'

'Never. I wouldn't dream of it.'

'Then,' Bernard pushed back his chair and rose, 'I'm going now.'

'I could have you detained, you know.'

'On what grounds?'

'Withholding information.'

'Rubbish! There's no such charge.'

'I didn't say "charge",' said Kenny. 'Those "special powers" you mentioned do come in handy sometimes.'

Reluctantly Bernard lowered himself back into the chair. 'Look,' he said, 'I'm as keen as you are to have Dominic put away but I don't want to see him hanged.'

'What about Rosie's father, wouldn't you like to see him hanged?'

Bernard shook his head. 'It isn't what I want, or what you want, Kenny. It's what Rosie wants.'

'And what may that be?' said Kenny.

'To have you for a husband.'

'Don't give me that patter, Bernard. She hates me.'

'No she doesn't. She's hurt and confused. In a sense her father means nothing to her. Heck, she can't even remember him. On the other hand she wants to meet him and see for herself what . . .'

'This has nothing to do with Manone,' Kenny interrupted.

'It has a lot to do with Manone,' said Bernard. 'It has a lot to do with Harker, Frank Conway or whatever you like to call him. All right, I'll tell you.'

Kenny sat up, raising the upper part of his body.

Bernard went on, 'It's an international conspiracy

– no, don't laugh: it is. I know it seems pretty bizarre to say so but we're at the sharp end of a Nazi plot.'

'Go on.'

'Manone and Harker are in it up to their ears. It started somewhere in Germany and moved to America. Carlo Manone was brought in. He got Dominic involved. Harker's the middle-man, the manager.'

'Who told you all this? Dominic?'

'God, no!'

'Polly?'

'I've seen with my own eyes what they're up to.'

'What are they up to, Bernard?'

'Don't you know?'

'No, I don't.'

'Not much of a detective, are you?'

'Detective enough to suspect that it's a spy ring,' said Kenny.

'The spy ring's out of your reach.'

'But Harker and Manone aren't?'

'Exactly.'

Kenny was still sitting bolt upright like a woodland animal that has caught the scent of danger. 'Flint, Manone, Lombard, Harker,' he murmured. 'They're funding this spy ring, aren't they?'

'Yes.'

'How?'

'First I want some guarantees.'

'I told you, Bernard. I don't deal.'

'Not even for Rosie's sake?'

'I can't protect Rosie now,' Kenny said. 'Much as I love her she's just going to have to take what's coming. I don't mean to sound harsh but this – this *thing* is far too important to let personal feelings get in the way. I thought you were a patriot, Bernard.'

'I'm a husband and father first.'

'Oh, how gallant!' Kenny said, sarcastically.

'If we play our cards right,' Bernard said, 'we can collar the agents. I don't know where they are or who they are or how valuable the information the Germans will glean from them might be, but I do know that Manone's supplying them with money and at a guess I'd say Harker and Flint are distributing it.'

'How much money are we talking about? Thousands?'

'Millions, more like.'

'Dominic Manone doesn't have millions.'

'He will have,' said Bernard, 'very soon.'

Kenny let his body slide in the wooden-armed chair. He was tempted to put his feet on the desk as Inspector Winstock had done in times of stress. Instead he shifted his weight on to his spine and stretched his long legs under the desk.

He was pleased, still puzzled but pleased none the less. He had lied to Bernard, of course. He knew a lot more than he had let on, enough to recognise that Bernard was telling the truth. He had read Fiona's carefully assembled clippings and typed translations, Winstock's scant correspondence with the Home Office, Harker's file from the FBI in America; enough, quite enough to have a picture of what was happening and how Manone fitted into it. Now Bernard had given him the key.

'If you make me one promise, Kenny, I'll tell you what Manone's got in hand and where you can find all the evidence you'll need to make your case.'

'What promise?'

'I want you to handle it personally and discreetly, without whistling up forty coppers and a Black Maria,' Bernard said. 'If you plan this properly, Kenny, you can cop the lot, not just Harker, Flint and Manone but the agents down south. That's what your superiors want, isn't it? They want the spy ring broken before it has a chance to leak information back to Adolf.'

'All right, Bernard,' Kenny said. 'You've made your point.'

'I need a promise,' Bernard said. 'Your promise.'

'I'll do my best. I can't promise more than that.'

'They're printing counterfeit notes off damned-near perfect plates.'

'Ah!' Kenny exclaimed. 'Ah-hah!'

'I know where the press is. I can take you there.'

'When?' Kenny said.

'Soon,' Bernard said. 'Soon, but not just yet.'

'Why not now? Why not today?'

'Because they haven't start printing yet,' Bernard said. 'And if they haven't start printing then they haven't started distributing and the agents are safely tucked away and you'll never lure them out into the open.'

For half a minute Kenny said nothing. What Bernard proposed made sense. If he could somehow tempt the agents into the open then Scotland Yard or Home Office hard nuts could pick them up one by one. Money was the bait, the money that Manone had been commissioned to print and Harker to distribute.

'All right,' Kenny said.

'All right – what?' said Bernard.

'I'll go along with you,' Kenny said. 'I'll give you a week.'

'It'll take a lot longer than that,' Bernard said. 'I'll tell you when.'

'When?' said Kenny. 'When what?'

'When the machines are up and running and Harker's ready for the drop.'

'Red-handed,' Kenny said, nodding. 'Of course.'

'Do we have a de . . . an agreement, Sergeant MacGregor?'

'I believe we do, Mr Peabody,' Kenny said. 'Yes, I do believe we do.'


Polly could not decide whether it was sentiment or convenience that motivated Dominic to take her to lunch at Goodman's Restaurant.

It had been years since she last she'd eaten there but she hadn't forgotten that it was in Goodman's that

Dominic had advanced his courtship, in Goodman's that they had celebrated their anniversaries. Three or four years ago the tradition had lapsed. No reason for it, no decision made to let it go. It had simply withered and faded away. He had taken her elsewhere – to Braggio's, to Brown's, to the Delphic – but never again to Goodman's.

Over lunch they talked business. He imparted a little of Victor Shadwell's history, more about Carfin Hughes, men whom Dominic trusted and admired.

He told her that the importation of manufactured goods and comestibles from Italy had been seriously affected by the threat of war and warehouse profits had dropped alarmingly. He outlined his arrangements for collecting untaxed 'interest' from Clyde coast café owners and explained how in exchange for monthly pay-offs – sums fixed regardless of profits – he provided security and, if asked, loans for expansion. He talked of his share in a plant for making ice-cream and his holding in Bonskeet's, presented her with a steady stream of facts and figures that, for the most part Polly found quite comprehensible.

It wasn't until they were driving back to Manor Park, however, that she put the questions that had been troubling her all afternoon.

She began tentatively, almost innocently.

'Does Tony make the collections from the Clyde coast clients?'

'He did. Charley Fraser does it now.'

They drove on through sunlight and barred shadow.

'Are all these clients listed?' Polly said.

'Victor Shadwell keeps a special ledger. You can see it if you wish.'

'Is Jackie's name in it?' Polly asked.

'Jackie? Oh, you mean the salon: no, that's recorded elsewhere.'

'Who "collects" from Jackie?'

'No one. He's family.'

'I see,' Polly said.

The interior of the car was warm. She had drunk wine at lunch. She was unusually aware of the luxury that surrounded her; leather and walnut wood, box-cloth, silk against her skin, the aroma of Dominic's cigar, his soft, unmuscular body nestling beside her. Approaching mid-life now, he looked smooth and comfortable, almost too comfortable to be real.

'Are you really thinking of making a run for it?' she said.

'I didn't say I was making a run for it.'

'Going away. You said "going away".'

'For a time. If I have to.'

'What will be the deciding factor?'

'What happens next.'

'Oh, Dominic, for God's sake!' she said, not crossly. 'Stop being so damned enigmatic. Why won't you tell me everything?'

'In case you let something slip.'

'Slip? To whom?'

'Kenny MacGregor,' Dominic told her. 'Bernard.'

'Bernard?'

'Tony, possibly.'

He steered the big car through a welter of afternoon traffic, seated well forward, the wheel close to his chest. She thought of Tony who drove casually almost indifferently, bossing the rest of the traffic on the road. She felt safer with Tony at the wheel.

'I thought Tony knew everything that goes on?' she said.

'He doesn't,' Dominic said.

'You have secrets from him too?'

'Sure. He has secrets from me, doesn't he?'

'I wouldn't know,' said Polly. 'I am, after all, quite new to the game.'

She waited for his challenge, a word, a hint that he had learned of her affair. All he needed to do was glance at her and say 'Are you?' with just the right amount of inflexion, but he gave her nothing, nothing at all.

After a few moments, she said, 'Where will you go if you do leave Glasgow?'

'I don't know yet.'

'America?'

'Not to Philly, not to my father, no.'

'Would he not make you welcome?'

'I doubt it,' Dominic said.

'Italy then?'

'Not Italy either.'

'Where?'

He adjusted position, pulled himself closer to the wheel.

'That, Polly,' he said, 'is not something you need to know.'

'Why didn't you tell me that my father was alive?'

He came back at her at once. 'Why didn't you tell me you were negotiating with John Flint to take over my business?'

'It wasn't a negotiation, not quite.'

'You worried them.'

'Good,' said Polly. 'I take it you mean my father as well as Flint?'

'Your father is dangerous.'

'I think I'd rather worked that out for myself.'

'He doesn't want to see you, or your mother, or any of you.'

'I guessed that too. Sad, isn't it?'

'Depends on how you look at it,' said Dominic. 'I didn't tell you, Polly, for the simple reason that I didn't feel it would benefit you.'

'No,' she said. 'I understand.'

'If it hadn't been for that damned interfering aunt of yours . . .'

Polly laughed, a small sound. 'Janet, Janet having her revenge.'

'I'm sorry about your mother,' Dominic said. 'And Rosalind.'

'And I'm sorry I disappointed you by talking with Flint.'

'I admit it wasn't what I expected of you,' Dominic said.

'Oh, but you expected – something?'

'Hmmm.'

'What?'

The car turned into the Avenue. Trees were showing green, new leaves trembling in the breeze from the river. Tulips had replaced daffodils in the border beds and a gang of eight or ten labourers were digging a trench behind the Ibrox gate. She didn't have to ask what the labourers were doing; signs of preparation for war had become too numerous to be remarkable.

She touched Dominic's sleeve, said again, 'What?'

Thirty yards from the gateposts of the mansion, from home, Patricia walked along the pavement, flanked by Stuart and Ishbel. Holding on to the girl's hands, Polly's children chatted and skipped happily. The girl looked fresh and confident and – loving: yes, loving, Polly thought, more motherly and loving than she had ever been. When war came Patricia would probably leave to take care of orphans or evacuees or load shells into boxes in a munitions factory; any sort of work was more useful than being paid to mother the children of a woman who was too selfish to mother them herself.

The car sped on down the avenue past the children, past the house. Looking back, Polly saw her son lift his hand in an uncertain wave and then lower it again.

'That was the children,' she said. 'Didn't you see them?'

'I saw them,' Dominic said.

Dominic steered around the long corner of the park, brought the car in against the kerb and braked to a halt. He switched off the engine.

'Dominic, what are you doing?'

He reached out a gloved hand, drew her gently to him and kissed her mouth.

'Listen,' he said, 'I want to tell you this. Whatever happens, I have not deserted you. I love you, Polly. I always have and I always will and, no matter what, I'll come back for you. Do you understand?'

'Yes,' Polly said.

'Do you believe me?'

'Yes,' Polly said again and for no particularly urgent reason began to cry.


It was late in the afternoon and Tony had been drinking steadily since lunch-time. He was propped in the attic window and not even the stiff little breeze that twisted over the pine trees managed to keep him alert.

The telescope nodded in his hands and his ear, resting against the window frame, was numb. If the guy had shown up five or ten minutes later Tony may not have noticed him at all. He wasn't drunk though, not even tipsy, just sleepy enough to be inattentive so that the man was in the yard before he spotted him.

Tony opened his eyes, rubbed a hand over his chin then, snapping wide awake, shouted, *'You. Stop right where you are,'* and fumbled for the rabbit gun.

'What do you intend to do, Lombard? Shoot me?' Bernard stood in the centre of the yard with his hands on his hips, overcoat billowing around him, hat tipped back from his face. 'Is that what the boss ordered you to do, to shoot me and put me out of my misery.'

'What do you want here, Bernard?'

'A wee quiet word, that's all.'

'Stay where you are.'

Tony closed the attic window, tossed aside the telescope and, with the rifle in both hands, made his way down the narrow stairs and out into the yard.

From the stables the sound of machinery was almost deafening, a fantastical *clickety-clickety-clacking*, like a gigantic knitting-machine. The wind accentuated it and carried it off in the direction of the roadway. There was no sign of Giffard, of course, and the racket in the stables would render him oblivious to any disturbance outside the thick stone walls.

Penny? Tony had no idea where Penny was; asleep maybe.

Bernard was waiting where Tony had left him, hands still planted on his hips. Easiest thing in the world to cock the loaded rifle, put a bullet through his chest and be rid of at least one complication. Plenty of places to hide a body too. Bury it among the trees or stuff it into one of the pits on the building site and cover it with earth and concrete.

'Go ahead, Tony, waste a bullet if you really feel like it,' Bernard said.

'You've got some bloody nerve coming back here.'

Bernard showed no sign of fear. He jerked his head in the direction of the stables. 'Has your tame printer got it working at last?'

'None of your business,' Tony said.

Where was Penny? Where the hell was the girl? He could toss her the rifle, tell her to do it. By God, she'd do it without turning a hair.

'I want my whack,' Bernard said.

'What?'

'You heard me, Mr Lombard. I want my share.'

Tony laughed uncertainly. 'You've changed your tune.'

'I've been thinking it over,' Bernard said. 'Rationally there's no reason for me not to get in on it. I mean, I'm family, aren't I?'

'How much do you want to keep your trap shut?'

'Fifty a week.'

'Too much.'

'Too much, when you're producing twenty grand?'

'We ain't producing anything yet,' Tony said.

'Sounds to me like you are.'

'That's noise, just noise. Wanna see for yourself?'

'No, I'll take your word for it,' Bernard said. 'I assume that since you haven't shot me dead Mr

Manone hasn't made up his mind what to do about me. Gone queasy, has he? Gone a little soft?'

'Soft or not,' Tony said, 'he won't give you fifty.'

'Fifty,' said Bernard. 'Clean money. None of your counterfeit rubbish.'

'Why don't you talk to Dominic?'

'I would if I could find him.' Bernard looked past Tony and politely tipped his hat. 'Perhaps your missus knows where he is?'

Penny was standing in the farmhouse doorway. She wore nothing but a bathrobe and a towel wrapped, turban-style, around her head. Her legs and feet were bare and she had the clean, athletic look that he, Tony, had begun to find more stimulating than any of the paraphernalia with which she teased him upstairs: just out of the bath she looked almost unspoiled.

He glanced behind him then, quickly, back at Bernard.

'Dominic ain't here. We haven't seen him for days. Call him at the warehouse if you want to strike a deal.'

'No,' Bernard said. 'You tell him what I've just told you. I'm not going to bother the boss with such a trivial matter as fifty quid a week. Heck, he can take that much from petty cash and never even miss it.'

'Not these days,' said Tony.

'Don't give me any sob stories.' Bernard jerked his head in the direction of the stables once more. 'You've got a money machine set up in there and as soon as it goes into production you're all going to be wallowing in dough. The day that contraption starts to cough out cash I want fifty pounds in a plain brown envelope on my desk at Lyons and Lloyd's.'

'Or what?'

'Or you're going to have to go to all the bother of shooting me, Tony, all the inconvenience of explaining away my disappearance to Dominic's wife and Dominic's mother-in law, to say nothing of the cops. Tell Dom what I want. He'll see how reasonable I'm being.'

'I had you figured all wrong, Peabody,' Tony said.

'You wouldn't be the first,' said Bernard and, with a nod to Penny, turned on his heel and left.

# Chapter Seventeen

Books were Rosie's salvation. If she had not had books around her in the gloomy weeks following her quarrel with Kenny then she would have broken down completely and been no use to anyone. Her deafness became a boon for she could shut herself away just by focusing all her attention on title-pages and foolscap and neat lines of copperplate writing. She catalogued like mad, filling slip after slip with descriptions of the volumes that Gannon hauled from the storeroom, pasting the slips into quires for the printer, for what, Mr Robert hinted, might be the last general catalogue that Shelby's would produce for a very long time.

Hard work and reading allowed Rosie little time to brood. At night in bed, however, she couldn't help but think of her father, her mother and her aunt and the odd triangle of betrayal and deception they had created between them. She pitied Janet in particular, Janet going about her dreary round with nothing to console her but the dairy, the church and the preposterous belief that one day Frank Conway would come back to reclaim her – a belief that had turned out to be not so preposterous after all. She wondered if she was destined to wind up like her aunt, a lonely old spinster clinging to dreams of what might have been and waiting foolishly for 'her man' to return and make everything right again.

She resisted her mother's attempts at reconciliation and refused to stand still long enough to listen to her explanations. Bernard was much more firm and now and then would grip her by the shoulders and force her to read his lips. In this way she learned that Kenny had been put in charge of the Special Protection Unit and would not be enlisting in the army, not immediately. A few days later Bernard collared her again and informed her that he thought he had found a solution to their problem.

'What problem?' Rosie shouted.

'The problem concerning your father.'

'Do you know where he is?'

'No, not exactly but . . .'

'Is he coming here to see me?'

'No. No, no.'

'Then there is no problem.'

'Rosie . . .'

'Leave me alone, Bernard, just leave me alone.'

Which, rather to her chagrin, he did.

★    ★    ★

'There's definitely something fishy goin' on,' Babs said. 'I mean, for God's sake, Polly, did you have to go tellin' him we'd been to see Flint?'

'I didn't have to tell him,' Polly said. 'He already knew.'

'Huh!' Babs screwed up her face. 'I'm disappointed in your Mr Flint, I must say. I thought he'd got more balls than that.'

'Babs!'

'All right then – bottle, if you prefer it.'

They were seated in a booth in the back of the Shamrock Café in one of the less salubrious streets in Ibrox. There was something comfortingly old-fashioned about the shabby parlour and the odours of coal-gas, coffee and ice-cream. It reminded the sisters of their girlhood when, out of Mammy's reach, they could talk uninhibitedly about boys and boyfriends, sex and marriage.

Baby April, fast asleep, was strapped into a pushchair beside them. Sunlight, fresh air and a small ice-cream cornet with a squiggle of raspberry syrup had all but knocked her out. The sisters spoke quietly, heads together over the cups.

'I never did understand your hubby,' Babs said. 'I mean, what does he think he's doing handin' you the business on a plate?'

'I don't know. I'm not sure.'

'Is he gonna pull the rug out from under us?'

'What?' Polly was startled by the question. 'I never thought of that.'

Jessica Stirling

'I wouldn't put it past him,' Babs said. 'I mean, otherwise it's weird, givin' you what you always wanted just to prevent you takin' it from him.'

'It isn't that at all.' Polly shook her head. 'Dominic is convinced that when war finally breaks out he'll be picked up and sent away, not because he's Italian but because the police will have special powers to lock up anyone they fancy without charge or trial.'

'Really!' Babs said. 'I thought they only did that in Germany.'

'Apparently not. Apparently in time of war . . .'

'Yeah, yeah,' said Babs. 'I see what Dominic's up to. Crafty, eh? Signs the lot over to you so you can keep the business tickin' over until the war's over and he can come back an' pick up what's left.'

'If anything's left,' said Polly.

'Hey, hey, what's this I'm hearin'?'

'There might be nothing but rubble and dead bodies.'

Polly's statement dampened her sister's enthusiasm for fully a half-minute then, with a smoky little sigh, she said, 'Dennis is in uniform.'

'Have you seen him?'

'Nope. He's in camp, tents an' stuff, in Ayrshire. Sends me postcards.'

'What about his wife?'

'Gloria? She cracked up totally. She's been round at our house screaming abuse at Jackie for encouraging Dennis to enlist.'

'Jackie didn't?'

'No, 'course Jackie didn't. He had to offer her money, a lotta bleedin' money, to get her to calm down and shut up. She wants me round there to help her sew black-out curtains, for God's sake, wants them lined with red velvet to match her new Axminster. I told her to go chase herself.'

'If Dennis is gone for long do you think she'll find another man?'

'I bet she will,' said Babs. 'She'll shake her tail at the first likely-lookin' handyman who crosses her path. Listen, have you got charge of Dominic's books?'

'Not yet.'

'When you do . . .' Babs hesitated.

'Come on,' said Polly. 'Out with it.'

'What Jackie pays him . . .'

'I see, you want the debt cancelled.'

'It ain't a debt,' said Babs. 'It's – what the word, Poll?'

'Usury,' said Polly.

'Well, there won't be much to "usury" with,' Babs said, 'not after Jackie closes the yard in Govan.'

'Is that what he intends to do?'

'No choice,' Babs said. 'With Dennis gone Jackie's stranded. Besides, car sales have fallen off since the war scare before Christmas. One more like that, or a war itself, an' we'll be in the poorhouse.' She stared at her sister out of innocent baby-blue eyes. Blinked. 'Won't we?'

'Of course you won't,' said Polly.

'Will you cancel the payments then?'

'I can't do that until Dominic . . .'

'I thought you were in charge now, in command?'

'Don't be ridiculous, Babs,' said Polly. 'Dominic's still running things. This isn't like the garage . . .'

'Salon,' said Babs.

'. . . isn't like the salon then, not in the slightest. Dominic's profits come from dozens of different sources, as well as the warehouse. Even if the authorities don't catch up with Dominic you can be sure they'll grab the warehouse.'

'What else does he own?'

'Apart from the warehouse, he doesn't own much,' said Polly. 'It's all investments, what Mr Shadwell calls capital deployment. As far as I can make out eighty per cent of the holdings are perfectly legitimate.'

'What holdings?'

'Shares in various firms.'

'Like what?'

Polly may have been in a confidential mood but she was not about to tell her sister about the Manones' complex financial affairs. It had already crossed her mind that if the worse came to the worse and all the menfolk were taken away then she might employ Babs to help her run what remained of the business. Babs would never be a queen of the boardroom but she had drive and initiative and a deviousness that would prove useful in dealings with men like John Flint. The threat of war might evaporate, of course,

Hitler might sign a pact with Chamberlain or a peace treaty with the French, but somehow she doubted it.

'Can you, I mean, handle this sort of stuff on your own?' Babs said.

'Dominic seems to think I can.'

'What about Tony?'

'Tony? What about him?'

'Won't he be around to – you know, help out?'

'I don't need Tony Lombard's help.'

'Aw, I thought you did. I thought you an' Tony were – chums.'

'Chums?' said Polly, contemptuously. 'Some chum Tony would make.'

'Okay,' said Babs. 'Sorry. I think I got the wrong end of the stick there.'

'I think you did,' said Polly.

The fact that her sister had guessed that she was more than friends with Tony Lombard worried her. She had reconciled herself to resisting Tony. Perhaps she had expected too much from him but it had excited her to have two men in her life and in her heart, two men who loved her.

Babs glanced down at her daughter in the pushchair. The child was so deeply asleep that her lids did not even flutter. There were no dreams in April's head, no longings, no memories, no desires or demands. Perhaps that was the only true innocence, Polly thought, an absence of memory and desire.

'What are we gonna do about Daddy?' Babs said.

'Dominic says he'll take care of it.'

'I didn't like the look of him, did you?'

'No.'

'I don't really wanna meet him again, do you?'

Polly paused before she answered. 'No, but Rosie does.'

'Rosie doesn't know what he's like.'

'Dominic says he's dangerous.'

'Now that,' said Babs, 'I *can* believe.'

'Do you feel anything for him?'

'Nope. I just want the bugger to go away,' said Babs.

'Honest injun?'

'Honest injun!'

'Then,' Polly tugged on her gloves, 'I think we can safely leave it to Dominic.'

'To do what?' Babs said.

'Get rid of him,' said Polly.


'Where the hell are you?' Tony shouted. 'I've been trying to get you for two days. I even phoned the house but all I got was that damned nursemaid.'

'Well, you've got me now,' said Dominic. 'What is it you want?'

'Peabody turned up at Blackstone yesterday.'

Dominic adjusted the receiver and swivelled his chair to give himself a better view of the river. He'd been working alone in the office since early morning and Miss Seavers, his secretary, had been fielding all his calls.

'I see,' Dominic said. 'Did he come alone?'

'Yeah. Oh, yeah!' said Tony, scathingly. 'He wants a cut.'

'A percentage?'

'No, straight whack.'

'How much?'

'Fifty a week.'

'That's reasonable,' said Dominic.

'Peabody isn't part of the deal, Dom, even though he is family.'

'How does he want it?' Dominic said.

'Clean cash in a plain brown envelope delivered to his desk every week.'

'All right,' said Dominic.

'Don't you even wanna talk to him?'

'No. Pay him.'

'What with?' said Tony.

'I'll pay him,' Dominic said. 'Leave it to me.'

He could hear Tony Lombard let out his breath. He knew it wasn't just Bernard's demand that had riled Tony; it was the other thing, the marriage. He smiled into the bakelite mouthpiece.

He counted to three slowly, then said:

'How soon will Dougie have us in full production?'

'Soon,' Tony answered. 'Real soon – so he says.'

'What does "real soon" mean, Tony?'

'He's talkin' about the weekend.'

'Good,' Dominic said. 'You will let me know, won't you?'

'Yeah, sure,' said Tony. 'If I can track you down.'

'How's Penny?'

'Fine,' Tony snapped and to Dominic's infinite satisfaction, hung up.


The baby had been crying. She was red-faced and pouty and her nose needed a wipe but she had been subdued by her mother's attentions and clung on to Babs and buried her face in her shoulder while Babs tried to work her charm on Miss Dawlish.

Miss Dawlish did not find children enchanting and ignored April completely. She wore a Harris tweed jacket over a starched shirt-blouse and her steel-grey hair was cut in pudding-bowl fashion. She was not unfeminine, though, and had large brown eyes and oddly delicate fingers. Babs watched her punch the keys of the comptometer and scan the slip that emerged from the counting machine. She punched in more figures, spiked an invoice, then looked up.

'He isn't here. He's out.'

'I can see that,' Babs said. 'Do you happen to know where he is?'

Miss Dawlish hesitated. She was loyal less to Jackie than to her job. She reminded Babs a little of Aunt Janet McKerlie and she felt a strange sort of pity for the spinster as she waited for Miss Dawlish to decide how much or how little she, Babs, needed to be told.

'Govan.'

'At the yard?'

'Yes,' Miss Dawlish said.

'When will he be back?'

'He's closing the Govan place down, you know.'

Babs transferred April from one hip to the other and said, 'I knew it was on the cards, yeah.'

Miss Dawlish smoothed a rumpled invoice, peered at it for a moment then said, 'Is he planning on selling this place too?'

'I don't think so,' Babs said.

'I shouldn't be saying this, but it isn't the same since Mr Dennis left.'

'How bad is it?' Babs asked.

'Bad.'

'Jackie – Mr Hallop won't give up the salon until he's forced to.'

'We haven't sold a vehicle in three weeks.'

'Parts?' said Babs.

'A few.'

'Are we still paying the bills?'

'Oh, yes. I make sure of that.'

'And the cheques don't bounce?'

'I transferred funds from the reserve to the commercial account.'

'Really!' said Babs. 'How much is left in the reserve?'

'It isn't for me to say.'

'That means damned little, doesn't it?' said Babs.

'Only Mr Hallop can give you that sort of information.'

'Does Mr Hallop realise how bad things are,' Babs said, 'or does Mr Hallop have his head stuck in the bloody sand, as usual?'

'I've told him until I'm blue in the face that something has to be done to rectify the short-fall,' said Miss Dawlish. 'He doesn't seem to listen.'

Babs leaned closer, the baby hanging off her arm.

'I'm listening, Miss Dawlish,' she said slyly. 'Tell me.'

For the past few days Polly had spent almost as much time closeted in Victor Shadwell's tiny office in the Global Building in Kinning Park as she had done at home. Mr Shadwell was a dry old stick but an excellent tutor. He had guided her through the ledgers and portfolios carefully, had explained what each entry represented and what the terms signified. Polly was startled by the extent of Dominic's holdings, though Mr Shadwell wouldn't reveal where all the bank accounts were housed and deftly evaded questions about Dominic's overall worth.

Late in the evening, over supper, she tried to discuss the day's lessons with Dominic but he seemed less interested in what she'd learned than in larger issues, the German invasion of Czechoslovakia and the final victory of Nationalist forces in Spain among them.

The following morning Polly came downstairs and saw the children off to school before she went into the sunny back parlour to eat breakfast and linger, brooding and dreaming, over coffee and a cigarette.

She'd barely finished her bacon and eggs, however, when Leah rushed in, waving copies of the *Glasgow Herald* and the London *Times*. 'They're calling them up. They're calling up the boys,' Leah cried. 'It's all here in black and white, Mrs Manone. See for yourself. All the boys, all the boys goin' off to die in the trenches.'

'Calm yourself, Leah,' Polly said.

She put down her knife, accepted the *Herald* and scanned the banner headline: *Conscription Disclosures*. She took the news in at a glance; young men, twenty and under, were subject to call-up for military training. War was closing in, no doubt about it. She felt no lurch of fear or panic, only a quickening of anticipation. Gloomy speculations, see-saw scares, unrealistic periods of relief were consolidating into inevitable conflict. Britain meant business after all. The government wasn't going to knuckle under to lily-livered socialists who would do anything but fight, that at least was something to be thankful for.

Leah was crying. 'I have brothers, Mistress Manone, two brothers an' they're going to die.'

'Nonsense!' Polly plucked up a napkin and thrust it at the stupid girl. 'It will take months, maybe years for the government to start drafting young men into the services. It may not happen at all if Hitler backs down.'

'We're all going to die,' Leah wailed. 'We're

all going to be shot by the Germans or gassed or blown up.'

'Stop it this instant,' Polly ordered. 'Take my tray downstairs and ask Mrs O'Shea to make you a cup of strong, sweet tea. Take your time drinking it. I don't want to see you upstairs again until you've pulled yourself together.'

'I'm – I'm so scared, Mrs Manone.'

'Well, go and be scared downstairs, if you please.'

The day-maid, still sobbing, scuttled off to the kitchen to look for solace in the teapot and Polly, tossing the newspapers to the floor, returned to her breakfast. She had only just spread marmalade on a slice of toast, however, when the front doorbell rang and Polly, tutting in annoyance, got up to answer it.

She wasn't dressed to receive visitors. In fact, she wasn't dressed at all. Under her housecoat she wore only a pair of cotton knickers and a vest. Her hair was mussy and she had applied no make-up and, she felt, still smelled rather of bed.

Licking marmalade from her fingers, she opened the door an inch or two and peeped out. Tony was leaning against the doorpost, arms folded, a cigarette in his mouth. He looked haggard and in spite of his easy pose, strained.

She stepped outside.

'Dominic isn't here,' she said, 'He's gone to the warehouse, I think.'

'I know. I saw him leave. Saw the nursemaid take the kids off to school.'

'What is it? What do you want with me?'

A sound in the hallway; she glanced over her shoulder and saw that Mrs O'Shea, not Leah, had come up from the kitchen to answer the bell.

Shrilly, Polly said, 'I have it. You may leave it to me, thank you,' and to her relief watched the cook disappear downstairs again.

'Did she see me?' Tony said.

'I don't know. Does it matter?'

'I don't want Dominic . . .'

'I don't have any secrets from Dominic now.'

'For God's sake, Polly!' he said, thickly. 'Don't send me away.'

He looked down at her, spying on her breasts under the collar of the robe. His eyes were sad, like those of a dog. She felt sorry for him, sorry for herself, sorry for betraying Dominic.

In three or four months she would be the boss, however, and if Tony was still around he would be answerable to her. He would not be her advisor, like Mr Shadwell or Carfin Hughes, he would be her employee. She could not allow her feelings to undermine the trust that Dominic had placed in her: everything had already begun to change.

'Let me in,' he murmured. 'Half an hour, twenty minutes, that's all.'

'I can't,' Polly said.

'Look, I need to talk to you.'

'There's nothing to say, Tony.'

'God, but you look lovely.'

'You won't butter me into bed, Tony, if that's your intention.'

'Tell them I'm looking for Dom,' he said. 'I am. I am looking for Dominic.'

She could not hold out against him.

She recalled the excitement of their first sexual encounter, how he had mastered her and taught her more about herself and the faltering state of her marriage than she had believed possible. And no guilt, no more guilt than Dominic had, no more guilt than Tony, no regrets at giving herself to him: no guilt until he told her that he loved her. She couldn't cope with that, with the pain and responsibility of loving and being loved. She loved him still, though, would love him forever, perhaps, live with him in mind day after day, yearning for him even when the planes came and the bombs fell and the world was crashing about her ears.

'All right,' she said. 'Come in. Come quickly.'

And, for the very last time, allowed him to enter her house.


Kenny was no more impressed by the Athena Hotel than Dominic. The difference was that the Highlander felt out of place there, not just because he was a copper. He'd been raised in a socialist household by a man to whom capitalists were the enemy and landowners, all landowners, were in league with the devil.

There had been nothing vociferous about Jock MacGregor's left-wing politics. The only times Kenny ever heard his father rant aloud were out in the sheep field when scrapie, say, had claimed another breeding ewe or feed was running low. Then his old man, outwardly so stoical, would let rip and denounce in no uncertain terms the government agencies that had reduced an honest man to reaching for the begging bowl or sliding into debt for the sake of a few measly pence. On the subject of war, though, his father had been strangely reticent. War seemed very far from the doorstep of a tenant farmer on Islay, nothing much more than a diversion to keep Westminster politicians from applying themselves to the problems of feeding the hungry, housing the poor and bringing prosperity back to the land.

When he pushed through the circulating door of the Athena Hotel, however, Kenny MacGregor could not help but feel his hackles rise at the brilliance of the foyer and the sight of so many haughty lackeys ready and willing to dance attendance on the rich. He had just started towards the reception desk when a familiar voice called out, 'Over here.'

Dominic Manone rose from the brown leather cushions of a steel-sprung sofa between two potted palm trees whose leaves were made of beaten copper on trunks of painted bronze. The foyer was all glass and mock marble, all sheen and shine, and for an instant Kenny wondered if it really was Manone who had signalled to him or some chimerical substitute whom he had never met before.

He looked different, did Manone, leaner somehow and lighter, lacking the sinister bonhomie of the host that, at Christmastide, had almost deceived Kenny into forgetting that the man was a crook.

They shook hands.

'Sit down,' Dominic said.

'What, here?'

'Why not?'

'Bit public, isn't it?' said Kenny.

'I've nothing to hide, have you?'

'I thought . . .'

'Ah, rushing to judgement again, are we?' Dominic said. 'Coffee?'

'No, thanks.'

They seated themselves side by side. The intimacy embarrassed Kenny. He had the feeling that every eye was upon him, speculating on why he'd been granted audience with the great, the almighty Dominic Manone. Nonsense, of course, daft and stupid nonsense. Nobody at all was bothered, least of all Manone.

'I assume,' Dominic said, 'you don't have a man still posted here?'

'No, not for weeks.'

'How is Winstock, by the way? I heard he was terribly ill?'

'He's recovering slowly.'

'He won't be back, will he?'

'I doubt it,' Kenny said.

'It must be very trying being a policeman,' Dominic said.

'It is.'

'But quite rewarding at times, surely?'

'It can be.'

'What would you consider rewarding, Kenneth?

'Putting you behind bars,' said Kenny.

Dominic laughed. 'Is that all you want, Sergeant MacGregor?'

'What else is on offer?' said Kenny.

'Oh, thousands,' Dominic said. 'Thousands of pounds or, if you prefer it, regular emoluments that would allow you to live very comfortably indeed.'

'For doing what?' said Kenny. 'Turning a blind eye?'

'You wouldn't be the first copper to do that,' said Dominic. 'With responsibility comes . . .'

'Temptation,' said Kenny. 'Aye, I've heard that one before.'

'However, I've no intention of offering you cash or any sort of financial inducement. I don't want you to turn a blind eye. I want you to open both eyes very wide and take note of what's staring you in the face.'

'You?'

'Me?' said Dominic. 'What use am I to you, Kenneth? It isn't me you need to bang up.' He spread his hands and at that moment seemed to be all Italian, not a dour and clever Scot. 'I pose no threat to social order. I haven't been a threat for a very long time, if truth be known. I'm just a young old has-been with a bit of a shady past. But,' he spread his hands again, 'I'm not a fool.'

'I never thought you were,' said Kenny.

'I'm not going to beat about the bush, Kenneth. I can give you what you actually do want, signed and sealed and delivered, but it has to be done my way and I have to have certain guarantees before . . .'

'Didn't Bernard tell you? I don't do deals.'

'Bernard's your man, not mine,' Dominic said. 'In fact, it was unfortunate that you got him involved at all.'

'I didn't get him involved. He got himself involved.'

'Fifty pounds in a plain brown envelope,' said Dominic, shaking his head. 'A signal we've gone into production. After it's delivered I assume Bernard will telephone you, you'll rake together a squad, descend on the farm in force and arrest everybody in sight. Is that the strategy?'

'I don't know what you're talking about.'

'Sure you do. And in case you're thinking that poor old Bernard's playing two ends against the middle let me assure he's not. Bernard Peabody would never, *never* sell out.'

'He sold out to you, didn't he?'

'He married my wife's mother,' said Dominic. 'I gave him a job.'

'In a shifty agency.'

'Not at all. Lyons and Lloyd's is legitimate. The

one and only "favour" Bernard ever did for me was arrange the lease of Blackstone Farm. There! Now you know. That's where the machinery's set up and where the printing will be done: Blackstone Farm, near Breslin.'

'What to stop me going there and . . .'

'Not a damned thing,' Dominic interrupted. 'You can raid the place tomorrow, tonight for that matter; but all you'll get for your trouble is an alcoholic printer and a more-or-less innocent girl.'

'And Tony Lombard.'

'Tony,' Dominic said, 'is expendable.'

'Are you saying I won't get you?'

'Not a hope in Hades,' Dominic said. 'Nor will you get Edgar Harker. Nor will you, or your cohorts in the Home Office, get the agents that are lying in wait down south. All you'll have is a girl, an old man, and one expendable second generation Italian who won't – let me repeat this – who *won't* sing.'

'I wouldn't be too sure of that.'

'Oh, but I am,' said Dominic. 'I'm absolutely sure of Tony Lombard's unswerving devotion – if not to me, to my wife.'

'Polly?'

'The one and only Polly, Tony's dear friend.'

'Good God!' Kenny said, sighing. 'You knew about it all along?'

'Now I suppose you'll assume I'm only out for revenge. Not so. In your book, Kenneth, I may be a rat but I'm not so much of a rat that I'd sacrifice my wife and family, and my best friend, just for the sake of getting my own back.'

'You're cleaning house, aren't you?'

'Pretty much, pretty well,' said Dominic.

'What about Harker, what about Rosie's father? How are you going to solve that nasty wee problem?'

'I'm not,' said Dominic. 'You are.'

'Am I? How?'

'By being patient.'

'What are you offering? The names of the agents?'

'I don't have the names of the agents. Harker doesn't have them either. What Harker *does* have, however, is the name, number and location of a source account from which the agents' payments will be drawn.'

'These are Nazi agents, spies? Right?'

'Of course,' said Dominic.

'So you're not a Fascist sympathiser?'

'No, I'm not,' said Dominic. 'Many of my friends and business partners are, or appear to be, but that's only because the Italian brand of Fascism provided them with an illusion of unity. They're not evil, not even misguided. Many of them don't understand what Hitler's all about, or that strutting little egoist, Mussolini, who fancies that conquering Abyssinia will turn him into Alexander the Great.'

'Or Julius Caesar,' said Kenny, nodding.

'Or Julius Caesar,' Dominic agreed. 'I take it you're still with me, Kenneth?'

'Can you deliver Harker? Can you uncover the names of the agents?'

'With your co-operation I can deliver Harker. Netting the individual agents is too much for either of us. Your Scotland Yard friends will have to carry out that part of the operation.'

'Why are you doing this? What will you get out of it?'

'I require two weeks grace, three at most.'

'Grace?'

'To print off the first consignment of counter-feit notes.'

'I can't possibly aid and abet a criminal act.'

'Harker won't come out of hiding until he has something to collect,' Dominic said. 'After sundry percentages have been deducted, he'll have around a hundred thousand in hot cash to pass to John Flint before he deposits the proceeds into a private bank.'

'At which point,' said Kenny, 'the individual agents will begin to perk up and take an interest?'

'Yes,' Dominic said. 'Soon after Harker makes the first deposit some other person – I've no idea who – will move in and arrange payments to small personal accounts in other banks across the country. Might be five, or ten, or fifty for all any of us can tell at this stage. At that juncture, not before, your colleagues down south can move in and pick them off one by one.'

'Including Harker?'

'Yes, including Harker.'

'So he won't be our responsibility? He won't appear in a Scottish court?'

'He probably won't appear in court at all,' said Dominic. 'Unless I've seriously misjudged the little weasel he'll spill his guts in exchange for a passport and a ticket to Siam.'

'Siam?'

'Anywhere,' said Dominic. 'Anywhere that isn't Europe or America. He'll simply vanish, never to be heard of again. History repeating itself.'

'What's Janet McKerlie going to say about that?'

'Janet McKerlie is the very least of our worries.'

'Our worries?' said Kenny. 'I haven't agreed to anything yet?'

'Rosie, I take it, wants to meet her father face to face?'

'I think so, yes.'

'And Lizzie?'

'I really can't say.'

'Small fry,' said Dominic. 'I really do hate to admit it, but we're all just small fry. Very soon Lizzie and the sisters three will have a lot more to worry them than confronting a ghost from the past.'

'Coping with a war, you mean?'

'I'm afraid so,' said Dominic.

Kenny sat back. He stared out over the foyer of the hotel and wondered how long it would be before the Athena's bars and dining-rooms would be filled with men in uniform, the same class, the same autocratic faces as filled it now only in best blues or browns, emblems of rank standardised and properly displayed at last: wondered how long it might be until the mock-marble staircases and metallic palms lay ruined among the rubble in the wake of Luftwaffe bombing raids. He had a sudden clear vision of carnage and destruction, of choking dust and acrid smoke, of Glasgow lying buried, like Pompeii.

'You want me to stay my hand for a couple of weeks, is that it?' Kenny said.

'Three at most.'

'And then what?' Kenny said.

'I'll let you know when Harker makes the collection,' Dominic said, 'and you can take it from there.'

'What about Lombard and the others?'

'They slip quietly away.'

'No charges?'

'No charges.'

'And you?'

'I'll tell Polly that the deal between her father and me fell through and he's gone back to the United States.'

'That isn't what I . . .'

'Polly will take my word for it,' Dominic went on. 'She'll impart the information to Lizzie and her sisters – and they'll believe her.'

'Point is,' said Kenny, 'do I believe you?'

'That's up to you.'

'What's the alternative?'

'There is no alternative, not if you want to snare the agents.'

'You still haven't told me what'll happen to you?'

'That depends,' Dominic said.

'On what?'

'On whether you trust me or not.'

'Huh!' Kenny exclaimed. 'I don't trust you, Mr Manone, not one inch.'

'Which,' said Dominic, 'is just as it should be. Do I get my fortnight's grace?'

Kenny sat motionless, hands between his knees. He wasn't puzzled by the offer or bewildered by the complexity of Manone's scheme. It was, in essence, really very simple. In exchange for a brief delay he would have the sort of material that the SPU had been set up to obtain and would be able to hand on to higher authorities a pretty-well foolproof plan for smoking out a nest of German agents. He would not be there at the death, at the kill, as it were, but he knew how the system worked and that what Dominic promised could be delivered, knew too that one way or another Rosie's father would vanish, never to be seen again.

'All right,' he said. 'I'll do it. But if you let me down . . .'

'I wouldn't dream of letting you down,' said Dominic and with an enigmatic smile, shook Kenny's hand to set the seal on their arrangement.

Dougie had been printing since mid-morning. Everything was running sweetly, so sweetly that he had carried on until three o'clock before switching the machinery off to let it cool. The racket had had died away before Penny came galloping up the wooden stairs and called out, 'There is a strange car coming along the track.'

'Is Tony back yet?'

'No,' Penny said. 'Where are all the finished sheets?'

'On the table, dryin' off.'

'Roll them and hide them between the straws.'

'An' spoil them?'

'It is a car I have not seen before, Dougie. It may be a policeman.'

'Okay, okay. Stall him long as you can, lass.'

Penny turned and ran down the staircase and out into the yard.

Hastily Dougie removed the plates from the clamp and rolled up the finished sheets. He stuffed the rolls behind the straw then, still with the plates in hand, heard the urgent honking of a motorcar horn below in the yard. He thanked his stars that the girl had been alert or lucky enough to spot the intruder. Panting, he shoved the plates into the straw bales too just seconds before Harker appeared on the stairs.

Edgar Harker came thumping up the stairs and on to the floor of the gallery.

'You're the guy, ain't you?' Harker said. 'Know who I am?'

'Aye.' Dougie swallowed his panic. 'I've a feelin' you've been sent to collect . . .' Behind the man's shoulder Penny signalled with a scowl and a shake of the head. Dougie hesitated, then concluded, 'to collect somethin' we haven't got yet.'

Harker turned to Penny. 'You wouldn't be holdin' out on me, sweetheart?'

'No, Eddie, it has proved more difficult than we anticipated.'

'Bloody impossible,' Dougie said. 'Och aye, I can get it up an' runnin' but I can't keep it runnin'. It chews the paper t' rags half the time.'

'Show me,' Harker said.

'There is nothin' to show,' said Dougie. 'We burn the spoilage.'

'It is not safe to leave spoiled stuff lying about,' Penny added.

Strutting like a rooster, Harker strolled around the machine, head back as if he could smell deception in the stink of ink and hot metal. He tapped the lid of the ink-box, one of the few parts that wasn't warm, and said, 'Where's the stuff that ain't been spoiled?'

'There isn't much,' said Dougie.

'How much?'

'Thirty sheets.'

'Where are they?'

'Dominic took them,' Penny said. 'I thought he had taken them to show you.'

'Well, he didn't,' Eddie Harker said. 'I hope for everybody's sake the son-of-a-gun ain't tryin' to double-cross me.'

'He's havin' them scrutinised,' said Dougie.

'Scrutinised?'

'To see if they will pass muster on the exchanges.' Penny took up the lie. 'He has close friends in the banking business.'

'He never mentioned them to me, sweetheart.'

'Dominic does not believe in giving away more than he has to.'

Harker grunted, lifted his head and grinned.

'Has he given you anythin' yet, darlin'?' he said.

Penny flushed and at that instant Dougie realised that the girl was afraid of Harker, more intimidated by him than she had ever been by Tony. Why, he wondered, would a beautiful hard-headed, self-possessed young woman like Penny Weston allow herself to be cowed by a cocky wee runt like Harker.

'Aw look, she's blushin',' Harker said.

'Leave the lassie alone,' Dougie said.

'I see you've found a pal here, sweetheart, a champion.'

'Eddie, please Eddie, I . . .'

He caught Penny by the hand, pulled her to him, his forearm pressing against her breasts. To Dougie's dismay, Penny did not resist.

'Tell you the truth, darlin',' Harker said, 'I didn't come for the money. I trust Dominic. I really do. I trust him 'cause I know what his old man'll do to him if he blows the deal.' He spread a stubby hand across Penny's stomach. 'So, tell me, how long until I see my dough? How long, honey, how long?'

'Two weeks,' Penny hissed. 'Three.'

'Well that gives us plenty o' time to play house,' Edgar Harker said. 'Where's your boyfriend, where's Lombard?'

'Tony's down in Breslin,' said Dougie. 'We expect him back any minute.'

'Then tell him he'll find us in bed,' Harker said and, to Dougie's disgust, steered Penny meekly downstairs and across the yard to the house.

# Chapter Eighteen

'Is Frank not here then?' Janet McKerlie peered into the corners of the drawing-room and clutched her handbag as if she feared that it would be wrested from her. 'Is that not why you've brought me here, for to meet Frank?'

'Janet, sit down,' Lizzie said.

'I should be at the kirk, y' know,' said Janet.

'Yes, of course you should,' Polly said, 'but for one Sunday evening I'm sure you won't be missed.'

'Oh but I will, I'll be missed all right.'

Polly guided her aunt towards one of the chairs that Dominic had placed in a half-circle around the fireplace. He hadn't told Polly why he had chosen to bring them all together on a blustery Sunday evening but if there was one thing that Polly had learned in her sessions with Mr Shadwell it was the value of patience, of waiting for the answers you wanted to hear.

Jackie had been sent over the river to pick

up Lizzie and Rosie while Charley Fraser, in the Wolseley, had navigated his way through the streets of Laurieston and had arrived on Janet McKerlie's doorstep only ten minutes late. She – Charley reported later – had come sweeping out like a damned duchess, swanking to all the neighbours or, more accurately, to the bunch of snotty-nosed kids that gathered, gawping round the big car at the kerb. Charley said he'd almost expected her to ask him for a handful of coins to throw out, like largesse at a wedding, but after she'd wigged him off for keeping her waiting she perched herself in the centre of the rear seat, popped a peppermint Imperial into her mouth and said not one damned word until he'd off-loaded her again in Dominic's driveway.

Once inside the mansion Janet had refused to relinquish her overcoat and hat, had refused to use the toilet at the end of the hall, had been as stiff and quivering as a greyhound in a trap at the prospect that the man she loved, Frank Conway, was waiting for her behind the drawing-room door. And when he wasn't, when all she found was what she'd been promised – her sister, her nieces and Dominic Manone – she'd entered a state of stubborn recalcitrance that would have put a mule to shame.

She refused a glass of sherry wine, tea, coffee or the delicious shortbread fingers that Mrs O'Shea had drummed up that afternoon. She refused to meet her sister's eye or, when invited to do so by Babs, to admire the handsome room which was even larger and more sumptuously furnished than Janet's sole experience of 'class', the Laurieston church minister's manse where Wednesday night prayer meetings were conducted for spinsters and widows. Apparently she also refused to accept that Frank Conway wasn't tucked away behind one of the old pieces of furniture waiting to spring up like a jack-in-the-box and sweep her into his arms.

Lizzie cherished no such silly illusions. Rosie and she sat side by side on the sofa, nibbling shortbread and sipping sherry, both watchful and cautious. They'd left Bernard at home in a raging sulk. He had demanded to be told precisely what Dominic was up to but as Lizzie pointed out, the only way to find out precisely what Dominic was up to was to do precisely what Dominic requested and turn up in Manor Park Avenue at seven p.m. on Sunday.

Polly had seldom seen her husband so at ease. For the best part of a week he had been purring like a cat that knows where the cream is hidden. She had seen little of him. When he had come home he had spent much time with the children, showing them a degree of attention that was almost, if not quite, smothering.

Polly had an inkling of what might be in the wind. Tony had told her that Dominic was in process of pulling off the biggest deal of his career and she had a feeling that her husband was tying up the loose ends of their life together and meant what he said about leaving. She felt no sadness at the prospect, no despair. Sprawled belly-down on the bed upstairs, she had wept after Tony had left her, wept because she felt guilty at last, horribly, tormentingly guilty at what she had done to Dominic and what she would do to Tony, and how much she would miss the excitement of living with a secret that was so intimately, so intimidatingly her own.

She watched her husband seat himself in one of the wing chairs and, his hands in his trouser pockets, stretch out his legs.

'I'm sorry,' he began, 'sorry that I had to bring you here when I'm sure we all have better things to do.'

'Dominic, please?' Rosie spoke up.

'Ah!' he said. 'Sorry,' and lifted himself forward slightly in the chair so that Rosie could read his lips more clearly. 'Better?'

'Yes.'

The little interruption did not disturb his rhythm, Polly noted. He smiled at Rosie and inclined his head as if to thank her for drawing attention to his negligence, then continued, 'It would be daft to pretend that none of us in this room aren't interested in Frank Conway and it's to tell you about Frank Conway that I've got you all together.'

'Where is he? Why isn't Frank here?' Janet demanded.

'He isn't here,' Dominic said, 'because at this very moment he's on a boat bound for New York. In other words, he's gone back to America. He will not return to Scotland.'

'Because of the war?' Rosie asked.

'Partly,' Dominic said, 'but rather, I fancy, because he didn't get what he wanted over here.'

'An' what was that, Dominic?' Babs said.

'He wanted me to co-operate with him on, shall we say, a get-rich-quick scheme cooked up by my father in Philadelphia. Now I'm not, as you all know, averse to making money but there were elements in Frank Conway's proposal that, candidly, disgusted me.'

'What elements?' said Rosie.

'A reasonable belief that profits from the enterprise would wind up financing members of the Nazi party,' Dominic said. 'Mainly for that reason I elected not to accept the proposal and refused to participate in it.'

'Nothin' wrong with Sir Oswald Mosley,' Janet broke in. 'He's a good-lookin' man an' a member o' the nobility.'

'Dear God!' Babs put a despairing hand to her brow.

'This wasn't to fund the Blackshirts, Janet,' Dominic said. 'The money was intended for Germany.'

'Some o' Adolf Hitler's ideas . . .'

'Auntie,' said Babs, 'shut up.'

'Don't you talk t' me like that, not after what I've had to put up with.'

Dominic raised his voice a little. 'Ladies, please, there's no need for argument. The fact of the matter is that Frank Conway has gone as suddenly as he appeared and I can assure you that none of us will hear from him again.'

'I will,' said Janet. 'I know I will.'

'Well,' said Dominic, holding up a hand to silence Babs's protest, 'well, perhaps you will, Janet, but I wouldn't count on it.'

'Did you know who he was?' said Rosie. 'Did you know he was my Daddy?'

'Not at first,' Dominic said. 'He passes himself off under the name of Edgar Harker now. I took him at face value. It was only latterly that I learned his true identity.'

'Did he tell you who he was?' said Lizzie.

'No.'

'Why didn't he come to see us?' said Rosie.

'He isn't that kind of father,' said Polly. 'Babs and I encountered him face to face, quite by chance. I didn't recognise him, nor did Babs. He was less than paternal, Rosie, believe me. He's a thoroughly unpleasant man.'

'I'll go along with that,' said Babs. 'Struck me as a right bastard.'

'Aye,' said Lizzie, quietly, 'perhaps he always was.'

She glanced up at Janet but the woman offered no defence of the phantom with whom she had been in love for so many years. She sat on the edge of the chair, clutching her handbag. Life for Janet McKerlie had stopped over twenty years ago, Polly realised. Perhaps, though, that was the way Janet wanted it

and dreary habit and false hope were all she needed
to sustain her to the end of her days.

'I know,' Dominic went on, 'that some of you
may be disappointed that he made no effort to meet
you while he was in Scotland and are inclined to
blame me for not informing you that he was alive
and back in Scotland. But it seemed the most sensible
thing to do at the time. Why? Because the police
were aware of his presence and might even have
arrested him, which would have been a disaster for
all of you.'

'Yeah, and for you too, Dom,' Babs said.

'Probably,' Dominic admitted.

'Is that why you chased him away?' said Rosie.

'I didn't chase him away. He went of his own
volition.'

'Back where he came from?' said Rosie.

'Yes.'

'Where did he come from?' Rosie persisted. 'And
why did he leave us in the lurch in the first place?'

'Things got too hot for him,' Lizzie said. 'He
thought he was in debt to the Manones – he wasn't
as it happens – an' went off to fight in the war.'

'Is that really true?' said Babs.

'I'm not sure,' Dominic said. 'I've a suspicion he
may have joined up and then deserted. I really cannot
say. All I do know is that he turned up in Philadelphia
soon after the war with a new name and went to work
for my father.'

'Is that where he's gone back to?' Lizzie said.

'Yes,' Dominic said. 'Philadelphia, possibly New York.'

Polly said, 'Did he take his wife with him?'

'I expect he did,' said Dominic, unruffled by her question. 'He married again, you see, more than once for all I can tell. Bigamy, however, is the least of your father's crimes. He was a danger to all of us, believe me, and it's better for all of us, especially you, Lizzie, that he's gone.'

'Is this supposed to clear the air?' said Babs.

'I hope so, yes,' said Dominic.

'Does it? Mammy,' Polly said, 'does it?'

And Lizzie, with a little sigh, said, 'Yes.'

At first she thought he had cost her the baby, that rough handling had restored the natural blood flow; that she had deceived herself, that all would be well when the bruises faded and she would be just as she had been before. She had sworn Dougie to secrecy and because he loved her in his fashion, he'd said nothing to Tony about Eddie's visit and had busied himself with running off a fortune in fine forged notes.

It was audible all the time now, the insatiable *click-clack-click* of the paper feeder, an accompaniment to the strange little pulses inside her. When she carried Dougie's lunch out to the stables or fetched him coffee she could feel the vibrations reaching up through the soles of her feet into her thighs and belly, shaking the tiny foetus inside her womb; felt that she'd become part of a device that would deliver her up as sharp and well-defined as the Britannia on a five-pound note. Then she would come out into the yard, breathe the fresh spring air, let the country wind soothe her, relieved that Eddie's brutal love-making had not cost her the child, that the child within her had survived.

There was money now, much money. Neatly stacked bundles of banknotes. Two hundred notes to a bundle. Each bundle bound with a strip of thick brown paper. She knew, of course, that it was not real money. But it looked and felt like real money. Perfectly authentic. She contemplated the money in a pleased, vague sort of way. Recompense for all the suffering her mother had undergone. Payment for her suffering too, a thin and brittle strand that bound her still to her father. Soon she would have her money. Money would free her to retrace the steps she had taken to get here. With Eddie. With her lawful wedded husband. Or not.

Tony was working hard now. He was over the stables with Dougie for much of the day. Dougie had shown him how to check each sheet of notes with the big magnifier, what to look out for, and the rate of wastage had dropped to almost nil. He, Tony, operated the guillotine by hand. He spread the notes to let them age, gathered them, counted them, bundled them as efficiently as any bank clerk, stored them in cardboard cartons.

They had a smell, those old new notes, a fine distinctive bouquet. Tony would pause to sniff one or, now and then, hold one out to her as if it were a tulip or a rose, would smile at her and wink. The money had brought him out of his sullen mood. He did not seem to mind that she would not allow him into her bed or be tempted into his. She told him that she was unwell, just a little unwell. He was tactful and solicitous – and busy. Busy with the money. Busy completing the job that Dominic had given him to do.

Once every two or three days he drove the Dolomite down to Breslin to stock up on groceries and once, just once, a Civil Defence volunteer had wandered up to the farmhouse to conduct an unofficial census of all those residents who still needed to be supplied with gas-masks. The machine had been switched off, sheets and plates swiftly removed and hidden. Dougie had come out of the stables in his overalls and had been charm itself to the volunteer who had drunk coffee and chatted and inspected the three gas-masks in an off-hand manner and had gone off again, quite satisfied, without realising that a man with a loaded rifle had been stationed in the attic window and that any sign of suspicion or alarm might have resulted in one volunteer less in the Breslin Civil Defence unit.

Then Dominic had come out to Blackstone. He had inspected the machinery again, had peeped into one of the cartons and had pocketed the tally slip that Tony had ready for him. Exact count: £63,430. Almost thirteen thousand notes. And enough paper in stock to print thirty thousand more.

Dominic had taken one of the bundles with him and, before leaving, had walked across the field for a bit with Tony, talking to Tony and, though she had spied on them through the telescope, Penny could not make out what they were saying, if they were talking about her or money or war.

Late that same night Tony came to her bedroom door, knocked upon it and asked if she would let him in. And she did. And he made love to her again.

They lay together afterwards, naked in the warm night air, smoking cigarettes, and Tony said, 'What'll you do when all this is over, Penny?'

'I will take my money and go back to New York.'

'Not Austria?'

'No, there is nothing for me in Austria.'

'Don't you want to marry a high-ranking officer of the Wehrmacht?'

'A German? No,' she said, then again, more emphatically, 'No.'

'You don't believe in backing winners?' Tony asked.

She leaned on an elbow and stared down at him. 'Do you think that they will be winners,' she said, 'truly?'

'There may not be any winners at all,' Tony said.

He transferred the cigarette to an ashtray on the bedside table and put his hands on her shoulders. She lowered herself an inch or two until her breasts touched his chest. Her nipples were sensitive and her breasts seemed heavier, though that, she realised, might just be her imagination. The bruises that Eddie's thumbs had left were no more than subtle shadows.

Tony said, 'You don't want to marry at all, is that it?'

'No,' she said. 'I would marry if the right man came along.'

'Hah! The old story,' Tony said. 'The old, old story.'

'What is?'

'Waiting for Mr Right. You could wait all your life for Mr Right.'

'Then perhaps I will – wait all of my life,' Penny said.

She suspected that she could force him to a decision, for behind his moodiness, beneath his toughness Tony Lombard was a sentimentalist who would not let her go, not if she was carrying his child. And it *was* Tony's child. She was eight or ten weeks into pregnancy and had been with no other man in that time.

'What are you smiling at?' Tony said.

'I did not know that I was smiling.'

He shifted his weight, drew up his knees a little. He had a broad chest, hairy but not ugly, broad shoulders too. 'So you wouldn't want to marry a guy like me?'

'A guy *like* you?' Penny said.

'Me,' Tony said. 'Get married to me.'

'Are you asking if I will marry you?'

'Yeah, I am.'

'When this is over?'

'As soon as this is over, yeah.'

'Will you go away?'

'We'll both go away,' Tony said, 'if that's what you want.'

'It is what I want,' Penny said. 'Somewhere far away.'

'Fine,' Tony said. 'Why don't you marry me and we'll clear out together?'

'I would,' she said, 'but Eddie . . .'

'Eddie? What the hell does Harker have to do with it?' Tony said. 'He isn't your husband, not legally.'

'You are right,' Penny said. 'I suppose you are right.'

'So you *will* marry me?'

'When it is over,' Penny said. 'When it is all over here, yes.'

'That's good enough for me,' said Tony and drew her down upon him and cautiously kissed her lips.

It came as a surprise to Lizzie, and something of a shock, to see Dominic's motorcar draw up at the kerb outside the living-room window and, a moment or two later, to find her grandchildren on the doorstep. She was nonplussed by her son-in-law's appearance on a Sunday afternoon, curious as to why he'd come. The fact that he'd left Polly at home in Manor Park suggested there might be trouble brewing between them.

'Don't look so perturbed, Mother-in-law,' Dominic said. 'We've had lunch, if that's what's got you hot and bothered.'

'You'll have tea then?'

'No,' Dominic said then, sensing Lizzie's agitation, instantly changed his mind. 'Please, yes.' He inclined his head towards the kitchen. 'Where's Bernard?'

'Out in the back,' said Lizzie, 'digging more holes.'

'Shelters?'

'Aye,' said Lizzie, 'More shelters.'

She turned her attention to her grandchildren. Much as she loved Stuart and Ishbel she was less at ease with them than with Babs's brood, particularly Angus whose enthusiasm for mischief seemed more natural than the little Manones' polite reserve. If she had spent more time with them she might have detected in Stuart a sadness that had no explanation and might have recognised in Ishbel some of her sister's prissiness.

'They're getting big,' Lizzie said, lamely. 'Aren't you getting big, Stuart?'

'Yes, Granny, I think I am.'

'Thank you,' Ishbel said.

'Thank you,' Stuart repeated.

There was more discussion about food and drink for neither child seemed willing to give offence by expressing a preference.

Lizzie came close to losing patience for she felt uncomfortable at having her son-in-law in her house without Polly and Dominic's elegant clothes and polished manners made everything here seem shabby.

She went into the kitchenette and put on the kettle. Though the back door was closed she could hear the rasp of a saw and someone, Mr Grainger probably, shouting orders. She had no idea what was going on and Bernard hadn't seen fit to tell her. Some new development in neighbourhood plans to thwart Hitler's bombs perhaps, or an argument about how much of the back lawn should be dug up to plant vegetables.

Dominic drifted into the kitchenette. Stuart and Ishbel remained at the table in the living-room. They looked bored, Lizzie thought, bored with being so well behaved. She recalled the clamorous life of the tenements, small rooms packed with unruly children, noise and fuss and quarrelsome voices, riotous games and impromptu free-for-alls. Though she liked Knightswood sometimes she felt the loss of . . . of what? Something she couldn't put a name to, a sense of endeavour and endurance, of energy and rebellion, qualities that Polly's children sadly lacked.

'Lizzie,' Dominic said, 'what did Bernard say when you told him that your husband – that Conway had gone back to America?'

'I don't think he believed me.'

'Would you like me to have a word with him?'

'Is that why you came today, Dominic?'

'Yes, that's why I came. Also, to let you see the children.'

'That's a funny thing to say,' said Lizzie.

'I feel sometimes that you have not seen enough of them.'

'It's not your fault,' Lizzie said.

'Ah, but it is,' said Dominic. 'Bernard's outside?'

'Aye, he is.'

She watched him open the door and step down on to the mud-slicked path that ran the length of the cottage row. It was, she supposed, as strange a world to him as Manor Park was to her but her son-in-law was too confident, too polite to let his distaste show. She had known from the first that by condoning Polly's marriage to this man she would in time lose her daughter – and that was exactly what had come to pass. She watched Bernard emerge from a slit trench ten or fifteen yards from the back door. Mr Grainger was in another trench forty or fifty feet away and the neighbours were shouting at each other, not angrily but with friendly raillery. Each had a spade, each had a cigarette hanging from his lips and Dominic, groomed like a tailor's dummy, stood between them, watching and waiting with a patience that Lizzie found unnerving.

She closed the back door with her foot, poured milk from a bottle into two clean glasses and carried them into the living-room.

'There you are now,' she said. 'Drink up.'

'Thank you, Granny,' Ishbel said.

'Thank you, Granny,' said Stuart.


'I've arranged an appointment for you with the Housing Officer of Breslin District Council,' Dominic began without preamble. 'Next Wednesday morning, ten a.m., at the Burgh hall.'

'Housing Officer?' said Bernard. 'What do we want with him?'

'Nothing,' said Dominic. 'He's interviewing for the post of deputy and I've suggested that you'd be an ideal candidate. Four sets of references have already been filed in your favour. I don't think there will be a problem.'

Bernard stuck the spade into the ground and leaned on the handle. He took the cigarette from his mouth, contemplated the wet end for a moment, tossed it away. 'Am I being sacked from Lyons and Lloyd's?'

'Let go,' said Dominic. 'Released sounds even better.'

'Why?'

'There isn't enough business coming through the

agency to justify the employment of two full-time estate agents.'

'You're not closing down then?'

'No. Allan Shakespeare will keep things ticking over.'

'Last in, first out?' Bernard said. 'The law of the jungle. This wouldn't have anything to do with Frank Conway, would it?'

'What could it possibly have to do with Frank Conway?'

'Or Kenny MacGregor?'

Dominic paused. He was conscious of the presence of the neighbour, Mr Grainger, who was digging away nonchalantly and pretending not to eavesdrop.

He stepped closer to the wall at the end of the communal drying green. Boards were propped against it, the remains of what had once been a sweet-pea frame and a stack of turves that would be laid over the roof of the Anderson shelter that Bernard had bedded in the ground. He drew Bernard away from the slit trench and put a hand on his shoulder.

'Fifty pounds in a plain brown envelope, Bernard? Do you take me for a idiot? No, you don't have to report to Kenny MacGregor. I'll do that for you.'

'You?'

'I'm closing the shop.'

'I thought you just said . . .'

'Not the estate agency, other things.'

'And you want me out, is that it?'

'Yes.'

'Supposing,' Bernard said, 'I don't fancy working for Breslin Council?'

'It's entirely up to you, of course,' said Dominic. 'I'm giving you a month's wages in lieu of notice. I want you out of the office by Wednesday. Allan will take over any transactions that you have on hand. The job with the Council is yours if you want it. If you don't . . .' He shrugged. 'I advise you to take it, Bernard. The pay's a bit less but the Council needs experienced housing officers and you won't, I'm sure, short-change them.'

'Are you sure they will take me on?'

'Oh, yes,' said Dominic. 'My friend, Carfin Hughes, has considerable influence in that quarter and he's given you a glowing recommendation.'

'Pretty cut an' dried then, isn't it?' Bernard said.

'Yes.'

'Has Conway really gone back to the States?'

'Yes.'

'What did our friend MacGregor have to say about that?'

'Kenny has bigger fish to fry.'

'Bigger fish?' Bernard chuckled, more like a cough. 'Not you?'

'I was never as big a fish as some people imagined me to be. In the current scheme of things I'm a minnow, a tiddler,' Dominic said. 'Will you keep the appointment on Wednesday, Bernard, please.'

'Don't have much option, do I?'

'If you do,' Dominic said, 'you won't be bothered again, not by me or by the coppers. You'll be as safe and secure as anyone can be at this time.'

'How safe and secure is that?'

'I'm not a prophet,' Dominic said. 'I don't know.'

'What about the farm? What about Blackstone?'

'Blackstone has been sold.'

'What?'

'Well, to be accurate it's in process of being sold.'

'Why wasn't I told? My signature's on the lease.'

'What lease?' said Dominic. 'There is no lease.'

Again the chuckle, the cough: 'By God,' Bernard said, 'you're certainly thorough, Mr Dominic Manone, I will say that for you.'

'Will you keep the appointment on Wednesday morning?'

Bernard looked down the length of the gardens. Grainger was still digging, little gouts of clayey soil spewing from his spade. Grainger was no navvy, no labourer. He was a clerk in Simpson Brown's clearing house; clean collar, shiny suit, tramcar to work every morning; two sons of twenty-five or thirty, eight or ten years to retirement and a modest pension. Eight or ten years! God, Bernard thought, where will we all be in eight or ten years, in eighteen or twenty months for that matter? He was no prophet either yet the long-term future appeared to be as bleak as it was uncertain.

Relieved and grateful to be out of Dominic Manone's shadow, free of his connection with the fraternity of less-than-honest men, he nodded.

'Yes, Dominic, I'll be there.'

'Good man,' said Dominic and without a word of farewell went back into the house for tea.

# Chapter Nineteen

If Gareth Winstock really had been dead and not merely 'missing', as it were, his ghost would surely have haunted no other place, give or take the odd public house, than the basement in St Andrew's Street for the chair at the head of the table remained respectfully vacant and the progress of the SPU's investigations continued just as lamely as they had done under his auspices.

Kenny saw to that for he had learned the art of prevarication from a master and had more motive than ambition to delay the case in hand. He still had Stone sitting outside Lombard's apartment in a radio van and Galbraith, on the hoof, strolling round Manor Park, but Fiona, his beloved sister, was growing short on patience.

'Are you going to throw it all away, Kenny MacGregor? Is that your intention? You promised me faithfully when you accepted the job that you'd do it to the best of your ability.'

'This is the best of my ability.'

'Is it? What happened to the message from Stone that Lombard had picked up a suitcase from his apartment and driven off with it?'

'I received the message.'

'What did you *do* about it?'

'Logged it, of course.'

'Why didn't you instruct Stone to follow Lombard?'

'I didn't have to. Besides, Stone's shift was almost up and I didn't want to run the unit into overtime.'

'Overtime! Overtime!' said Fiona, in her best Lady Bracknell voice.

'We do have a budget,' said Kenny, 'and right at this very moment I'm trying *not* to exceed it. Good management is very important, Fiona, as you are constantly reminding me.'

'So are results.'

'Results will come.'

'Oh, will they?'

'Yes, they will,' Kenny said.

'You don't even read my foreign résumés.'

'I do, when I'm not too busy.'

'Busy! You've been twiddling your thumbs for the best part of a month, Kenny. I'm amazed that Percy hasn't had you on the carpet.'

'Percy is otherwise occupied,' Kenny said. 'If I'd asked for extra money for overtime, though, he'd have been down on me like a ton of bricks.'

'My God! What an attitude!' Fiona said, outraged. 'When are you going to pick up Manone and the others? I mean, if you were really worth your salt you'd have that damned villain Carfin Hughes behind bars by now and half his high school cronies with him.'

'Nobody will ever put Hughes behind bars. He's far too slippery. Besides, he's a lawyer. Can you imagine the ructions upstairs if we had the audacity to lift an esteemed member of the legal profession for questioning, let alone arrest. In addition to which . . .'

'I know, I know: we've nothing to go on.'

'I could lift Flint, I suppose. If you want me to.'

'It isn't what *I* want, Kenneth. *I'm* nothing around here. *I'm* just a female civilian who does your typing and wastes time translating material nobody bothers to read. Frankly, if you weren't my brother I'd resign tomorrow.'

'Did you bring any scones?'

'Scones!' Fiona spat out. 'Hitler's trampling all over Europe, Jews are being beaten senseless in the streets of Berlin, the Italians are on the point of signing a pact with Germany, Franco has pulled Spain out of the League of Nations, and all you can think about is *scones!*'

'An army marches on its stomach, you know.'

'Oh, God! Kenny, I ask you!'

'Instead of nagging me, Fiona, why don't you ask me why I didn't send Stone chasing after Tony Lombard and his precious suitcase?'

'All right then. Why didn't you send Stone chasing after Lombard?'

'Because I know where Lombard and his suitcase were going.'

'Oh!' Fiona exclaimed.

Kenny savoured a small moment of triumph over his sister. He let her stew for almost half a minute while the ruckus upstairs in the corridor grew louder and Detective Constable Galbraith's boots clumped on the stairs.

Fiona could contain herself no longer. 'Where?'

'Blackstone Farm.'

*'Where?'*

'Out by Breslin.'

'Doing what?'

'Printing counterfeit money.'

'Why don't you bring him in then?' Fiona said, glancing at the door.

'I intend to,' Kenny said. 'I'm going to bring him in myself.'

'When?'

And Kenny said, 'Tonight.'

Two hundred five-pound notes were laid out on John Flint's desk like a gigantic hand of Patience. Johnny could hardly keep his hands off them and while Harker talked, lifted a note here, a note there and stroked it, smirking, before returning it to its place in the pattern.

'Lovely,' he murmured. 'Isn't it a lovely sight.'

'For Chrissake, stop gloatin',' Eddie Harker told him. 'It's only the tip o' the iceberg, Johnny boy. There's a million more where that came from.'

'A million, a whole million?' Johnny said. 'Is that a fact?'

'Can you cope with it?'

'Oh sure, sure I can cope with it.' Johnny looked up at Harker with the most profound expression he could muster. 'Money, I can always cope with but I never imagined I'd ever have a million quid lyin' on my desk.'

'You won't,' Harker said. 'What you will have are consignments o' twenty thousand, cash value, at a time. An' listen, bucko, if one note, one lousy wee fiver slips through your fingers, I'll know about it an' you won't see another tosser.'

'Of course, I'll account for every penny,' said Johnny soberly. 'I'll give you a statement of price on every packet in every consignment. But the rate's bound to vary, Eddie. Nobody's gonna buy more than five grand's worth from me at any one time.' He fingered another note, stroking it with his forefinger. 'The stuff's so bloody good, though, I reckon we could get off with not scrubbin' it at all.'

'Maybe later,' said Harker. 'What we need to do first is test the market. We also need to pull in some honest cash. This operation ain't been cheap.'

'I can well believe it,' Johnny said. 'I'm just glad to be a part of it.'

'Keep your nose clean, Flinty,' Eddie Harker said, 'an' you'll make your fortune along with the rest of the guys.'

'Along with Dominic, you mean?'

'Yeah. Dominic.'

'When can I expect a first delivery?'

'I'm pickin' it up tonight,' Eddie Harker said. 'I need keys to your van.'

'My van?' Flint's euphoria vanished. 'I didn't know you'd be usin' my van.'

'You know now, don't you?' Harker said.

'How big is the shipment?'

'Twenty thousand notes.'

'A hundred grand, my God!'

'Packed in two boxes.' said Harker. 'I want you here at ten-thirty when the movie show gets out downstairs. There'll be enough goin' on in the street so the cops, if there are any cops, won't notice. I'll park round back an' bring the boxes up by the stairs. Have the door open, won't you?'

'Smart,' said Johnny, nodding. 'Very smart.'

'You got a safe cleaned out?'

'All ready an' waiting,' John Flint said. 'Who's makin' the collection?'

'I am,' Harker said.

'You an' who else?'

'Just me,' Eddie Harker said. 'Me an' my little friend here.'

'What is that?' Johnny said. 'A gun? Is that a gun?'

'What does it look like?' Harker said. 'Chopped liver?'

'Guns? I dunno about guns. I'm not very clever with guns.'

'You don't hafta be,' said Harker. 'I'm just takin' precautions.'

'Precautions?' said Johnny, dry-mouthed. 'Against what?'

'In case anyone tries to get smart.'

'You – you wouldn't actually use it, would you, Eddie?'

'You bet I would,' said Harker.

There was no real reason for drinking, none at all. It had been weeks since she'd felt the need to tipple at the gin bottle in the early part of the afternoon. Victor Shadwell had cancelled her morning appointment, however, and she'd felt a little lost and lonely without a lesson to fall back on. If she'd been just a pinch more attentive, a shade more clear-headed she might have noticed tension in the girl. But she was in no mood to dilute her new-found power by helping out with housework or arbitrating in squabbles below stairs.

She was in the front lounge, lying on the big leather sofa listening to dance music on the wireless when Dominic arrived home.

She sat up, slid the highball glass under the sofa and peered at the clock on the mantel above the fireplace. Ten past four. She hadn't even heard Patricia leave to collect the children. She rose, swaying slightly, and looked towards the window.

The weather was indecisive, bright one minute, raining the next, more like April than May. A blustery wind shook the evergreens and sprinkled blossom petals from the park on to the wet lawn. Polly stood motionless, a hand over her mouth. She heard a car door slam, the front door open, the thump-thud of her children clambering upstairs to the playroom where Patricia would have laid out milk or lemonade and a plate of chocolate biscuits to keep them going until supper.

'Patricia?' she said, not loudly.

No answer: voices in the hall sounded furtive and threatening, like plotters. She took a step towards the door, changed her mind, seated herself in the sofa. She reached down and pushed the highball glass further out of sight, tugged down her skirt, clasped her hands in her lap.

'Dominic,' she called out, 'is that you?'

His head appeared around the door.

'Oh, there you are,' he said. 'I thought you'd gone out?'

'Lesson,' Polly said, 'cancelled.'

'My fault,' said Dominic. 'I needed a consult with Victor this morning.'

'Might,' said Polly, 'have told me.'

'Would it have made any difference?'

'Probably,' Polly said, 'not.'

He didn't enter the room. Nothing visible but his

head peeping around the door-jamb, like the sort of game her nephew Angus might invent to tease her.

'I collected Pat and the children in the car,' he said. 'I was passing the school and it seemed a bit daft not to.'

'Fine,' said Polly. 'Good.'

'What are you doing?'

'Having,' Polly said, 'a little nap.'

'Yes, you have been overdoing it somewhat lately,' Dominic said.

There were sounds upstairs, faint whisperings, muffled thumps to which her husband paid not the slightest attention. She glanced up at the ornate ceiling, saw – or thought she saw – the chandelier sway slightly, followed its motion not with her eyes but her head.

'Sorry if we disturbed you,' Dominic said. 'Finish your nap. I'll keep them quiet for a while.' He closed the door before she could think of anything to say. Then he opened it again, showed her his face once more. 'By the by, I won't be home for supper. I'm meeting Hughes for dinner in Glasgow.'

'Should – shouldn't I,' Polly said, 'be there too?'

'Not tonight, darling,' Dominic told her. 'No, definitely not tonight.'


The night was a lot less dark than most of those on Islay. There was a long clear pink afterglow in the sky to the west and a gaseous haze hung over Clydebank and dappled the underbelly of the cloud that covered the small towns and villages.

Kenny had put on a stout pair of boots. He reckoned the rain showers would have left the farmyard muddy and the fields slippery and felt that boots would give him an advantage if a hot pursuit was called for.

Dominic had picked him up outside the picture house at Anniesland Cross. It had still been light then, almost full daylight. They had driven over the Switchback at a leisurely pace.

Rain had hastened the arrival of summer and fruit orchards glowed with blossom and tall trees were in full leaf at last. He didn't know this side of Glasgow at all well. He had walked the Roman wall with Fiona once or twice and had been dragged along the ridge of the Campsie Fells one sweltering Sunday afternoon some years ago, but it was, for Kenny, *terra incognita*, and he began to wish that he had studied the large-scale maps of the area just a little more carefully. He had a sense where Breslin was and where the farm lay in relation to the little town but Dominic did not take that route and Kenny was startled when the Wolseley jounced abruptly off the road into what appeared to be a cow pasture.

'Where are we?' Almost the first words he'd spoken since Dominic had picked him up: 'This isn't Blackstone?'

Dominic switched off the headlights but did not cut the engine.

The car continued slowly up a mud-slicked road-way towards a line of villas on the skyline. Peering from the window, Kenny realised that they were on the edge of a builders' estate, surrounded by half-finished bungalows.

'Blackstone's just the other side of the hill,' Dominic said. 'I'm going to take the car through the field and park out of sight of the farmhouse.'

'Is someone expecting you?'

'Yes.'

'Friend or foe?' said Kenny.

'That remains to be seen,' said Dominic.

Kenny thought he knew where they were. The office maps weren't sufficiently up to date to show the building site but he guessed they were heading for a prominent knoll that overlooked the old farmhouse.

'Are those the villas that Bernard sold?' he asked.

'Yes.'

'Bonskeet's must have made a tidy profit on that lot?'

'Yes,' Dominic said, 'but a loss on the rest of the site.'

'What? Why?'

'Cancelled reservations. Mortgages hard to come by. Nobody interested in investing in property this close to the shipyards. At Bonskeet's board meeting last week it was decided to mothball the site, board it up and leave it as it is.'

'Until after the war?' said Kenny. 'If there is a war.'

'Hmmm,' Dominic murmured.

Sitting forward, brow close to the windscreen, he eased the Wolseley through a field gate between thorn hedges, across an open field and around the base of a grassy hillock where, almost arbitrarily, he braked to a halt.

'This is it,' he said. 'We're here.'

'Where's the farm?'

'Down there, dead ahead.'

'How far?'

'Quarter of a mile, or less.' Dominic opened the driver's door. 'Are you ready for this, Sergeant MacGregor?'

'As I'll ever be,' said Kenny.

She had been to the toilet three times since supper but the irritating urgency had not been relieved. She was on the point of going to the closet again when Tony called from upstairs: 'He's here.'

'Who? Dominic?' Penny shouted.

'I don't know where the hell Dominic's got to.' Tony answered as he ran down the stairs. 'He should be here. Christ, he said he'd be here.'

'What will we do if Dominic does not come?'

'Give Harker the dough, I suppose,' Tony said. 'Dougie, is it ready?'

'All ready.'

Dougie was seated by the hearth with the cat on his knee. He was tickling the back of her ears with his finger and looked absolutely calm except that the cigarette hanging from the side of his mouth twitched and shed little flakes of ash and when he put his hand to his mouth to remove it, his fingers were trembling.

'Bugger it!' he said, scowling at his hand. 'I could fair do wi' a drink.'

'Later,' Penny said. 'We will have a drink together, later.'

'I'm goin' t' hold you to that, lass,' Dougie said.

Getting up from the armchair, he opened the window above the sink and eased the cat out on to the ledge. He paused, watching the headlamps of the van buck and flicker as it rounded the hairpin at the top of the track and began the descent to the yard.

He closed the window and turned.

'It's him,' he said. 'It's Harker.'

'Is he alone?' said Penny.

'Looks like it,' Dougie said.

'Thank God for that,' said Penny.

'Now all we need is Dominic. Where the hell *is* Dominic?' Tony asked, and a voice just behind him answered:

'Right here.'

Kenny didn't dare switch on the electric light or use his pocket torch in case he alerted Harker to his presence in the stables. There was just enough light from the window, however, to illuminate the printing equipment, a ramshackle Heath Robinson device that looked as if it were held together by baling wire and string. He inspected it as best he could, alert for voices in the yard or the sounds of the men entering the stables below where two cardboard boxes were packed and ready to be collected. Sealed with gummed tape and twine, the boxes were not so bulky as he had imagined they would be but it would have cost him several minutes to open one, and he probably didn't have several minutes. Dominic had timed it to perfection. They had arrived at the side of the farmhouse just seconds before headlights appeared at the top of the track. Dominic had told him to hide himself in the stables and had pushed him towards the door before he could protest. He, Dominic, had gone into the farmhouse through the front door, moving as silently as shadow in his black alpaca overcoat.

Kenny had barely had time to dart across the yard to the stables before the beams of the van's headlamps spilled over the damp cobbles and Frank Conway – alias Eddie Harker – climbed out of the cab. He wore a jerkin, American style, and a cloth cap; a small man whose massive shoulders and heavy moustache lent him a ludicrous air of menace. He loitered by the vehicle, patted his hip, his breast then leaving the van door wide open, headed towards the farmhouse.

'Eddie,' Kenny heard Dominic say, 'how nice to see you.'

From the window Kenny watched Harker and

Dominic shake hands and enter the house: the door closed.

At that moment Kenny knew that Dominic was up to something. He had been deliberately excluded from whatever plotting or negotiation was going on inside. He didn't even know how many of Dominic's 'gang' were present. He hadn't seen the blonde girl, the printer, or Tony Lombard. He wondered if Manone had shoo-ed them away or if, as seemed likely, they were all gathered inside.

He had told Manone, 'no deals', yet here he was doing exactly what Dominic wanted him to do. He was tempted to charge down the wooden stairs, race across the yard, break into the meeting and arrest the damned lot of them. Instead he clambered back up to the gallery where the machinery was situated. He had no idea how much time he would have before Harker emerged from the farmhouse again.

He just hoped it would be enough.


'Hiya, kid,' Eddie said. 'Miss me, did ya?'

He swaggered across the kitchen, insinuated an arm about Penny's waist and thrust his face up to hers. She kissed him perfunctorily on the mouth.

Tony, hands in pockets, watched sullenly.

'No time for jig-jig, sweetheart,' Harker said. 'Got work to do.'

He detached his arm from about her, glanced at his wristlet watch.

He said, 'Where's the stuff?'

'What's the rush?' Dominic said. 'Have a drink, a cup of coffee. I assume you're not delivering the goods directly to your German friends.'

'What I'm doin' with it, Dom, ain't none o' your business.'

'I see,' Dominic said. 'I'm just the factory foreman, am I?'

'You got it, son,' said Eddie Harker. 'Now, where's the goddamned stuff?'

'In the stables, packed and ready to go.'

'Packed?' said Harker.

'I didn't think you'd want to take it away in a shopping basket.'

'I wanna see it,' Harker said. 'I wanna see the money.'

Dougie was seated in the armchair by the hearth and looked, Penny thought, rather incomplete without the tabby on his lap. The cigarette in his mouth no longer twitched, though, and his eyes were bright and attentive.

'Do you intend to count it?' Dominic said. 'It'll take all night.'

'I didn't say "count it".' Harker said. 'I just wanna make sure it's there.'

'Dear God, Eddie!' Dominic said. 'You *really* don't trust me.'

'I *really* don't trust anybody,' Harker said. 'How many boxes?'

'Two,' said the girl.

'I want them opened.'

'Jesus!' Tony said, softly.

'What do you think, Eddie,' Dominic said, 'that the boxes are stuffed with newspaper? Why would I want to cheat you at this stage in the proceedings?'

'I want them opened,' Harker said.

Dominic signalled. 'Tony, go and bring . . .'

'Tony,' Harker said, 'stay right where you are.'

'I'll go,' said Penny.

'Not you either, sweetheart,' Harker said. 'You might be my lovin' wife but when it comes to hard cash . . .'

'So she really is your wife,' Tony said.

Harker swung round. He glanced first at Tony, then Penny, and, feigning amazement, said, 'You didn't tell him? You didn't show him your ring? I thought you'd've shown him your ring. Nice, shiny, new wedding band. Ain't you proud to be my little wifie? Oh, dear! Oh, my! Looks like somebody round here ain't been entirely honest. Sure, she's my wife. We got married in New York and honeymooned at sea. Didn't see much o' the ocean, though, did we, honey?'

'The marriage isn't legal. It will never stand up in a court,' Dominic said. 'Did you forget you already had a wife in Scotland, Eddie?'

'That was a long time ago,' Harker said, 'an' Scotland's another country.'

'It's this country,' Dominic said. 'And you're back in this country now.'

'Yeah, but not for long. Soon we'll be snug in our little love-nest in New York. Won't we, sweetheart?' Eddie glanced again at his wristlet watch. 'Love to stay an' chat, folks, but I gotta be on my way. Why don't we all go out to the stable an' lemme take a look inside those boxes. Okay with you, Mr Manone?'

'Fine with me, Mr Harker,' Dominic said and touching Tony's arm as he passed, moved to open the door.

Kenny had come too far and made too many concessions to let impatience spoil it now: he must wait for Harker to take possession of the money. Once he had Harker bang to rights he would decide what to do with the rest of them. He would keep Harker here as long as possible of course – days if necessary – until Fiona made contact with Home Office authorities and a squad was sent up to take Harker away. He had no knowledge of how the law operated in such cases but had no doubt that Home Office had 'departments' trained to deal with enemies of the state and powers much more flexible and draconian than those of any Scottish court.

Crouched by the window, he watched Dominic and Harker cross the yard. He glimpsed Lombard in the doorway, the girl too, the long-legged blonde whose photograph was still in his wallet. Twilight had dwindled, cloud covered the hills, sealing in the night. From the top of the stairs he could only just discern the men below. Fortunately he had an unimpeded view of the cartons.

'There,' Dominic said. 'Twenty thousand pounds. It's all yours, Eddie.'

'Open one,' Harker said.

They stood just inside the doorway, looking down at the boxes.

'You open it,' Dominic said. 'I don't have a knife.'

For an instant Kenny thought Harker was about to strike Dominic, then, cursing, he hunkered down, cut the twine and ripped off the gummed tape. He peeled away the paper and flipped open the flaps of the carton.

'It's bloody dark in here, man,' he complained. 'Ain't you gotta light?'

Dominic took a torch from his overcoat pocket, clicked it on and directed the beam to the box. The tableau suddenly became dramatic, almost theatrical.

Harker thrust a fist into the box and extracted a bundle of banknotes.

'Closer,' he said.

Obligingly Dominic focused light on the object in Harker's hand.

'Now do you believe me?' Dominic said. 'Open the other one too if you like.'

'Nah!' Harker said. 'I trust you. Never didn't trust you. Just wanted to make sure.' He stuffed the wad back into the carton, closed the flaps and smoothed the paper wrappings. Stooping, he lifted the box and tucked it under his arm. 'Bring the other one to the van, will ya?'

'Of course.'

Dominic allowed Harker go past him into the yard. He looked down at the remaining box then up the staircase to the pitch dark gallery and with a flick of the wrist flashed a signal to Kenny.

Then he switched the torch off and stepped outside.

The gunshot was sharp, not muffled. It rang in steely little echoes between the buildings and left a tingling reverberation hanging in the air. Kenny was on his feet and bounding downstairs before the first crack faded.

*'Manone,'* he shouted. *'My God! Dominic, what've you done now?'* He leapt over the remaining carton and out through the door.

He caught sight of Harker sliding down the side of the van, jerkin thrown open, arm flung wide, a gun in his hand. Then something heavy struck him on the side of the head and he fell forward on to his knees, already blacking out.

The object struck him again, from behind this time.

And Kenny was gone.


Something rubbing against his leg impinged on his consciousness. He had been knocked cold once before, on the boxing mat in the police gymnasium, but on that occasion had been swiftly brought round by a dash of cold water administered by Sergeant Ridley, his opponent. Now he remained addled and mentally numb. He kicked at the creature that was clambering up his leg and heard a grating Glaswegian voice say, 'Mind the cat, please. Mind the cat.'

Kenny opened his eyes.

Shoals of pink and lavender tadpoles swam in front of him, scattering when a trident of pain drove among them.

Kenny groaned loudly.

'Here, get this down ye.'

A hand closed on his wrist, a glass was fitted into his fingers.

He inhaled whisky fumes and without further assistance steered the glass to his lips and drank. More tadpoles, black this time, more little tridents of pain as the whisky trickled down his gullet into his chest.

He gasped and sat up.

'Never fails,' the voice said. 'Raise the dead wi' a good malt, so y' could.'

'Wh – where's Harker?'

'Gone back where he come from.'

His head felt enormous but when he probed it with exploratory fingers he found no obvious lumps or swellings. Pain radiated down the side of his face, however, and he couldn't form his words properly. He wondered if this was how Rosie felt when she lost control of her vocal cords and experienced a weepy little rivulet of pity for poor Rosie. He blinked, rubbed his eyes, looked round.

If he had been a touch shabbier then the wee man who stood beside the armchair would have been an ideal model for a Glasgow artisan. In his days on the streets Kenny had encountered hundreds just like him.

'Who are you?'

'Giffard.'

'Are you the printer? You are, you're the printer.'

'Aye.' Giffard generously offered the bottle. 'Want another one?'

Kenny shook his head: a serious mistake.

'Wh-what time is it?'

'Ten t' ten.'

'How long have I been unconscious?'

'Half-hour, give'r take.'

Kenny struggled to hoist himself out of the chair. His head throbbed, his knees were like jelly. He sank back. 'I've got to get to a telephone,' he said. 'Is there a telephone here?'

'Nup.'

Giffard raised the bottle to his lips, took a tiny sip then corked it and slipped it into his jacket pocket.

'He – he was shot, wasn't he?' Kenny said.

'Who, who's that?'

'Harker.'

'Nobody here by that name,' Giffard said.

'I saw him. I saw him, and he was shot.'

'Don't know who you're talkin about.'

'Conway then. Frank Conway.'

'Frank's been dead for years,' Giffard said. 'Maybe you saw a ghost.'

'Someone hit me: was it you?'

'You fell down the stairs.'

'All right. All right.' Impatience made Kenny's head throb but it also restored his concentration. 'I suppose you'll be telling me next that Manone wasn't here either, or Tony Lombard or – or that girl.'

'They were,' Giffard said, 'but they've gone.'

'Did they take Harker with them?'

'No, he left,' Giffard paused, 'on his own.'

'He's dead, isn't he?' Kenny said. 'I can have you arrested as an accessory after the fact, you know.'

'After what fact?' said Giffard.

'You've been printing counterfeit banknotes.'

'Have I?' said Giffard innocently and then, as if weary of the game, added, 'Aye, you've got that much right. Considerin' you've got the fake plates in your pocket I can hardly deny it, can I?'

Kenny's hand shot to his chest. He was still wearing his overcoat but it had been unbuckled and unbuttoned. He struggled, wriggling, patting his pockets.

The cat moved cautiously away.

'Is this what you're lookin' for, Sergeant?' Giffard said.

He held the plates, laid on a towel, in both hands.

Kenny reached out. 'Give them to me. They're mine.'

'I know they are,' Giffard said. 'They're evidence.'

He bent his knee and dragged one of the cartons across the kitchen floor with his foot. 'An' so's this. I mean, you're not goin' to get very far wi'out evidence, are ye?'

'Oh yes, I see,' Kenny said. 'What's in that box? Old newspapers?'

'Ten grand in new fivers,' said Giffard. 'There's another ten in a box in the van outside.'

'Harker, Conway, whatever you like to call him, left the van behind, did he?'

'He departed in kind o' a hurry.'

'Whose van is it?'

'John Flint's,' Giffard said. 'If you're quick off the mark you'll find another thousand quid in Flint's safe at the Stadium Cinema – so Dominic tells me.'

Kenny pushed himself to his feet. The printer was only a messenger whom Dominic had left behind to tie up loose ends and complete the deal that had never been a deal in the first place. He was sure that Harker was dead, the body buried in the woods or, more probably, whisked away to some last resting place where it would never be found. He was sure too that Manone, Lombard and the girl would already be in hiding or en route out of the country. All that was left was a salvage operation. 'What else did Dominic tell you to tell me?'

'Not t' go wastin' your time.'

'Pursuing him, you mean?'

'He gave me this,' Giffard said. 'He said this's what you really need an' all the rest's irrelevant.'

Protected by a wallet of alligator hide, the booklet was hardly larger than a warrant card. Giffard handed it over and Kenny opened it.

He knew at once what it was and what it signified: a pass-book for a deposit account in Grant Peters private mercantile bank in Carnarvon Street, London, W1. He saw by the entries that there had already been movements of monies in and out of the account and that the current balance was eight hundred and four pounds. If Giffard's plan had worked in a week or two that sum would have been swollen by ten or twelve thousand pounds and traffic through the account would have increased tenfold.

'Where did Dominic get this?'

'I think Harker left it behind. Dominic said you'd know what t' do with it.'

'I do,' said Kenny. 'At least I know people who do.'

'He said if you was to put the twenty thousand together wi' John Flint an' this pass-book you'd get everythin' you need for a promotion.'

Private bank or not, duty of secrecy notwithstanding, the compulsion of law would see to it that Edgar Harker's contact and his clients stood revealed. If the faceless experts in the Home Office's secret departments were as devious as they were reputed to be then Adolf's agents would soon be scooped up.

Kenny closed the book carefully and put it in his inside pocket.

'Giffard,' he said, 'who pulled the trigger, who fired the shot?'

'Shot? I dunno what y' mean.'

'Was it Dominic Manone?'

'Was it?' Giffard said. 'Was it Dom or Tony, or Penny maybe?' He grinned, showing brown teeth. 'Or maybe it was me. How do y' kill a dead man anyway, an' who's to blame if you do?'

'I've no answer to that,' Kenny said.

'Which is probably just as well,' said Giffard.


Polly had eaten dinner alone in the dining-room and had spent an hour with the children afterwards, helping them with a big jigsaw puzzle that Patricia had spread out on an oilcloth on the floor. She was sober enough at that point but oddly detached, empty of all longing, all positive thought.

Patricia had returned from her room about half-past eight o'clock to see the children into bed and hear their prayers and had sat with Stuart for ten or fifteen minutes afterwards, talking quietly to the boy.

Bored by her son's constant need for reassurance, Polly had gone downstairs into the living-room and had mixed herself a stiff gin-and-tonic and, when that was finished, another. She'd left the curtains open for the sky over the park was a pretty colour, tinted pink and lavender. She had no desire to switch on the wireless. The news that May day had been depressing and a word, an odd, exhilarating, zig-zaggy sort of word,

*Danzig* had cropped up again and again, repeated in the solemn orations of news readers and announcers.

No one came near: not Patricia, not Mrs O'Shea. No one came calling: not Babs, not Mam, not Tony. Especially not Tony.

Polly drank a third tumbler of gin-and-tonic and, later, a modest snifter of brandy to settle her stomach and about eleven went upstairs to bed. She lay down and fell asleep instantly, and when she wakened again it was morning.

Sunlight patched the floral curtains. The bedroom looked uncommonly tidy. Clothing she'd dropped on the carpet last night had been picked up and put away. Her housecoat was draped on one of the antique chairs. There was no trace of cigar smoke in the air, no impingement of sound from the bathroom. She lay propped against the pillows listening to the unusual silence, steeling herself to get out of bed. She did not feel bad. Her hangover was mild, a little distemper of the stomach, a slight ache above the eyes. Gin was a safe drink after all. Who had told her that? Tony, was it Tony?

She swung herself out of bed, put on the housecoat, went out of the bedroom and along the corridor to the bathroom. She used the toilet and then, at the sink, splashed water on her face. She opened the mirrored cabinet in search of the aspirin bottle. One aspirin tablet and a glass of water would remove the last traces of her headache. She took down the bottle, then stopped.

The glass shelf on the top row of the cabinet was empty.

Shaving brush and shaving bowl, the razor and even its stand were missing. The elegant jars of male astringent and hair cream were missing too. Toothbrush. Nail scissors. Laxative. Dentrifice. Missing.

Polly went out into the corridor and ran back to the bedroom. She glanced at the dressing-table. His hairbrushes and comb were gone. She pulled open drawers. Shirts, socks, ties, underwear, handkerchiefs, a leather box of cuff-links, two expensive wristlet watches – all missing. She darted to the wardrobe, threw open the doors on empty hangers.

'Dominic,' she shouted, her head splitting now. 'Dominic?'

She ran to the top of the stairs and leaning over the rail, called his name again. By now she expected no answer.

'Mrs O'Shea, Mrs O'Shea.'

The woman appeared below. She was dressed in her apron but there was no evidence of flour on her hands. She looked up stiffly, frowning.

'What is it, Mrs Manone?'

'Where is my husband?'

'He's gone, Mrs Manone.'

'Gone? What – what time is it?'

'Quarter after seven,' Cook told her.

She had assumed it was later, much later, well after nine.

Shocked, she spun away from the rail and into

the playroom, through it to Stuart's bedroom. The bed was unmade, his toy-box tilted on its side, his toys strewn on the floor: in Ishbel's room, the same. She was running now for all her worth, thumping, clumping barefoot on the narrow staircase. She hurled herself into Patricia's room on the upper floor, saw sunlight and in the pool of sunlight an empty bed, not slept in or remade, the pinewood wardrobe door hanging wide open, its hangers empty too. She turned and ran down the narrow staircase again, battering herself on the walls, and flung herself against the rail.

Cook was just where Polly had left her, below in the hall, looking up.

'Where are the children?' Polly said, panting. 'Tell me where they are?'

'They went away with Mr Manone.'

'When?'

'Six, a wee bit after.'

'God! God! God! He's taken my children. He's taken away my children.'

'Aye, Mrs Manone,' Cook told her, 'and he's taken Patricia too.'

# Chapter Twenty

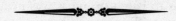

The announcement of intention to marry came as no surprise. Banns were read in St Margaret's Church in June and the minister, Mr Heatley, was thoughtful enough to have a 'signer' by him so that Miss Rosalind Conway could share the moment. A handful of dark souls in the congregation muttered that 'girls like that' should not be permitted to marry and should in fact be sterilised to prevent them passing on their defects. But for the most part all went well and Rosie, and Lizzie too, were happier than they had been in a very long time.

If she ever thought of her father and regretted that they hadn't met, Rosie did not speak of it. Kenny'd had a word with her, a quiet, loving but informative word and whatever he'd told her — and what he told her was Rosie's secret — it somehow settled her mind and, in a curious way, matured her.

There had never been any question of her not wanting to marry Kenny.

All it took to bring about a reconciliation was for Kenny to eat a just a little slice of humble pie and Fiona to take the girl out to lunch and do a bit of finger-wagging. Fiona MacGregor, stern and rather spinsterish, put the arguments for marriage so convincingly that she sent Rosie rushing back into Kenny's arms to patch up what was now referred to as 'a tiff'. Some tiff: it was perhaps as well that Rosie didn't know a half, not a quarter, of what had taken place out on Blackstone Farm that night in May or how cleverly Dominic had plotted to send her father back from whence he came.

From Polly, Rosie learned that Dominic had taken the children to seek sanctuary in America, that Tony Lombard, Dom's right-hand man, had vanished off the face of the earth and that her father's new bride had also disappeared. She was too prudent to ask Bernard if his transfer from Lyons & Lloyd's to Breslin District Council's housing department had also been part of Dominic's devious and elaborate scheme to thwart justice.

What she did not know, because neither Kenny nor Fiona were willing to breach their oath of confidentiality, was that Home Office Special Branch, acting on a package of information received from Glasgow CID, had discreetly netted thirteen persons, including five women, who were alleged to have threatened the security of the nation. There was no press coverage of the arrests or trials, but all thirteen, several prominent British nationals among them, served short custodial sentences and were still behind bars when war broke out.

By that time Kenny had been promoted to the rank of Detective Inspector and was involved in rooting out Republican terrorists and there was no possibility of his being released to serve in the army.

The wedding, however, came first.

It was a hot July Saturday, blisteringly hot in fact. The tyres of the hired car in which Rosie and Bernard drove to church hissed on melting tarmac and Bernard, clad in the better of his two blue suits, looked as if he were melting too.

Only Rosie appeared cool, perfectly poised and beautiful in a bridal gown of icy-white satin. The veil draped her brow in a delicate little glissando and her cheeks were paler than the carnations in her bouquet. She stared reflectively out at the streets during the short journey – not at the drab, towering tenements of her girlhood but at wide tree-lined boulevards – and held Bernard's hand.

Tonight she would be with Kenny in a little hotel overlooking the Firth of Clyde and would give herself to a man for the very first time. The prospect of lovemaking did not frighten her. Kenny, like Bernard, was kind and thoughtful, and would not demand too much of her. On Tuesday they would return to the flat in Cowcaddens which they would share, at least for a little while, with Fiona. It was the sensible thing to do with everything so uncertain and Fiona talking eagerly of 'joining up' as soon as war was declared.

Rosie had imagined that she would weep in Mammy's arms on the night before her wedding, that the old childish need for security and protection would rush at her out of the shadows. It didn't happen, though: perhaps because she was the last of Lizzie Conway's wayward girls to leave the nest and she would soon be Mrs Kenneth MacGregor not poor wee lonely Rosie, the little sister.

She could see St Margaret's against the skyline, its tall steeple like a tower, parched grass, parked nearby the car that Jackie had borrowed from the salon to drive Babs, the children and Lizzie to church. They would all be inside, her family and her friends. Albert, old Mr Feldman, her teacher, her nieces May and June dressed as flower girls, Angus, in kilt and sporran, as a page. Babs was her matron-of-honour and Bernard would give her away. On the bridegroom's side were Kenny's mother and father, down from the island, Fiona, and several policemen, including DC Galbraith who had been persuaded to perform the duties of best man.

There would be no Aunt Janet, though. Rosie had written to invite her and Kenny had even threatened to arrest her and bring her along in a Black Maria but Janet had not deigned to reply. With Frank gone she had crept back into her shell, retreated into the shrivelled little world of hope and habit in which she had eked out an existence for far too many years.

Polly would be there, however: Polly all alone, Polly stripped of her family, watchful now and cautious but still exuding that effortless air of class: Polly with her limousine, her chauffeur, her Paris dress, and a hat that cost the earth: Polly who had encouraged her husband to take the children out of harm's way, who had sacrificed her happiness for their sakes and who, with an indomitability that was entirely false, would keep the home fires burning and business ticking over until the war was over and Dominic Manone returned: so Rosie thought, sadly, as the hired car turned at the crossing and drew up before the church.

Bernard released her hand and reached for the door handle.

'Wait,' she said. 'Please, Daddy, wait.'

He turned to face her, his eyebrows raised. 'Cold feet?'

'Oh, no,' she said. 'Oh, no.'

'What then?'

She brushed aside the veil and, reaching up, kissed him.

'Just that,' she said, then let him help her from the motorcar and escort her, proudly, up the steps to the church.

She lied only to save face, of course.

'My God!' Babs said. 'You mean he just grabbed the kids an' skipped? I'd kill Jackie if he did somethin' like that to me.'

'Dominic did not just skip. We discussed it,' Polly said, 'and I agreed it would be safer for the children to be abroad than trapped here under a rain of German bombs.'

'Did Dominic have to clear out?'

'No, but it seemed the sensible thing to do, to go with the children.'

'Go where?' said Babs.

'New York,' said Polly, without hesitation.

'I thought his old man lived in Philadelphia.'

'He isn't staying with his father, or his brother. I doubt if they'd make him welcome even at this difficult time.'

'An' here I was thinkin' all Eye-ties were one big happy family,' Babs said. 'Will you be goin' to join them?'

Polly shook her head. 'Someone has to stay and look after our interests.'

'What's Dom gonna do for money?' Babs said.

'He has funds,' said Polly. 'He sold most of our assets.'

'Planned it all in advance, eh? Wish my Jackie could be more like him sometimes,' Babs said. 'What happened to Patricia?'

'Patricia has been paid off,' said Polly.

It was easy to lie, to elaborate and embellish, hide that which she did not wish to reveal, even to herself.

Had she learned the trick from Dominic or had it been lurking in her genes all along? She'd always thought of herself as her mother's daughter: now she was not so sure. Mammy had been ruthless when she'd had to be but there was a softness in her mother that Polly did not possess. She recalled her lost loves, young men she had known before Dominic swept her off her feet, remembered them without sentiment, wondered where they were now and what they had made of themselves, if they were happy, happier than she was.

'Who paid Patricia off?' Babs said. 'You?'

'Dominic.'

Easy, all too easy to write your own version of events, for the past was strangely malleable when you got right down to it. Lies told to her sister were not malicious or damaging, were merely intended to deceive. She had to save *something* from the debacle, something apart from the responsibilities that Dominic had thrust upon her, something that was uniquely her own.

'Well,' Babs said, 'I suppose Tony will help out?'

Polly pressed her lips together. 'Tony? No, no, no. He's gone too.'

'Aw, really! Babs's eyebrows arched. 'Gone with Dom, has he? Didn't want to be left behind?'

'I don't know where Tony is,' Polly said, trusting that her tone would imply that she didn't much care. 'I don't need his, or anyone's, help.'

'Not even mine?' said Babs.

Polly gave no answer.

Babs had sense enough not to persist. She laughed. 'Bloody hell, won't be a guy left if this goes on. Dominic, Dennis, your Tony, the old man. Billy too. Billy's had his call-up papers. Jackie'll be back in the pit in his overalls come Monday, and he ain't gonna like that one bit.'

'You mean you'll continue to run the garage.'

'Salon,' Babs said. 'Aw hell – garage. Yeah, we'll stay open as long as we can. I'll take over the book-keeping an' Jackie'll do the repairs. Spot of hard graft'll do the bugger no harm an' I'll be on the premises to crack the whip. I take it,' she paused, 'I take it we won't be needin' to give you a cut any longer?'

'No, your debt's cancelled,' Polly said.

'Is that you speakin', or Dominic?'

'Me,' Polly said, firmly. 'I make all the decisions now.'

'I see,' Babs said. 'You really are gonna go it alone, aren't you?'

'You bet I am,' said Polly.


There was no mystery as to where Dominic had taken them. He had left a letter with Carfin Hughes which the lawyer delivered into Polly's hand less than twelve hours after Dominic's departure.

By then she had been to Tony's apartment in Riverside and had found it locked. She'd gone at once to the tenement where Tony's parents lived and had learned from them that Tony had left the country. His graceless old father approved; he didn't want to see Tony interned or, worse, forced to fight on a side that was doomed to defeat. Polly left the Lombards strengthened by resentment, and returned home to keep her appointment with Carfin Hughes.

Dominic's letter contained no mention of Tony, Penny Weston or for that matter of Patricia. Polly allowed Hughes to console her, to tell her it was all for the best and that it surely wouldn't be long before war started and, God willing, war ended and Dominic and her children would be able to return to Glasgow. He watched Polly read the letter, trying to gauge by her reactions just how much support she would require in the difficult months ahead and just how far he might push her. She seemed calm enough, well in control of herself. She even had the temerity to indicate that she'd agreed to Dominic taking the children abroad and said that she would far rather have them with their father in the United States of America than evacuated to some remote corner of Scotland.

Soon after Hughes left, Polly drank a single gin-and-tonic and, steeling herself, went downstairs to interrogate Mrs O'Shea about her part in the deception.

Mrs O'Shea would have none of it: her friend Patricia was only concerned with the children and had no designs on Mr Manone, Cook declared indignantly. Polly could tell by the woman's manner that

Leah and she, Patricia too for that matter, had all been well aware what had been going on upstairs when Mr Lombard had dropped in for tea.

That night, her first alone, Polly cried herself to sleep.

She missed Dominic more than she missed the children, missed Tony most of all. She was haunted by a sense of failure, of finality, like a great weight pressing upon her. She wept, and whimpered apologies to the empty wardrobe and vacant chairs then, just as dawn light stained the curtains, curled up on top of the eiderdown and fell into a dreamless sleep.

Leah did not turn up for work next morning; Polly never saw the girl again.

Mrs O'Shea also handed in her notice, one week, as stipulated by the terms of her employment. Polly accepted without hesitation. The Irish woman's departure would remove the last of her guilt, the last lingering shreds of conscience. Carfin Hughes would find her another housekeeper, some efficient widow or retired domestic who would take over management of the household, a task rendered all the easier by the absence of children.

Polly was not in total control of herself, however, not yet. She was tempted to drink herself into oblivion and for that reason hurried out of the house and went walking, all alone. She walked twice around the park and then out into the streets, striding on though her calves hurt and her shoes chafed and she felt as if her heart would break at the loss of all the good things Dominic had given her; why, she wondered, had it not been enough?

As she limped back through the rain to the empty house, though, she began to construct the lies that would protect her, lies that would in time become truth, to alter the reality of her situation so that she was no longer an abandoned wife or an adulteress but a woman ennobled by her own virtues, martyr to circumstance and the selfishness of men.

By the time she felt strong enough to admit to her mother and sisters that Dominic had left her, a postcard arrived from Southampton. It depicted an ocean-going liner with a cheering crowd on the rail and a flutter of bouquets and bunting. Three laborious lines of print in blunt pencil expressed her son's excitement at the voyage that lay ahead. He signed himself *'Yours Sincerly, Stuart,'* a piece of copybook formality that made Polly smile.

Her children might no longer be with her but she hadn't lost them entirely and she was tempted to believe that they would come back one day stronger and more mature – more interesting too – for their experiences.

In the course of that warm, unpredictable summer Polly received many postcards and letters from her children, prosaic little essays composed no doubt at Dominic's insistence. Only one communication came from her husband. In a brief transatlantic telephone call he informed her that he had rented a family house on Staten Island, a big clapboard house with spectacular views over the Hudson. He had brought his aunt Teresa over from Rome to housekeep and the children were settling down remarkably well and would go to the local school at the start of the fall term.

Polly asked after Patricia.

Dominic told her that Patricia was well, and in love with America.

He did not enquire about the state of the business which did not surprise her for she was sure that he was receiving regular reports from Carfin Hughes. It was odd hearing his voice, though, so thinned and roughened by a transatlantic cable that he no longer sounded like Dominic, like her husband.

She did not have the gall to ask about Tony.

Day and daily she waited to hear from Tony, to receive a telephone call, a letter, some scrap of information to assure her that only necessity had driven him from her and that she was absolved from blame. From Tony, though, there was nothing, only silence – and that silence was her punishment.


Five days after her sister's wedding, Polly called Hughes to a meeting in the office in Central Warehouse. So far the lawyer had been generous with his time. He was polite and courteous, a man of good breeding, though he was never less than punctilious in posting the itemised bills for his services. He had even charged her for advertisements in the *Glasgow Herald,* though they had failed to turn up a satisfactory housekeeper.

Polly was inclined to take up Babs's suggestion that Miss Dawlish, the clerk from the garage, might fill the bill, for the Hallops were finding it more and more difficult to balance the books and might soon have to let the clerk go. Miss Dawlish was interested in becoming Polly's housekeeper and had assured Babs that she was a good plain cook and had looked after her ageing father long enough to know how to manage a household. Polly had too many other things on her mind to rush to an immediate decision on a mere domestic matter, however, for she had received a telephone call from an unexpected quarter, a call that demanded not just her attention but guile and forethought too.

Carfin Hughes arrived promptly at half-past four o'clock. He looked a shade more harassed than usual for he had been presenting a court case that had dragged on to the point where his punctuality was challenged. It was also hot and smelly on Clydeside and the cab-driver had been garrulous and had shouted the odds about what he would do to Hitler if he ever got his hands on him.

Hughes spent a good five minutes in the washroom, carefully removing all traces of sweat from his brow, before he ascended to the office on the upper floor.

Victor Shadwell was already present. He was seated before the desk, facing into the glare of sunlight.

Shipyards and docks seemed awfully far off in the motionless haze that overhung the river, and the river itself had the listless viscosity of mud so low and sluggish had the water become.

'I would like to point out, Polly, that I do not usually make house calls,' Carfin Hughes began, not testily, 'not even warehouse calls.'

'She's had an offer, Fin,' Victor Shadwell said.

'An offer?' Hughes said. 'What sort of an offer?'

'For the warehouse,' Polly said.

'Lease or purchase?'

'Purchase.'

'From whom did this offer come, and why was it not made through me?'

'It wasn't made through you, Fin, because the gentleman who made the offer believes that I am a softer touch,' said Polly.

'Who is this "gentleman"?'

'John Flint.'

'Flint!' Hughes exclaimed. 'My God! That villain!'

'Is he?' Polly said. 'Is he any more of a villain than any of us? He was investigated recently, as you no doubt recall, and in exchange for his co-operation all charges against him were dropped.'

'I cannot say about that,' said Hughes.

'Did you not represent him in the hearing?' said Polly.

'It wasn't a hearing,' Hughes said.

'Negotiation then,' said Polly.

'I – I was present, yes, during the interviews.'

'Would it be straining confidentiality too far to enquire if Johnny Flint is your client? Polly said.

'I am not his legal representative.'

'Then why were you present at the interviews?' Victor Shadwell said.

He wore a light linen suit and had a Panama hat upturned on his lap. He was so desiccated and wispy now that he appeared to be hardly there at all.

Carfin Hughes was not deceived. 'I was brought in, invited.'

'By whom? By Johnny?' Polly asked.

She too looked slight, almost frail in the glare from the window. The glass had been masked with a lattice of brown sticky tape but the sunlight was strong enough to cast shadows on the floor and desk. In the bright light, the woman seemed to be little more than a voice, a quiet, decisive, almost inflexionless voice that unfortunately reminded him of Dominic Manone.

Hughes shifted the position of his chair and brought Polly into view again. She was prettier than ever in a summer dress, make-up perfect, hair cut short and styled to show off the shape of her face; not for the first time he felt a tug of desire, a perverse longing to strip away the lady-like trappings and reveal the tart from the Gorbals that Polly Conway Manone had been before Dominic got his hands on her.

'I was brought in by Flint's solicitor,' Hughes explained. 'Be that as it may, tell me about this offer Flint's made for the warehouse. I mean to say, what can a fellow like Flint possibly want with a warehouse?'

'We were hoping,' Victor Shadwell said, 'that *you* would tell *us.*'

'I?' Hughes said, ungrammatically. 'I? What makes you suppose that I would be *au fait* with some book-maker's underhand schemes?'

'Is it underhand, Fin?' Polly said. 'On the surface at least, it seems to be perfectly legitimate. Johnny hopes to purchase the Central Warehouse as a going concern on behalf of the Lincoln Stephens Small Arms company who, not unsurprisingly, are obliged to expand to cope with massive government orders.'

'A factory?' said Hughes.

'No, a warehouse,' Polly said, 'to stock stores and supplies for their main factory at Corkerhill.'

'Did Flint tell you all this?' Carfin Hughes said.

'Absolutely,' Polly said. 'There seems to be some urgency in the matter and a decision and an agreement on price have to be reached within the next few days. He suggested that I consult you as soon as possible.'

'Flint told you to consult me?'

'Oh, come on, Fin,' Polly said. 'Just because I'm female and new to this game doesn't mean to say that I can't smell a rat in all of this? Johnny Flint's connection with a long-established firm like Lincoln Stephens is tenuous at best. Dominic has no stake in the company, at least none that Victor knows about.'

'None,' Victor Shadwell said. 'And I would know, you know.'

'But you do, Fin,' said Polly. 'You *do* have a stake in the Lincoln Stephens.'

'I emphatically deny that to be the case.'

'What therefore would you advise me to do, Mr Hughes?' said Polly. 'Submit to a first offer for the property, take what Flint offers?'

'In six months the property will have no value whatsoever. It's situated in the midst of the most productive shipbuilding yards in Britain, a fact that will not have escaped notice. There's little or no imported stock arriving from Italy. I can tell you that Dominic was only too well aware that the warehouse would soon be no more than an empty shell.'

'Perhaps,' Polly said. 'But I'm not, I'm no empty shell, Fin. And you haven't answered my question yet.'

'Yes, Fin,' said Victor Shadwell, 'please do answer her question.'

'I would advise you to take Flint's offer.'

'Sell at any price?' said Polly.

'Yes.'

Polly wished that her sister had been here. Babs wouldn't have been so lady-like, so polite. Babs would have given the not-so-old devil a tongue-lashing.

'The building's in sound condition,' Polly said. 'All the floors are equipped to carry non-combustible small-wares of whatever description and the location is ideal for a company that needs ready access to the docks. As for air raids – well, if the yards go up in flames then half of Glasgow goes with them.'

'Who told you that?' said Carfin Hughes.

'Nobody told me,' Polly said. 'I looked, and saw for myself.'

'I suppose,' Hughes said, 'you're going to be stubborn and let a prime asset go to waste rather than get what you can for it before it's too late.'

'On the contrary,' Polly said, 'I'm perfectly pre-pared to talk terms.'

'With John Flint?'

'With you, Fin,' Victor Shadwell said. 'She means with you.'

'I'm not empowered to . . .'

'You're a registered stock-holder in Lincoln Stephens, are you not?' Polly said. 'Victor was kind enough to check the records. John Flint is nothing but a front, put in by you to broker the sale, so that *on your advice* I'd sell the place below its actual worth. I wonder what the Law Society would have to say if told them what you're up to?'

'I do believe,' Hughes said, 'that the Law Society is best left out of it.'

'I won't sell,' Polly said. 'I will, however, lease the warehouse.'

'Lincoln Stephens do wish to purchase.'

'I will not give up ownership,' Polly said. 'Nomi-nally the property may be mine but we both know that it's Dominic's and one day he'll come back for it.'

'If there's anything left,' said Carfin Hughes.

'A blackened patch of ground,' Polly said, 'will still be his.'

'What sort of rental would you be looking for?' Carfin said.

'Two hundred and forty pounds a month,' Victor Shadwell said.

'Oh, come now!'

'Two-year lease,' Polly said. 'Insurance to be met by the tenant.'

'That is usurious. Insurance rates have doubled in the past three months.'

'There are eight senior staff on the payroll,' Polly said. 'I would expect them to be employed by the new management.'

'No, no. You're asking too much,' Carfin Hughes said.

'If,' Polly said, '*if* you weren't an interested party, *if* you were acting exclusively and objectively on my behalf, wouldn't you consider it a good deal?'

'I might,' the lawyer admitted. 'I might at that.'

'Will you put my proposals to the appropriate party?'

He laughed, an odd little *haw-haw-haw*. She knew that she had been tested and had passed with flying colours and that Carfin Hughes was gentleman enough to acknowledge it.

He said, 'Is there room for negotiation, may I ask?'

'None,' Polly said. 'Would you like the terms in writing?'

'That would,' Carfin said, 'be handy.'

'Good,' Polly said. 'Thank you for your time, Fin.'

'You mean . . .'

'You may go now.'

She rang the bell on the desk and the secretary opened the door to show the lawyer out. Carfin hesitated before he got to his feet.

'Am I to assume,' he said, 'that my services to Manone Enterprises are to be terminated and another legal adviser employed in my place?'

'Certainly not,' Polly said. 'Better the devil you know, Fin. In fact, if you aren't otherwise engaged you may take me to dinner on Saturday evening.'

'May I really?'

'You may.'

'Eight o'clock?'

'Eight will be ideal,' said Polly. 'Will you send a car?'

'I will,' he said. 'Of course I will.'

Then, smiling sardonically, he gave her a little bow and left.

Polly closed the glass-panelled door then turning to Victor Shadwell pulled a face and burst out laughing.

'Don't,' she said, 'don't say it, Victor, please.'

'Don't say what, Polly?'

'That Dominic would have been proud of me.'

'The thought,' the old man said, 'never even crossed my mind.'

On that Thursday morning the newspapers were filled with the latest developments on the border of Poland and Silesia and the wide-ranging powers that the British Prime Minister had been granted to 'arrange' for war. Mobilisation had begun in earnest and Central Warehouse had lost all but a handful of its staff to call-up. In consequence the change of management had been effected much more efficiently than Polly had anticipated.

She had got what she'd asked for; Fin Hughes had seen to that. Unless the British economy crumbled completely at least she wouldn't starve. She was relieved to be rid of the warehouse. It smacked too much of Dominic, was too much his domain. She also nurtured a certain patriotic pride in having surrendered the building to a small-arms manufacturer and felt that by her sacrifice she had already made a contribution to the defeat of the Nazi dictator.

Evacuation of women and children was inevitable. In August, after the schools reopened, little was being taught but discipline and drill. Babs had no scruples about keeping her three out of class for an afternoon. In fact, she was dying to get behind the wheel of the big Wolseley, to try her hand at driving something more powerful than a three-wheeled Beezer. She jumped at the chance to take the family on a picnic and allow Polly to do a little business at the same time. She guessed, of course, that Polly was up to something, but Polly was always up to something these days.

Polly was waiting in the driveway when Babs and the children arrived. Miss Dawlish, Polly's brand new housekeeper, had packed a hamper and stowed it carefully in the luggage boot along with rugs and cushions. It was a magnificent afternoon, hot and still, the sky cloudless. The children, Angus in particular, were excited at the prospect of a drive into the country with Mummy, Granny Peabody and Aunt Polly. Baby April had recently found her voice and babbled happily and gave her aunt coy, twinkling smiles from beneath her sun bonnet.

Babs tugged on her driving gloves, knotted a scarf over her hair and, leaving Miss Dawlish and Polly to settle the children into the back seat, slid behind the huge steering wheel and cautiously surveyed the array of dials and switches. She had no intention of making a fool of herself or of imperilling the lives of her children. She turned the key in the ignition and with Angus scowling critically over her shoulder, checked the petrol and water gauges.

Doors slammed; Babs hardly noticed.

Polly said, 'Now are you sure you know what you're doing?'

'Aw yeah, absolutely,' Babs said.

Miss Dawlish leapt back into the doorway as Babs released the handbrake, depressed the clutch, tapped the accelerator and, tearing leaves from the hedge *en passant*, lurched the car through the gate into Manor Park Avenue and swung its long snout towards the Paisley Road.

'Nothin' to it,' she said through gritted teeth. 'Piece o' cake really.'

An hour later Lizzie was installed in the back seat. Bolstered by her grandchildren and with April on her knee, she gazed out at stretches of moorland and hill ridges that she had seen only from a safe distance, a landscape that seemed very different now that she was part of it.

Signs of war were everywhere; little regiments of school cadets marching along pavements in peaceful suburban villages, a troop of volunteer fire-fighters struggling to tame the ferocious flow from a water main, a convoy of camouflaged lorries weaving down a back road, an open-sided truck with ten or a dozen girls clinging to ropes, all waving, all shouting, their cheeks reddened by unaccustomed sun; also raw brick shelters, emergency water tanks, policemen who weren't policemen riding about on bicycles, and overhead, floating high above the hills, the first silvery barrage balloons that any of them had ever seen.

'Elephants,' Angus cried out. 'Look, Granma, elephants in the sky.'

There were no flowers left in Bluebell Wood which lay behind the decaying gates of the Garscadden estate, but the trees were old and shady-cool. The Wolseley was parked in shadow, the picnic things

spread out on a rug under the boughs of an oak
that Polly said had been there for two hundred years,
though no one, not even Angus, was going to swallow
*that* tale.

They could no longer see elephants in the sky, no
longer hear the *pam-pam-pam* of an artillery battery
practising in the depths of the hills, could no longer
smell the cloudy metallic reek of Clydeside foundries
or the tang of the sea from the river, only the hot,
fecund odour of weeds and wheat fields and hedgerows rife with flourish and the bland dog-rose.

'I thought you'd business to do,' Babs whispered
to her sister as they set out sandwiches and cake and
unscrewed the tops of tea flasks and bottles of ginger
pop. 'What sort of business can you have in the middle
of nowhere?'

Polly got up from her knees and smoothing down
her dress looked uphill through the trees to the crest
of the ridge.

'I'm going for a walk,' she said. 'I'll be about
an hour or a little longer. Keep me something to
eat, please.'

'Goin' for a walk?' Babs said. 'I'll come with . . .'

'Alone.'

'God, it's a guy. You're meetin' a guy. Is it
Tony?'

'I'm not meeting anyone,' Polly said. 'No one,
you understand.'

Babs wrestled with the stopper of the ginger pop.
Angus was lying full-length close by, ostentatiously

licking his lips. May and June were prowling around the hamper like two demure little predators. There were flies too, black flies. Lizzie flapped her plump hands to shoo them away from April's face and tried not to listen to her daughters' conversation which, she felt, was not for her ears.

'Where are we, exactly?' Babs said. 'Are we near Breslin?'

'No.'

'My God, Poll, you've pulled some stuff before but this . . .'

'If you must know, Dominic has property near here,' Polly said. 'If I've read the map correctly I can get to it by taking a path up through the wood.'

'I'll drive you there by the road.'

'No,' Polly said. 'I'd prefer you to stay with Mammy and the children. Please, don't make a fuss, Babs. It's something I have to do on my own.'

'Is that why you brought us here?'

'Yes, partly.'

'An' I thought you just fancied a nice day out in the country. I should've known better.'

'Mother,' Polly said, 'I'm going for a little stroll. I shan't be too long.'

Lying was easy, lying was simple. She looked at her mother, big and comfortable even in the heat of an August afternoon, at her cheap floral-patterned dress, moth-eaten straw hat, wrinkled cotton stockings and shoes with worn heels, and felt a transient wave of remorse pass through her, the lie within the lie.

'Where?' Lizzie said. 'Where is there to go round here?'

'The top of the hill,' said Polly.

The footpath led over a stile and across an empty back road. Garscadden wood lay behind her, ahead a field of ripe barley whispering in the sun. She followed the path by the side of the field, climbing gradually towards a line of conifers, dense and dark above her. She skirted the plantation, emerged on the edge of another field, and suddenly the valley of the Clyde was spread out below her, from the braes above Paisley to the mountains of Cowal, faint on the horizon and shimmering in the August heat. How small and contained Scotland was, she thought, how precious; then she heard laughter and, moving on, caught sight of the girls she had passed in the truck on the road.

Bare-armed and bare-headed, one was driving an ancient tractor while the others, six or seven in all, followed along in its wake, dropping seeds into shallow furrows. Polly had no idea what the crop would be. She gave the energetic crew a wide berth, slid between the strands of a fence and headed up the flank of the pasture towards the farm.

He was leaning on a gate. At first she took him for a farmer. He wore a faded cotton shirt, sleeves rolled up, and a hat, a fedora of all things, set back from his brow. He was smoking a cigarette and a drowsy, rather dusty tabby cat was perched on the gatepost beside him.

'Afternoon,' the man said, amiably.

'Good afternoon,' said Polly.

'Are ye lost, lassie?'

'I'm looking for Blackstone Farm.'

'Ag'n'Fish?'

'Pardon?'

'Are you,' he spoke clearly, affectedly, 'from the Ministry of Agriculture and Fisheries?'

Polly laughed, shook her head. 'What gave you that impression?'

'You're too dolled up to be here t' dig for victory. Welfare?'

'Welfare?' Polly said.

'Aye, the girls've a welfare officer. I've never met her so I reckoned it might be you.'

'It isn't,' Polly said. 'Is this your land?'

'It used to be, aye.'

'May I ask,' Polly said, 'who you are?'

'Dougie Giffard's the name.' His hand went to his hat, a finger flicked the brim. 'I think you're Dominic Manone's good lady wife. Am I right?'

'Yes.'

'It's mine, the farm,' Dougie said. 'All legal. I have the papers in the house.'

'I know it is,' Polly said. 'I'm not here to dispute your ownership.'

'Very generous,' Dougie said. 'Dominic – Mr Manone – was very generous.'

'What are the girls doing?'

'Ploughin' an' seedin',' Dougie said. 'So they tell me.'

'On your land?'

'Naw, I sold most of it off. Fifty shillin's the acre, thirty-three acres. I kept the farmhouse.'

'Do the girls lodge here?'

'No room here. They're billeted temporarily down the road in Drumry church hall until better accommodation can be found for them. I give them a bit of dinner at midday an' let them use the you-know-what, those o' them who are too modest t' go into the woods.'

'What do you do for a living, Mr Giffard, now that you're no longer employed by my husband?'

'I suppose I'm what you'd call a man o' means.'

'Eighty pounds won't keep you for ever,' Polly said.

He turned away, propped an elbow on the gate and looked towards the farmhouse. There was laundry on a rope in the yard and, in spite of the heat, a thin spiral of smoke rising above the chimney.

He said, 'Would you care t' come over to the house, partake o' a glass o' somethin', take a look round?'

'Thank you all the same,' Polly said, 'that won't be necessary.'

'What will be necessary then?' Dougie said. 'What is it brings you here?'

'I'm looking for Tony Lombard.'

'Tony's gone,' Dougie said. 'Long gone.'

'Do you know where he went?'

'Nope.'

'I think you do, Mr Giffard.'

'Have you not heard from him?'

'Not a word.'

'Ask your husband,' Dougie said. 'He's bound to know.'

'Please,' Polly said, 'just tell me where Tony's is.'

'He went away with the girl, with Penny.'

'Oh!'

She was less than surprised, less than dismayed.

'Tony never told you anythin' about her, did he?' Dougie said.

Polly shook her head.

'He's goin' to be a daddy,' Dougie said.

'A daddy?'

'Aye, sometime fairly soon, I think. October or November.'

'I see,' Polly said.

'They sailed for Canada when the balloon went up then moved on pretty quick to the United States,' Dougie said. 'The last I heard, Tony was lookin' for work on the docks in Seattle.'

'Not New York?'

'Nope, not New York.'

'Does he write to you?' Polly said.

'She does. Penny does.'

'Why does Tony have to work? I thought – doesn't he have money?'

'Not near as much as he might've had,' Dougie said. 'Aye, there *was* money. We were rollin' in money for a week or two, a lot more money than the police ever confiscated. They took away my printer, though.' He shook his head sadly. 'I could've had a nice wee jobbing line set up if they hadn't took all my stuff away. Still, I suppose I got off light, all things considered.'

'How much money *didn't* the police confiscate?'

'Thousands, thousands an' thousands. None o' it real, alas.'

'Where is it now, Mr Giffard?'

'Search me,' Dougie said innocently.

Polly didn't care enough about the counterfeit money to press him.

She said, 'He can't marry her, of course. Tony, I mean.'

'Can't he?' Dougie said. 'What's stoppin' him?'

'She already has a husband. She's married to my father.'

'Is she?' Dougie said then casting pretence aside, turned to face Polly. 'She's not married t' anyone, not now. Even a good Roman Catholic boy like Tony Lombard can marry her wi'out a qualm o' conscience.'

'He's dead, isn't he? My father's dead?'

'He might be.'

'Did Dominic – did my husband murder him?'

'Can't say.'

'Was it Tony?'

'Who knows!'

'You were here, damn it. You know, don't you?'

'He was kind t' me,' Dougie said, 'your husband, more generous than I'd any right to expect. He left me well provided for. I don't need much, just enough to keep me an' the cat fed. I can sit out the war right here, quite comfortably.'

'And do what?' said Penny. 'Do what?'

Dougie thrust out his under lip, shrugged. 'Keep an eye on things.'

'What things?'

'Just things.'

Polly closed her hand on his arm.

Dougie didn't draw away. He wouldn't meet her eye, though. He stared across the corner of the field at the land-girls and the tractor, hardly bigger than a toy, churning up the pasture under a milky blue sky.

'He's buried here, isn't he?' Polly said. 'My God, Dominic's paying you to make sure he stays buried, that he's never found?'

'That, Mrs Manone,' said Dougie, 'is pure conjecture.'

'Oh yes,' Polly said. 'Pure conjecture. Am I right, though? Am I not right?'

'You might be,' Dougie said. 'An' then again . . .'

'I might not.'

'You don't really want t' know what happened here that night, do you?'

She turned this way then that, looking at the plantation, at the shallow furrows that scored the clay, at the knoll above the farmhouse. Anywhere: he could be anywhere. It mattered not. She didn't want him back, whatever was left of him. She felt only relief that Giffard's little lies and evasions had finally exposed the truth. Her father was gone for good this time, lost not in Flanders but here on the fringes of the city he had scorned and abandoned.

She couldn't mourn and would not condemn. She would take it no further, not one step beyond this place, this point in time. She must leave her father – and Tony – behind, and move on.

Polly shook her head.

'No,' she said. 'No, I don't want to know what happened.'

'Then go away, Mrs Manone,' Dougie said. 'Go away an' do what I've done.'

'And what is that, Mr Giffard?'

'Dig in, lass' he told her. 'Dig in.'

When she reached the shelter of Garscadden wood she stopped running, running from where her father might lie, crashing through fern and bracken as if she feared that he might reach out of the earth and catch her still.

Only when she had crossed the back road and entered the shelter of the trees did she finally slacken her frantic pace. Boiling hot, dripping with perspiration, her dress clinging to her skin, she was tormented now by an irrational fear that when she arrived at the top of the hill and looked down she would find that they had gone too; Babs, the children, Mammy vanished as if they had never been. But they were not gone, had not vanished. They were precisely where she had left them, picnicking on the grass under the shade of the oak tree.

Relief, vast and exhausting, flooded over Polly. She slumped shakily against the trunk of an elm and, screened by its leaves, looked down at the car, at the little girls, at Angus, like a monkey, swinging from a branch, at Babs scowling as she peeled an orange; at Mammy, Mammy with April on her lap, woman and child both drowsy, both hovering on the verge of sleep.

As she knelt in the grass at the base of the elm tree, looking down, Polly knew that a part of her life had drawn to a close. She was no longer Dominic's wife, no longer Tony's lover, no longer a mother to Stuart and Ishbel. She had allowed herself to be replaced. For that she had only herself to blame.

Dig in, Giffard had told her. Dig in.

Perhaps he was right. Perhaps that was the only way to survive and she had better heed his advice. She had asked too much of life, more than her mother had ever had or ever wanted, and she had paid dearly for her greed; yet in the lengthening shadows of that hot August afternoon something quite unexpected happened, something so strange that it took Polly's breath away: there, on the very eve of war, she felt at peace with herself at last.

And calmly, almost serenely, she walked the rest of the way downhill to join her family and take tea in the shadow of the oak.